# A Month of Sundays

Jade Olivia

Copyright © 2024 by Jade Olivia

Edited by Jenine Corneal - @imajinconsulting

All rights reserved.

No part of this book may be reproduced in any form or by any electronic or mechanical means, including information storage and retrieval systems, without written permission from the author, except for the use of brief quotations in a book review.

This is a work of fiction. Names, characters, places, brands, media and incidents are either the products of the author's imagination or are used fictitiously. The author acknowledges the trademarked status and trademark owners of various products referenced in this work of fiction, which have been used without permission.

The publication/use of these trademarks is not authorized, associated with, or sponsored by the trademark owners.

# Prologue

DeAndre looked up from the second glass of brandy he was drinking today since arriving at the venue. He was thankful for this moment of relaxation just as his friend Melody had promised.

She assured him that the wedding – cementing her second marriage – would be drama-free and the most relaxing one he'd ever participated in as a groomsman. And, for the most part...this was true. There were no outlandish bachelor party plans or unnecessary rehearsals leading up to the big day. In fact, these few hours before the ceremony allowed the wedding coordinator to lead a short, convenient rehearsal for the bridal party before the bride and groom's first looks. DeAndre thought to himself, how surprisingly unfazed Melody was about the entire ordeal, even as the bride. He was glad he could come to Rapid Springs the day of the wedding then head back to California where he'd begin training before the next season.

What Melody failed to mention, though, was how chatty her fiancé's cousin, Carter would be.

"When you hit that ace after you turned, yoooo," Carter said, "man, I wanted to cry and I don't get soft like that."

Carter, who was also one of Hosea's groomsmen, DeAndre and Jordan - Hosea's brother, were sitting on lush sofa chairs in one of the mansion's parlor rooms, waiting for the wedding coordinator to return with proper instructions for the rehearsal's itinerary. Carter had been talking DeAndre's ear off about his match yesterday and it had taken everything in DeAndre not to politely tell him to shut the hell up.

No one was as serious about tennis as DeAndre was, but most of these conversations with fans turned into arguments of epic proportions. Discussions that held no regard to what DeAndre thought about his own game. He'd learned over the years, though, that most people didn't even know what the hell they were talking about. People who were fans of DeAndre's fell into either one of two categories: those who followed tennis religiously – knowing the exact schedule of matches, tournaments and openers, and those who were only fans of him – amazed, shocked and maybe a little jealous that a Black man from Port Springs…one of the roughest neighborhoods in the country, could break into the lily-white world of tennis, smashing records since he was 15-years-old.

Carter was shaping up in DeAndre's mind to be the latter.

"When they were trying to hand out that penalty to you, I didn't think that was right. Messing with your shit all because your foot wasn't even an inch into the serve line?" Carter asked before frowning as if he smelled something foul. "That was crazy. What even goes through your mind when they pull that shit on you?"

DeAndre took another sip of his brandy, taking a beat longer to respond, considering this was the first word he got in edgewise since Carter's diatribe began.

"It is what it is," DeAndre shrugged, dismissing the idea of even bringing up some of the bullshit he went through on the court. There was no way he was opening that can of worms.

"Gotta take the good with the bad, even when it's not called for."

"But, you stand your ground, D, I mean…you call it how you see it, cussin' them out and everything. That's how you do it. I never watched a game of tennis before you played."

Carter scoffed, "What I look like watching tennis?"

He did have a point.

Standing about a foot under DeAndre's 6'7' height, Carter looked every bit like the dudes he grew up in Port Springs with. He had tattoos from head to toe, including a lightning bolt extending from his temple to his cheek, and a permanent scowl that never faded from his features. Two slits in his eyebrows made him look much more menacing than DeAndre knew he was and his whole demeanor reminded DeAndre that men like Carter and even Hosea were never supposed to like tennis, let alone watch or attend the games. Guys like him put DeAndre's entire career – and his life – into much-needed perspective. He was always reminded that he did get out of Port Springs in one piece, which was why he put the city on his back, representing it no matter what court, country or state he was competing in.

So, if he had to lend an ear to harmless rants and empty conversations - so be it.

"'Preciate that you even follow my game, man," DeAndre said, placing a hand on his shoulder. "It's a boost when I get love from my people."

He stood, extending his hand to give Carter dap. The two embraced and DeAndre swore he saw a faint smile brush across Carter's features, looking like a school kid finally meeting his favorite player for the first time.

"Good morning, gentlemen."

Kathy, the wedding coordinator, rushed in with the verbal cadence of someone on the run.

"Mostly everyone is on time," she said.

Short and stocky with glasses sitting on top of her tightly coiled hair, Kathy tucked her clipboard under her arm securing it with her elbow. The stark black band of the watch was enough to make her look like a spy kid if it wasn't for the long, straight cobalt dress she wore. DeAndre could tell that Kathy only wore gowns like this per her client's request as her wide stride didn't work well with the cut of her dress. Observing her frustration, he smirked at seeing her pull up her dress so she could move faster.

"The Matron of Honor and one bridesmaid have arrived. We're still waiting on the last one, but..." she glanced at her watch again, biting down on the left side of her lip. "She should be here shortly. C'mon guys let's get downstairs to get this started."

A few moments later, the entire bridal party, which also included Melody's sister, Monica and their cousin Denise, were gathered in a private salon waiting for the ceremony to begin. The third bridesmaid still hadn't arrived, but Kathy was satisfied with the timing of everyone's entrance when they practiced the procession without her earlier.

Guests filed into the common area an hour later, taking their seats which were outfitted with cream fabric tied into a bow on the back of each one. Florists, hired for the occasion by Melody, appeared late dressed in tuxedos, making a show of arranging a bevy of flowers through the entire space as guests took their seats. Wrapping an array of vines around the columns next to the wedding arch in the front of the room, the team of florists moved with precision and speed, placing large bouquets of white gardenias and pink peonies in the far corners of the space, garnering everyone's attention to the floral grandeur. Melody had a penchant for drama, in every sense of the word. And even though her new husband had calmed her down in some ways, she could never deny onlookers a show.

After Hosea walked down the aisle, garnering his own small round of applause, the solo pianist played the melody to Brian McKnight's "Love of My Life," which was the bridal party's cue to begin their procession...if the bride was present. After a wait that lasted longer than the ten-minute grace period, Kathy's mouth was closed into a straight line that wouldn't budge, showing signs of frustration that the ceremony was starting late. Hosea, looking nothing but dapper in his suit, stood with his hands behind his back, swaying in place. He looked surprisingly calm, but that could have been because his wicked poker face was unreadable. Monica, the Matron of Honor, stood next to Carter with her small bouquet in hand, a nervous half smile plastered on her face.

Besides, the mysterious bridesmaid was still nowhere to be found. Kathy sighed and glanced at her phone.

"I haven't gotten any word that this wedding is canceled..."

She turned to look at DeAndre with a slight shake of her head.

"Looks like you might have to go down the aisle solo after all...we have to get this started."

Smoothing out the front of his suit jacket, DeAndre wiped off a few specks of dust.

"Well, here you are...Charmaine?" Kathy asked.

Her question was followed by the sweetest, softest, chortle DeAndre had ever heard. He looked up at who it came from and lost his breath for a second.

## A Month of Sundays

"No, it's Imani. I'm the substitute bridesmaid and was helping Melody in the back," she said. "They're definitely getting married today, so no money wasted."

With a heart shaped face, brown eyes and lips tinted with a soft pink hue glowing against her brown complexion, her height in heels came just under DeAndre's forearm...she was so petite. Monica pulled Imani closer and the two chatted for a moment before Monica glanced at Kathy.

"Let's do this," Monica said.

Monica's eyes fell on DeAndre, then cut to Imani next to her before switching back to him again. Monica's countenance went from one of concern to one of caution, her eyes narrowed.

*Whatever you're thinking, don't,* she was saying to him, wordlessly.

Monica, Melody and DeAndre had all been friends since DeAndre first moved to Rapid Springs about fifteen years ago, neither of them ever crossed that line of being anything more. Plus, they felt they knew too much about each other for that nonsense. But, the one other thing the Monroe sisters vowed to never do...was hook him up with any of their friends.

Known to be a player in every sense of the word, DeAndre was too busy juggling the many women he came across from different time zones and area codes to even consider settling down with anyone. It wasn't as if he wasn't open to it. He just never came across a woman unpredictable enough to hold his attention.

But, this goddess in front of him...made him question where the hell she came from.

Kathy gestured for all of the couples to quickly line up in the order they had rehearsed, then signaled to the pianist to start the procession. Imani didn't even look at DeAndre as she walked over to him, placing her arm underneath his. Since Melody and Hosea only had three couples in the bridal party, they were the last one. The second couple, Jordan and Melody's cousin Denise, marched down the makeshift aisle in slow succession, allowing DeAndre and this intriguing woman to step forward to wait their turn at the doorway.

There was no way he wasn't going to say anything.

"Hi, I'm DeAndre."

"Hi," she said, looking straight ahead.

# Jade Olivia

He initially thought this beautiful woman was rude as hell until the grip she had on his arm tightened, her hand trembling. He realized something was wrong...was Miss Beautiful nervous?

Not many guests were in attendance, but DeAndre could tell the seats were brought closer together to make the crowd look fuller. There wasn't much room between them and the aisle. DeAndre took a glance at the crowd now, only to find a few people, mostly women, smiling at him from ear-to-ear.

Thank God Melody had that no-cell-phone rule in place. He looked down at his partner, who had now bitten down on the far corner of her bottom lip and placed his other hand on top of hers to comfort her. He inched closer to her ear, inhaling a good whiff of her soft musk scent with a hint of vanilla. Small, ginger red curls were fluffed on top of her head with the sides tapered.

"I won't hold it against you if you have to only look at me," he whispered.

The woman cut her eyes up at him, her eyelashes fluttering. Her face perked up slightly when a small smile ascended that made DeAndre's heart skip a beat.

"I'm Imani, by the way," she whispered quietly.

"No way I could've done this without you, Imani. Too nervous."

She met DeAndre's gaze again, holding it a little longer before a smile lit up her face - this time a little brighter. Catching Kathy's cue next to him, DeAndre led Imani down the aisle, managing to pull his eyes away from this striking woman.

Imani was gorgeous and most definitely caught him by surprise like an unexpected gift.

# Four Years Later

## Chapter 1
# The Desired Reaction

Imani, clasping her dangling earring closed, glanced at her best friend with a grimace. Kaylee looked lovely, but there was no way she was stepping out the door like this.

"Be honest, could you see Mother Reba wearing this on Sunday? " Kaylee asked.

Her midi dress, complete with mesh flesh tone stockings, hugged her body in all the right places. But it was definitely the stockings that looked like they had belonged to one of the oldest members of the church of which the two have been longtime members.

"Well..." Imani chuckled, stretching her bottom lip across her teeth in mock guilt. "It's not what I'd think to go with for a Friday night."

Kaylee groaned and placed her hands on her hips.

"Most of my clothes are in the laundry and you know I barely have any going-out clothes nowadays, anyway."

She walked to Imani's bed and collapsed into the soft mattress, laying on her back. The two were on their way to a birthday party for Randall Price, a friend of her aunt's client, Melody Monroe. Well, Randall was *really* a friend of someone else...but, Melody had given her the invite with the option of bringing a guest. It didn't take much convincing for Kaylee to agree to be Imani's guest, but Imani also knew that going to parties on the regular wasn't either of their MO's anymore. Imani had no issues with going, but she couldn't even remember the last time Kaylee even mentioned going to a gathering that wasn't church-related.

"If you're not comfortable with this," Imani started, "you know I can just Uber."

"No, I'm fine. I'm going with you, like I said I would. Just wish I was one of the cool kids like you." Kaylee smiled, gesturing at Imani's ensemble - a stretchy one-shoulder top and boyfriend jeans, paired with silver heeled sandals. Her sparkly drop earrings fell just above her shoulders.

"You have the juice, too," Imani chuckled. "Just have to tap into it."

Imani went to her closet, glancing at the colorful disarray of clothes stacked and hung all over. She pulled out a few options and placed them on the bed, before picking out a denim jacket with cutouts on the sleeves and tossing it in Kaylee's direction.

"Put this on and ditch the stockings," Imani said.

Doing what she was told, Kaylee turned to the standing mirror that was tilted upward. Her expression was hopeful, as if she was expecting to see a difference, but her shoulders ultimately sagged in disappointment.

"I look like a 12-year-old playing in my big sister's closet."

Imani chuckled and placed her hands on Kaylee's shoulders, resting her head against them.

"You're way too hard on yourself, plus it's not like the party's gonna be that big of a deal anyway."

"Says the woman who was personally invited by Melody freaking Monroe to a house in Rapid Springs, darling," Kaylee shrieked sarcastically.

"Pretty sure she invited me in case she gets a tear in her dress and needs someone to hem it."

Kaylee laughed, taking one of the pillows from the bed and chucking it at Imani.

"Point is," Kaylee continued. "I want to look more...natural, like, 'yes, I'm always here in the Rapids, walking my poodle with my Chanel bag on my arm, don't you recognize me?'" She batted her eyes in quick succession, adding a high-pitched accent to her tone.

Imani chuckled, "Oh, you're spot on there, girl."

## A Month of Sundays

"I'm gonna look in my closet to see what shoes I have to match this better," Kaylee said. "I'll be back and we can head out in, like…20?"

"Still want me to do your makeup?"

Kaylee smiled, sheepishly. "Eehh, then let's make that another hour."

Imani went to gather the clothes she had taken out, putting them back in the closet with no sense of organization. She was trying to act as if the party wasn't a big deal, but it was one of the handful of invites she received from Melody that wasn't attached to an assignment. Imani's Aunt Ethel had been one of the personal seamstresses to the Monroe family dynasty for over ten years. Many years ago, Imani started assisting Ethel with Melody, the family's most famous member and reality star, on an as-needed basis.

Ethel was an old-school pro with decades of experience as a seamstress, but Melody was clear with her that she appreciated Imani's youthful perspective. She even started hiring Imani to style her for more informal occasions, like personal dinners or events where she'd likely be photographed out and about. It wasn't long before Melody and Imani built a rapport that toggled somewhere between friendship and mutual respect.

Imani never claimed to be friends with Melody, no matter how many texts and invites she received from her, mainly because she didn't put too much stock in *trying* to be friends with her in the first place. Celebrities and those of influence constantly had to manage people and whether or not their motives were genuine. Imani wasn't playing that game of proving herself to them or anyone - she was just doing her job to the best of her ability.

"Wow. I can't even believe this," Kaylee walked back in the room with her phone in hand.

"Larry is gonna increase the rent again," she continued. "And this'll be our last month with the current rate."

Imani shook her head, annoyed that her landlord wasn't willing to keep their current rate as is, despite her and Kaylee's shining record as tenants. The two had been living in this apartment since Imani moved back six years ago and never bothered Larry with innocuous requests or messed up his place. Even with all of that, though, the reality was that Larry was merely following the increase in pricing that was spreading throughout the entire area of Port

Springs, a once under-served majority Black neighborhood that was transforming into an enclave for trust fund babies.

"Good thing I've been at Artgo," Imani said. "I'll be able to cover my half."

Kaylee sighed.

"I don't know, 'Mani," she said. "This rate is not just a $50 increase. This is nuts and there's only so many hours I can take at work with classes."

Kaylee had been in law school for two years now with a cushion of funds that her parents put to the side for her to focus on her degree while they handled her living expenses. But, even that cushion was dwindling by the year.

Imani folded her arms in front of her, tapping her fingers on her elbow. She knew there was no way she could afford to take on the entirety of the rent for long, even with her full-time salary as an assistant curator at the Artgo Museum and the freelance assistant stylist gigs with the Monroes but, she'd figure it out.

"Let's not worry about it. I have a few commissions coming up at church that could help out."

Kaylee looked at her, pity lacing her features.

"You're saving up to get yourself another car," she said. "I don't want you to have to dig into what you're saving already."

"Well, we gotta do what we have to. Not like I have too many options."

Unlike her roommate, Imani didn't have parents to go back home to if mess hit the fan nor was she sitting on a cushion of cash to help her stay afloat.

Kaylee gathered her lips to one side of her face. "I'll see what freelance writing assignments I could maybe get. I don't know....this is just...ugh...Larry knew what he was doing."

"I hate to say it," Imani said. "But, Michael was right. He suggested we look around for another spot this time last year, but I said we'd be fine."

"Should've known he has the Holy Spirit on speed dial whispering to him when it comes to you."

Imani laughed, this time grinning harder. "He wasn't trying to be a know-it-all about it, you know, but he hinted at it."

"He's such a sweetheart. And, I know you'd much rather him be who you're going with tonight than me."

Imani eyes widened and mouth slacked.

"Kay...that's not it!"

# A Month of Sundays

"It's ok. He's your man, your man, your man, so I get it."

Imani wiggled her eyebrows in jest. "When you put it that way…"

The two laughed as Imani thought about her boyfriend of four years, who had been adding to her life since they had been together. Imani was not the type of woman who believed in soulmates, but she knew that having Michael in her life was an indirect result of her relationship with God being strengthened. She hadn't felt this adjusted in a long time and Imani loved Michael for helping her with that.

"Mind if I give him a call before we head out?" Imani asked. "He should be out of his meeting with Pastor Goodman. I promise not to hold us up."

Imani put her hands together in a praying position, smiling with faux innocence.

"Go 'head, girl. I'm following your time, but you know traffic going to the Rapids will be something tonight."

"Before I forget, though, let's take a pic," Kaylee said, her phone in her hand, angling it in different directions. "We look great here."

Imani put up a peace sign and smiled just when Kaylee snapped a selfie that she posted to her Stories, which Imani then reposted to her own feed. Clicking out of Instagram, Imani then hit Michael's name under her contacts list, as a burst of energy shot through her system. She hadn't spoken to him all day and was missing him like the sappy girlfriend she never thought she'd be.

Michael appeared on her phone after two rings, his masculine features and kind smile on display.

"Hey, sweetheart," he said, still smiling at her. His dimples made her melt every time.

Imani made a gesture of moving her head from side to side, posing like she was taking a picture.

"Don't you look nice?" he chuckled. "All ready to head out, huh?"

"Hi, Minister Michael!" Kaylee cut in, waving her arms above her head as Imani moved her phone for him to see her briefly.

"Hey, Kaylee," he laughed. "You know there's still a day left before you can start calling me that."

"Well, unless the Lord has other plans between now and then…it's all just a formality as far as I'm concerned."

## Jade Olivia

Imani turned the phone back to herself and saw Michael still smiling, but with a flash of hesitance in his features. He'd be presented as an official minister during a church program tomorrow, after going through a year-long training, and Imani knew he was feeling the weight of it. She knew how much pressure he was putting on himself to carry out his walk as a minister for the right reasons, with the right intentions, and with humility. So, while Michael was flattered at Kaylee's confidence, he was also trying his best to take it with a grain of salt.

"So your meeting with your dad - I mean, Pastor Goodman...didn't go overtime?"

Michael grinned at what Imani called her most common slip up. He never had an issue with her mentioning Pastor Goodman as his father because...he was his father. But, Imani felt like it was much more appropriate to refer to him by his title when they spoke about him in the context of church matters.

"No, it went well." Michael stretched out his arms. "Just have a ton of meetings and events to attend with him over the next few months."

"Yeah, I'm sure," she said. "Look, I already knew you wouldn't be able to come tonight, considering...everything," Imani started. "But, I do miss you and wish you could."

"I miss you, too," he said, "and, we're hanging out in a more neutral setting tomorrow. We're still grabbing a bite to eat after my ordination, right?"

Whenever Michael said things like this, Imani couldn't help but feel like a heathen of a girlfriend, the wild child dating God's Son who could lead him into irreparable danger. But, she knew she was getting stuck in her head. Michael insisted that he loved her in every way and never made her feel guilty about her decisions. For what it was worth, Imani had done a total 180 from the time the two met to where they were now.

"Yeah, I'm already smelling that French Toast," she smiled.

"And, the biscuits," Michael said, pushing himself back into his seat as he rested an arm over his head.

Imani rolled her eyes and laughed, "Here we go...you and those biscuits need to wed in Holy Matrimony."

"I already have plans with someone else for that."

Imani smiled at Michael's words, feeling them still her for a moment.

## A Month of Sundays

Michael started hinting at marriage a few months ago and Imani wondered where it was coming from. Of course, she felt like marrying Michael was the natural next step in their relationship. She wanted marriage and that was the only next step, if he was following the trajectory of the other ministers and his father. But, Imani still erred on the side of caution, wanting him to settle into his upcoming role as a minister first.

"Ok, lovebirds," Kaylee said. "Y'all can watch each other breathe on your own time. Imani still needs to do my makeup."

Once Imani got off the phone with Michael with an air kiss, the two piled into their small bathroom with Victoria Monet's latest single streaming through Imani's phone. Kaylee sat on the edge of the sink while Imani used kohl eyeliner to line her lids with meticulous precision. She then placed dainty faux lashes over Kaylee's own, making her sit with her eyes closed. Imani always told Kaylee that she didn't need much makeup, not that Imani was a professional makeup artist by any means, but she was really good at it. Kaylee always begged Imani to do her makeup for special occasions.

*You're still an artist, just using a different canvas*, Kaylee always encouraged her.

For the past year, Imani had to remind herself –*you're still an artist*–even though the way bills, rent and other responsibilities managed to take over her life…had her singing another tune.

*You're also a 30-something-year-old*, her brain would counter, as she thought about the money that she needed to have, which wasn't coming in fast enough unless she made the effort. She loved her art…breathed it even. But, instead of trying to make it work as her main source of income, as she tried in New York years ago, she currently had relegated it as a self-proclaimed, "heart hobby." Something that only sustained her spirit yet wasn't substantial enough to put any food on her table.

Kaylee opened her eyes slowly, revealing purple-rimmed almond orbs curved into a slight cat-eye.

"You look uuuhh-mazing!" Imani beamed.

Kaylee turned to look at the mirror, fanning out her fluffy head of curls.

"Oh, I want the world to know like Miss Diana Ross, girl!"

The two laughed in the mirror as Imani snapped her fingers in time to her friend's prissy, playful poses. Kaylee was like the goody-two-shoes sister she never had, who never looked at her crazy, for her "worldly tendencies" as Aunt Ethel loved to say. Both women knew the heart they had for God and their faith, but they were still two completely different women. Where Imani had tattoos etched on multiple places all over her body, Kaylee still blushed when she admitted to having a belly ring at 13. She took it out less than a month later, of course.

Imani was the artist – painting the living room walls on a random Saturday when she was bored or switching up the color of her short, curly cut just because. Kaylee was the conservative – careful to follow the rules written in a furniture instructional guide to a T and not even considering buying a dress that was more than an inch above her knees. The friends balanced each other and held each other accountable... two factors that allowed Imani to thrive.

Victoria Monet continued her wordplay over infectious harmonies when a faint hush of the music on Imani's phone signaled a notification.

She tapped onto the Instagram tab that appeared at the top and a thread of her direct messages appeared. She received a response to the reposted selfie in her Stories that she had forgotten about that quickly. Connected as a reply to her post, a gif of Bugs Bunny and his heart beating out of his chest made Imani burst into raucous laughter, spilling from the depths of her insides.

She couldn't even deny it – *this* was the exact reaction to her look that she wanted and it wasn't from Michael.

"Ready to go?" Kaylee asked, her car keys in hand, pulling Imani out of her reverie.

"Yeah, lemme give you the address." Imani grabbed her clutch as she pulled together her stuff and looked around to make sure she hadn't forgotten anything before following Kaylee.

Locking the door behind her, Imani looked forward to having a good night and refused to let her mind wander on things and people, who she had no business focusing on.

# Chapter 2
# Thirsty

The familiar tremble in the back of DeAndre's legs was all he needed to feel to know he was on his third release of the night.

"Oooohohhhohhohohohooooooo!" Jazmine screamed, facing the partition that was a literal wedge between her and Clive, his driver.

He let his eyes collapse and mouth go slack as he gripped her ass tighter. DeAndre already knew he was going to have to give Clive another bonus before the end of the year just because he, yet again, put up with all of his antics with the highest level of professionalism that DeAndre didn't always reciprocate. He and Jazmine were on their way to his best friend Randall's birthday and all DeAndre needed was to put his attention elsewhere momentarily.

For the time being, Jazmine's ass had it...every bounce and ripple motivated him to keep maneuvering her up and down his shaft.

"Hooow? Whaaaa? Uugggghh," she continued moaning, gripping the leather car handles with white-knuckled fists. With one more thrust to the left, thanks to the speed bump Clive drove over, she let out the loudest scream followed by an avalanche of moisture that almost made his condom-laden member slip out of her.

Jazmine was the one woman he felt always got wet faster, and somehow managed to stay that way the longest. She was always a good enough time and a trooper to match his stamina, if he was being honest.

# Jade Olivia

She looked behind herself to DeAndre with lustful admiration and disbelief, pushing her long, black curly waves over one shoulder.

"I...don't think I have an extra pair of panties on me."

They laughed as Jazmine shifted out of his lap and into her seat next to him, her scent wafting through the leather interiors.

"C'mon now," he said. "You know you have to make sure you got more than what you think you need wit' me."

This was their third round in the car and DeAndre was nowhere near done. All he needed was a few minutes of reprieve, give or take, and he could go again. Just like his game, he could always go again.

"I should've known, especially after that win," Jazmine shook her head and sighed. "Aren't you supposed to be injured anyway?"

DeAndre let out his own deep breath this time.

"Yeah, something like that."

His injury was definitely something all those months ago. A pulled hamstring that damn near had him seeing stars, laid out on his back against a clay court in Paris. But, to everyone on the outside looking in, DeAndre Harrison's "career threatening" injury was old news - a slight inconvenience that he magically got over not even a year later - because he did the one thing that not many managed to do at his age. He returned to tennis a few weeks ago, completely dominating the court as if he hadn't been injured at all. He won by the skin of his teeth, to be fair – by a two-point lead. Yet, he won and that's all the reporters and his team focused on.

But, for DeAndre?

All he felt during that match was an insatiable, unfamiliar fear of losing.

"Did I help you heal?" she smiled, lust dripping from her tongue.

DeAndre looked up, acting as if he was in deep thought, then looked back at her, sizing her up again with his eyes.

"You definitely part of the rehab plan."

She chuckled, biting her bottom lip. DeAndre saw the effect he had on her and felt good about himself for being so damn generous with his gifts and talents.

After all, he had just won one of the most pivotal matches of his career so far, which put him right where he needed to be to get to the SW Tournament

## A Month of Sundays

next year. All he had to do was continue rehabilitating his leg in therapy and get his mind right. His trainer told him to get as much rest as he could, just to give himself a bit of a break before his next match this week at his home court in Rapid Springs, The Royal. For now, he was gonna enjoy this weekend celebrating his best friend's big day and keep himself...distracted.

"How far are we from the spot?" Jazmine asked.

"Tryna get rid of me already?"

"Never that," she smiled.

When her phone pinged, though, it didn't even take her five minutes to start scrolling mindlessly, blue light radiating her doll-like features, pulling both of them out of their exchange. But, it didn't faze him - he knew what Jazmine was about and she damn sure knew what he was about.

They'd been messing with each other for a minute now, all for the simple fact that she never caused any issues. She was one of the good ones. No weird subtweets, Instagram posts, TikToks and most importantly, no clingy behavior. It also helped that she had her own thing going on...a business he couldn't think of at the moment.

DeAndre was never really sure what the women he met up with did, until they mentioned it. As long as they had something to occupy themselves with - their relations were clear, consensual and truly mature in his opinion. DeAndre just appreciated having them to pass the time, quell his boredom off the court and keep his mind off of other things...and off of someone else.

*What she gonna pop out in tonight?*

It was a question he had been working on relegating to the back of his mind, but thoughts of Imani always had a way of creeping back in. It made sense that would be the case right now, since she'd be at the party. He wanted to make sure he heard Randall right, when he first told DeAndre a few weeks ago.

*"Yeah, yeah, shawty gonna pull up, probably with Melody,"* Randall had said. *"But, she got a plus 1."*

DeAndre pulled out his phone to check Imani's Instagram but the profile populated without him even typing in her handle.

*@Imaniation_oo*

He remembered hunting down Imani's Instagram with the quickness after they met at Melody's wedding about four years ago. She told him she was an artist, but DeAndre had been so captivated by her conversation, he slipped up and didn't get her number before she abruptly cut him off and left. Without even a last name, he played detective on IG after the reception at damn near 2 in the morning, scrolling through profiles of women named Imani. He finally came across an account with only three posts and no profile pic. Two of them being sketch drawings – that included an upside down picture of her by herself - deep mahogany complexion glowing under the sunlight. He shamelessly double-tapped all three photos just before sending her a direct message.

*Where did you go?* he typed, not even caring how thirsty he might've seemed. She was worth pulling out all the stops.

It had taken her three days to respond to him.

*Hi, DeAndre. It was nice meeting you, but my boyfriend came to pick me up.*

Her response was like a glitch in the matrix.

He wasn't surprised that someone was smart enough to get her before he did, but something in her message only activated his curiosity even more. Her rejection had been so...polite. Like a "I'm so sorry for the inconvenience, but no, I really can't help you." Most women he came across, even if they were in current relationships, acted very much single and readily available. On the other hand, Imani was so genuine...so sweet... that it made him jealous of another dude he knew nothing about. DeAndre never got jealous but he was rarely satisfied with a flat out 'no' neither.

*Got you. You plan on posting more of your work?*

Even if he couldn't have her, there was no reason why they couldn't keep in touch...right?

*We'll see,* she had replied.

After the wedding, he'd randomly run into her at Melody's house from time to time and it was a pleasant surprise each time he did.

*"She's my stylist - a very good one at that. If I even think you're barking up that tree, I'm running over your legs with the Lambo,"* Melody warned him. *"I don't need her to resign after you wiggle your way in and have her crying to me that you ghosted her."*

Whenever DeAndre ran across a woman he had an ounce of 'like' for, his mind would quickly figure out how soon he could sleep with her and if he would keep her around afterwards. Yet those thoughts hadn't even crossed his mind when he met Imani. Not that he'd be stupid enough to refuse it if she wanted to. He wasn't *that far* above it.

But it had now been four years since then... Imani was still Melody's assistant but her Instagram account had grown to around 700+ followers. Her posting had become much more frequent, and just as creative. DeAndre would purposely wait a few days before checking her profile for recent posts just to have something interesting to look at after training or a match. Her drawings, paintings and pottery were some of her most common pics, but every once in a while, she'd bless his timeline with those gorgeous, chocolate brown squinted eyes and soft pouty lips he wanted to kiss with such urgency. They had a casual flow of occasional messaging through DMs, though DeAndre was always ready to take their conversation offline.

It didn't take long for him to pick up on how easy it was for Imani to feel like she was overstepping, so he never pushed to get her number or to give her his. He was satisfied with keeping their exchanges friendly, for her sake, as hard as it was for him. She definitely had a hold on him, and he would do just about anything to talk to her now...to be with her right at this moment and, he knew he *fucking* couldn't be.

He tapped Imani's profile picture on the left side of the screen. It was circled in red, tempting him like a dangling carrot. He had already responded to her first post, in her stories for the day, of her and another woman smiling together. Even in a photo with another woman who was also attractive, Imani stood out like a singular rose in a garden. Another image followed - of Imani hugging *Michael* and, just like the masochist he was - DeAndre held his finger down, examining it from every angle. Her arms draped comfortably around his neck with her cheek resting on his, the dazzling smile on her face was in direct contrast to this dude's cool and calm one. That breezy confidence in his smile stemmed from the privilege he had of being her boyfriend, unfortunately for DeAndre.

The whole thing got under his skin.

Shortly after her first response to him all those years ago, Imani made it known through her Instagram stories that she was spoken for, shouting out Michael for his birthdays or for corny #NationalBoyfriendDays or whatever other trending topics people wanted to hop in online. Tonight, would be different. Michael was no longer going to be relegated to just a social media post, he was probably coming with Imani as her plus one, which meant DeAndre had to stand and see this man's face - in the flesh - for the first time.

"Mr. Harrison?"

Clive's voice cut through the silence that enveloped the backseat for at least fifteen minutes. He had slowed on the cobblestone driveway, packed with an array of vehicles parked every which way. They were directly across from the mansion that was the venue of Randall's party.

"There aren't any spaces free."

"It's a'ight, man," DeAndre said. "You could just pull up here and we'll head out."

Clive parked where he could on the property that was formerly DeAndre's personal residence. Once parked, Jazmine was the first to step out of the car on the left side, tossing her hair over her shoulder before adjusting the top of her leopard print strapless dress. Her black strappy heels clacked against the tiled pavement as she made her way around the front of the car. She had been to a few events with DeAndre over the years and was the definition of being seen, but barely heard.

DeAndre started to get out of the car from the right but turned back to Clive.

"Aye, you got my other keys?"

Clive pulled out the key fob imprinted with the Ferrari emblem from the glove compartment and handed it to him. DeAndre made sure to have one of his other cars dropped off and parked before the party just for convenience.

"Let me know if you still need me," Clive said.

"'Preciate you."

He patted Clive on the shoulder and stepped out into the warm evening air, extending his lean frame.

DeAndre remembers when he had casually mentioned to Randall that he was going to sell this house. The place reminded him of his days as a newbie starting out, when he was just proud to be the first in his family to even own a home. But Randall convinced him to keep it in his real estate portfolio as a rental for events or TV and film shoots. His boy made it seem like the property would only be used as a serious investment. When DeAndre suggested he

### A Month of Sundays

could use it for his 35th birthday party, he thought Randall would keep the celebration intimate.

Upon hearing the muffled sound of heavy bass now seeping from behind the glass doors and windows, DeAndre could only imagine what was going down inside. He straightened his chains before stealing a glance at his Audemars.

"It's barely 8 o'clock," he said under his breath, "and, this fool already losing his damn mind."

Running a hand from his fresh haircut down to his face, DeAndre led Jazmine up the marble steps to head inside.

# Chapter 3
# Familiar

Imani was babysitting a sour lemon drop cocktail and dancing alongside Kaylee to the DJs mix of early-2000s hip-hop and R&B with more recent hits, having a good time.

No one was having as good of a time as the birthday boy Randall though.

She and Kaylee had arrived at the party a little before 8 and Randall was already light on his feet when he greeted them.

"My homegirl, Imani!" he shouted, lifting both arms in the air. Randall was far enough away from them in the living room, but Imani could tell he was already multiple drinks in.

"Whaddup, girl?" he asked for the entire crowd to hear.

Imani grimaced as he wobbled towards her and tried not to laugh at his expense. She was hoping he was being looked after as he moved through dancing and moving bodies packed like sardines in the massive living room. But, once she saw his wife Eve a moment later, pushing her head up from behind him, navigating through the crowd and apologizing to guests on Randall's behalf, Imani knew he was safe.

.As Randall's wife, Eve - a petite Latina with a bevy of blonde curls pinned to the top of her head, was clearly prepared for whatever Randall was going to do. Imani wasn't even sure how she kept up with him in the first place. She didn't know them too well, but from the handful of times she saw the couple at

## A Month of Sundays

Melody's house, Imani saw Randall just as he was now - the life of the party - while Eve had an energy equivalent to a yogi on retreat.

Once Randall and Eve finally reached them, Imani was slapped with the pungent, overhauling smell of Hennessy.

"Wait, wait, wait," he said, shifting in place, looking at Imani before pointing a lazy finger at Kaylee.

"That's not a dude," he continued pointing between the two of them, "and, she ain't your man."

He said it more like a statement than a question as Kaylee looked on with wide eyes like she'd been caught in the middle of something. Before Imani could jump in to save Kaylee, who was about two seconds from apologizing simply for being there, Eve positioned herself between Randall and Imani. As Randall's wife, Eve - a petite Latina with a bevy of blonde curls pinned to the top of her head, was clearly prepared for whatever Randall was going to do. Imani wasn't even sure how she kept up with him in the first place. She didn't know them too well, but from the handful of times she saw the couple at Melody's house, Imani saw Randall just as he was now - the life of the party - while Eve had an energy equivalent to a yogi on retreat.

"Imani," Eve said, an uncomfortable smile broadening on her face, "It's so good to see you and," she turned to Kaylee, "it's nice to meet you-"

"This is my best friend, Kaylee," Imani continued.

Eve looked between the two of them, apologetically, and turned back to Randall.

"Let's try to get some more fresh air, baby," she said to him, in a pacifying tone. "We'll see what other friends you have out here who want to celebrate you."

Barely standing properly on his own, Randall looked at her, drunken eyes lit up in thought.

"See, you right, baby," he said.

Imani could still smell his breath as he walked past them, his entire frame facing Eve. "That's why I love you 'cause you know me. You know all these fools here need to be coming to see me, celebrating the day I came to bless... these mofos."

Eve continued nodding her head with an appeasing smile as she patted his back, pushing him towards the glass doors leading to the backyard. She stopped for a moment, letting Rand walk ahead at a safe distance before quickly turning to Imani.

"Not sure when Melody is supposed to make it," she said. "But try not to dip out early. At this point, you're the only one who I don't want to punch in the face."

Imani quickly glanced around to take in her surroundings. Although the party didn't fall straight into loud frat party territory, guests were all over the place – dancing in every square inch of the house, grooving on top of the bar and making out on the couches and sofa chairs. It seemed like they only wanted to egg Randall on with whatever antics he could get away with.

"Don't worry," Imani glanced back at Eve. "I'm not going anywhere."

"Oh, shit!" Randall shouted over the crowd, his hand cupped over his lips. "Hol' up, hol' up, hol' up…if it isn't my brother from another mother, my homie, the GOAT…the real Don!"

In the middle of a mid-2000s hip-hop cut, the DJ scratched the record, pulling the crowd's attention to the source of Randall's outburst. He was at the front door, embracing whoever it was in a bear hug, concealing his friend's face, but Imani just…knew.

Her breath caught as the realization of who it was, hit her like lightening.

"Uh oh, uh oh, uh oh," the DJ started, "Who we got? Who we got in here?"

He then played three consecutive bomb sounds as guests around Imani looked over those in front of them to find out who Randall was talking to.

The friend in question pushed himself away from Randall's hug, smiling and shaking his head at his clearly drunk friend, giving everyone a full view…of all of him. Imani's nerves went haywire in a matter of seconds.

"Damnnnnnn," the DJ announced. "One of the greatest to ever do it, is here to celebrate the man of the hour! DeAndre Harrison's in the building y'all!"

Randall then made a scene, wailing his arms in front of DeAndre, who threw out a casual salute to the now re-energized crowd. Dressed in a simple black shirt and a layer of two slim diamond chains, DeAndre and his mahogany complexion accented by stark white teeth looked as if God himself had spent hours concocting the perfect hue of brown. A full beard

## A Month of Sundays

lined with precision below a fresh fade accented the angular features of his face that were just rugged enough without being too pretty. Imani had surmised that there was nothing *pretty* about DeAndre when she had met him years ago. Same as then and just like now, he was both beautiful and rough all at once.

DeAndre didn't greet the crowd any further, exhibiting the nonchalance of a casual guest trying to find the best spot to settle themselves. Imani's gaze soaked up every inch of him like she was calling him telepathically...only, she'd be crazy if she did.

*Imani, look away...look away,* she thought. She had to stop staring before....

When DeAndre's almond shaped eyes caught her own, she felt a shiver down her spine. Imani saw him maneuver his way through the crowd in her direction and turned to Kaylee, taking a heavier sip of her cocktail than she needed. Just on the verge of choking, she started coughing.

"You ok, 'Mani?" Kaylee asked, patting her on the back.

"Yeah, I'm fine."

Imani turned to fully face Kaylee who was swaying rhythmically to the R&B classics the DJ was spinning. She wasn't even trying to get a view to take in DeAndre any further.

"Guess Melody won't be the only celebrity here tonight," Kaylee said, eyes sparkling with excitement.

"Oh my gosh, don't look," she grinned at Imani. "I think he's on his way over here."

Imani's hands suddenly became clammy and it wasn't from the sweat of her cocktail glass either. She and Kaylee continued dancing as Imani tried her best to calm her nerves. She just didn't understand why she was frazzled over this dude.

They were friends.

No, that sounded too generous.

DeAndre and Randall were friends - best friends, which made sense as to why he'd be here. DeAndre was more of a casual acquaintance to her. An extremely fine acquaintance who randomly dropped comments on her IG posts and sends hilarious GIFs to her selfies that made her giddy like a damn teenager...

## Jade Olivia

"He might not be," Imani said, her statement sounding far from believable, even to her.

The two met more than three years ago at Melody's wedding when she became a bridesmaid, saving the day at the last minute. Melody's ex-friend Charmaine bowed out at the ninth hour and Imani went from helping Hosea's mom fasten the tail of buttons on Melody's gown to becoming a stand-in, tying a cobalt blue dress at her waist, thankful she had on proper undergarments. She had no idea who she was walking down the aisle with but, once she saw that it was DeAndre Harrison, she pulled her face into an expression that would make any poker player proud.

And, her stoicism worked for a while, too.

She managed to stand next to him, per the wedding coordinator's instructions, without acting starstruck. She even held it together when she tucked her arm underneath his, feeling his lean muscle and his warmth at the tip of her fingertips. But once she drew closer to the open door, when the two were next in line to walk out, Imani wanted to run. She suddenly felt cold, her teeth began chattering as she involuntarily tightened her grip on DeAndre's arm. Stage fright was never something she thought she had, but in that moment, she felt like everyone could see how much of a screw up she truly was.

*A bamboozled, scatterbrained artist who came back home because she didn't listen to her aunt who tried to warn her about getting caught up.* Thoughts like those and the humming in her mind were at an all-time high, when DeAndre placed a hand on top of hers, moving closer to her ear. The warmth of his breath seemed to make her entire body melt.

*I won't hold it against you if you have to only look at me,* he had said.

It was the wildest, cockiest, funniest thing anyone could've said to her, in that moment, and it pulled her completely out of her mental escapade.

*Who is this dude?* she had thought.

Of course, she *knew* who he was, but she wasn't expecting to be intrigued at all. Yet, she remained enchanted during every conversation they had later that night. They were so in sync, it felt right...too right.

"Imani."

The baritone in his voice had the same effect on her now that it did when they first met - like an assembly of butterflies taking flight from deep within.

## A Month of Sundays

DeAndre said her name for the first time at the wedding like he was placing it somewhere, making sure it fit. Then, he kept saying it all night, with more familiarity and comfort, like they were *that* close.

Imani was still looking at Kaylee, who was now standing with her mouth agape and eyes wide with an expression nothing short of, *He knows you?!*

Imani counted to three in her head before turning to meet his gaze with confidence.

All that confidence she mustered up evaporated immediately.

DeAndre's chocolate brown eyes held an intensity that was only smoothed by his captivating smile. He was looking at her like he had been waiting to see her all day.

"Glad to see you," he said, eyes crinkling at the corners.

Just when she was getting her bearings, he pulled her into a hug, snaking his arm around her waist and sending tingles from her chest all the way down to her toes. She tasted the spice of his Bergamot scent through her nose as she placed a hand just under his shoulder, feeling the slight curvature of his back. Fortunately for her, they released themselves at roughly the same moment, though Imani felt his hand linger on her waist a little longer. She felt like she just downed a shot of the highest shelf of liquor at the bar.

"Hey, DeAndre," she said, releasing a breath. "This is my...my best friend, Kaylee."

As if pulled out of a trance, Kaylee offered her hand in greeting and had no shame in showing her obvious excitement. DeAndre gave her a kind smile along with a handshake.

"It's nice to meet you, Kaylee."

"This is gonna sound so crazy," she started, "but, my grandma loved watching you play at the Grand Deux tournament a few years back. She prayed for you that whole week and didn't even bat a lash when you won."

"We used to watch a lot of your matches just before she passed. She used to say how handsome you were and she wouldn't have passed you up if she was at least four decades younger...God bless her," she laughed.

No matter where she was - in church, at home, even at a party with guests stripping down to their underwear to backflip in a pool - Kaylee was always going to be herself. Imani watched DeAndre for an inkling of indifference on his face, but he actively listened to her fan out, a genuine smile playing on his lips.

"Didn't think you'd be so tall, but it makes sense, considering how wide in diameter a tennis court is," Kaylee continued. She scratched the inside of her ear, looking around.

"I'm gonna stop talking now before I embarrass myself even more."

DeAndre chuckled in response, warming Imani's own insides.

"It's all good. Thank you, Kaylee, for real. I definitely need them prayers."

Imani stole a glance at him scratching the side of his beard. *What did that mean?*

"I didn't realize you two knew each other," Kaylee said, looking between both DeAndre and Imani now. "How'd y'all meet?"

"At Melody's wedding," Imani said before DeAndre could answer. She tried to say it as casually as she could, even while his gaze seared into her. They hadn't seen each other in person for about a year, since she stopped assisting Aunt Ethel with Melody full time once she got her job at Artgo. Internally Imani shook her head, time had passed yet he still gave her goosebumps.

"I'll leave y'all to yourselves," he said, after a beat. "I just wanted to say hi."

His eyes were on Imani before shifting to Kaylee, "Enjoy yourself."

"Thank you, DeAndre," Kaylee said. "Yeah, it was nice meeting you...oh, 'Mani, we should tell him about Kid's Day at church. It's a few months from now and a really fun day for our ministry. I just know if you were to come, the kids would be so amped to play–"

"He's probably busy, Kay," Imani said, low enough for her to hear.

"I'll be there," DeAndre countered like Imani didn't say anything at all. He said it with such finality that she couldn't even respond.

"How can we get in touch with your team? Like I don't know...your manager or agent or whomever?" Kaylee asked, getting down to business.

"Imani knows how to find me."

He wiped underneath his lip with the side of his finger, stealing another glance at Imani with a smirk. His gaze alone had her on fire, it was like he was taking his sweet time pulling back all of her layers one by one.

Just then, a hand with a full rhinestone-studded acrylic nail set appeared on DeAndre's chest. The owner of it approached from his right side, body for

## A Month of Sundays

days squeezed effortlessly into an animal print dress. Imani knew there was no way he showed up by himself. She rarely ever saw him alone.

"Hey," she said. "I'm getting a drink at the bar. Coming with me?"

Mysterious woman sounded like she was going to sleep or had just woken up. All of a sudden, Imani felt a pang of annoyance.

DeAndre turned to her, with a smile that wasn't as wide and open as it was for Imani, though it was still a smile of satisfaction. Imani had tuned out quickly enough to miss what he said to the woman before she walked away to said bar, presumably. DeAndre then turned back to them.

"Have a good time tonight," Imani said, cutting him off just as he looked like he wanted to say something. Seeing this "friend" with him reminded Imani exactly how single he was, while she was completely committed and devoted to the person she needed to be with. These weird feelings she had when he was around were merely displaced – they had to be...right?

DeAndre must've picked up the sudden tension Imani was feeling because he stood still, looking at her...assessing. Imani folded her arms around herself, instinctually, as he suddenly released a titillating smile.

"Glad *you* can have a good time tonight," he said. He did a once over at Imani as he walked past her, brushing himself against her shoulder slightly. His familiar woodsy scent trailed behind.

*Don't look to see if he's watching you. Don't do it*, Imani scolded herself, bringing her drink to her lips again. She couldn't stand how seeing him tonight made her want to see more of him.

The familiar chords of Usher's voice were heard on full blast as the vibe of the party slowed down to something Imani could finally dance to, a break from the hip-hop they played earlier. Imani swayed her hips in response to the switch of the vibe.

*"My mind was changed, I'm glad you made it...Intoxicated, your vibe's amazing,"* Usher crooned.

"Oh my gosh," Kaylee said. She grabbed Imani's free hand, pulling her further into the dancing crowd. Her feet moved in time to the song, as she pointed her finger towards the ceiling.

"You know this is my song," she gushed, as she did a two-step with a smile taking up her entire face.

"Just don't waste my tiiiimmmmme," she sang in an exaggerated tone to Imani. The two hiked up their knees, jumping in sync with one another before pushing their hips together in a synchronized bump.

A renewed feeling of exhilaration ballooned in Imani's chest as she looked at her best friend. If anyone had told Imani four years ago, that she would be living back in Port Springs with a chosen family including Kaylee - who supported her and a great boyfriend like Michael who loved her with all he could give, there was no way she'd believe them. Yet, it was all true. She was no longer the chick from three years ago searching for belonging. Imani finally fit in where she needed to be. She didn't have complete clarity of what the future held, but she knew with God and her chosen family, she'd never be alone again.

Imani and Kaylee's backs were pushed against each other when Imani looked up to find a woman, shielded in a long sleeveless fur vest with fire engine red hair cascading down her back and matching nails, dancing up to the two of them. The woman's ample chest, decorated with layers of dainty necklaces, sat in a low-cut dress that hugged the signature curves she told everyone was purchased with the best money she ever spent.

"Okay, Imani!" she said, falling in line with their rhythm.

"Melody!" Imani smiled even wider. "This is my friend, Kaylee...thanks for the invite, by the way."

"Of course, girl," Melody said. "It's good to see you out."

For the first time tonight, Imani agreed. It felt good to be out.

## Chapter 4
## For The Streets

Imani turned down the AC in the car as Kaylee straightened herself in her seat, facing the steering wheel.

"Go back inside, 'Mani," she said, "they might be cutting cake or something."

"They're not, Kay...Randall is 35, not 12."

Imani opened her clutch, resting it in her lap and pulled out her lip gloss to re-apply it.

"I don't know what these rich people do."

"I could just go back home with you," Imani said. "I'm already in the car and it's not like Randall would miss me."

"We haven't even been at the party that long," Kaylee said, "and, the only reason I'm leaving is because I got called in."

In addition to being a student, Kaylee also worked part-time as a department store manager, which meant late nights and early morning shifts. She, Imani, Melody and Eve were all dancing when Imani saw Kaylee stop to read a text. She had gotten word from her co-manager that she needed someone to fill in for a colleague who called out sick. Imani insisted on walking Kaylee to her car where she was debating if Kaylee's emergency was a sign that she should leave as well.

"Just enjoy yourself," Kaylee continued, watching Imani push her head back. "Melody and Eve already said that one of them would take you home, so you're fine. You know you don't want to leave, it's barely the end of the night yet."

Imani knew that Kaylee was right. Even with how crazy drunk Randall was at the start of the party, there was no sign of it slowing down. More people had showed up and there was even a game of Spades being played near the pool outside.

Shifting in her seat, Imani tucked her lip gloss back in her clutch and looked at Kaylee for a beat.

"Okay, fine," she shrugged, "I'll head back in, but I don't want to be out too late."

"It's not like I'll be back at the apartment or asleep," Kaylee laughed, "just text to let me know you're good."

As soon as Kaylee drove off, Imani walked back inside, looking for Melody and Eve. She and Kaylee had left them near the wall next to the bar, but they were no longer there. Imani walked towards the backyard that was lit up with lights from the underground pool and uplights interwoven on the cement. She didn't think they were in the pool tonight, but she at least wanted to see if she could spot them where there weren't as many people. Imani managed to maneuver through the crowd to the door leading to the yard, prepared to pull it open, when her eyes fell on DeAndre sitting on a sofa seat across the room with the mysterious woman. Someone outside tapped on the glass, signaling that they were coming back inside, making Imani stop stargazing long enough to move over, giving them room to pass.

Her eyes drifted back to DeAndre and the mysterious woman talking as her hand rested on his knee. The two started laughing at whatever comment or joke they shared and Imani couldn't pull her gaze away, something about them just drew her in. The mysterious woman laughed, moving closer to DeAndre, damn near placing her titties in his lap. He then whispered in her ear, making her smile with full on desire.

Whatever he was saying to her, Imani knew he could definitely back it up.

DeAndre was often photographed with different women pretty much anytime he was out and Imani swore they all descended from the same family of stunning people. A woman always followed behind him and his crew whether they were out to eat or attending a more public event. He rotated through various women at the same rate someone would change their undershirts. Don't even get her started on the women she'd see during his matches on TV, clapping for him when he scored. They always stepped out looking like Instagram models in a sea of Polo shirt touting tennis fans. She never understood how men like him were able to keep up with so many, but he seemed to do it with such ease and little to no drama – at least, drama that didn't affect him directly.

It helped that a majority of them were not famous themselves, but what Imani liked to call "ambiguously recognized." They had enough of a following on social media to be potentially recognized on the street, but they never attracted much of a crowd. Women like that were often hanging on the arms of men like DeAndre, waiting for their appointment – an event, date night or weekend trip – which they were always willing to remain flexible for. Imani wasn't a part of the ecosystem of the wealthy, but she was around it enough to connect the dots.

DeAndre finished whispering in her ear when the woman stood up, adjusted her dress and pulled him up from his seat. With his lean build elongated, DeAndre let the woman lead him to wherever she planned on taking him. Imani watched them leave and had this sudden urge to follow them…a million questions coming in succession in her mind.

*Where were they going?*

*What were they doing?*

*What was he going to do… to her?*

DeAndre *looked* like he could teach a Masterclass on how to handle women.

"You…tryna go with them?"

Imani's heart accelerated, hearing Melody's question. She placed a hand on her chest and gasped, she hadn't even heard Melody near her, while Eve stood next to them speaking with another partygoer.

"Where did y'all end up?" Imani cleared her throat, switching the subject, especially now that Melody may have seen her ogling DeAndre.

"Making sure Rand doesn't end up drowning in the pool," Melody said. "He got caught up talking to some of the guys playing dominoes, so he should be occupied at least for another few minutes. We were coming back in to get some drinks."

Imani nodded, following behind Melody and Eve walking to the bar. Once they reached the bartender, the three women ordered drinks. As Melody turned to face the room, Imani noticed a few people smiling at her in that way people did when they knew someone famous was among them and insisted on acting natural. This was one of those parties where guests weren't stuck on taking sneak photos for social media, but just secure enough in the access they had, to casually mingle with the celebrities they fawned over. Some guests still in attendance were now forming small groups to play dominoes over a folding table, Twister in a corner towards the back of the living room and card games with stacks of cash and dice on the floor.

"Looks like it's empty over there," Melody pointed to an empty table a few feet away, "Oh, and I think I see...Uno cards? Y'all broads about to get it today."

A few minutes later, Melody, Imani, Eve and two other women who Melody let join in were all sitting down, waiting for Melody to deal out all the cards for their hand. The game started respectfully enough as each of the women felt each other out – politely letting the others know when it was their turn or offering a simple smile when one pulled out a Draw 2. But, after a few rounds of hand holding, the proverbial gloves came off and Imani felt like she might as well have been playing with dudes.

"Uno out, hoe!" Melody cackled, slamming her last card in the middle of the table and sticking her tongue out.

She stood up, turned to the side and jiggled her rounded cheeks in perfect succession, giving partygoers who weren't playing Uno an eyeful. To think that this side of Melody was the tamest Imani had ever seen did not go unnoticed.

"I thought we were playing numbers, though?" Eve asked, taking another sip of her wine. She went through the three cards Melody stacked in the pile like a teacher correcting a student paper.

"Here come the losers trying to switch up the damn rules," Melody said, rolling her eyes.

Imani laughed at Melody's arrogance and the side eye Eve gave her.

"No, Eve," Imani said. "Melody won this round fair and square. If we're going again, I'll deal this time."

## A Month of Sundays

Imani closed her hand and gathered all the cards as she looked up at the crowd, which had finally started to die down. It was that time of the evening when people were saying their goodbyes and indulging in their last drink of the night from the open bar. Randall was still MIA, but Imani figured if Eve wasn't worrying about it, then no one else had to either.

"Y'all ready?" she asked, now shuffling the cards.

DeAndre appeared suddenly out of nowhere, walking over to their table with his little friend nowhere to be found. For some reason, seeing him now, imagining what he and that chick *might* have been doing, made Imani's blood simmer a little.

"Hold on, y'all," she said, getting up. "I need to use the restroom. Be back."

Without even waiting for a response, she stepped away from the table in the opposite direction from where DeAndre was coming from. She was walking beyond the living room and the kitchen when she realized she had no idea where the bathroom was.

*Whose idea was it to even have it at this place? They couldn't have gotten a venue with one floor,* she thought. She just needed to gather herself.

"Excuse me," Imani asked a woman who was very clearly *not* giving the time of day to the guy talking to her, "do you know if there's a bathroom on this floor?"

"Straight down, first door to the left, love," she pointed behind her.

When Imani got to the door, she turned the knob to find it locked and knocked twice.

"Just a minute," someone said, voice muffled.

Imani fortunately didn't have to wait long when the door opened as mysterious woman herself stepped out, in all of her refreshed glory. Looking at her now, much closer, made Imani do a double take. The chick was beyond stunning with her flawless makeup and body bouncing effortlessly. DeAndre sure knew how to pick them, that was for sure.

"Sorry about that," she said, then smiled at Imani, flashing her dimples. She held the door open for Imani who was left stunned.

If the woman had been mean or gave her a crazy look, Imani would've had every bit of ammo to pile onto her sudden frustration. Instead, Imani took a breath and offered a small smile herself.

"No problem," she said. "I should've gone to the restroom sooner."

The woman let the door go once Imani had a hold of it and moved out of the way.

"Hey," she said. "Where'd you get that choker from?"

Imani put a hand on the choker she forgot she was even wearing.

"It's from a designer I know in New York," she responded.

Imani smiled at herself, remembering when she got the custom piece from Victoria, a high-end Black designer Imani met at an event in the city. When she finally saved enough coin to get it, she joked with Victoria that she'd one day be able to buy and select all her Avant Garde pieces to help fill her exclusive-designer closet.

"Love it," the woman replied. "Can you send me the link?"

"She doesn't sell her pieces online, but I can give you her website and you could reach out."

"Perfect. I'll type in my IG for you."

Imani handed her phone to this woman she had no clue about and had assumed just moments ago was blowing off DeAndre in the back of a bush somewhere. Two things could still be true, but at least the woman was nice. Imani had to get a grip – DeAndre was well in his lane to be dating anyone he wanted.

The woman gave Imani back her phone and took out her own.

"Let's take a selfie. I want to make sure I ask her about that piece," she pointed to the choker, "or anything like it."

"Sure."

The two put their heads together with Imani behind when the woman snapped the picture.

"Thank you..." the woman said, waiting for her to fill in.

"Imani," she said. "I didn't get your name?"

"Jazmine. My IG is all there for you. It was nice meeting you, gorgeous."

Imani returned to the living room where she found Melody and the rest of the ladies still sitting at the table. Smiling at each of them individually, Imani's expression fell once she saw who was in her seat. DeAndre was now there, sitting with his legs spread comfortably. She walked over with her arms folded in front of her but all airs of annoyance were gone, now that she settled on

## A Month of Sundays

DeAndre obviously having a very active dating life. She had never actually interacted with anyone linked romantically to him before, and seeing one of them reminded her of the reality she willingly accepted. Michael was hers alone and DeAndre belonged to Jazmine...and the many women he entertained.

She thanked God in heaven, for not being one of them.

"There you are," Melody said to her.

Imani could feel DeAndre's full focus on her before she even looked at him. She tried to ignore the tug in her stomach when their eyes met again.

"DeAndre, you're in my seat," she swallowed with a smile.

"It's a comfortable one, too."

He sat back on it even further, if that was at all possible, daring Imani to break eye contact. DeAndre raised his arms, crossing his hands at the back of his head. He wore a short sleeve shirt and the muscles in his arms flexed.

"Can you get out of my seat?" she asked.

"Can you say please?"

Imani's eyes narrowed as she tried her best to keep a straight face and not look as flustered as she felt. His expression was cold as ice before a mischievous smile rose up his cheeks. She melted like hot lava from the inside out.

"Please...DeAndre," she said.

Giving Imani another once over and biting the corner of his lip, DeAndre met her eyes again. Imani felt her middle throb in response.

"Since you said my name so well, I guess I will."

He stood up slowly, the distance between them barely existing once he was at his full height in front of her. Imani had to lift her gaze well above her height to maintain eye contact.

"D, get the hell away from our table," Melody chimed in. "This game is for women only, no men allowed, especially scallywags like you."

DeAndre looked at Melody, who once told Imani that he was like the annoying brother she never had, getting all the attention from the family just for existing.

"I don't even know what that shit means," he said, giving Melody a playful scowl before turning back to Imani.

"Where's Kaylee?" he asked.

"She had to leave a while ago."

"So, you've been here by yourself?"

Imani squinted her eyes at DeAndre slightly before stealing a glance back at the table.

"I'm not - though," she said, pushing her head back slightly. "I know people, too."

He held a look on Imani before chuckling to himself and shaking his head. He walked off again, heading to a few of the other guests still present. Jazmine wasn't around, from what Imani could see, and she assumed he went off to find her.

Imani sat down in her seat next to Melody and noticed she and Eve were the only two left at the table now.

"I don't know why you just won't slide your panties to the side for that man," Melody said, cutting the stack of cards on the table. "Get it out of both your systems."

"Mel," Eve chided, shocking laughter spilling out of her mouth.

Imani felt a knot the size of a frog form in her throat.

"Number one - I wouldn't do that," Imani started, "and, number 2, I'm definitely not single Melody - you met my boyfriend."

"Oh right, Matthew...no - Mitchell," Melody said, squinting up at the ceiling with a finger at her lips..."Miles?"

Imani rolled her eyes.

"Michael."

"Michael, Michael," Melody continued. "Yes, Michael is sweet. He's the church boy, right?"

Imani's brow spiked.

"He's a little more than that, but yeah. We've been together for almost five years."

Melody nodded then sighed, "Guess that'd make things complicated."

"Imani," Eve said, smiling from ear to ear. "I didn't know you were with someone."

"Yup," Melody responded before Imani could, as if Eve was talking directly to her. "He's stopped by the house a few times, picking her up. He seems like such a darling. Completely opposite to that playa from the

## A Month of Sundays

Himalayas over there," Melody dipped her head in the direction DeAndre went off to.

Yeah, the two were on complete opposite sides of the spectrum as far as Imani was concerned as well.

Eve, Melody and Imani played a few more rounds of Uno when someone called for Eve to come to the backyard. Melody and Imani shuffled behind her and the three found Randall laid out on the sofa, wrapped in toilet paper with a cream substance covering the bottom half of his face below his nose. Eve looked at him like a mother discovering their child got into a mess she knew she had to clean.

"Rand, baby," she encouraged, shaking him gently. "Open your eyes."

His wife grabbed a handful of napkins from the table and began slowly wiping the cream off his face. He opened his eyes, still bloodshot and bewildered looking, as if he forgot where he was. Once he saw Eve though, he settled for a moment before his face scrunched up in full panic mode.

"Baby yo- what the fuck's on my face, yo?" Randall asked. "I smell like that cheap ass Axe spray."

Melody and Imani were behind Eve, speechless, holding onto each other by the arms. Melody's lips were pursed while Imani held a hand to her mouth, both of them trying not to break into hysterical fits. Imani had no clue where Randall was or what he was up to but seeing him out here now looking like a mummified Santa Claus wasn't it.

The two snapped themselves out of it enough to give Eve and Randall some help with the mess. A few moments later, Imani walked out to the front of the mansion with Melody, Eve and Randall - free of shaving cream residue. The party was officially over as the remaining guests all left with their friends in their respective vehicles. Randall was sending off the few people who had remained while Eve sat in their Mercedes truck waiting for him, after giving Melody and Imani their goodbyes. Eve mentioned there was a cleaning crew coming tomorrow at the crack of dawn to clean everything up, but Imani was still at a loss for words on the mess Randall and everyone was leaving behind. Imani wasn't the tidiest, by any means, but she never attended a party where folks weren't offering themselves as tribute to pile at least some of the trash into large bags.

Melody was texting when she looked up at Imani.

"Roy is coming up the street for us now," she said, referring to her driver. "You need a ride home?"

Before she could answer, DeAndre approached them, jumping in and not even bothering to see if he was interrupting their conversation.

"I can take you home, Imani," DeAndre said. "Just let me talk to Rand and handle somethin' real quick.'"

"Hol' up," Melody said, looking at him like he grew another head before turning back to Imani and pointing a finger at him. "You're riding with him?"

Imani looked at DeAndre for a moment, shocked with how he tracked her down to the few seconds before she was going to leave. Something in his face suddenly burst the bubble of anxiety that she didn't even know she was holding. It felt like she had been wanting to say 'yes' to him all night and this was finally her chance. At least Jazmine would be there.

"Yeah, Melody," she said, nodding her head slightly. "I'm good."

# Chapter 5
# Home

Imani hugged herself against the slight chill in the Spring evening, walking ahead of DeAndre to his car which he mentioned was in the driveway. The steel matte gray vehicle was the only one left, sitting so low that Imani thought she'd basically be on the ground.

As she continued her stride, a twinge of panic manifested into the fussiness of a toddler – she literally felt her forehead dip in consternation.

*What is wrong with me?* she thought.

The problem arose when she realized she'd be riding in the car with DeAndre alone, sans Jazmine. When he told Imani that Jazmine wouldn't be with them, she regretted declining his offer a few moments ago. Melody had even tried to give her a way out but there was no use beating herself up over it now. It was just a ride. She'd hopped into Ubers with drivers who were fine before! She was a grown woman who could stay focused on making it home.

Once Imani got to the passenger door, she went to pull the handle, only to find there wasn't one. She turned to DeAndre who was now even closer, walking like he had absolutely nowhere to be.

"How do you even get in this thing?" she asked, placing a hand on her hip.

Once on the driver's side, he bent halfway to the level of the car. Almost magically, both his door and Imani's slid open at the same time, angling upward.

"You can get in now, grumpy," he teased, raising his brow at her.

The soft leather seats felt like pillows against Imani's entire body and it took everything in her not to let out an audible sigh of pleasure. She had never thought much of luxury cars, but she could definitely feel the difference between this and Kaylee's Prius. DeAndre climbed into the driver's seat, his woodsy scent - which was at a safe distance at the party, now hit her with full force. She had to get used to how close they were, too. They were mere inches away from each other, even with the middle compartment as a buffer.

"Sorry," she blurted, her manners superseding her attitude. "Thanks for offering me a ride."

"You're welcome," he said. "But, you never have to thank me for anything."

"So, where's Jazmine?" Imani blurted out again.

Again, she knew Jazmine wasn't going to be with them ,but Jazmine was nice…Jazmine was pretty…Jazmine would've been a physical barrier.

DeAndre scratched behind his ear, looking at her.

"She's straight," he said, then paused. "You know her?"

"We met in the restroom," Imani replied. "She complimented me and seemed nice, like *not* a person you'd just leave behind."

DeAndre feigned amusement.

"Happy she was so accommodating."

He placed his hand on top of the steering wheel and started the engine, which made a loud purring sound that Imani swore she felt rumble through her backside.

"DeAndre, wait."

Imani put a hand on top of his for a moment to stop him from driving, without realizing she was actually touching him until it was too late. She pulled back her hand like she just touched a hot stove. No…no - no touching was happening tonight. Like - at all!

Imani looked out the window and gazed at the front of the mansion.

"We're not leaving her here - are we?"

"Why do you care?"

"Because you arrived with a date, who's not here with you now. That's not very nice."

DeAndre chuckled, scratching his brow. "Calling it a date is a stretch."

### A Month of Sundays

Imani narrowed her eyes.

"I just don't get how she left so quickly. She didn't know anyone else there - did she?"

He looked at her, surveying her eyes, and actually looked stunned. Was she being naive? Ridiculous?

"A'ight, Imani, you're right. She only knew me," he met her gaze, with a serious expression.

"She told me she wanted to go home and I requested her magic carpet to fly here and take her back."

Imani rolled her eyes.

"Look, I just wanted to make sure she was safe. Don't you like her?"

DeAndre chuckled.

"You know, you and these words...are something else."

Imani sighed, folding her arms and settling into her seat.

"She's fine where she is," he said, "are you?"

"I'm fine."

She folded her hands over her clutch, clearing her throat.

DeAndre turned his attention back to his phone. He then glanced back at Imani, expectantly.

"You have an address for where you need to be?" he asked.

Imani had forgotten that she and DeAndre never exchanged personal information, not even phone numbers, and was glad he didn't pressure her to do so neither. Even with his random comments and messages on social media, DeAndre truly respected the boundary Imani had set. She *did* have boundaries, after all.

"Let me just type my place in," she said, reaching for his phone. When Imani returned his phone to him, she found DeAndre staring at her, dumbfounded.

"So, I can have your address, but I can't have your number?" he asked. "That don't sound ass backwards to you?"

"No. It sounds like you have the one thing you need...to follow instructions."

DeAndre shook his head, turning up the music before pulling off. A playlist with Jeezy, Rick Ross and Jay-Z was on rotation in the background, but not on full blast, as the two had been talking since they left the mansion grounds.

"I'm sorry if Kaylee came on kinda strong," Imani started.

"Nah, she's cool," he shrugged, "at least *she* was showin' love."

"What does that even mean?"

"Just saying what I observed." He scratched his chin, looking ahead.

Imani shook her head, taking in the full moon glowing from the dark sky above.

"I didn't expect to even see you tonight," she said. "Thought you'd be recuperating from the last match, to prepare for your next one in a few days."

Any game that DeAndre was competing in, was must-see TV and an event that no one in Port Springs missed. To a Port Springs native, it was the equivalent of a televised presidential inauguration.

"Yeah, just needed to take it easy before practice again."

He let out a breath, that Imani felt read more like exhaustion than anything else. She couldn't help her curiosity.

"Are you good?" she asked, looking at him fully again.

"I'm straight. Why you ask?"

"I mean…I know you won and everything, but…Mike and I were watching the game and I just kept noticing that you looked…I don't know, not like yourself."

Imani noticed the mien of annoyance that flashed in his eyes before he toggled them to her.

"Did he cry for me?"

She shook her head. "Seriously, DeAndre, you should consider taking a break."

"I already took one," he said, a slight edge in his tone.

But she didn't take it personally, assuming it had something to do with his injury.

Imani grimaced, "I know…I'm…sorry. What you do is so far above my head, I shouldn't even comment."

"Nah, it's not you."

He licked his lips as if agitated with himself. Jay Z's "Lost Ones" continued streaming in the background as the two sat in silence for a beat.

## A Month of Sundays

"My knee getting jammed up really fucked with me, ya' know?"

Imani didn't *know*, but she could imagine. She had never been to a game of his in-person yet, watching him on TV on that court a few months ago - laid out, felt like she received a punch to the gut. She had never seen him that vulnerable in a match before and Imani didn't know what to say. So, she didn't say anything. No messages, no comments on Instagram. She couldn't even wrap her head around how to respond in a way that didn't seem pacifying.

"How're you feeling now?"

She had asked the question so quietly, but the way it was held in the air resonated loudly.

"That's what I'm trying to figure out."

He had such a "larger than life" presence when he played but, seeing him now reminded Imani of how much of a weight it could be. She couldn't imagine the pressure he felt to continue to perform at such a high level each time. Imani looked at his profile with a sudden urge to rest a hand on his leg and pull the side of his face close to hers with the other, gently kissing the space behind his ear. The urge was so strong…so clear in her mind, that it scared the hell out of her.

"Well, you can take your time," she said. "You are one of the greatest to do it, after all."

Imani noticed the second her compliment resonated because his cheeks rose into the cockiest smile.

"Say it again."

He tilted his head, looking at Imani, really expecting her to repeat herself. She rolled her eyes, resisting the urge to willingly indulge him.

"I won't."

They laughed.

"I also don't have a clue about tennis. I won't even lie. But, your stats are…" Imani threw her voice like a sports commentator, "Unbelievable, they say!"

DeAndre chuckled at her imitation, switching lanes on the parkway.

"Okay, okay," he said.

"But, what about you? How've you been? Haven't seen you in about a month of Sundays."

Imani felt like God had just thrown her a sign. The only other person she ever heard say that phrase was her father.

She looked at DeAndre, his eyes still peeled on the road, leaning back with one hand on the steering wheel, seemingly unaware of what he said. She smiled at the familiarity, the sudden intimacy, and took a quick breath to avoid an awkward silence.

"I'm on Instagram," she said, "I'm around."

"Barely."

"I've gotten better."

Imani poked at the small heart tattooed on her forearm, outlining the shape with her fingertip.

"You're still doing your art?"

"Always," she said. "Taking commissions here and there, but I work at the Artgo Museum full-time now."

DeAndre's brows shot up in surprise.

"The one over on 48th and Stanton?"

She nodded, smiling at what all Port Springs natives said when she mentioned the neighborhood relic. Though Artgo had a recent resurgence as a mecca for art, it was more of a community center for the area back when Imani and DeAndre were kids.

"Damn, haven't heard about Artgo in a while."

"Yeah, it's good. I have a chance to work with the main curator who's also a Black woman, so that's...interesting."

"As long as you're happy," he said, shifting his eyes to hers for a moment.

The two fell into simple conversation shortly after and it didn't take long for Imani to see why. Just like when they met, the most unassuming thing about DeAndre was how easy it was to talk to him, at least for Imani anyway. Even though they were worlds apart in terms of experience, talking to DeAndre felt like talking to the guy from around the way who was funny, laidback and crazy smart.

Talking to DeAndre felt like...home.

Minutes later, he slowed the car down once they ran into a sea of traffic that didn't seem to be advancing anytime soon. They spoke about Rand's party. DeAndre didn't live at the mansion that held the party anymore, but he still kept it as an investment. Though he never expected anyone to host a massive blowout like Randall just had.

"I'm just impressed that he never ended up in the pool," Imani said, referring to Randall and his drunken state. "The way he was acting, I thought he was gonna flip over or get pushed in."

DeAndre laughed. "Nah, he told me when I came in that he was staying far away from it, so he wouldn't get got...I don't know where those fools got that shaving cream from, though."

The two of them laughed so hard, Imani felt her stomach cramp. She was finally able to release the laughter she was holding onto for dear life, tears gathering in her eyes.

"I could talk to you for hours."

DeAndre said it so faintly, in the midst of their laughter, that Imani thought she imagined it. But, no, she heard it and caught the brief sense of want in his eyes.

Imani's eyes fell to her lap, a shiver running down her spine before she looked up at the window again.

"There's literally nowhere to go at this point," she said. "You know another way?"

"I do...but, I want to take you somewhere first. It's along the way."

Imani looked at him, narrowing her gaze again.

"Where?" she asked, cautiously.

"My place."

Imani blinked - eyes the shape of large domes.

"Chill," he said, putting up his hand for emphasis. "It's not like that."

"How can I trust that it isn't?"

"Because if it was, I'd say, 'Imani, we're going to my place so I can sleep wit' you.'"

Her breath caught in her throat.

"But I didn't say that," DeAndre continued, turning to her for a beat, "Did I?"

"That...wasn't necessary," she countered, breaking his eye contact. Her voice was so weak, she didn't even recognize herself.

"Well, I'm gonna always tell you what you need to know," he said. "For real."

Imani took a breath. They were either going to sit here, waiting in traffic for an undisclosed amount of time - wasting even *more* time, or ...they could just take the shorter route.

"Can't you just take a picture of it and send it to me?"

"I could...but I want you to take in all of it, get your artistic opinion. And, when's the next time I'm gonna be able to show you in person? You work full-time now anyway, like you said, right?"

Imani took a quick glance at her phone. It wasn't even that late. The hour was...decent. She looked up at the traffic again, this time, hearing car horns blaring in the midst of a total standstill. Imani closed her eyes for a moment and took a breath.

She should've *never* agreed to this ride in the first place.

"Ok," she said. "I'll check it out for a few minutes then I need to get home. I'm serious."

# Chapter 6
# Impulse

DeAndre was grateful to every higher force of nature for the amount of self-control he exercised, watching Imani walk around his house while only the two of them were in it. When he initially approached her at Randall's party, it didn't take long for him to notice who *wasn't* with her. He was so enraptured, it had also taken everything in him to not grab her face and kiss her lips. DeAndre hadn't even made it all the way in the house for the party before he spotted her - looking like the physical manifestation of his wildest dreams.

"...You really can add anything with the amount of space you have," she was saying now, standing next to him.

The two of them were in the middle of the spacious common area between the foyer and the living room. Imani was surveying the large wall in front of them, between two windows overlooking the side of the house, to help DeAndre decide how he should decorate it.

"The sky's the limit. You just have to decide what you want."

*I want you.*

He had thought it more than once tonight, multiple times at the party and in the car, to the point where it played in his head like a broken record. To try and tone it down, he did what he always did when she planted herself in his head and wouldn't leave, fuck it out...or at least... try to. It didn't work, though.

## Jade Olivia

Even with Jazmine working overtime, doing straight gymnastics on his dick, it never worked. Imani had prime real estate in his head.

"That's what I need your help on," he said, scratching the back of his ear before putting his hand back in his pocket.

He shrugged.

"I don't know where to start when it comes to all the art stuff, but I know I want to walk in here and feel like..."

Words always came up short for DeAndre when he made impulsive decisions. Purchasing this house last year was one of those decisions. All he remembered was stepping through the french doors and envisioning it as...

"An oasis?"

Imani asked, facing him now. Her doe eyes, against her silky, sepia brown skin, settled back on him. He smiled at her, feeling a twitch in his cheeks. That was exactly what he wanted.

"Yeah."

She turned, walking further away and closer to the wall, as DeAndre watched her every move. Imani was much shorter than him, but her neck and arms were elongated by her posture alone. Almost swan-like in appearance, she stood with her back facing him and could easily be mistaken for a ballet dancer. The shirt she had on left her right arm completely uncovered. Since she kept her hair short, a bevy of tattoos were visible from the nape of her neck near her choker necklace, down to her wrist.

"How often are you even home?"

He moved closer to her now, smelling her amber fragrance, positioning himself to face her.

"Not that often, to tell you the truth," he said. "My staff and team are here more than I am. But, I refuse to have a home I'm livin' in to feel like another hotel."

Imani looked up at the space again.

"Would you ever consider moving to another state permanently?"

DeAndre scoffed. "Hell no. My heart will always be where I'm from, ya' know?"

She gave him a small smile before nodding slowly.

## A Month of Sundays

"Yeah, I know," sounding dazed before turning to the wall again. "Well....it IS a great canvas."

DeAndre watched her eyes plastered to the blank wall, her kissable pout slightly agape, like she was in deep thought. He could care less how the wall was done, especially if he could convince her to paint it for him. She could decorate it with unicorns and glitter if that was the type of time she was on. But he also knew she wouldn't do that – her work was really that good.

"You could go crazy with it, too," he added, "I trust you."

Her eyes glided to him then, a smile threatening to break free. She folded her arms and tilted her head.

"I have to see if it's really something I can do," she said. "I have other projects and commissions; I'm booked."

"Busy and blessed?" he raised a brow in jest.

Imani nudged his arm with her elbow and laughed, finally freeing that smile from its state of bondage. He loved hearing her laugh, feeling the sound spread on his body at the pace of sweet honey being poured.

"Okay, DeAndre."

He also liked how it felt when she said his name.

Imani may have been hesitant at the moment, but DeAndre had already made up his mind. He was going to make sure she would create something just for him.

"Cool wit' staying here for a minute?"

He walked to his office on the opposite side of the house, searching through a pile of papers on his desk before pulling out the first drawer and finding what he needed. He walked back into the common area with a small book and pen in hand, to the circular table. Scribbling away, he felt Imani watching him.

"Wait, is that a check?"

"Yup," he said, ripping it off the perforated line and handing it to her. She looked at it, then quickly darted her eyes up at him again.

"I never said I would do it," her brows furrowed. "No need to give me a… deposit or anything."

He chuckled.

"It's not a deposit. I prefer to just pay in clean numbers…Cash App or Venmo won't let me transfer this to you in one shot anyway."

Imani shook her head, now avoiding gazing in the direction of the check again.

"I can't accept that."

"You workin' for free?"

Imani rolled her eyes at him.

"No, I don't."

"Then?"

He maneuvered the check towards Imani again, still holding it between them. After another moment of hesitation – a bit too long, DeAndre took a deep breath.

"Just hold it for now and let me know within a week if you want to take on the project."

"How do you know I won't spend it and ditch you?" she hiked her eyebrow.

DeAndre chuckled, then shook his head. The little hints of sarcasm she piecemealed him felt as satisfying as drops of candy for a quick sugar rush.

"Something tells me...now that you say that, there's no way in hell you'd actually do it."

Imani cut her eyes, gathering her mouth to one side in reluctance. She then pinched the corner of the check between her thumb and index finger before giving it a slight tug. Her eyes, dipped in reluctance, toggled up to him.

"I'm not looking at this now, just so you can watch my reaction to how much it is."

DeAndre gripped it between his fingers tighter as Imani tugged on it once, then a second time when she realized he was messing with her.

"Whatever you want to do," he said with a smirk, finally letting go of his side of the check. "Lemme know if it's enough."

"Uhh...Okay. Thanks," she said, taking another breath.

"So, could I...see a little more of the house?"

"No problem...want something to drink?"

After refusing his offer to quench any thirst, DeAndre showed Imani the remainder of the first level they were on - from the den to the kitchen and his office. He didn't bother to offer her a tour of the second wing of the house or upstairs. The entire time they toured from one area to the next, Imani kept looking above her, to the left and right, clearly overwhelmed by the immensity of it all. Her reaction was palpable and it even made him look at this spot with fresh eyes. *Did he really need all of this?* he thought. He just knew he wanted her to at least get used to it, though, as she'd be working in it for a few weeks - at least.

They ended the tour outside, in the backyard, on DeAndre's personal tennis court – the main selling point of the house, he admitted. This was the first house he had purchased with one that was the perfect surface and size in diameter–no customizations needed. Painted in an immaculate green color, the clay court came with the mansion from the previous owners who were avid tennis players themselves. They didn't play on the Pro level, DeAndre had learned, but they took it seriously as a hobby and invested resources into it. The court was so well done that all DeAndre's staff really had been doing was keeping it routinely cleaned.

With his hands still in his pockets, he watched Imani walk past him onto the court, heels tapping against the rubbery surface. The evening wind was picking up, brushing against the leaves, but it was still comfortable enough to stay out. She stopped at the middle of the center service line and turned around to face DeAndre who was a few steps away from the baseline. Imani's motion triggered the court's sensory lights so they beamed down on her, giving her an iridescent glow. His heart was racing just looking at her so comfortable in his space which suddenly made him want her here all the time.

The court overlooked the floral landscaping that his mother had insisted on getting done to add a view of interest to the yard, that would've otherwise just been unimaginative clay ground.

"This is…wow," she said, grinning at this point. Even though he was further away from her, he could see her beam with excitement.

"And again…I don't know what would be impressive or a big deal, but it's really sporty."

DeAndre chuckled, placing a hand at the back of his neck.

"I guess that's one way to put it."

Imani shrugged her shoulders.

"I don't know…I feel like I'm in your office or something. This is what you'd consider work, right?"

DeAndre pulled down his hand.

"Not sure if it feels like work," he shrugged. "More like an impulse. I'm not really clockin' in and out."

Imani just looked at him, still for a moment, before she caught herself.

"Sorry," she said, looking down at her hands. "It's just when I tell people that about what I do, they look at me like I'm nuts...like, it's not that I don't love it, I just feel like art is more instinctual. How can I explain it? Like if I don't do it for too long, I get kind of irritated."

Imani avoided DeAndre's eyes before folding her arms again.

"Yeah...I get irritated," he said, "when I don't win."

Another laugh spilled over from Imani, but DeAndre didn't even break a smile, feeling his jaw tighten at the mere thought. He hated losing, to the point where he didn't even talk about those matches when reporters brought it up after a game. Reporters always want to know what you may have *learned* from your recent loss. Hell, he learned that he needed to go even harder the next time around.

"Oh my God," Imani started, "And, you know what I can't stand, either?"

She walked over to sit on one of the benches on the edge of the court, a few feet from where DeAndre stood.

He went over and sat on the bench next to her, awaiting her response.

"When you search for the right color to paint with," Imani said. "Like, obsessing over it, researching it and all. Then, you buy this gorgeous red, open the tube, test it on a blank page and then...it's purple."

Imani looked at him, mimicking the seriousness shown on his face, before breaking into a cackle, her face crumbled in laughter.

DeAndre, realizing what she was doing to ease the tension, bent over halfway at his knees and burst into laughter himself.

"You real corny, Imani."

"I'm sorry," she said, still recovering with a hand placed on her stomach, "I'm not trying to belittle how important it is to you...just...felt like I lost you for a minute, ya' know?"

DeAndre did feel like he was getting in over his head for a minute, starting to dive into conversations that didn't even exist yet.

"*Losing is an excuse for the weak-minded,*" David would say, "*You weak now?*"

## A Month of Sundays

It was the start of almost every conversation he had with his father after a loss, even as a kid, and he knew it was high time again to have another one. This latest injury was the closest thing he ever felt to weakness.

"Yeah, I know," he said simply, breaking out of his reverie with a smile.

There weren't many people who could redirect DeAndre's focus. Randall was always the one to hype him up before and after a game, no matter the outcome, and that included lightening up the mood when the game didn't end in his favor. Imani did something like that just now...and was much better at it than his boy.

"Do you have anything else in your life you're looking forward to?" she asked.

DeAndre tilted his head, narrowing his eyes at her.

Imani shook her own head.

"It's not a big deal," she said, in haste. "That sounded like a much deeper question than necessary on a Friday night."

"Nah...I love the question," he said, his heart speeding up by the minute. If anyone had told him a few years ago that he would be turned on by basic conversation, he'd laugh in their face before walking away with another chick to sleep with.

"I don't," DeAndre said.

Imani's head pushed back slightly with widened eyes.

"And, not in a depressed kinda way...I got other things going on outside the game. A couple projects, but I really want to stay grounded in the community. Trying to find more opportunities to do that."

"Yeah, I could see that."

"You think you could help me with that?"

Imani watched him, sizing him up with a raised brow.

"I don't work for free, remember?" she asked, before breaking into a smile.

He shook his head, laughing again.

"Oh, you right, you right," he said, his tone playful.

The light from the court continued illuminating the glow of her skin. He would never get bored looking at her nor her eyes and lips, which his eyes were drawn to. He felt himself drawing closer to her - he wanted to kiss her right now.

No, he needed to kiss her right now. Her lips were painted with the perfect shade of red, outlining her pout which seemed to open so effortlessly...

"Traffic should be clear," she said, pressing her lips together then, as if wiping away the desire that just passed between them...or was it just him...or was it just her?

She pushed herself up from the bench, leaving a trail of her sweet scent.

"Should be," he said, releasing a breath. "Let's get you back."

Imani grabbed her bag from where she abandoned it on one of the tables in the backyard and followed him back to the front of the house.

Once the two were in another one of DeAndre's cars - a Range Rover without scissor doors, to Imani's relief - it didn't take long for him to get to her apartment. Traffic had indeed cleared up, making their ride swift and quiet, but not awkward. DeAndre felt good being with Imani, all the same, and was already looking for another excuse to see her again. He parked in front of Imani's apartment complex and turned the car off, while his playlist filled the air with hip hop.

Imani was facing the window on her side not moving an inch, her arms folded.

"Hey," he said, softly.

Still nothing.

He hadn't touched her for what felt like so long, even though he had given her a hug earlier at the party. DeAndre placed a hand on top of hers, rubbing his thumb over her knuckles, feeling the softness of her skin against his own calloused hands. Imani slowly turned her head towards him, then, her honey brown eyes fluttering open as he moved his hand away.

Her eyes adjusted, focusing on DeAndre before she chuckled.

"Wow, guess I'm the old lady in the club," she said.

He could get used to watching her wake up, too.

"It's all good," he said. "And, it's only..." He took a quick glance at the dashboard. "A few minutes to 1."

Imani looked at the dashboard, eyes wide at the time.

"God, it's late," she said. "Anyway, thanks for the ride...again."

DeAndre leveled another look at her.

## A Month of Sundays

"I already told you - you don't have to thank me."

From just this night alone, he was willing to give her damn near anything.

"But, I want to," she said. "So, I will."

With her clutch in hand, she went to open the door when DeAndre had a thought.

"You comin' to the match?"

Imani slanted her body to get a better look at him.

"On Sunday? Not sure if I'll have the time to...I'll be doing Aaliyah's fitting after church. I also didn't get tickets."

He tilted his head again, staring at her with confusion. At times, DeAndre had to look at her, just to make sure she wasn't joking around.

*You don't need tickets because you know me,* he thought.

"What?" she asked, picking up on his expression. "I've never been to a game of yours, but everyone talks about how crazy it is to get tickets."

"Wait a minute," DeAndre squinted. "You've never seen me play?"

Imani shook her head.

"Well, we gotta change that."

"Well, it won't be this weekend...but, it could be nice," she shrugged. "I'd be curious."

"I'll make sure you're in if you come Sunday...later...or whenever. I got you."

"Whatever you say, D," she said with a chortle.

"Nah, I'm serious. If I tell you I got you, I do."

"Yeah," she said, looking at him directly. "I just have to make sure. Michael and I are—"

"Yeah, yeah," he said, under his breath but still audible. He pushed the top of his head back on the headrest and held her gaze.

"I know," he said.

DeAndre didn't even let her finish, already growing frustrated that she dropped *another* mention of dude before the night ended.

Imani looked at him for a beat before giving him a small smile, eyes twinkling under the yellow streetlights.

"Have a good night, DeAndre."

59

## Jade Olivia

With that, she climbed out the car, closing the door behind her. It wasn't until he saw her disappear inside the entrance that he pulled off, letting his mind run back to their time together all over again.

# Chapter 7
# Safety

Before Imani became a member of New Leaf Church, she heard so much about Michael Coleman she swore she knew him long before they even met.

As Pastor Coleman's youngest son, Michael was the golden child – following his father's footsteps into ministry. He looked like one, too - clean shaven, usually outfitted in a blue, black or gray suit unless he was running with the toddlers in Children's Church.

"I remember when that boy was running after his dad," Ethel had said, shaking her head with a smile. "Now…he's growing up to be him."

Imani thought he was cute and looked like the straight-A kid in school who wanted to do well on all fronts, follow the rules to a T and smile proudly at all the fruits of his labor. There was something innocent about Michael that Imani gravitated to that felt safe – the total opposite of what she encountered in New York – and she only hoped they would eventually become friends.

After a meeting with the creative arts ministry team lead, Imani was in the vestibule, waiting for her new church friend Kaylee to come meet her. The two were in talks of moving in together, since Kaylee needed a roommate she could trust and preferred to find someone who was already at New Leaf. Imani had been living with Aunt Ethel for a little over a year, gathering enough savings, from working as her assistant, to at least afford a one-year apartment lease.

Imani knew she'd figure out the rest. She was more than ready to leave her aunt's apartment in assisted-living housing, especially since the clause that allowed tenants to have relatives under 65 live with them for up to a year was at the brink of expiring.

Imani was packing her art supplies in her bag, when she heard one of the office doors in the back close. When she looked up, Michael was there, locking the door behind him. He turned around and found Imani's eyes on him.

"Hi, Sister Imani," he smiled.

Imani pushed her head back in surprise.

"Hi there," she said.

Michael chuckled.

"Yeah, your aunt has spoken a lot about you before you actually moved back here," he said. "And...since I've seen you come and go with her...I guess, I just put a face to a name."

"Oh, well...you're right," Imani smiled.

"I'm Michael," he said, extending his hand to her. When their hands held onto each other, the ease Imani felt in that moment was instant.

They started seeing each other on their way in and out of meetings. A few weeks passed before Michael finally had the courage to ask Imani on a date - a request that she saw coming. Michael was the kind of guy who showed every bit of emotion on his sleeve and seemed like the type to have planned his request and the date over the entire time they knew each other. He took her to a restaurant on the boardwalk of Springsdale Beach - the nearest beach for Port Springs' residents. And, after a casual meal, Michael suggested they get some ice cream along the shoreline to watch the sunset.

"Has anyone ever told you that you're so easy to want to take care of?" Michael asked, before casting his eyes down and shaking his head.

They were sitting on a bench eating their chocolate chip fudge ice creams, Imani had hers in a cone while Michael ate his in a cup. She turned back to him with her mouth slightly open in shock, revealing the ice cream and extra fudge she had in hers on her tongue.

"I'm sorry," he laughed. "I probably shouldn't have said that out loud."

Imani smiled, taking another chunk out of her ice cream cone. She had spoken a little more openly on this first date than she thought she would, mentioning her parents and exactly how she ended up moving back in with her aunt. Imani told him almost everything. At least, everything he needed to know.

"I don't expect you to tell me everything you've gone through," he started, "especially, since it's your past, but... you're amazing just the way you are."

Filled with emotion, Imani nodded, avoiding eye contact in an effort not to burst into tears in front of him. How had he said the one thing she had been yearning to hear? She felt it in her heart like a sign from above, but hearing someone say it, was a feeling she couldn't put into words.

"I guess we should go," she said, "I have to get back to my Aunt's house or she'll start calling until I pick up, like I'm still the kid she met at 12 years old."

The two chuckled as they stood up from the bench and walked back to Michael's car. About an hour later, Michael parked at Aunt Ethel's house and opened the passenger side for Imani, escorting her to the front steps. With Ethel's front light on, Imani managed to see to the bottom of her tote as she fished for her keys. She was prepared to open the door, when she turned behind her to find Michael still standing there. He rubbed his hands at his sides, looking nothing short of someone who was waiting for his name to be called.

"Are you okay?" Imani asked, her eyes shifting, suddenly feeling the same nervous energy Michael had. She tried not to show the effect it had on her, but she was always gauging someone's energy. It was second nature to her at this point.

He stepped closer to her and Imani smelled the mint dark chocolate ice cream, from earlier, on his breath. It was mixed with a pleasant cedar scent.

"Imani..." he asked, his breathing shallow. "Can I kiss you?"

Her eyes widened, surprised by his advance.

"Ugh..." she stammered.

Michael laughed, awkwardly, stepping back again to soften the blow.

"It's not that," Imani started. "I...guess...I never thought you'd want to kiss."

He looked at her again, eyes suddenly more than sure. "I do...I do...I wanted to respect your boundaries, though."

Michael looked from her lips to her eyes and back, chest beating through his shirt with anticipation.

"Thank you for that," she chuckled. "But, just a piece of advice?"

She stepped even closer, giving him the greenlight.

"Don't hold back."

Michael inched halfway to her lips and stopped, allowing Imani to close the space between them. The kiss was probably the sweetest, and kindest one she'd ever experienced at that point. It was a kiss of reverence.

Michael pulled away, slowly, and let out a shaky breath. He looked at her, fully enchanted.

"You're amazing."

Michael and Imani's relationship moved forward with the same compassion and care that he poured into her from that day. He supported her during some of her toughest moments with depression and self-doubt, praying with her and affirming her through words that he'd text to her in the middle of the night as sleep evaded her.

*I know today isn't a good one, but you won't stay there.*

These messages and so much more were saved in her phone for reference and memorialized in collages she'd hang on the wall in her bedroom. Imani didn't remember talking to Ethel about Michael much, but Ethel had gathered *something* was happening between the two when Imani would hang around after service, waiting for him to greet other parishioners.

Watching him now, greeting them with such patience and poise after his ordination as minister, Imani was so proud of the man he was – his loyalty, love and devotion to her. She swore it was the closest thing to a perfect love she'd ever have.

"Thank you, Mother Connie," he said, hugging one of the oldest elders in the church. "I felt your prayers all through this journey."

Michael skirted his eyes to Imani as she, Aunt Ethel and Kaylee approached him from her seat at the front of the pew. As Mother Connie left, Michael smiled, looking exhausted, but overjoyed.

"You did so well up there, sweetheart," Imani said, pulling him into a soft hug, careful not to wrinkle his ministerial robe. "How'd it feel?"

"Like I was sweating bullets," he said, smiling. "Out of all the times I've been up there to speak or make announcements...being up there for this...was a whole different experience."

## A Month of Sundays

"Where's Mark and Andrew?" Imani asked, referring to Michael's two older brothers.

Michael sighed and shook his head.

"They stayed for the ordination," he said, "but left just before it ended."

Michael had an awkward, estranged relationship with his brothers that Imani knew weighed heavy on him.

Imani rubbed his back as Aunt Ethel and Kaylee looked at him empathetically.

"We gotta just continue to lift those boys up in prayer," Aunt Ethel chimed in.

"Always," Michael swallowed. "I still love them...we all have to eventually decide our path, even if it takes longer to get there for some than others."

Imani watched him, warmed by his maturity. His selflessness really was unbelievable.

"Ok, Minister Michael," Kaylee beamed, lightening the mood. She gave him an exaggerated wink as the four of them chuckled.

"We should be getting out of here, right, Ms. Ethel?"

Kaylee turned to Ethel, taking the older woman's purse out of her hands.

"Yes, indeed," she said. "Gotta cheer on my team today...my boys will make the playoffs this go 'round, in Jesus name."

They all laughed as Michael and Imani hugged and kissed them goodbye before they left. Michael and Imani then stood in the sanctuary alone. After a few moments, Michael held Imani's gaze, looking at her much longer than anticipated.

"Penny for your thoughts?" she asked.

"I just...thought so much up there...about you being by my side. Now that I'm in this new role, I want you to be in a new position in my life."

Imani swallowed, suddenly feeling like she was back riding on a familiar train. The topic of marriage was always the largest elephant in the room that everyone around them wanted to openly acknowledge. The younger women in the church would praise Michael for his God-fearing love for Imani while the elders often complimented Imani for her own level of class and "sophistication"- the perfect First Lady in the making. But, none of these compliments or praises made Imani feel any different about it - now was not the time for them to get married.

"A new position?" she asked.

"Premarital counseling sessions with the pastor are starting up again in a few weeks," he took Imani's hands, engulfing them with his. "And, I want us to take it this go 'round."

She smiled, looking over his light-skinned features. He had a look similar to the pastor - his father, paired with his mother's keen eyes.

Michael had mentioned counseling a few times before, promising that each time a new session was coming up would be the time they would attend. It was a two-month commitment that Michael or Imani would always end up backtracking on for whatever reason. Mainly because of Michael's ministerial responsibilities piling on as well as his 9-5 day job as a marketing executive. There was no need for Imani to bring that up, though. She wanted to remain hopeful that they'd get to it, and definitely knew they needed it before making any decision about marrying each other.

She took a breath before turning to follow him down the middle aisle of the church, outside of the double doors.

That sounds like a great idea," she tightened her squeeze around his hand.

"Yeah?" he asked, one eyebrow raised.

"For sure," she nodded with a wide smile.

He clearly wasn't trying to rush marriage, choosing to follow the path of what is taught through their doctrine. There was no matrimony by way of Justice of the Peace for someone like Michael and Imani appreciated taking it slow. Maybe, going through counseling would alleviate some of the hesitance Imani had about marrying him?

The two walked back to the Pastor's office where Pastor Coleman and First Lady Coleman were preparing to leave. When Michael and Imani stepped into their office, the two were beaming with pride for their son. Michael removed his robe, allowing both of his parents to embrace him with a pride that was beyond palpable. Each time Imani witnessed the affection and love the Colemans had for Michael, she couldn't help but yearn for the same parental love, - a love that was taken from her so soon.

## A Month of Sundays

"Imani, aren't you proud of this Man of God?" Pastor Coleman said, his baritone voice resounding through the room.

Imani often joked with Ethel that Pastor Coleman sounded as if he did voiceovers for car insurance commercials on the side.

"Absolutely," she said, beaming. "But I'm not surprised."

Imani was smiling, but as soon as her gaze met the First Lady, her expression faltered. Mrs. Coleman looked at Imani pensively with a close-mouthed smile that didn't reach her eyes. She was always *kind* to Imani, from the time she and Michael started dating. But, she always seemed to hold back from her, like she didn't want to catch herself saying something to Imani that she'd regret.

"It's nice to see you, Mrs. Coleman," Imani said, extending her arms to meet her in a hug.

"You, too, Imani," she said, patting Imani on the back sheepishly, "It's good seeing you...as always."

Imani blinked, still not sure what this tension with her man's mom was all about.

Pastor Coleman and the First Lady spoke with their son a little while longer before Michael invited them out to eat with him and Imani. His parents declined, leaving Imani and Michael alone on their first brunch date in weeks. That was another thing that Imani appreciated about her relationship with Michael, he always made an effort to include Imani in the inner workings of his immediate family. If there was an event they were attending or if his mom invited him over to Sunday dinner, Michael always spoke to Imani's internal need for connection and to have a family of her own.

∼

"Do you ever wonder what they use to make these biscuits so...savory?"

Imani looked up from her plate at Michael when he asked the question, eyes narrowed in a state of euphoria.

They were at Ronnie's Diner, which was furnished as an ode to the diners of the 1950s - bright red chairs and booths along with the waiters' attire of boat hats and stark pastel aprons. The checkerboard floor tiling squeaked as patrons were escorted to their tables. Michael loved coming here when they first started dating, relishing in how nostalgic it all was. Imani wasn't sure how he could see nostalgia in the 1950s, as a descendent of the Black American South, but she never bothered to burst his bubble.

He took a sip of his coffee, not even clearing his mouth of the soppy biscuit and she chuckled at his expression that was beyond content. He looked like a kid at a candy store.

"Love, you're acting like we weren't here a month ago," she said, placing her hand over his.

"I know, let me stop," he said, as if realizing how silly he looked. He interlaced his fingers with Imani's and held her gaze, his eyes crinkled at the corners.

"Just felt like I haven't had a meal in days. It's been crazy at the firm this week and I'm off to another business trip in the next few days."

He turned his eyes up towards the ceiling.

"And, you know Pastor still wants me to attend some of these funeral services during the week when I'm here."

Whenever Michael conducted church business with Pastor Johnson - his father, he never called him Dad, even if he was talking about him outside of the church like he did now. Imani couldn't help but feel like Pastor Johnson was almost part-human, the way Michael described him sometimes. Even after four years, she'd remind herself that the two were, in fact, father and son.

"I can imagine, will you have a break coming up soon?"

"I got to, especially now that my girl is about to be the head curator at the Artgo."

Imani raised her brow.

"It's just an assistant position."

"Does it matter what it is, though? You're in the infrastructure. God's got you."

Imani smiled, but sobered a bit, thinking about this gig that she now had in the bag for the past year. Having a job at Artgo was the art world equivalent of being drafted into the NBA. It was hard to get into and those who worked there typically stayed for the long haul, at least until they were well into their retirement years. But, the more Imani thought about the opportunity, the more she *didn't* want to stay there for that long.

This was her first corporate job in years, where she actually had to wake up

## A Month of Sundays

early in the morning to get ready, commute and spend a *full day* in one space. Over the past few years, she got by with odd jobs like assisting Aunt Ethel, bartending or crafting hearts with foam at coffee shops. She hoped she'd flourish in this newfound structure she was forced to yield to, simply because she was in need of health insurance.

Imani added creamer to her coffee and mixed it with a spoon, taking note of her colorful manicure - each finger painted either red, pink or white.

"How was the party last night?"

Imani's spoon dropped from her fingers, clacking against her mug, as a mention of the party immediately triggered images of DeAndre's house.

"Fine…just a small birthday party, celebrating one of Melody's friends."

Michael hiked a brow, incredulously.

"Must be your friend too, if you're celebrating something as intimate as a birthday party."

The image of Randall with his arms raised, neon green sunglasses and an open bottle of Hennessy in one hand shouting, "*I don't know half of y'all, but thanks for partyin' wit ya' boy,*" flashed across her mind.

"I mean, parties like that aren't really about personal connections. Usually, it's for networking."

"So, did you network?"

Imani swallowed, heat radiating from her.

"Yeah."

"I could imagine getting into the corporate side of art, you need to know a lot of people from different walks of life to build your rolodex?"

Imani thought back to how easy it was for DeAndre to write out a 5-figure check to her before she even confirmed him as a client. Michael never openly said to Imani that her art wouldn't be profitable, though he never failed to bring up Artgo as if it was all she did. But he'd be surprised at how much she'd potentially make from her art, if she set her rates at even a fraction of what DeAndre gave her so freely.

"Exactly…Melody knows lots of people, so it was nice just being around."

"It's good you enjoyed yourself."

"I did," she smiled.

"And, so did Kaylee," she tacked on.

## Jade Olivia

Imani took a generous sip of her coffee, thinking about how excited Kaylee was to meet one of her favorite athletes of all time. So excited that she'd tell anyone who'd listen. She didn't think Michael would care either way but, she felt compelled to say something.

"DeAndre Harrison was there," she added, "it was his friend being celebrated, but Melody was there, too."

"Oh, wow," his brows raised. "That's big, how was he?"

There wasn't just one word to describe who or how DeAndre was – how he looked or smelled or walked was hard to describe with just a singular word. Experiencing him was like watching an illusion. No matter how often you did, there was always something new to notice from every angle. It was also why she didn't look him in the eyes for too long if she could help it.

"Regular, I guess," stirring her spoon, "we spoke a little about my art – he might be interested in a few things."

Michael shook his head and took another swig of his tea.

"Seems like he's a lot to deal with off the court," he sighed. "But he gets better, performance-wise, every year. Gotta give him that."

Imani blinked, her mouth slightly parted. She was astonished to witness his selective hearing in real time.

"Don't you think that's…a bit of an assumption," she said, instead, "considering you don't know him?"

"And, you do?"

Imani's cheeks heated.

"I don't…I mean, every time I see him with Melody when I'm working or out with her, he's nice."

"Sweetie, everyone's nice to a pretty woman."

Imani's lips arched into a smile without reaching her eyes. She wasn't even sure what to do with that statement.

He put his hands up in mock surrender. "Part of it is the nature of the game, competition. I get that…but, all his antics…" Michael blew out a breath, swelling his cheeks.

"Gotta rise out of that neighborhood mentality. He's been playing for, what? Over 20 years? He's no longer the Port Springs dude with dreams…got all these kids idolizing everything he does and what does he do? Threaten to beat down an umpire?"

Michael stopped his ranting, now fully aware that Imani hadn't responded.

"Didn't realize you followed him so closely," she said.

"I mean, if you know an inkling about tennis, you can't avoid knowing who DeAndre Harrison is."

Imani nodded, remembering what he said during Melody and Hosea's reception years ago.

*"What Kanye say? Everybody feel a way, but at least they feel something? I can really care the fuck less as long as they not talkin' about my game."*

"Yeah, you're right."

∽

Feeling Michael's smooth, sand-toned skin under her fingertips, Imani glided her hands down his arms before placing her hands at his belt. The two were kissing each other with such longing, a feeling she hadn't felt from him in a while. Imani playfully pushed her tongue in his mouth. She moved her hand to his buckle, just above his burgeoning erection, making Michael break the kiss and pull her hand away.

"Oh, geez. Baby..." he breathed before releasing a chuckle. He opened his eyes, searching hers begrudgingly.

"I'm doing my best to keep it together here...and honor you."

Imani looked at Michael who appeared to be trying to convince himself more than anything. He was right, though. They had both vowed when they first started dating that they wouldn't be each other's stumbling block in the relationship, leading them into the depths of hell before they became man and wife.

Imani took a breath, traces of heat still prickling her skin.

They had been together for four years and even though Michael courted her appropriately – never being with her alone after hours, going on dates without encouraging "fleshly desires" and sometimes even foregoing dates all together for a moment in time. But, Imani's resolve was getting harder to control.

Michael represented safety and security for her, two things she didn't think she'd ever have and, if she was being honest, he felt familiar. He couldn't lie to her, even if he tried nor would he ever want to. The loyalty they shared was something that still made her heart swell as much as it did when they first met, and his dedication to it turned her on even more. But Imani knew what she promised to God, too. Something she knew would be like dousing a dumpster with lighter fluid.

"Guess both of us would've gotten carried away," she said.

After smoothing the wrinkles on the front of her shirt, Imani walked to the kitchen to get herself something to drink. Michael was behind her and she could feel his eyes on her.

"You know you're not the only one who feels the way you do," he said.

Imani turned in his direction, placing two plates in front of her on the small kitchen island. "I know and it's okay...it'll all be worth it when it does happen."

She smiled at him, this time agreeing with what he was saying. It wasn't like Michael lacked sex appeal. With a clear complexion and dimples that showed up even when he spoke, he wasn't anything any woman in her right mind would complain about. Michael reached for both of her arms, pulling her closer without their bodies touching.

"We've made it this far and I don't want to mess this up for you. I know you have standards you want to keep."

"Yes, and I'm grateful you respect that. You hold me accountable...that's the best love anyone could ever give me."

Michael searched her eyes, a pang of sympathy in them.

"Any nightmares recently?"

Imani sighed, her breath shortened for a moment. "It happens when I'm in transition to or from something...like this job situation...trying to figure out where I'm living."

"Hey, hey," Michael said, reeling her back in before she ventured too far over the ledge. He placed her head between his hands, looking her over again. "Your mind has the power to be your heaven or hell, but that doesn't mean we're not human. I'm always praying for your peace, honey."

When they first started dating, Imani rolled her eyes at his nickname, teasing him that it was more fitting for someone about six decades older. But,

## A Month of Sundays

just like him, the name became a balm for her, fitting the moment just right each time he said it, especially during moments like this when those skeletons were chasing after her.

"Mom's birthday is in a few months," she said.

He took her hand and propped it to his lips for a kiss.

"And, what do you have in mind to do then?"

The older she'd gotten, the harder it was to remember her parents' interests. Every year since they met, Imani dedicated both her parents' birthdays to doing things they'd do. This year she couldn't think of anything.

"I'll have to pray on it, first."

"Fair enough," he said.

"Anyway," Imani said. "I'm craving some more of that cheesecake from Downtin's. You want to share a slice with me?"

Michael smiled and nodded.

"Didn't even know I wanted more food until you said it. Let's do it. I'll do a Dash order."

He went to his phone, pulling up the restaurant and menu to order the decadent dessert, complete with strawberries and chocolate syrup, for delivery.

"I got their card in my wallet," Imani said. "Finally gotten stars punched, better believe I'm redeeming this 10% off reward."

Dumping the remnants of her cloth tote onto her bed - keys attached to a yellow fluffy pompom, hand sanitizer, sketchbook and other random items she knew she had to clean out her bag, Imani unzipped her faux leather pouch and took out her small red wallet...only *not* to find her smaller purple wallet, that definitely had the Downtin's punch card inside of it. She looked at the pile in front of her again, taking stock of everything there, turned her bag upside once more and felt the slow creep of annoyance tickling the recesses of her mind.

Yeah, she wasn't the most organized, but she could always keep track of her essentials – phone, keys and wallet. She also didn't allow any of those items to be out of her bag for long.

"Hey, love. Have you seen my purple wallet?" Imani called out to Michael in the living room as she felt her way through her other tote bag that she rotated throughout the week.

"No," Michael said, hesitation in his voice. "Haven't seen you take that out in a minute, actually. Do you remember the last time you saw it?"

Imani let her head drop to the side. Now, she was officially annoyed.

"*Sweetie,* if I did," she said, "I wouldn't be looking for it."

Imani pulled out all of the tote bags, sparkly clutches and colorful pouches in her closet, as her breathing picked up speed. She was glad that nothing she needed immediately was in that wallet – her driver's license and debit card she used every day were in the one she currently had. But, her work ID, the Downtin's card and a photo of her parents were in the one that was missing. She hated knowing that photo wasn't in reach.

*Okay, Imani. Get a grip. You didn't throw it out. It's here,* she thought to herself.

Michael appeared at her bedroom door.

"Try not to worry too much about it," he said. "It'll come up when you least expect it. Pretty sure that by the time we finish dessert, it'll present itself."

# Chapter 8
# Jackpot

His knee may have still been on the mend, but DeAndre felt adrenaline pumping through his veins fueling him to push through any subtle discomfort he was feeling at the moment. Coach Walters was adamant about having him work on his footwork and backhand today, something DeAndre was known to struggle with. He moved quickly from one corner of the court to the other, slamming down on his right foot for the last ball, which he shot back over the net to the left side of the serve line.

DeAndre let out an all-consuming breath, walked to the bench behind him and picked up a white towel to wipe the puddle of sweat dripping down his face.

"Always got what it takes to win, D," Coach said. "You're physically ready for SW. You just gotta decide if you're ready in here." He pointed to his temple, illustrating the point he was making earlier to DeAndre when Coach arrived for practice.

Winning these few matches before the SW Tournament shouldn't be an issue. He had already won that match in Colorado, but both Coach and DeAndre knew that none of these matches compared to SW. This would be his 23rd year competing in the SW Tournament. If he managed to win next year's competition, he would officially have 21 SW Tournament titles to his name, beating his own father's prediction. Busted up hamstring, be damned! He was willing to play the game five more times if he had to.

For now, though, he was merely practicing for his game tomorrow night – an exhibition match between him and Ivan Pavlov, a young player from Russia who was moving up the ranks quickly at The Royal Court. The Court was near to Port Springs, DeAndre's neighborhood, and he was confident he'd feel all the love from the crowd, no matter how Pavlov was coming tomorrow.

After patting his face with the towel again, he saw his mother and Stephanie – his publicist Stephanie approaching him and Coach Williams.

"You looked good out there, son," Andele said, hand on her hip, peering at DeAndre behind Givenchy sunglasses.

Despite himself, DeAndre's lips rose into a small smile. He felt a swell of pride release in his chest, reminiscent of his days in the beginning when his mom never missed a match of his. No matter what went down, she was always there, cheering for him.

"But, it's all in vain if you don't win tomorrow."

DeAndre's smile dropped. Of course, his mom hadn't been to a game of his in years, either.

He did a great job pressuring himself to perform at the highest possible level, all of the time. There was no need for his mother or anyone else, besides his coach to add to it, yet many insisted on doing it anyway.

"Alright, D," Coach started, "We're done. Remember to get some rest and I'll see you on the Court tomorrow."

"Aye, Coach, you went easy on my boy today?" Randall called out, approaching the four of them, while sipping on a smoothie. Coach looked at Rand and put on his sunglasses, his forehead dipped in the middle.

"I see that you're up bright and early for a change, Randall," he said.

It wasn't that everyone hated Rand, but most of DeAndre's team saw his childhood friend as a complex distraction, someone who could easily take him away from structure and discipline and plunge him back to the unpredictable mindset of the streets. Little did they know, Rand was a major force that kept him focused all the way up to this point.

Stephanie and Andele were in a deep conversation when Stephanie brought her attention to DeAndre, a tight smile on her caramel features.

## A Month of Sundays

"We gotta discuss a few things," she said, holding her phone in a death grip. She cut her eyes at Andele, then looked back at him, blinking twice for emphasis.

Stephanie was a recent hire on DeAndre's team who'd been working with him for a little over a year. She had come with shining references touting her as professional, bright and a cut above the rest. For the most part, she was living up to the challenges that came with her job. But dealing with DeAndre's mother wasn't a responsibility she realized she was also signing up for.

Andele and the private communications firm she established at the beginning of his career was the marketing machine behind his career for 15 years. But, about five years ago, DeAndre knew it was time to cut ties with his mom professionally, hoping to re-foster the mother-son relationship they once had or at least tried to have. Now retired, Andele spent more than enough time subtly reminding Stephanie of the amount of money and opportunities that came DeAndre's way, all from the cumulative years of her effort.

"Give me a few minutes and we'll talk," he said, knowing that his mom was on the verge of asking him *something* and would likely leave him alone once she did. Stephanie nodded, moving to one of the backyard tables next to the court.

"This court is much better than the old one," Andele said, continuing to sip her smoothie. She shifted her weight, bouncing slightly on the balls of her feet enclosed in stark white Nike's. She turned to look at DeAndre who was drinking Gatorade, sweat gliding off his ebony tone body like rain droplets.

"Only reason why I went with the house," he said between sips. "Think it's cleaner, too."

Andele raised her brows before looking across the front of the yard. "Hope you actually keep those hooligans out of here this time..."

"Uhhhuhh..." he nodded.

Not even five years ago, DeAndre was known for having crazy house parties that would often result in cops being called and paparazzi camping out in a gated community that guaranteed its residents peace and quiet. Once he was actually served a noise ordinance from the cops, after ignoring all of the neighborhood letters. DeAndre knew he had to move differently. So, he stopped throwing them - his last party was easily two years ago - but Andele loved on it every so often.

"You know it's true. I'm shocked that you didn't decide to get further out of the city."

He leveled a look at her.

"Why haven't you moved?" he asked.

Andele squinted, pursing her brown lips at her only son – her pride and piggy bank.

She always made little slick remarks about the people DeAndre hung out with or some of the choices he made. But he'd remind her every once in a while, that she didn't have much say about the choices HE made with HIS money, especially as one of the few people in his life who benefited from it the most.

As soon as DeAndre's career skyrocketed, he did what every kid from the hood dreamt of once they got a little change - he bought his mom a crib. It didn't stop there neither – soon enough, it was another house then a few cars, a couple trips and shopping sprees and it went on and on like a never-ending cycle with no limits. DeAndre provided a lifestyle for Andele a lifestyle that was beyond what even her fellow retirees could fathom. Unfortunately he was constantly coming to grips with the ramifications of his actions. He had indulged her way too much until all that was left was the shell of the mother he once had. Andele always appreciated life's finer accoutrements, even when the family was living in a one bedroom apartment in the hood of Port Springs. But, her appreciation soon became unabashed, flexing as she showed off all that she acquired, the wealthier her son became.

"I'm comfortable where I am," she said, "plus, I'm still close to family... speaking of which, Tyrone is coming over in the next few weeks to stay a few days. He just graduated from Smithwood, and you know how it is...20-year-old trying to figure it out."

" Y'all letting him figure it out...on his own, though - right?"

DeAndre grabbed a small towel from the rack next to the benches, wiping sweat from his forehead before draping it across his shoulders.

"Of course...but you know how Patty is...always figuring out a way to make sure her son is going down the right path."

DeAndre shook his head, sliding his tongue across the inside of his mouth. This was a standard routine with just about anyone in his family, whether he knew much about them or not. It was funny how a relative "figuring it out" typically meant that DeAndre would provide the answer. Uncles were hired as security guards, cousins were the assistants to his assistant and he could've sworn he had a 'godfather' that ended up working for ESPN due to a connect he had. The solutions weren't always in the form of money, yet, that's typically where they ended up. He'd been doing favors like these for so long that he couldn't remember being in a room with anyone he hadn't given *something* to, just to be left alone or absolved from guilt.

Considering where he came from, DeAndre didn't think twice about giving money and resources to friends, family and people he cared about – it was instinctual for him at this point. He just wished it didn't feel like that's all they wanted from him.

Andele followed DeAndre back into the living room where Randall was lying on the L-shaped couch, watching a throwback episode of *The Wire*. Eyes glued to the TV, Randall looked like he wasn't worse for the wear after his crazy birthday blow out the night before. He only had DeAndre by about a year, but the man had the energy of a freshman in college.

"A'ight, just have him call Rand and we'll see what's up."

Andele smiled, satisfied with, once again, not having to explain much to get exactly what she wanted. DeAndre scratched his neck, slightly annoyed, but grateful he didn't have to hear her nag about it.

"Hey Auntie," Randall said, getting himself up to give his best friend's mom a hug.

"Rand, you're now a year older, do you feel wiser?"

"Gotta get back to you on that part, but we'll take older for now." They all laughed as Randall continued eating his gourmet-prepared egg and cheese omelet.

"Hope you takin' it easy on the critiques with this guy," he said, angling his head at DeAndre. "You know it's been a minute since he's been back."

The match tomorrow against Pavlov was the first one for DeAndre after about three months, post-injury. Per Coach's instructions, he was working on easing himself back into his routine instead of rushing to knock out every match he could before the year was out. That energy- he was reserving for next year's season.

"Aye, aye...it could be a minute, a month or a year, my hand still ain't like no other, feel me?" DeAndre joked.

The two slapped hands, laughing and sharing the handshake they'd had since they were kids.

"He's handling his own out there," Andele said, "I have to admit. But, like David says, 'it's all about the mindset in the end.'"

DeAndre and Randall's laughter sobered quickly as DeAndre's smile dimmed a little. "Spoke to him recently?" DeAndre asked.

"Just last week but you'd know that if you took more of his calls."

"I spoke to him last month," he replied, "I did my duty."

Andele grinned, her eyebrows shooting up.

"Oh, you know your father always has something to say."

She laughed as if they were all sharing some common inside joke like his father was in the backyard, turning ribs on the grill instead of biding his time away staring at a concrete ceiling.

DeAndre scratched behind his ear.

"Right."

There was no time for him to bring up David, especially now, nor was he trying to give his mom the space to do so. Thankfully, she walked back outside towards the court, to take a FaceTime call from one of her sisters.

"Yo, D...I found you a little present."

Randall was back in the kitchen, waving a small card affixed between his index and middle fingers in the air. DeAndre walked over, past Chef Sebastian tending to pots with smoke billowing up to the ceiling. The smell of onions, peppers and aromatic spices filled the air. DeAndre inhaled the aroma and patted his chef on the back as he met Rand on the other side of the island.

"Looks like you and Imani had a good time."

DeAndre narrowed his gaze at the card in Rand's hand, before grabbing it to get a better look. It was a basic white card with a magnetic strip in the back, stamped with the Artgo Museum's logo at the top and a photo of Imani's heart-shaped face in a tiny square underneath.

"Where'd you get this from?" he asked.

Randall drummed his finger against a small purple wallet.

"Saw this out near the foyer and since I don't think you'd walk around with a colorful purse, had to do some fishing around inside to see if I could figure out whose it was. Thought it was one of the housekeepers...but, nope..."

DeAndre smirked, opening the wallet and haphazardly looking through the credit cards and receipts crumpled in its grooves. A sliver of a photo peeked out near the front, beckoning his attention. When he pulled it out, he found two older adults smiling back at him - the man in the photo resting his arm across a woman's shoulders as she stared at the camera, blushing. The man had an assured smile along with deep brown features and the more DeAndre looked at him, the more his features felt familiar. Despite himself, DeAndre felt like he just hit the jackpot, elated for this fated moment that seemingly fell out the sky and onto his lap.

Before he let Rand see him damn near giddy, he neutralized his expression.

"Nothin' went down," DeAndre said to him, "If your nosy ass must know."

Randall laughed, scratching the center of his stomach.

"Hey, I ain't tryna know what you doin' with her," he said, "I just want you to be aware of the kinda woman you dealin' with."

DeAndre knew full and well the kind of woman Imani was, which was why he couldn't just leave her *all* the way alone.

"Here we go," DeAndre said, with the now closed wallet in hand, already walking in the opposite direction of Randall's incoming rant. Only Hosea and Rand knew his true feelings for Imani. But, as the friend who had been married the longest, Rand thought he had more stake in his claims of how women operated.

"I'm just sayin', dog," Rand started. "Eve and Imani...they from the same school of women...they either," he stuck out a closed fist before counting off, starting with his index finger, "wit' someone who gave 'em a commitment...or wit' someone who's trying to figure out how to do it."

DeAndre rolled his eyes. This dude swore he knew Imani more than he did and Rand had only met her a handful of times.

"Get that noise out my house, man," he scowled as Rand laughed.

"I'm tellin' you," Rand said. "She's not keeping a dude around who ain't baggin' her officially...eventually...she ain't gonna keep being open to you and your hoe-ish BS for very long."

To be fair, though, Imani wasn't very open with DeAndre at all. DeAndre treated the nuggets of intel she gave him like gold coins, hoping to gather enough to reach some higher unknown level. The little he did know of Imani, made her seem like the kind of woman that would be honest about a shift in her relationship. As far as DeAndre was concerned, Imani was still with her dude, but the level of commitment they had was unclear. He didn't see no rock on her finger.

"We don't even be on that type of time," he shrugged. "She barely says anything to me...so. I'm gucci. We're friends."

The words he hated saying were enough to make him want to spit them out.

"Whatever you say, my young grasshoppa," Rand said, closing his hands in a prayer-like gesture then nodding.

DeAndre heard Stephanie walking behind him, and when he turned, saw her shaking her head at her phone. She let out a sigh before looking up at him.

"You need to calm down with these women at your matches."

He slid his hand over his fade, as he tried his best not to laugh.

"What's up now?"

"The Court had to issue a statement to let everyone know they don't condone violence and, any act of violence could cause them to end the game prematurely."

DeAndre folded his hands, placing them in front of him, and stared at her, waiting for the part where it had something to do with him. Stephanie placed her hand on her hip, her eyes instantly snapped back to her phone.

"They issued the statement on their Instagram but the Head of Marketing over there emailed it to me...personally," she said, looking him directly in his eyes again.

"They know those women who fought in the stands a few weeks back were because of you."

While some chose drugs or alcohol in which to indulge, DeAndre's poison was always women. He liked being inside of them, having them up under him and the subtle shifts in expression they had when he simply looked at them. They were like pieces on a chess board – he could mess with one for a time before letting it go, resting assured it'd be in the same place when he returned. DeAndre *was* single, after all. Therefore, he never felt bad about the women he had available to him at any given moment for any amount of time. What they chose to do once they were out of his presence, had absolutely nothing to do with him.

"Me?" DeAndre asked, eyes wide with his hands turned inward on his chest innocently.

A video of two women fighting at another court DeAndre played at was trending everywhere on social media. Apparently, one of the women messed with him a few years back and was shocked to find out that her friend, who she came to the match with, had messed with him too, and was now trying to sneak her way back to DeAndre somehow. DeAndre was always honest with any woman he dealt with, letting them know very matter-of-factly that they weren't the only one nor would they ever be. But, they either wouldn't listen or rarely take him seriously. Many thought they were THE one who could change him.

There would only be one exception in his mind.

Yet, even with his transparency, some of them managed to get more carried away than others.

"Yes," Stephanie said, eyes widening. "They're beefing up security this weekend because of it and, considering that we just made sure that violation from you breaking your racket is paid for can we just tread lightly, please?"

Stephanie grimaced, sarcasm laced in her features.

He scratched his shoulder, letting his head fall to the side. Regarding the last tidbit of what Stephanie said. DeAndre never actively looked for problems, but he couldn't let dumb calls on the court slide. He couldn't guarantee that would ever change.

"Yeah, I got it," he said, "I got it."

Stephanie folded her arms.

"You're a great client, DeAndre," she said, "I don't have to convince anybody of your influence, even if they don't want to admit it. But you gotta help me...help you. You have an amazing career, but it's nowhere near where it could go."

From the start of working with him, Stephanie reminded him that she could do more for him professionally than he even thought possible. DeAndre wasn't the type to get caught up in what anyone told him, typically, but he believed Stephanie and felt like she was on his side. He just knew he had to ease up on his little antics. He would...eventually.

DeAndre chuckled to himself before looking at Randall.

"Aye...I got that much control over what these women do?"

"I ain't know you had powers like *that*, my G, damn," Randall mocked before letting out the most obnoxious shrill of a laugh. DeAndre scratched his forehead, smirking at their exchange.

"I pray for the woman," Stephanie sighed, "who'll convince you to turn a new leaf."

# Chapter 9
# Overstuffed Luggage

Imani looked at the reflection of the 17 year old girl watching herself in the brass gold 3-way mirror. She spun in a circle swaying left and right, beaming in the midi black dress which was originally a much longer smock dress that dragged to her ankles.

"Imani! Ms. Ethel! I absolutely loveeeeee it."

"I can tell," Ethel laughed. "I'm glad this ended up working out because it would've been crazy trying to figure out what you were wearing only a few days before the dance."

Melody's stepdaughter, glanced at Imani with a knowing smile.

"I knew we could do it. Thank you, Imani! You knew just what to do!"

Imani laughed with a shrug.

"I figured the first dress had the material for the style you were going for, all we had to do was get it perfect."

"I can't wait for Melly and dad to see it. I think I'm ready."

Aaliyah stepped down from the circular platform and went to put on the sparkly gold Lanvin heels her stepmother Melody bought to match the dress. Ethel and Imani were there to style Aaliyah for her Senior Spring formal and make last minute adjustments on her outfit for the occasion. They were in her spacious bedroom that was a vision of every teen girl's dreams with its light gray walls, a white plush fur rug, strings of tea lights darting across the four corners of the ceiling, and a heavenly gold canopy draped over a plush queen mattress.

As Hosea's daughter from a previous relationship, Aaliyah lived the best of both worlds. She stayed in a quaint one-family home with her mother - Hosea's ex and her mother's husband for half the month. The other half of the month she stayed with Melody and Hosea indulging in the accoutrements that came with having a stepmother who was both a hotel heiress and former reality show star. Having custom dress fittings with a personal seamstress was par for the course.

Imani followed Ethel and Aaliyah down the black circular staircase, carrying a pile of fabric scraps from their work on Aaliyah's formal dress. When her phone vibrated in her jeans pocket, Imani gathered the fabric in one arm and glanced at the Instagram notification flashing across her screen.

*Are you coming?*

It was one of many messages from DeAndre, making the case that she needed to come to his match today with Melody, Hosea and their kids to pick up her wallet – the one that hadn't shown up in her apartment after all, since it turned up at his house instead. She had barely gotten any sleep last night, thinking about the photo of her parents in said wallet and where it ended up. It had never even crossed her mind that it could be in DeAndre's possession.

She also realized a few cards she often used were in that wallet, too.

As for her ID, Imani had been working at Artgo for a little over six months now and constantly lost it, so much so that HR had started charging her for replacements since they had issued so many to her. She didn't feel like hearing Rebecca - one of the annoyingly perky HR managers, 'gently reminding' her about museum policy after she signed in at the front desk for manual access to the offices upstairs.

Her phone had chimed shortly after she arrived at Melody's house with her first direct message from DeAndre – a photo of her Artgo ID, nestled between his fingers, with a *"This you??"* for good measure. She could've kicked herself for making such a careless mistake. She must've pulled out her wallet to tuck his check inside, but never put it back in her bag.

*Sorry, can you have someone drop it off to Mel's house?* she had asked.

## A Month of Sundays

*My team is busy prepping for today. Won't be able to make it to the other side of town.*

Imani watched the three-dot ellipsis dance on her screen.

*Melody is coming. You could just come with them,* he wrote. *I'll have it in the back for you and you can grab it after the game.*

*I have to see. Just bring it and I'll figure it out. Deal?*

*Cool. I'm gonna see what I can get from Downtin's in the meantime. That membership card you got is clutch.*

*Get out of my wallet, D,* she typed, adding a rolling eyes emoji.

Their on-and-off message exchange started from the time Imani arrived at Melody's house. She was trying to come up with another way to get her wallet from him without actually going all the way to Royal Court. But it wasn't worth it to pay an Uber to drop her wallet across town, especially since someone from DeAndre's team would have to be at a location to wait for the driver to pick it up in the first place.

She was running out of options.

Imani was also trying to avoid DeAndre like the plague, only because seeing him the night before was unearthing feelings that she zipped up like an overpacked piece of luggage a long time ago. They had plenty of interactions with each other beforehand through IG direct messages, occasional likes and innocent enough comments, mostly on her page, from him. But seeing him physically made her melt from the inside out. She reminded herself that the only man she needed to be melting for was Michael.

She shoved the phone back in her pocket and continued walking across the black and white checkered floor to the kitchen island where Melody, Hosea, and their sons - Judea and Caleb were gathered. The four of them were all dressed casually, ready for the hour-long commute to Royal Court where DeAndre was playing. Caleb was playing with blocks in a corner underneath the kitchen TV and Hosea was helping their nanny pack Judea's baby bag while Melody nursed Judea. She only looked up when she heard Aaliyah's heels clacking against the tiles.

"Baby? baby!" Melody squealed in Hosea's direction, pointing at Aaliyah. "Our superstar has arrived. This is how you do the formal!" She put her free hand above her head, snapping her fingers with Judea still suckling on the other side.

Hosea looked over at Aaliyah and smiled, radiating calm approval, the total opposite of his wife. "Wow. You look incredible, baby girl."

"Thanks, y'all!" She spun around, garnering applause from them. "Ms. Ethel and Imani work miracles...I could get used to this kinda treatment."

Hosea's smile collapsed as he looked over at Melody. "See, you give 'em an inch..."

"Hush, Sé," she said, referring to her husband.

"You look absolutely stunning, Aaliyah. If those dusty girls don't pick you as formal queen it's only 'cause they want to be you."

"Thanks, Melly," Aaliyah laughed. "I can't wait for next week! I gotta FaceTime mom...Ms. Ethel, you gotta tell her everything...Dad, my phone's dead. Can I use yours?"

Imani went searching for a garbage bag to discard the fabric and watched Aunt Ethel, Aaliyah and Hosea walk into the living room as Melody moved about the kitchen, burping Judea with light taps on his back.

In the few years they'd known each other, Imani witnessed Melody's growth. Nothing filled Imani with as much joy as seeing her as a wife and mother – two titles that Imani had dreamt for herself since she was a child. She was the kid in elementary school making clothing for her baby dolls, nursing them back to health after an imaginary scrape on the knee that required mending or taking off an extra layer of clothing when they were running a make-believe fever. Imani's dad would always worry about her fetishizing motherhood too early, hesitant that her young mind only conceptualized having a baby as just having a doll instead of a very real, very adult responsibility. On the other hand, her mom observed Imani with a knowing sort of pride that her daughter realized so young that she wanted such a cherished role.

Her mom used to tell her, *"You're gonna be such a great mom when it's your time."*

The feeling never wavered, even when her parents passed away. It didn't take long, once she and Michael officially got together, for them to start a running list of potential baby names in their phones. Imani may have been hesi-

## A Month of Sundays

tant about when marriage would happen, but having a family was non-negotiable.

Melody walked closer to Imani with a new garbage bag.

"Sorry, girl," Melody said, "figured you were looking for this. Here you go."

While handing the bag to Imani, Melody peeked over her shoulder, looking at the three of them huddled over Hosea's phone before turning back to Imani.

"I was trying to hear if Naima was gonna say any mess on that call," Melody said.

Imani folded her lips in a tight smile, keeping a laugh at bay. She already knew if she gave the slightest response, Melody would proceed with one of her petty rants about Aaliyah's mother. She stared incredulously at Imani, a scowl forming on her face.

"What?" Melody continued. "I'm playing nice with her, but I still got my eye on her little brown nosing-ass. You know she told Aaliyah that the manicure we got together was too mature? The girl will be 17 in under a year."

Melody shook her head and Imani swore she was rocking Judea faster.

"Broke broads always got somethin' slick to say."

"Mel..." Imani interjected. "Let's just be excited for Aaliyah, right?"

Melody stopped moving and rolled her eyes, but the smirk she mustered let Imani know she managed to divert her impending vitriol.

"You're right, and there's even better things to be excited about," she said. "Especially, since we're having another one."

Imani gathered the top of the garbage bag, now full of fabric, into a knot.

"Another what?"

Melody looked from left to right, conspicuously, and held out a flattened hand.

"Ok, it's been like only six weeks, but..." She looked at Imani with a cheesy grin, wiggling her eyebrows.

It took Imani a minute to get the hint, but her heart raced once she did.

"Oh my God, Melody!" Imani grabbed her hand with a light squeeze.

"You're pregnant...again...already?! You were at the party last night–"

"Yeah, but wasn't drinking," she clicked her tongue against her cheek.

Imani shook her head, amazed at the thought of Melody being able to potentially conceal yet another pregnancy, especially since Imani saw her in undergarments at least twice a month while assisting her aunt.

"I know," Melody giggled, morphing into a cackling schoolgirl.

"Hosea doesn't know anything yet, and I plan on having Caleb help me tell him this time. He's old enough now."

Imani clutched a hand to her chest.

"That's too sweet. The fact that you'll be juggling 3 under 5." Imani gestured a head bow in her direction. "Truly an inspiration."

Melody laughed, smoothing the bang of her straight dark weave - hanging like a shiny rope down her back. "I really should tell him to get up off me, but when my man comes to bat, he swings every time."

"Please...TMI." Imani faked like she was about to gag and crossed her arms in front of her face, making a playful sour face. Meanwhile, Melody thrust her hips forward with Judea lying milk-drunk in her arms.

"What y'all in here talking about?"

Hosea's low voice made Imani straighten up almost instantly. Unlike Melody who was as cool as a cucumber, Imani's face begged to tell the truth no matter what.

"Nothing, babe."

Hosea approached the kitchen, brows dipped in hesitant curiosity as he looked between them. He walked over to Melody and held himself closer to her face saying something before taking Judea from Melody's arms. Whatever he said made Melody giggle all over again like a certified creampuff. Outside of her kids, Hosea was the only one who Imani had ever seen who softened all of Melody's edges.

Occupying herself to give them their privacy, Imani thought that Michael could make her laugh, but she couldn't remember him ever making her swoon.

"Please make sure all my supplies from upstairs are in the car, 'Mani," Ethel said, walking into the kitchen. "I'm not leaving my tools tonight."

Imani looked at her, suddenly thinking of her way out.

She dashed upstairs, gathered her aunt's pin cushions, needles and darting tools. Then she returned to pack up Ethel's sketchpad and other papers into her tote adorned with an array of Michelle Obama's photos.

"Auntie, do you need your car tonight?" Imani asked.

## A Month of Sundays

    She typically only asked to use Ethel's car when she was running errands for her on the weekends. Though she didn't admit it, Ethel was skeptical of anyone driving her car, even her niece who she taught how to drive. Just as Imani predicted, Ethel put a hand on her hip, watching Imani suspiciously.

    "Now you know I have my bingo night," Ethel said.

    "But, I thought Bingo was every other weekend?"

    "Pearl is doing a special weekend now that her grandbaby got accepted to his top college pick," Ethel grinned.

    "Wants to see if Lady Luck will be there for her again."

    Imani's shoulders deflated as she hid her eye roll from her aunt.

    "Why do you need the car anyhow?" Ethel asked.

    "I left my debit cards and ID for work tomorrow with…someone and they can't drop it to me."

    "What about your ID?" Melody asked, now in earshot of the conversation.

    Imani was close to mentioning DeAndre's name but stopped herself once she saw Ethel still looking over her glasses at them.

    "A friend has my ID for work tomorrow and I wanted to see if they could just have someone drop it off to me, but it's too much of a hassle at this point. They'll be at DeAndre's game today and suggested I come."

    Imani shrugged her shoulders.

    "But I don't have a ticket."

    "You mean that big home match he's playing?" Ethel's eyes widened. "They were trying to get group tickets for church but someone dropped the ball."

    Melody looked at Imani, narrowing her eyes with her lips pursed. Imani could tell Melody *wanted* to inquire further but wouldn't at the moment for Imani's sake.

    "Come with us then," Melody said. "We'll drop you home after."

    Imani knew the odds of her *not* going to the game were slim because, no matter what, she still needed to get that damn card wallet. The only thing she had to do was sit for a game then get it afterwards. It was really that simple.

    "Hope it's not too much trouble. I appreciate it."

# Chapter 10
# A Quiet Day for Tennis

Considering Imani had never been to a tennis match before, she was surprised with how much busier the stadium was in-person. She, Melody, Hosea and the kids all arrived at the Royal Court about a half hour later, witnessing fans cheering and shouting to friends they flagged down, while dancing to the music projected on the screens at opposite sides of the stadium. Fans rushed to get to their seats like they didn't want to miss the opening act at a concert.

On television, most of the focus was on the players on the court with only a handful of crowd views once the game began. Imani wasn't expecting this much commotion beforehand at all.

Inside, they were escorted to a ground level section with five ascending rows of benches flanked with security on both sides. Randall and Eve were seated towards the end of the row above them, waving to greet the five of them warmly.

"Ready to see Mr. Phenomenal?" Randall asked, leaning over the bench and grinning at Imani.

If Imani considered DeAndre a distant friend, Randall was a total stranger, even with seeing him drunk on his tail days ago. But, Randall was always so inviting, making her feel like they'd known each other for years.

## A Month of Sundays

"We'll see about that," Imani smiled, "I'm impressed that you're not drinking water with sunglasses right now."

Randall laughed, patting his stomach that had no trace of fat or pudge anywhere.

"Liver built different, Imani. It's REAL different."

Settled into her seat in the second row, Imani noticed one group of men sitting in front of them with lanyards hanging around their necks and sunglasses shielding their faces. She then turned back to the row behind her, where Randall and Eve were situated, to find another group had joined them. The group of Black men were in hoodies with fitted hats pulled low scrolling through their phones and conversing with each other. A woman who *wasn't* Jazmine - sat at the tail end of the row, isolated from the men, taking multiple selfies, holding her phone up at various angles. Unlike Jazmine, this woman favored Imani's deep complexion and had a blunt bob that was cut to perfection. The pang of annoyance Imani had at the party presented itself again as she turned back around, hoping to distract herself with Caleb playing with his dad.

"Care to explain why you didn't tell Ethel that your wallet was with DeAndre?"

Imani's eyes collapsed as she took a second to answer Melody who was sitting next to her. After Melody's initial hunch that Imani was leaving out bits of information back at the house, Imani came clean – not about spending the entire evening with him, but she did reference her and DeAndre's message thread earlier. She knew Melody wasn't done processing her brief confession in the car though and was bursting to initiate her own interrogation at the right time. Even with Judea nestled in her arms, ready for his next feeding, Melody was always ready for the tea.

"I just didn't want her to start asking questions and...," Imani sighed.

"...put together that you were most definitely with him last night?"

Imani chose not to answer and merely crossed her arms as Melody shook her head.

"I'm not even gonna ask where you two were, but hesitating to be honest about what you're doing is...a little sketchy."

"I don't want her to think I even know DeAndre like that, which I don't."

Melody stared at her waiting for the details.

"Well, if you're going to this secret hideout with him where you forget your shit...you know him like that."

"It wasn't a secret hideout," Imani corrected, irritated. "It was at his house."

Melody turned fully to Imani, eyes as wide as saucers, with Judea smacking his lips together.

"I...Melody...I didn't," Imani stammered. "It wasn't like that."

"Oh...bitch."

"He just wanted me to view a space that he'd like me to paint," Imani said. "He wants to commission a piece from me."

When she didn't hear Melody say anything, Imani was convinced her explanation was enough. Their eyes met, and Melody burst out laughing, covering her mouth with a manicured hand.

"That man is relentless," she said, eyes wide, "Good Lord."

"It's not even that big of a deal," Imani said, "I'm still trying to figure out if I have the time to even take it on."

Melody lifted an eyebrow, "Ooooh, I'm sure you'll manage."

Instead of acknowledging that comment directly, Imani shook her head. She was already more than ready to leave as she looked behind her again, this time scanning the entire stadium above. A few kids several sections ahead were milly rocking in their seats, shamelessly interrupting the wave that the rest of the fans were trying to spread through the crowd.

Imani turned around and took another glance at the deep purple court in front of her, thinking back to the gorgeous one at DeAndre's place. His home court appeared smaller than this one here, even though it was just as pristine and immaculate. Standing in the middle of his court last night, Imani had done her best to imagine what it could be like playing for thousands of fans in these seats now. There were easily more than 10,000 people here and Imani couldn't even begin to fathom what was going through DeAndre's mind. She was certain he went through this at least a million times over the course of his career, but the energy from this crowd alone was so electrifying.

*How did he ever get used to this?*

Imani shook her head, freeing herself from a thought she couldn't ponder. She didn't need to wonder because it didn't matter. She had to watch the game, go backstage to get what was hers and leave. No need to extend her stay.

"When's this thing over?" Imani sighed, turning her attention back to Melody.

"Buckle up, sugar cakes," she said. "It's not like we're gonna be outta here in a half hour."

After a few minutes, the lights in the stadium dimmed as the megatron looming above the court lit with graphics of the Royal Court logo and images of both DeAndre and his opponent. The deep baritone of the sports announcer revved up the crowd as an array of purple, blue and white lights danced in figure eights across the court.

*"When the pressure is on, when the stakes couldn't be higher, who will rise to the top? Ladies and gentlemen, tonight will be legendary. Are you ready?"*

The entire stadium roared in response, but Imani swore the crowd on her side was trying to outcheer the fans across from them.

*"Making his third consecutive appearance at the First Ring, hailing from Moscow, Russia - Ivan Pavlov!"*

The fans across from Imani cheered the loudest when DeAndre's opponent began his walk from the far left side of the stadium. Ivan walked out waving to the crowd on both sides, as a spotlight followed him to his side of the court. However, he didn't pay much attention to the fans on Imani's side. She was clearly sitting on the side of DeAndre's supporters who started stomping their feet against the cement. The stomping was faint at first and it gradually escalated to the collective sound of an impending stampede. Stealing glances at the crowd as they worked themselves up into a frenzy, Imani felt her body tremble.

Imani glanced curiously at Melody again, her brows creased. This wasn't panning out to be the quiet day at the tennis court after all.

"What in the–?"

"Oh, right," Melody responded before a faint smile broke across her golden tan face. "This is your first one…girl, D's matches bring the whole hood out. It's a good time, though."

The techno instrumental playing in the background for Ivan's short introduction was cut short suddenly as the lights in the entire stadium went out. In the middle of the court, sparks of light flickered with the effect of a blown fuse.

Cheers from the crowd rose to the higher sections of the stadium. The stadium remained pitch black, until a video of sound waves reverberating in frequency flashed across the jumbotron. The opening chords of an acapella version of a familiar Kanye West verse rang through the crowd.

"La la la la, wait 'til I get my money right. La la la la, then you can't tell me nothin,' right?"

With the crowd finishing the lyrics of the track, the instrumental version flooded the stadium as strobe lights circled the court, stirring up the crowd to whistle and cheer even more. A few of DeAndre's fans started slapping their hands against their seats, more than ready for their hometown hero to step out.

"Making his sixth appearance at the First Ring, the seven-time champion and number one in the world, hailing from Port Springs, USA..." The crowd's cheers escalated to deafening levels, as the announcer's voice broke through "DeAndre Harrison!"

"Uncle D, Uncle D!" Caleb shouted suddenly, jumping up and down in the middle of Hosea's legs.

The claps, shouts and noisemakers some managed to sneak into the stadium seemed to reverberate in Imani's chest as DeAndre, with a bag hanging from his shoulder, walked out from the doors on the right side of the court with ease. For all the excitement and pandemonium around him right now, he remained focused with barely a smile on his face, as he put a finger in the air to acknowledge his fans. DeAndre was only a few inches taller than Ivan, but his confidence and swagger alone made him look ten feet tall in comparison.

Once Ivan and DeAndre placed their belongings on their respective sides of the court, the crowd's cheering subsided. Everyone's eyes were glued to both players' movements as they shook hands to signal the start of the match. A ball person threw DeAndre a ball a few moments later, which he caught then bounced with his racket against the court effortlessly.

"Cue players are ready. Ready. Play."

Throwing the ball up with one hand, DeAndre hit it against the racket with his other, shooting the ball straight to Lorenz's side.

It didn't take long for Imani to be enraptured by the game.

She wasn't even blinking by the tail end of the last half of the match, as her eyes followed the ball from one side of the court to the other. Imani had no

## A Month of Sundays

clue about the mechanics of tennis and barely knew any of the terms that Michael would throw out from time to time when they'd watch these games, yet she was still at the edge of her seat. The entire crowd was right there with her reacting to Ivan's serves along with DeAndre's returns. Imani knew that Ivan was a little younger than DeAndre and it definitely showed in his apparent agility. But, DeAndre was still giving him a run for his money with a refined strength and ease that only came from decades of experience. Watching DeAndre run across both sides of the court, pivoting with his feet to hit the ball whichever way it came, captivated Imani to the highest degree. The cords of his deep brown muscles flexed and pulsed each time he came in contact with the ball, peaking Imani's attention and suddenly making her a little restless. The aggression DeAndre expressed in his game on television was on full display in person as his grunts and guttural sounds were heard all over the court. Imani crossed her arms and legs, preparing herself for DeAndre's next move.

Ivan and DeAndre were returning each other's serves for a while until Ivan made one last shot. The ball landed near DeAndre, and just when it seemed it was moving out of bounds, DeAndre knocked it with an unexpected backhand.

The move re-ignited the energy of the entire stadium as DeAndre's fans stood up on their feet - screaming, shouting and cheering. Even Hosea and Melody stood, clapping without abandon for DeAndre, who threw his racket ahead of him once the end of the game was called in his favor and laid down on the court, his arms and legs out wide. DeAndre then pushed himself up from the ground, beating on his chest, sweat cascading down his entire frame, totally ignoring Ivan who stood midcourt awkwardly waiting for the closing handshake. DeAndre ran to a bench in the middle of the stands and jumped on it, extending his arms on both sides as the crowd cheered for him even further.

"Who runs this shit?!" he projected, putting his hand to his ear, encouraging the crowd's cheers.

"Whose court is this?! Who's up in here?!"

Fans started chanting his name, reciprocating DeAndre's full energy, every person in the crowd crossed their arms into an 'X,' a sign Port Springs natives used to represent the city.

Imani observed it all, frozen in amazement and awe at how he captivated

## Jade Olivia

the crowd. Before now, she knew DeAndre was pretty epic, but she wasn't expecting such a visceral and powerful performance.

He really was one of one.

Once DeAndre stepped off the bench, he walked to the sports reporter standing at the other end of the court, waiting for him with a mic in hand. A cameraman was a few feet away, ready to capture the post-game interview. The fact that DeAndre had enough energy to even talk to someone after what he just did on the court was insane.

Melody tapped her on the shoulder, pulling Imani's mind back into their space in the second row, far from where DeAndre was on the court.

"Let's get ourselves back there before he's finished," she said, "it'll be a lot getting through this crowd otherwise."

Escorted by security, the five of them arrived at DeAndre's locker room where an array of people, whom Imani assumed were all a part of his team, occupied themselves with post-game activities. A small array of fruit and snacks were arranged on a rectangular table that Imani walked over to after a few minutes, with Caleb holding her hand.

As she gathered snacks on a plate for Melody's oldest son, who yelled out the name of every fruit he knew how to pronounce, Imani's gaze fell to the woman with the bob who had sat a row behind them back in their section. She was sitting in a corner a few feet from the table now with one leg over the other, clutching a purple purse against her stomach. Imani noticed her tight, all-black jumpsuit that cinched her entire frame paired with strappy stiletto sandals. Feeling her lips curl up as if she was smelling something sour, Imani felt an itch crawl down her back.

*Who wears that to a tennis match?* she thought, looking at the woman who was engrossed in her phone, but this time chatting and laughing on a call.

A viral video that trended online a few weeks ago showed two women fighting in the stands at one of DeAndre's matches out of state. Clawing at each other and gripping long weaves with sharp nails, the women allegedly had a common history with him, even going out of their way to subtweet each other after the whole melee. Imani rolled her eyes now at the memory of seeing it, slightly annoyed with herself for even watching two Black women mess each other up over a man who claimed neither of them. But, if DeAndre chose to leave women with an impression that wasn't true in the first place, that was his prerogative. She hoped this woman with him now didn't think being with him would lead to anything serious. Did she even know about Jazmine? Or the other women he was often seen with?

Either way – not her circus, not her problem.

The door pushed open moments later as the men who were in the row ahead of Imani in the stadium filed in one by one, followed by DeAndre who looked like the king of his domain, dressed casually in a stark white T-shirt with dark wash jeans and Jordans. Straightening two thin diamond chains that hung around his neck, he wore a singular diamond bracelet on each wrist and a thick diamond band on his right hand. Imani felt her breath catch as he smiled, walking over to Melody and Hosea who extended their congratulations for a job well done. The three of them were in conversation as Imani watched from the corner she still occupied with Caleb near the snack table. She wasn't visible to DeAndre unless he turned around, and realizing she was on the verge of looking like a starstruck fan just staring, Imani drew closer.

But Catwoman, well into her phone a minute ago, moved much faster.

"The champ does no wrong," she smiled, angling her full body to his side as DeAndre extended his lean arm around her shoulders. He pulled her further into him, spiking up Imani's heart rate, and whispered in her ear.

*Was he using the same lines on all of them?* Imani wondered.

The woman then walked away as Melody and Hosea did the same. Hosea zigzagged through bodies to get to the snack table with Judea in his arms while Melody garnered Caleb's attention.

"Baby boy, are you telling Ms. Imani, every food you know?" she teased, smiling at her fixated toddler as he bit into one of his apple slices, while holding onto Imani's hand tightly. She beckoned Caleb to her as the two went to join Hosea.

DeAndre was pulled into a conversation with someone else after they walked away from him, but Imani saw him pause once he heard her name. He turned around, his serious face breaking into a bright smile once his eyes landed on her. She literally could've evaporated right then and there, feeling heat rise up in her cheeks as he took her in. Suddenly, Imani was hyperaware that she was wearing the same outfit from Aaliyah's dress fitting earlier today and *really* felt like Melody's assistant now.

"Hey...there," she said, mustering up the most casual grin she could. She wasn't shy but felt like her praise would spill out like word vomit if she tried to say anything else.

"You came out. What's good witchu?"

DeAndre pulled her into him, this time wrapping her in a bear hug with both of his arms across the center of her back. His scent – this one, a fresh cedarwood had her nearly drunk all over again as she held some resistance to avoid melting her entire weight against him.

. Letting her eyes close for a moment over his shoulder, surrendering to the feeling *just* this once, Imani knew DeAndre's hugs could brighten her on the cloudiest of days.

She pulled away first, straightening herself with a closed smile as DeAndre fixated on her.

"You enjoyed the match?" he asked.

*It was the most incredible thing I've ever seen in my life.*

"It was good," Imani said aloud, folding her hands in front of her, not knowing what to do with them.

DeAndre mimicked her stance, folding his own hands behind his back, with a tilt of his head.

"You think I could improve on somethin'?" he asked, hiking a brow.

*No. You're absolutely incredible in every single way. An icon.*

"Why would you even ask me that?"

He had to remember when she told him she wasn't a tennis fan at his house that night. She did. But, Imani also remembered everything when it came to him.

"Best feedback comes from those who ain't attached to it," he said to her, his face illuminating with a slow, genuine smile.

Thoughts ran through her mind as she placed a finger behind an earring, clearing her throat. She started to squirm under his stare and wasn't even sure what to say.

"I don't know, DeAndre," she said, folding her arms across her chest, "...you hit the ball, it landed on the other side, then...you scored, right?"

## A Month of Sundays

As if working to assess Imani's true thoughts in real time, DeAndre watched her with his eyes crinkled at the corners. He bit down on his bottom lip with his teeth, holding onto a smile.

"Yeah, Imani," he chortled, "that's exactly what happened."

The two looked at each other for a beat until Imani took another breath, eyes dancing around the room.

"My wallet? You have it?"

DeAndre snapped his finger. "Right, my bad....aye, Rand?"

Randall walked over to Imani and handed her wallet to her. Eve came over as well to speak with Imani for a few minutes before migrating back to Hosea and Melody again. After Randall and Eve were out of sight, Imani opened her wallet, inspecting the cards and counting each one at least twice to make sure nothing was missing.

"Don't worry, I ain't run up your credit."

DeAndre's snarky comment made her pause as she looked up to find him smiling at her with his own arms folded. With everyone else in the room either in separate conversations or handling other tasks, DeAndre was the only one actively watching her as she fumbled though her wallet like a frantic woman who finally retrieved her stolen belongings – an overreaction to an otherwise benign situation.

Imani may not have known him all that well, but he hadn't proven to be someone she couldn't trust.

"Where'd you even find it?" she asked.

"It was in the foyer, not too far from the kitchen you didn't let me get you anything out of," he said, without hesitation.

Imani's eyes widened as she shook her head, a laugh spilling over. She was starting to look forward to hearing his slick mouth and she knew she *definitely* had to go now. Refusing to respond directly to that comment, she noticed Melody - a short distance away, already signaling that they were on their way out.

Imani stole another glance at DeAndre with a smirk.

"Be sure to get some rest...champ."

# Chapter 11
# An Answered Prayer

For better or worse, DeAndre learned everything about being a man from David Harrison.

He learned how to maintain his appearance by watching his father shave with a steel razor in front of the bathroom mirror twice a week, lining it with unparalleled focus. He learned how to treat a woman with tenderness, by watching from the kitchen doorway as David pulled Andele by the hands to dance with her next to the stove, while a song from Heatwave played on the radio near the sink. He also learned how to remain confident by default, even when folks were quick to suggest humility. To David, an insistence of humility was the easiest way for others to bring one down to their lowest level. He used to always say that people loved to drag others down to the pit just so they didn't have to reach much higher to do better.

"You gotta pull from the excellence that's your birthright," he'd say. "Never let anybody see you fold."

DeAndre, with fear and reverence for his father, would merely respond with a "yes, sir" after David said something along those lines on occasion or just before he demanded DeAndre redo a homework assignment with errors. David was often slow to speak, but there was no stopping him once he did. He worked multiple shifts as a custodian at several high schools as well as elementary schools in the area, but his self-assurance and pristine appearance – never wearing shirts with stains or socks with holes as he complained that his work colleagues often did - made DeAndre's classmates assume he was a highfalutin corporate executive. Even if David didn't embody what he often preached as a blue-collar worker himself, all he needed was a physical manifestation to get behind that represented everything he stood for and knew to be true.

To this day, DeAndre is convinced that his father damn near manifested the summer when Andele enrolled him in tennis classes as a teenager for the first time, beckoning an unexpected answer to an unfulfilled dream.

Andele had learned about a free summer program in the area while photographing a community event at Port Springs Park. She spent a lot of time shooting pictures as a freelancer for the Springs Tribune back then and would often look through business fliers that residents would staple to the park's massive flagpole. After tearing a tab from a poster advertising the array of sports classes at Port Community Center, she called the center that day to find out if there were any courses still available for registration. Learning about the program at the last minute, Andele managed to get him registered for the last spot.

"Tennis is all they have open," she said to DeAndre later that day. He looked up at her - standing in the doorway of his room, from his position on the bed. He hit a growth spurt a week after school let out and was officially too tall for the mattress.

"Can't have you sitting on the couch with idle hands for twelve weeks. You interested?"

At 14 years old, DeAndre really didn't have a preference for much of anything and was just getting by as a student during the school year. He was the kid who teachers swore was smart but needed the right dose of motivation to excel. Andele and David were doing everything in their power, everything they could afford - at least, to help him get some. DeAndre didn't have too many friends, besides his rambunctious neighbor Randall, who he'd known since middle school and would sometimes cut classes with if they felt like it. That summer, Randall was away visiting his cousins down South, which meant DeAndre didn't exactly have a full social calendar to fall back on.

## Jade Olivia

"Ok," he shrugged.

On the first day of tennis classes a week or so later, David insisted on taking him to see what they truly signed up for. Many of those free "enrichment" programs for kids in Port Springs usually came in the form of second-class handouts with babysitters cosplaying as instructors using sports equipment that was falling apart so David kept his expectations low.

Walking with David through the doors of Port Community Center, DeAndre saw five other boys standing in a small semi-circle in the middle of the gym, watching a man shuffle through papers on a clipboard. The door that slammed behind DeAndre and David once they were inside, brought the group's attention to them. The only sound heard was the high buzz of the gym's barely functioning air conditioner.

"You gotta be kiddin' me," David said under his breath. Standing only an inch or two above his son, David placed a hand, decorated with an array of gold rings, on DeAndre's shoulder.

They were the only two Black people in the room.

"Is this Tennis 101?" David asked, the baritone in his voice echoing against the gym's walls this time.

"Yes...sir," the man said, adjusting his glasses to look between them and his paper.

"You can come and join us," shifting his attention to DeAndre, "I'm just taking roll call, so you aren't late yet."

"We're never gonna be that," David countered, a tinge of defensiveness in his voice.

DeAndre learned early on about the unease his parents had with White people, not to the point where they were blatantly calling them out of their name or refusing to speak to them, but they weren't hesitant about calling out disrespect or expressing themselves if they felt slighted. David was a child of the post-Civil Rights era, after all, and had DeAndre listening to old tapes of Malcolm X speeches in the car since he was five.

Turning his back on the group to face his son, David held DeAndre's gaze.

"If any of this shit seems fishy to you," he said. "Let me know. You got me?"

DeAndre nodded, "Yes, sir."

## A Month of Sundays

"And, I'm not just talkin' about if you feel like comin' or not. Do I make myself clear?"

David placed his palm at the side of DeAndre's neck with one last look of warning, giving it a light squeeze before leaving.

But, after that first day of class, DeAndre couldn't imagine *not* going every day. He gravitated to tennis immediately, feeling this sense of ease and vigor that he couldn't even fully comprehend. Whatever it was, though, the coach - Mr. Perry, took notice of his agility after about a month or so of watching DeAndre's form, which he claimed exceeded that of the other kids in the session by a long shot.

"I just gotta tell you the truth, Mr. Harrison," he said to David, wiping his glasses with a cloth, "I think DeAndre is a rare talent...so much so, that I don't know if sticking around here would do him any good."

Mr. Perry, David and DeAndre were all sitting in the coach's office, which was just big enough to fit the three of them. DeAndre's closet at home was much smaller and didn't have nearly the same amount of breathing room.

"What're you suggesting?" David asked, eyes narrowed in suspicion.

"There are a lot of tennis programs out of state and across the country that would give DeAndre a huge leg up. On a local level, there are other programs that are more...structured, too. I mean, he already has the speed and coordination, but there's nothing like getting fine-tuned by a team that can really push him."

Mr. Perry put his glasses on, pushing them up his nose to steal a glance at DeAndre. "That's if...DeAndre wants to go any further with this...I hope he does - I really think he should."

David looked over at his son this time, his eyebrows dipped in the middle. His father rarely ever smiled, there was no telling whether or not he was proud or slightly displeased. DeAndre could see he was pensive this time.

"What're you thinkin'?" he asked.

According to the Book of David, the shrug DeAndre felt like responding with didn't qualify as an answer – he had to speak up.

"I like playing," DeAndre cleared his throat, "A LOT."

David's brows shot up in surprise before he let out a chuckle, scratching the top of his head.

"If you want to see for yourself," Mr. Perry said. "You're more than welcome to sit in for a match."

DeAndre remembers when his father stayed for a class, waiting quietly as Mr. Perry went through demonstrations of the drills for the day. He honestly couldn't remember what he did, just like he couldn't recall much of anything he did on the court now. But, he always remembered how David looked at him that day…like he stumbled on a treasure trove.

On the drive back home, David asked DeAndre all kinds of questions, including what made him interested in tennis in the first place.

"You and Rand watch any matches on TV?" he asked, "'cause you sure as hell ain't get this interest from me or your mama."

"No, sir."

"You think you'd want to do this?"

DeAndre could've very easily said no, insisting that he only wanted to get through the summer and move on to the next grade if he could. But, something about David's intense curiosity made DeAndre reconsider his answer. It felt like his dad was trying to level with him out of respect this time instead of lecturing him like a delinquent.

"Yeah," he said with one nod, staring at him in the eye. "I do."

Once DeAndre let David know of his newfound passion, his father went into overdrive immediately. That one practice he stuck around for based on coach's suggestion turned into multiple practices that Mr. Perry continued doing with DeAndre throughout the next school year. David started recording them with a video camera and would convince Mr. Perry to watch the footage to give tips on technique and form. David also started reading up on tennis himself, borrowing multiple books from the library, and of course, watching the games. There was a point when all DeAndre remembered seeing were tennis matches playing on their one television set in the living room like white noise in the background.

Once David and Mr. Perry grew more comfortable with each other, Mr. Perry gave David references for private coaches. However, he was honest about the amount of money and investment needed to train DeAndre to become even halfway decent. The Harrisons weren't exactly poor, but DeAndre knew when times were lean based on the few new clothes and sneakers that Andele was able to purchase for him before the seasons changed. Tennis training costs were a lot for them, then, and DeAndre never pressured his parents for any help outside of what Mr. Perry offered.

David took it upon himself to go beyond local resources – spending boatloads of mysterious money on coaches and out-of-state academies that neither DeAndre nor Andele knew the full scope of. It didn't take long for DeAndre to figure out how he got the cash, though.

His father never explicitly said he turned to hustling to afford it all – it wasn't like DeAndre's life was a drama in which he saw David cutting up drugs under a lightbulb in the kitchen. However, DeAndre was privy to his parent's conversations and overheard Andele beg him plenty of times to stay home even after he returned from his custodian shifts.

"You're doing God knows what to pay for all of this…and for what?" Andele asked, her voice a loud whisper spilling through the thin walls of their bedrooms, pleading with reason. "You can't even guarantee this is gonna work out the way you think it will. He's not even 18 yet. We don't know if this is gonna stick or not."

"This is all based on a hunch right now - I know," he'd say. "But, I feel like… this…baby - this is somethin' different."

After his suspicions were confirmed, DeAndre still assumed that his father knew what he was doing. David wasn't a friend up the street who was trying to get extra money for a video game. But he found out anybody could get caught, or even if they didn't at the moment - their conscience had a way of convicting them of their wrongdoings. After one of Port Springs' most notorious drug kingpins finally got arrested by the cops in a police raid one night, David knew it was a matter of time before he'd have to pay for his own actions. He had gotten involved in distributing both drugs and guns, making him a hot target for police at the time. So, to avoid any sort of embarrassment or dramatics that would potentially scar the family, David turned himself in.

DeAndre thought it was the craziest decision his father ever made and was shocked that David took counsel from the pro-bono attorney who claimed they wanted to help. None of it made a difference though David still got served a prison sentence that, to DeAndre, didn't even fit the crime. Andele and DeAndre visited him once a month in prison during the first year of his sentencing until David demanded that they stop. When DeAndre tried asking his father to at least give a hint of what he could've done, David refused to give him any detail.

"Don't worry about all that…what I don't want you to keep doing, is wasting your time comin' up in here to run your mouth and cry all day," David said, "when what you really need to be out there doing is focusing on your game."

"Make this your last visit for a while. You already know what to do, so just… do the shit. I need you to be so good…so excellent, that nobody can ever discredit you. That's what you owe me. You got me?"

Even now, DeAndre still wasn't sure if hustling was the only crime on David's hands.

And, just like David demanded, DeAndre stopped worrying about it, giving the game his all. But, the rub was that David wasn't there to witness any of it. The tournaments DeAndre started to win, the endorsements he began to receive and the opportunities that took him around the world were all shared with David through Andele, who balanced her two roles as single parent and a convict's wife. After a televised match, David would call Andele's phone like clockwork, wanting to hear every detail so it felt like he was there. His phone calls were congratulatory at first, with David laughing about a forehand he hadn't seen coming or how DeAndre's footwork was improving.

But, as DeAndre's star accelerated, all that started to change.

He started picking up on David's subtle hints of jealousy right around the time he secured his fifth Grand Slam singles title. It was such a great year in his career and proved to critics who were still doubting him that the kid from Port Springs was here to stay. The money was no longer funny, by any stretch of the word, and DeAndre was enjoying every bit of it as a barely 21-year-old phenom. DeAndre was having a good time up in his big ass crib with his bevy of cars and the line of women around the block waiting for him after he picked up trophies around the world. He hadn't realized how quickly his life could change nor did he realize how quickly his relationships would, too.

"Just know your ass can still lose," David would say on those phone calls. "There's always someone better than you, waiting for you to mess up. Stop wastin' what you have on stupidity."

David's hints eventually took on an even more blatant and rude tone, as

## A Month of Sundays

time passed and DeAndre acquired more titles and wealth. His father went from being his hero and guide, to ultimately being a man he tortured himself to acknowledge. It was the guilt and pressure that made DeAndre pick up his calls eventually, realizing that a part of his success was built on the road that David paved. Neither of them ever said it out loud but DeAndre worked tirelessly to ensure David's decisions, no matter how scrupulous, weren't made in vain. Part of why DeAndre still couldn't let tennis go was that he felt so indebted to David for his sacrifices.

"What was that move you made so late in the game, DeAndre?" he asked now, his voice raspy with exhaustion.

DeAndre knew David would call him tonight, considering it was his first major game in Port Springs in months. He made sure he was back home around the time he predicted the call would come in to avoid having to manage a conversation with his father in public.

"If you were playing like you needed to," David continued, "Ivan wouldn't have had the chance to return your serve…would've been a much quicker game - in and out."

As usual, DeAndre didn't even respond, choosing to just let the old man ream him until he ultimately couldn't take it anymore, coughing up a lung from all the hate he was spewing. One of the best tools DeAndre had taken advantage of and was thankful for early in his career was meditation. It wasn't only useful for stretching his body, but it stretched his mind to the point where a room, or in this case a phone call – could turn silent. He used it so often during games and worked it like a muscle during practice that he didn't realize when he'd go into his head in his everyday life. He was thankful he always had the skill in his toolbelt.

It helped him win games, beat out his competition and gave him the mental fortitude to make decisions he didn't think he ever would, including hanging up the phone on David's ass.

Tapping the end button with his father's voice reverberating on the other end, DeAndre tossed his phone onto the couch next to him and clicked into Netflix on his living room screen.

DeAndre had a fairly busy evening before he called it quits for the night. After the game, he took Mia, the one he always had to make an effort to not mistakenly call *Mya,* back to her hotel for the sex she so obviously wanted to give him before they even left the stadium. They went to a restaurant, afterwards, to join Randall, Eve and a group of guys from Port Springs that he didn't have a chance to see often. The men, who also came to the game, were mostly Randall's friends and loose associates he'd known since they were all kids.

He still vividly remembered his life before his career, playing his heart out at that community center. But everyone around him, except Randall, seemed to forget about all of that. Even Rand's friends from today showered DeAndre with so many compliments, so much praise, that it was almost unsettling. He recalls wanting to pretty much *be* these guys when he was growing up, admiring their swagger and bravado like big brothers he never had. They used to joke with him all the time back in the neighborhood, nudging him along when he tried to get himself involved in mess to prove his toughness after David went away. Now, they were looking at him like a specimen in a petri dish, some otherworldly figure to whom they couldn't relate.

Being a public figure was still such an odd thing to him.

Nevertheless, Randall had invited them to the game, granting them seats to DeAndre's player's box at The Royal. DeAndre almost always knew who'd be in his Player's Box at any one of his games, especially since he had to grant permission. He also made sure each guest had the option of bringing a plus one of their choosing, which could be a toss-up depending on who he initially invited.

Not finding anything interesting on Netflix, DeAndre went to his phone again, ignoring the notification signaling Mia's text message. He tapped into Instagram and a new photo appeared on Imani's profile as soon as his timeline loaded. The photo was of her and Caleb from earlier today. They sat next to each other, holding ice cream cones in front of their faces with their eyes crossed. Caleb had his tongue sticking out while Imani wrinkled her nose, balling up her mouth, playfully.

*Star crossed lovers united again,* she captioned.

Double tapping the image, DeAndre felt his mouth creep into another smile. He then tapped into his direct messages, going straight into the message thread with Imani. DeAndre couldn't believe that she had actually shown up to

## A Month of Sundays

his game, especially when she had insisted she wouldn't on Friday, and didn't give him a straight answer earlier today.

He recognized that communication with Imani was never all the way clear.

*Thanks for coming today*, he typed, sending the message.

Out of the bevy of emotions he experienced, within a span of several hours, seeing Imani was the surprise that made up his entire day.

# Chapter 12
# Potential

"Take one more breath in."

With her eyes closed, Imani breathed in air through her nostrils and held it before awaiting further instructions.

"Now, let out the largest breath you've done all morning and open your eyes."

Imani opened her eyes, peering at her coworkers and the rest of the Artgo staff standing in a circle around the second floor's spacious exhibition room. Sunlight beamed from the sunroof overhead, pulling Imani out of the late morning lull that typically hit her, after the smoothie she'd pick up from the cafe downstairs.

This was far from the yoga classes Imani occasionally attended on Saturday mornings.

The woman who led the Artgo staff through a twenty-minute group meditation was none other than Stella Rose - a world-renowned artist with a career that Imani had admired since her teen years. While her colleagues looked more than ready to leave, Imani was smiling from ear-to-ear, feeling renewed and downright giddy.

Even before she knew anything about the art world, Imani knew about Stella Rose from the coffee table books her mom would buy. Helena was an artist herself, but a much more casual one, and would often purchase large,

## A Month of Sundays

colossal-sized books filled with photographs of Stella's collections or borrow them from the library, stacking them all over the living room floor. Stella was like Imani's personal Bob Ross when she was a kid and she used her work to practice with whatever cheap, commercial store paints she could afford with her allowance money.

Now, more than three decades later, Stella was still a recognizable force in the art scene, though her career was slowing down as age creeped up on her. She wasn't producing as much original work at the same pace she used to, but Stella always managed to get support from art institutions and museums based on her legacy alone. Artgo was the latest one to extend a helping hand, offering her a half-year residency to complete her work that would potentially be a part of AireFete - a highly selective art show bringing together exhibitions from major art museums around the world. Having this residency was mutually beneficial for Stella and Artgo, granting the artist time, space and resources while the institution received credit for having a juggernaut's work shown on their behalf.

Lauri, Imani's direct boss and Artgo's Exhibitions Curator, walked towards Stella to meet her in the middle of the room, initiating the group's applause. Smiling from ear-to-ear, Lauri placed her hands on Stella's shoulders and squeezed.

"I think we can all agree that we're delighted to have someone as skilled, passionate and dedicated as Stella be a part of the Artgo family."

Everyone continued cheering as Imani watched Lauri shower the artist with praise and admiration. Both Lauri and Imani's jobs involved engaging other artists in the community and initiating relationships that were beneficial to the museum. Imani was still getting a handle on that part of her role, but Lauri was an absolute pro, working any room she stepped into with the grace and poise of someone who had a rolodex of contacts who'd vouch for them.

"I'm so honored to share space with you all," Stella smiled, clasping her tawny brown weathered hands in front of her. Wearing a hot red fedora - a signature look of hers for years, Stella made an effort to look everyone in the eye.

"Even though I've done a few things in this life of mine, I'm always so humbled by the support I can still receive from you all...this newer generation. I know I can be a little....," she circled two fingers at her temples and crossed her eyes, "all over the place, but just know I'm here for you as much as you're here for me. I can't wait to sit and meet every one of you and I look forward to the work we'll do together."

The crowd gave her another round of applause before breaking away to ultimately return to their desks or other responsibilities. Imani was making her way towards Stella and Lauri when her coworker Gloria fell in-step with her.

"Can you believe we got someone as big as Stella to work with us?" Gloria asked, "for damn near a year at that? The fact that we went from helping that old White man make paper dolls about the Antebellum South to this, is something to be studied."

Imani chuckled at her colleague who always managed to make the monotonous days of being in the office much more humorous.

"I'm not surprised. Lauri's connections are incredible. I'm sure she didn't have to do much heavy lifting to get her to agree."

"Yeah, you're right. Black girl magic, for real."

Imani nodded, but still felt like she was feeling Lauri out, even after six months. Now, Imani wasn't looking for any handouts just because they shared the same skin color, but it felt like Lauri didn't even want to hear any of her ideas half the time, shutting them down before Imani could even elaborate. For the public love Lauri showed Stella just now in front of the majority white Artgo staff, no one would ever guess Lauri was Imani's harshest critic. Gloria was an assistant curator just like Imani and had been at Artgo for about two years now. But, she didn't work directly under Lauri like Imani did, which meant Gloria still viewed her through rose-colored glasses.

"Anyway, I gotta get back to my desk before this meeting with acquisitions," Gloria said. "Did I tell you about the materials we're getting from Bayard Rustin's estate?"

Imani's jaw dropped as her eyes widened.

"No."

The team Gloria was on always seemed to get the projects that Imani would kill to be a part of, while Lauri would fill Imani's calendar with museum tours, taking notes during board meetings, and writing catalog entries for the art

## A Month of Sundays

collections coming in. All administrative tasks of a curator, which Imani was extremely bored with.

"Yeah, it's cool," Gloria smiled. "But, you're working with *the* Lauri Shelton as her direct employee. You got it made, Imani. Just gotta work it in your favor. It's been little under a year since you've both been in your roles. Gotta start letting her know who you are."

Imani rolled her eyes.

"Right, but it feels like she doesn't even give me a chance," Imani said, folding her arms together.

"I don't want to even hear that," Gloria said. "Have you told her about your work?"

Imani hung her head to the side and looked up at the ceiling.

"Got it," Gloria nodded, her lips flattened in a straight line. "I'm assuming that's a 'no.'"

"It never feels like the right time."

"Don't you have one-on-one meetings with her, at least, weekly?"

Imani tapped her heeled boot against the floor, shifting her eyes.

"Yeah."

"So?" Gloria chuckled, holding her hands out in front of her. "That's time right there!"

Imani shook her head. Gloria just didn't get it. Lauri was hard on Imani *and* the majority of ideas she had. If she was quick to shut down the artists Imani suggested to hold exhibitions at the museum, she couldn't imagine what Lauri would say about her work. Imani never shied away from constructive feedback or others opinions on her art - that was pretty much the bulk of her MFA program years ago. But, especially as a Black creator, she wasn't actively looking for someone to tear her work apart. Imani felt like she was at a stage where she wanted support, if anything. Constructive feedback, suggestions for improvement, but support would be lovely.

"Look, I'll tell her when the time is right," Imani sighed, grazing her hand over her gold chunky wraparound necklace.

Gloria shook her head.

"Ok," she said. "If you say so, but Lauri is also cushy with the judges in AireFete this year. Might want to make sure you let her know soon."

"For what? It's not like I can apply to that."

Gloria shook her head.

"Swear you actively block your blessings, girl."

With that, Gloria turned to leave, letting Imani know she'd text her with ideas she had for lunch today. Imani looked around the room once more to find Lauri who she knew wanted to meet after Stella's introduction with the staff. She eventually found them laughing and chatting with each other in front of a large landscape painting capturing the mountains and lakes near the Catskills. As Imani made her way over, Lauri's eyes landed on her.

"Yes, yes...Imani," she said, keeping her smile in place, "I want you to meet Stella."

"It's so nice to meet you, Stella," Imani said, careful not to squeeze the woman's hand too hard out of sheer excitement. "I've just always admired your work, so this is surreal."

Feeling the coolness of Stella's hand, Imani now saw the woman's maturity upclose - the age warts at the sides of her face, the wrinkles around her neck and the cloudiness in her brown eyes. But, her energy - the joy Imani remembers radiating in pictures of her in all those books she poured over as a kid - glowed right through her. This was a woman with experience and a whole lot of wisdom that Imani could see she was willing to share.

"I'm so delighted when a young person has heard of me," Stella beamed, her thin lips pried into a smile, "It's truly humbling. So, are you an artist yourself?"

Imani swallowed - the question had completely caught her off guard. She looked at the woman with a nervous smile.

"I am," she cleared her throat before taking a cautionary glance at Lauri. "I have my time on the side and after work hours...but, I can't wait to support whatever vision you have in mind, Ms. Stella."

Imani wasn't sure why she was so nervous about just owning up to her practice. She had a full book of clients, not to mention DeAndre potentially being a huge prospective one. She didn't understand why she opted to play much smaller.

"Hmmmm," Stella said, nodding with a knowing smile. "I see."

"Well, Imani and I have to meet before my next meeting in another hour,"

## A Month of Sundays

Lauri said, before turning back to Stella. "If you need anything else from us, you know where to reach us."

Stepping back into Lauri's spacious office - complete with a clear glass table shaped as an arch and floor to ceiling windows looking out into Artgo's backyard lawn - Imani closed the door behind her and sat across from her boss at her computer.

"I want to go over the architect exhibition for the banquet in the next few months," Lauri started, scanning through emails through blue cat eye frames. "Do we have confirmation on location?"

"Yes. Karen got back in touch with me and she said one of his homes is available for the date. Just need to go over if there's any equipment we need for setup."

Every year, Artgo hosted a huge banquet to thank current funders, attract prospective ones and give the art community a space to mingle and network. The banquet was like the Met Gala of the industry where artists from across the country come out to have a good time, imbibe good drinks and make much-talked about appearances. While guests received notifications of the banquet date months in advance, the most exciting thing about Artgo's banquets is the themes and locations aren't revealed until the week prior. The invitations are given like mystery pieces, then, which typically keep guests on their toes, guessing what the Artgo staff has up their sleeves.

This year's theme - "Black Spaces, Black Homes: An Introspection of African American Architects"- highlights Black architects from the twentieth century, centering the late great Paul Revere Williams. California was blessed to have the legendary architect's actual homes he designed, but Imani had been in touch with Mr. Williams' estate who connected her with a good friend of Mr. Williams in Rapid Springs. His friend consulted with Paul when he was building his home from the ground up, a fact that Imani had only learned when she requested Paul's architectural renderings and drawings. Imani would've been fine with obtaining a few of Paul's pieces to display during the banquet, but the idea of having access to a local home that had Paul's iconic touch never even crossed her mind. Imani felt on top of the world, transfixed that guests could literally hold space in such an iconic home.

But, when Imani had presented this new discovery to Lauri a week ago, her boss only gave a small smile before moving on to other topics on the itinerary. The interaction left Imani feeling somewhat rejected, but she was trying to move forward anyway. She had to get over taking this job so personally - she just needed insurance for crying out loud.

"Okay, and the invitations this year?" Lauri asked, looking between her screen and her keyboard. "Do we have graphics approved for that?"

"I was actually wanting to do something different this year," Imani said, opening up her laptop. Even though she wasn't ready to show all of her work to Lauri, Imani would take advantage of one-off opportunities like this to show her skills. Unbeknownst to Lauri, Imani had a rough design of this year's banquet invite on her desktop to compare to a PDF design from Artgo's Marketing team. Placing her laptop on Lauri's desk, Imani bit her bottom lip, shifting in her seat.

"I spoke with an artist friend of mine who's into this year's theme and she loved the idea of having the invitation look similar to a collage," Imani said, pointing to her work. "Like, how people do vision boards and typically include dream homes, she wanted to play that up to get folks excited about the banquet."

Lauri dragged Imani's laptop closer to her, examining the details of the option. She placed her hand on her chin and leaned forward before looking at Imani, an eyebrow arched.

"You want to invite our top donors to our banquet with a vision board?"

Imani's smile fell.

"Lauri," she said. "It's not literal. It's more figurative of how aspirational homes have been to us for centuries. Considering that we're having many of these Black architects in the space, it'd be interesting to see a montage of their work."

Lauri took off her glasses and took a deep breath.

"I hope you didn't pay this artist anything for this mock-up," she pointed, pushing herself to the back of her chair. "Who did this, again?"

Imani could've sworn she saw Lauri actually snarl at her. There was no way she was revealing herself to this woman now.

"It's someone I went to school with," Imani said. "You know I'm always scouting talent."

## A Month of Sundays

Lauri leveled a look at Imani with a smirk.

"You do," she said.

"It seems to be a challenge," Imani said. "Is there any advice you have for me when looking?"

"You know the mission of this museum is to highlight American art with focus," Lauri said, pointedly. "It's always subjective, but there needs to always be a cohesive message."

"I felt like I've been doing that, coming to you with artists who I know and are familiar with–"

"Artists who are your peers," Lauri said, "who lack direction."

And, there it was again. Lauri always seemed to tell Imani one way or another that the artists she'd propose to host exhibitions weren't clear on what they were actually trying to say with their art.

"Imani, you obviously have a very strong...preference for who you want to see here and I appreciate that. I just want it to be based on merit, okay?"

"Yes," she said. "Is there anything else that needs to be discussed?"

After Lauri's quick run through of the rest of the topics, Imani stood up, closing her laptop and picking up her notebook. She had her hand on the doorknob when Lauri called out to her.

"Tell your friend they have potential, just not there yet."

Imani turned, expecting to see Lauri's gaze meet hers, but her boss just looked over her screen and scanned her papers on her desk absentmindedly. Imani balled up her lips to the side, walked out the door, letting all of her responses to that comment fall out of her mind.

# Chapter 13
# Purple Flowers

Missing out on a majority of his family and friend's events was one of the many sacrifices DeAndre had to make throughout his career, so he took full advantage anytime he had a chance to attend and, today was one of those days.

He was glad to finally make it to one of Melody's fabulous celebrations – this time, Aaliyah's Senior formal send-off after years of sending gifts to apologize for his absence. Walking down the curved, red brick walkway of Melody and Hosea's Mediterranean home, he pushed open the front door with a bouquet of purple roses in hand. He wasn't sure where everyone was congregated when he first stepped in, but once he saw gold, black and purple balloons decorating the courtyard, he headed toward the back.

A few acquaintances DeAndre were familiar with, as well as Melody and Hosea's friends hung out near the pool on one side of the yard or underneath a black-and-gold striped tent on the other. A decadent buffet of teen-friendly finger foods covered two long tables in the center. Melody made sure this occasion was an all-out affair, complete with official photographers, a DJ and a focal wall of purple hydrangeas. Some of Aaliyah's classmates and their parents were set to arrive at the house shortly or for Aaliyah and her friends to ride to the dance in a party bus.

Scanning the small crowd now, it didn't take DeAndre long to see Randall,

## A Month of Sundays

Eve and Hosea sitting near the patio furniture. He was only a short distance away from the three of them when his godson Caleb - Melody's oldest, came running to him nearly tackling DeAndre.

"Uncle D," Caleb said in his 4-year-old voice, holding onto DeAndre's legs.

"Okay little man, okay," he said, placing the flowers on top of a standing table near him to crouch down to Caleb's height.

"What's good witchu?"

DeAndre kissed him on the cheek, allowing Caleb to fall into his chest and squeeze his small arms around DeAndre's neck.

The sweet moment didn't last very long before Caleb suddenly pulled back, pushing both arms down to his sides, widening his stance and scrunching up his face at DeAndre. DeAndre, in turn, stood up a little straighter imitating Caleb's pose.

"You ready?" DeAndre asked, a scrunched expression plastered on his face.

From his right side, he saw Imani approaching them. DeAndre would notice her fine, chocolate ass anywhere.

He and Caleb then slapped hands five times in succession, exaggerating their arm movements more each time as Caleb fell into toddler giggles. The whole charade was a little thing DeAndre started doing with Caleb after one of his matches. Melody and Hosea had brought him to his first game only last year and the little guy actually held out his hand to DeAndre backstage, after the game, as if he wanted to give him dap. DeAndre quickly improvised since Caleb's hand was way too tiny to even grasp all the way and so their silly handshake was born.

By the time he looked back over at Imani, she was easing her way closer with a small smile, allowing him to give her an instinctual once-over. Why wouldn't he openly appreciate an Angel walking among them?

"Hey," he said, feeling his cheeks lift.

She was dressed in a black sleeveless, cropped ribbed turtleneck, paired with purple bell bottom pants offering a small peak at her midriff. Gold necklaces of varying lengths hung at the front of her top with the longest one stopping just above her chest. Of course she'd wear the theme colors of Aaliyah's occasion, in homage to her. Imani was classy like that.

"DeAndre, hey," she said.

Her thin, gold hoop earrings glinted in the light when her head fell to the side.

DeAndre went in for a hug when Imani stepped to her right, allowing a man behind her to present himself. He hadn't even noticed the guy and had a feeling akin to seeing a fly on the wall that wasn't there a moment ago, as the guy appeared.

Standing a few inches taller than Imani, the man had a wide smile with deep dimples. Imani's attire reflected the informal nature of the outing, while this dude looked like he was coming from a business convention - opting for a shirt and suit jacket combo paired with dark jeans. Dude finished off his outfit with brown casual sneakers, making him look every bit like DeAndre had imagined.

He knew exactly who this corny light-bright dude was.

"I'd like you to meet my boyfriend, Michael."

Imani, sounding relieved that she was finally introducing them to each other, looked to Michael who extended his hand to DeAndre.

"It's nice to meet you," he said, all 32 teeth beaming, "I'm a big fan."

DeAndre glanced from Michael's hand to his bright, shiny face then to Randall and Hosea near the couches behind them. With their hands cupped in fists over their mouths, witnessing this entire exchange, the two clowns must've known Michael would be here with Imani this time, especially since he didn't come with her to Randall's party.

"What's up, man?" he finally said, shaking Michael's hand. "Good to meet you."

Not allowing his gaze on Michael to waver, he settled into the uncomfortable feeling of not having exactly what he wanted for the first time...in a long time.

"For sure, for sure," Michael said, "Um, so I'm always curious to ask this of athletes...what's one of the little routines you do that get you...really...ya' know...pumped for a game?"

DeAndre scratched behind his ear and observed Michael, waiting for him to admit he was joking. But, Michael continued watching him, expectedly, waiting for his response.

"I don't know..." DeAndre said.

## A Month of Sundays

He wiped a hand over his mouth, thinking about the meticulous routine he went through before and after every match especially now that he had to have multiple hydrotherapy sessions for his leg, about how well-documented his routine was - anyone could open any sports magazine to find interviews with psychologists who worked with DeAndre personally, and google any of his videos training with the top coaches in the world in several regions and cities. There were even actual routines named after him for rookie players to follow at tennis programs across the country. Nothing in his routine was little, it was part of a whole lifestyle and insinuating otherwise was practically an insult.

This dude was already being disrespectful. He *knew* he wouldn't like his ass.

DeAndre scratched under his chin subconsciously rubbing his recently trimmed beard.

"I just..." he shrugged, training his eye on Michael, "do me."

"Got it," Michael said, nodding with his eyes wide as a deer in headlights. "I respect that."

Imani smiled vaguely listening to the two men converse, but stood nestled into Michael's side with her hand resting on his shoulder and his arm around the back of her waist. Observing how they looked together, like Urkel bagging the flyest chick in school, put a sour taste in DeAndre's mouth.

Melody walked out a moment later, dressed to the nines in a long green duster jacket billowing around her, with a production crew not far behind.

"Hey, D..." she said, giving him a hug with a cameraman, mere feet away from them,

filming the interaction.

DeAndre didn't have to ask why, since everyone knew she was actively filming her limited series that would air on streaming platforms pretty soon. Anytime someone attended any event at Melody's house, that person automatically gave Encore Network producers the go-ahead to potentially use their likeness and image on the show. DeAndre remembered a time, much earlier in his career when he was fighting to be taken seriously, when he hated going anywhere with Melody for this exact reason. He wasn't trying to make any reality show cameos back then. But, now that Melody and Hosea were co-producers of their series, she had much more control of what eventually aired, mitigating the risk of anything being misrepresented.

"...Okay, everyone's here. Let's all go to the living room and prepare for Aaliyah's grand entrance," she sang, clapping her hands together.

Once the DJ transitioned into one of Nicki Minaj's classics, Aaliyah made her grand entrance into the backyard from the courtyard, blushing and waving, in sparkly gold heels and a form-fitting black dress that stopped just above her knees. She hugged the few friends who had arrived with their parents and dates, then greeted her parents' friends. When Aaliyah approached DeAndre, she gasped, and her eyes lit up at the bouquet DeAndre planted between them.

"These are gorgeous, Uncle D...oh my God," she said, taking a generous sniff of the floral scent. "They're the perfect purple...thank you!"

Even though Aaliyah wasn't Melody's biological child, she had certain expressions like her stepmother that made DeAndre sometimes wonder otherwise.

"You're welcome," DeAndre said, giving her a hug. "You look beautiful, Aaliyah."

DeAndre shifted his gaze to Hosea a few feet away.

"You alright wit' babygirl growin' up on you, homie?" he joked aloud.

With an impassive expression on his face, Hosea maneuvered his hand under his chin in a swift motion. According to Melody, Hosea and Aaliyah's father/daughter bond had gotten much better over the years since their marriage. But, DeAndre could only imagine how odd it was for Hosea to witness Aaliyah's childhood years slipping away while simultaneously trying to make up for them.

Once Aaliyah's date - a tall awkward teen who was on her school's basketball team arrived, all her friends posed in front of the flower wall for a mini-photo shoot before the party bus picked them up. After several moments of promises to keep their parents updated on their whereabouts, the kids left, leaving the adults with an impromptu kickback complete with food, drinks and music.

DeAndre grabbed a Ginger Ale from the bar when his gaze fell on Imani and Michael across the room, chatting with Melody, Eve and one of Melody's other friends. Michael sat on the sofa chair while Imani sat on the arm, leaning

## A Month of Sundays

her weight against him - the two laughing at Melody's dramatics. Every so often, her hand would fall on top of his head, stroking tenderly while Michael sat there, not matching her energy but looking like a man content, nonetheless. DeAndre's eyes stared at the sight, in disbelief that Imani was somehow attracted to ol' boy. If he at least matched her swag, he'd understand – he'd still be as pissed as he was now, but DeAndre would get it. But, her being with this man just didn't add up.

The whole thing seemed to go against nature.

DeAndre joined Randall and Hosea on the couch where they were talking amongst themselves, nursing beers. Rand turned to DeAndre, following his line of vision, then fell into a fresh wave of laughter.

"You gettin' a real kick out of this shit, ain't you?" DeAndre asked, cutting his eyes at his best friend who was the only one given roasting privileges.

"Aye, Sé..." Randall said, tapping Hosea on the shoulder with the back of his hand.

"So, check this out...I done seen this dude literally approach another man in the club to tell him, 'I'm about to take your girl...and, do it!" Randall snapped his fingers, "within minutes!"

He continued, in an animated tone, pointing a finger at DeAndre. "Now, this same nigga out here sweatin' to step...to...Carlton Banks?!"

Randall collapsed into Hosea, laughing hysterically - even Hosea chuckled.

"I'm ready to see this shit play out like a pay-per-view fight," Randall added.

DeAndre cast a look at the two of them with a deadpan expression. Hosea was at least trying to hold it together but Randall was beside himself with laughter.

If this was even ten years ago, DeAndre was certain he would move by instinct in the same way Randall described. But, Imani was completely different than any woman he'd ever met before. He quickly surmised that coming at her like that would never work, single or not.

"A'ight...ain't nobody sweatin' nobody," DeAndre shrugged, "I ain't lookin' for no smoke."

"But, you ain't gonna turn a blind eye to it neither," Randall added, "remember what I told you, bruh...committed."

## Jade Olivia

DeAndre looked at Rand for a beat, ignoring the reference he was making to their conversation earlier in the week.

"She's where she is and I'm..." he paused, at a loss for words.

"Not with her," Randall said.

"Alright, easy, easy," Hosea added tactfully, smiling in good humor.

Out of nowhere, Randall suddenly broke into a coughing spell, patting his chest a few times. It lasted much longer than a cough from just choking on something minor.

"Damn, man," Hosea said, tapping Rand on the back after his cough still didn't let up. "You good?"

"That's what yo' ass gets," DeAndre tacked on, taking another sip of his ginger ale.

Releasing one more cough into the crook of his arm, Randall held his chest with his eyes closed before opening them like he just emerged from a body of water. He looked at Hosea with renewed clarity.

"Yeah, homie...just this cough been on my neck , but I'm a'ight," he said. "You got water?"

When Randall followed Hosea to the kitchen, DeAndre looked back to where Melody was holding court with her conversation, but the group had dispersed.

"Alright, y'all..." Melody announced, walking towards the middle of the room. The camera crew from earlier had left not too long after the teens did, so Melody was off the clock. She was comfy walking barefoot in her home, sans cloak, in leggings and a plain gray T-shirt.

"Up for some friendly competition?" she asked, jiggling a bucket of Jenga blocks in her hands.

The remaining friends followed her to the large table in the dining room. Melody opened the bucket from the bottom, placing it upside down on the table, then pulling it up and over a neat stack of blocks.

"Since it's, like, ten of us - let's pair off," Melody said, before turning to Hosea.

"Sé, get the bag of candy from the fridge..."

Hosea looked at Melody, a mischievous smirk on his face with an eyebrow raised.

## A Month of Sundays

"It's not in the fridge, baby…" he said.

They exchanged a knowing look , only meant for them as Melody chuckled at Hosea, shaking her head.

"Y'all, I'll be back," she said, "talk amongst yourselves for a minute."

Once Melody left, DeAndre brought his attention to his phone, taking a look at the Wild Wild West of IG messages that he did a thorough check on every once in a while. He was a fairly casual Instagram user, overall, and only had it so he could post whenever and whatever he wanted. DeAndre could care less about following "brand" trends or performing antics on social media in order to be relevant.

It wasn't that he didn't enjoy the direct access social media gave to other options though, mainly women, if he chose. DeAndre mostly stuck to the rivers and lakes he was used to, satisfied with the ones he so thoroughly curated over the years. Yet, every so often, he'd be impressed with a new woman's assets.

Yet not quite as impressed or intrigued as he constantly was with Imani. No woman would ever hold a candle to her. But, right now, she was off the table.

"Hey, DeAndre," Michael said, pulling his attention. It was weird hearing Michael call him with such familiarity as if the two were cool like that, but DeAndre let it rock.

He looked at him, met Imani's gaze quickly, then turned his attention back to Michael. She was smiling and holding Michael by the arm, playfully stopping him from whatever he was going to do.

"I'm just trying to tell her about the amount of intellect and agility you need in order to play tennis," Michael said, giving him another cheesy smile. "Like, it's not just about getting lucky with a swing…a lot of strategy goes into it…you'd agree with that, right?"

DeAndre gave him the most lackluster head nod known to man, sizing him up.

*What was this dude's angle?*

He took another sip of his drink, not even caring to figure out the answer to his thought. For some reason, Michael just talking to him annoyed the hell out of him and all he wanted to do was wipe that stupid ass grin from his face.

"I could agree," DeAndre said. "Maybe she should take some private lessons wit' me to help her out."

Imani's smile froze as her eyes widened, her head shaking in short spurts.

"Oh Imani," DeAndre continued, smiling harder than he had in a while, "You didn't tell him?"

He looked back at Michael who stood there with his face frozen in time.

"I hired her to do a painting in my crib," he started, his smile falling. "So, I'll take her private...with tennis lessons and all that."

DeAndre watched Michael's eyes slant slightly and knew right then and there that Michael wasn't as happy-go-lucky as he pretended to be. Anybody breathing would recognize the innuendo he just made and DeAndre was ready to let another one go, just for general purposes. He may not have been trying to take Imani, but he could hold her attention.

Michael then turned back to her.

"You never told me about this, honey," he whispered.

"Because I haven't actually agreed to anything yet," she stressed, eyes throwing fire darts at DeAndre.

DeAndre tilted his head.

"But, I told you I'd need an answer within a week," he said.

"And, today is only Thursday."

"A week will be two days from now, Imani."

Michael was now caught in the middle, his eyes darting back and forth as they spoke.

"I know what day it is, DeAndre," she smiled sarcastically, folding her arms across her chest, sitting up straighter. "You'll get an answer from me...just like any prospective client would. I ask you to respect my process."

Michael was now as loose as a damn bobblehead as DeAndre chose not to comment, taking his foot off the gas with a small smile dancing across his face.

As silly as it was, DeAndre was kind of turned on by this little banter they had, just because Imani never made it easy. He thinks it started from the bits of small talk they used to have when he'd see her at Melody's house after they first met. He'd initiate conversation with her and Imani would answer in short phrases, focusing on her priorities as Melody's assistant stylist. She was quiet, but never missed a beat in conversation. Imani just intrigued him, like a puzzle he enjoyed analyzing, even if it took much longer to solve.

"Okay, lovely people, let's pair up!"

## A Month of Sundays

Melody called out to her guests once she was back in the room, this time with a small burlap bag in hand. She went around to each person, letting them reach into the bag for the first thing they touched without looking.

"Once you get your piece, look for the person with the same type of candy," she said. "That's your team partner."

DeAndre pulled a piece out of the bag without much thought. Twirling the Hershey's Kiss between his fingers, he looked up again, only to find Imani staring at him with her own Hershey's Kiss in hand.

∼

Michael and Imani were in Michael's car heading to her apartment, as nightfall set in. Their time spent at Melody's house after Aliyah's send-off was interesting, to say the least, and they hadn't said much of anything to each other once they left well after midnight. Soft gospel music played in the car, making for a quiet ride while the sounds of the highway lulled Imani somewhere between wakefulness and sleep.

"Do you plan on doing the commission?"

Michael's voice reverberated as Imani paused before turning to him.

"What is it?"

His eyes shifted.

"With DeAndre...you're taking it?"

Imani took a breath, placing her hands on her lap – her shoulders lifted.

"It would be a great opportunity," she said. "Why wouldn't I go for it?"

"You get great opportunities all the time," Michael shifted in his seat uncomfortably. "What's the difference with this one?"

Imani blinked.

"Because...having DeAndre as a client would be a goldmine," she responded, "the potential referrals I could get from him alone would be incredible."

Michael sighed.

"Honey, not all business is good business."

*Was he being for real right now?*

Hearing his line of questioning now, Imani decided not to bring up the fact that she needed the money, especially with her and Kaylee's rent increase. She chuckled, folding her arms over her chest, and realized that part of this probably stemmed from her not mentioning it to him beforehand. Though honestly that was because she didn't think she needed to tell him. The conversations she and DeAndre had the night of the party were casual. Plus, she rarely told Michael who her clients were until it was confirmed and streamlined.

"What does that even mean?" she asked. "DeAndre's not in the mafia or something."

"How'd you get on his radar anyway? Didn't you meet him for the first time at the party?"

Imani's back stiffened.

"No, I've seen him a few times at Melody's house. He's seen my work on Instagram before," she cleared her throat. "...and I told you we talked about it at the party."

"Okay, but talked about it enough to where he offered you a gig? Based on looking at an Instagram page?"

Imani blinked, feeling her forehead dip. These little digs he was shooting her way were really starting to irritate her.

"I...Michael," she stammered. "How do you think I get clients? I don't know what other evidence he'd need to see that I can do what he wants. He's seen me before...so, just put two and two together."

"Who put two and two together?"

Imani scratched the side of her leg, shifting in her seat.

"I don't know," she shrugged. "What's your point with all of this?"

"My point is that..." Michael paused, shaking his head before taking another breath. "I just...need you to be careful when you're taking these clients and all. You'd be working in his home?"

"Yeah, but it's huge."

Michael gave her a weird look.

"We just left Melody's," she said, "so you know they all look the same."

The glimpses Michael got of the celebrity-driven world Imani was exposed to only came from the few visits he had made to Melody's house. Tonight, had actually been his first time seeing her house filled to capacity with guests. But, when he'd pick Imani up once in a while after a styling job, Melody would be

## A Month of Sundays

taking calls and meetings with producers and her team, all circulating in and out of her space freely. This gave Michael more than enough intel for Imani to reason with him. Even though Melody's lovely home didn't quite compare to DeAndre's.

"The gig is going to be about two months - tops," she continued, "...could be even less, depending on how often I can schedule access to the area I'm working in."

"So, you'd be able to just step into his place?" Michael scowled.

"No...people like him have staff everywhere that'll let me in," she said. "All this will be happening on the weekends...during the day...We'll likely never even see each other...he's barely in town."

Releasing a breath, Imani didn't know how she was saying things she couldn't confirm with such confidence. She hadn't discussed any professional terms with DeAndre yet, since she still hadn't made her final decision. She felt a little bad about not knowing much, but there was no need for Michael to get caught up in details that would be ironed out later. What mattered was that she was taking the gig, especially now that he brought it back up.

It *was* a great opportunity and whatever strange thoughts she had concerning DeAndre, she could push all of that to the side to get the job done. Everything fell out of Imani's mind when she was creating.

"I guess..." he said. "You're right."

"I'll be done with it before you know it," Imani reassured him.

Michael looked at her again, balancing his gaze between her and the road.

"Just promise me we'll still carve out time to see each other," he said. "I know it's been crazy for us this week, but I want to make sure we stay connected."

Imani nodded, placing her hand on top of his.

"Love, you don't ever have to worry about that."

Imani placed her hand on Michael's cheek. The last Imani remembered before her eyes closed was the reassuring smile Michael gave her.

Everything was going to be fine. Imani was going to be fine.

After being in New York for a little over two months, Imani finally took up an offer from one of the interns she was working with that summer, to attend a Friday night happy hour. She had dodged their offer to hang out more than once before, opting to just turn in for the night back at her shabby shoebox of an apartment her Aunt Ethel was helping pay the rent for each month. Imani was getting into a productive groove with her art, balancing her day job while carving out time on evenings to finetune her voice and narrow her message so she preferred to head home rather than to hang out. Before then, she felt like she was absentmindedly scribbling on the pages of her notebook, unaware if anything made sense.

But New York stimulated a new energy in her, a new pulse to create from her heart.

"Just letting you know we'll be at Tao's," Shawn - one of the interns, said to her, pointing in the direction of the glass door behind him. She glanced up at him and the other three interns, and realized he was signaling to her to be considerate, assuming that she would yet again - decline.

But Imani felt different tonight. Amped up from last night's art session in her room, she decided to take a much-needed break.

"I'll come with," she said, "just give me five minutes to get my stuff together."

Imani always wondered where she'd be now if she hadn't agreed to hang with her coworkers that night. That night jump started a series of events that changed the course of her life.

Seeing DeAndre today reminded her of the same bain of existence she had in New York after that night. People like DeAndre made Imani nervous only for the simple fact that people like him pulled out an unadulterated side of her that tinkered between fantasy and reality. They convinced her that she was better without rules, without order – drunk off of pure desire. She was uncomfortable getting close with people like him because people like DeAndre - always had a good read on her, whether she wanted them to or not.

Imani had been *this* close to being game partners with DeAndre at Melody's house. But, even when that didn't happen, their connection was still just as apparent.

She noticed the awkward tension in the air between him and Michael, since DeAndre called out their potential professional agreement, but tried not to think too much of it. He switched with Michael's designated partner, allowing Michael to be with Imani, just to clear the proverbial air.

## A Month of Sundays

"*Not tryna disrespect, man,*" DeAndre said, barely looking Michael in the eye.

Imani did the absolute best she could not to feel the tug at her stomach once DeAndre walked away.

Shaking herself out of the funk she suddenly felt, Imani focused on playing the game from then on, thankful that she wasn't forced to play nice with a stranger - this was her man, for crying out loud.

After only a few rounds, it was clear that Michael wasn't as competitive as DeAndre, which also meant he played a lot slower than was necessary. They had been playing Jenga for a while, when the tower of blocks dwindled to a mere skeleton. The game that started out casual was now much more strategic, as partners paid attention to their every move which required ultimate focus.

Michael was examining the barely-there tower with a fine toothcomb, searching for any blocks he could easily push and pull. All the blocks were positioned disjointly, leaving one to believe that pulling any of them would end the game. It may have seemed like there were no blocks to salvage, but Imani saw one. This *one* block looked as if it would knock the entire tower down if it was touched, but Imani knew better. Glancing around the table at the other paired partners, Imani waited to see slow realization dawn on their own faces. But, everyone looked just as dumbfounded and confused as Michael did. She couldn't have been the only one to see the answer, though....right?

There was no way.

Sitting next to Michael, Imani looked from Michael's intense expression of concentration back to the players staring at him, when she and DeAndre's eyes crashed into each other.

On his face, Imani saw that she wasn't the only one who saw *it*. DeAndre got *it* too and got *her*. He smiled at her knowingly before Imani's own lips curled slightly. She tapped Michael gently on the shoulder.

"The block in the middle of this row..." Imani pointed with her pinkie, "is good. Just have to be gentle."

Michael pushed his head back, brows dipped in further confusion.

"Honey, that's the shakiest one...it's basically tilted to the side already."

"Yeah," Imani said, "But, you should just...trust me on this one."

She made eye contact with him and smiled as his forehead opened.

"Should probably listen to her, homie," DeAndre said, staring at Michael with a head tilt and a smile. Michael turned to DeAndre, sitting in a seat to his right, before looking at Imani then back at the tower.

Instead of going to the suggested block, Michael went with one that was two rows below, closer to the bottom of the tower - the safest choice. He managed to tug part of the block out of the tower before giving it a small shove that pulled the tower forward, causing it to fall down on the table, splattering everywhere.

Guests clapped and yelled at Michael's loss while DeAndre watched, shaking his head. Michael - growing red in the face, stood up from the table without a word and let out a sigh.

"I'm heading to the kitchen for some water," he turned to Imani, "want something?"

"No thanks," she said, before he walked away from the table.

Imani reached for the Jenga box and handed it over to an expectant Melody. Melody grabbed one end of the box and pulled the whole thing out of Imani's hand, leaving a slight burn on her finger.

"Oh, shoot," Imani said, pulling her hand back.

The burn stung the top of her index finger as a hint of blood pooled at the side when she gave it a squeeze. Imani sucked her fingertip.

"Crazy papercut," she mumbled to no one in particular.

"You need someone to kiss it?"

DeAndre asked low enough for only Imani to hear, but it registered loudly in her head.

"Uncle D and...Ms. Imani sittin' in a tree," Caleb projected under the table, right at Imani's feet.

"K-I-S-S-I-N-G..."

Imani's heart raced as she held her finger, now sensitive to the touch. DeAndre's comment along with Caleb's insinuation drove her into a mental frenzy.

*I should leave. I need to go. Wait, why am I leaving?*

"Caleb!" Melody yelled low through clenched teeth.

"Get...over...here...now," squatting to her son's level to pick him up. "You're going to bed, that's enough adult time for you."

## A Month of Sundays

Imani scratched her neck, feeling warm, before she involuntarily looked at DeAndre. His head was tilted downward, pretending to be focused on his phone with a smirk on his face. Melody walked back over to Imani, with Caleb clutching her hand.

"Come upstairs for a band aid," she said.

Walking into Melody and Hosea's cream-colored ensuite, Imani stepped closer to Melody who was reaching for band-aids at the top of a cabinet. She handed Imani the band-aid with a spike of her brow.

"What?" Imani asked.

"Y'all need to stop...seriously."

Imani blinked, wrapping the bandage around her finger.

"Who needs to stop?"

"You and D."

Imani put up her other finger to counter her before Melody closed her eyes and shook her head.

"Look, I don't know what y'all got going on," she started, "but I don't want any drama up in my house...I'm a new woman now, Imani, swear to you! I don't need grown men fightin' around me."

"Who's gonna be fighting?" Imani shook her head, refusing to even let Melody answer.

"I don't even know why you keep bringing DeAndre up. There's nothing going on."

"Better say that to church boy."

"What?"

"A 4-year-old is feelin' something between y'all at this point," Melody said.

"This flame y'all have going with each other is," she started, bringing her red bedazzled claws to the sides of her mouth "blaringgggg."

Imani rolled her eyes.

"Me and DeAndre are friends," she said. "Geez, Melody. Nothing more... nothing less."

Melody made a beeline past Imani to the door.

"All I'm saying," Melody said, "is if church boy starts askin' questions, you better give him some solid answers or...girl...just cry."

Imani shook her head as she followed Melody back to the party, slightly annoyed that she even entertained that conversation. Friends had chemistry, otherwise they wouldn't have a friendship. Anything anyone was witnessing between her and DeAndre was from a rapport they built with each other years ago, which was...casual at best. They knew each other enough, but they didn't know each other like *that*, no matter how many game moves they predicted together.

Michael was now back in the living room and once Imani was closer, he pulled her into him, giving her the tightest hug at the waist.

"Let's dance," he whispered in her ear.

Imani held his gaze as he led her to the dance floor.

*This was where she needed to be*, she thought.

She walked forward, watching Michael move his shoulders to the music with her back facing the other guests. The entire gesture was a rarity since Michael preferred not to dance at the handful of events the two attended. But Michael indulged her this time, laughing and spinning her before pulling her closer again.

The rest of the evening went by without any of the concerns Melody tried to warn Imani about earlier. There was no drama in her house and by the time Michael and Imani were leaving, DeAndre was nowhere in sight. Imani found herself scanning the living room until Michael pulled her towards Melody and Hosea to say goodbye.

DeAndre left just like that, without saying goodbye.

As they walked out of Melody's home and into Michael's car, Imani was struck with the thought that she wouldn't have to see DeAndre ever again. With her now full-time work schedule, Imani didn't have the open flexibility she once did to support her aunt on a styling job with Melody. The chances of seeing DeAndre on a whim would be even more slim, especially if she rejected him as a client. But, these thoughts came to her before Michael brought DeAndre up in the car a few moments ago. Michael's voice slowly filtered through Imani's subconscious as she stirred awake in her seat.

"...Glad traffic wasn't that bad," he muttered.

Michael bringing up DeAndre just now reminded Imani that DeAndre was presenting her with the right opportunity, which was always going to be her professional priority.

### A Month of Sundays

Imani felt a warm sensation near her lap and jumped, opening her eyes wide.

"Honey, are you okay?" Michael stared at her, worry etched across his face. "Fighting demons in your sleep?"

He gave her a weary smile as Imani gathered herself, noticing they were now parked across from her apartment.

She *was* fine.

"Yeah, just...more exhausted than I thought I'd be."

# Chapter 14
# Confirmation

DeAndre looked over at the umpire, sitting high on his perched chair, as his opponent Roberto Vasquez paced from the left to right side behind the serve line. This was the third time he wasn't ready and it was starting to piss DeAndre off. An opponent has to be ready for a serve at all times unless he wanted a violation, which the umpire had lazily given to him only once. DeAndre positioned himself and served to Roberto who put his hands up as the ball bounced to the right side of the court. The umpire blew his whistle, signaling that he hadn't been ready for the serve...again. The whole thing was starting to irritate DeAndre as he turned to look back at his coach. Coach shook his head, putting his hands up, tracking exactly what was happening.

DeAndre took a breath and walked closer to the tall chair, his blood hot.

"Yo!" he barked.

The umpire's startled blue eyes landed on him.

"This is the fourth time dude is going over the clock and you only tracked him for one violation. C'mon, man, why you pullin' this shit?"

The crowd cheered for DeAndre, only fueling what he already knew was mistreatment.

"I haven't said anything for this entire match, but it's getting fuckin' ridiculous. Are you dumb?"

## A Month of Sundays

DeAndre pointed out to the crowd as the umpire shook his head, icy blue eyes cut into a slight squint. "I don't care what he got going on with his serve, but with mine, he needs to be ready for it."

The crowd cheered for him as he walked back over to the serve line. This was the mess he hated dealing with, but knew he'd have to if he was going to continue competing. In his twenties, he remembers enjoying the rise he'd get from seeing the surprise on the faces of people who fell victim to his vocal venom and had the mental bandwidth to curse anyone out who was wrong during a match. He always knew why he went through it – the subtle microaggressions that never went over his head. However, he now felt like he earned the right to not have to deal with this - it was getting tiring. How long was he gonna have to put up with this?

He ended up winning the match by 40-0 from a serve that Roberto eventually failed to return not even ten minutes into the game. Hearing the crowd cheer made DeAndre smile as he waved to them after his on court interview. But, the entire win did very little to warm his overall icy mood.

Stretching in the holding room after the game, DeAndre still couldn't get over seeing Michael and Imani on Saturday night, no matter how hard he tried. He forced himself to stay at Melody's house after reluctantly switching game partners and even after seeing Michael shoot himself in the foot with that weak-ass Jenga move. But, seeing him pull Imani close, dancing with her the way he wished he could have, guiding her hips to the music the way he wanted to - made him want to beat his ass.

So, he left before they did - offering no sort of farewell to Imani at all.

He had to stop playing himself like this. She very clearly was in it with that cornball - he saw it with his own two eyes, which meant he should focus on other options that didn't require much on his end. As if by osmosis, DeAndre felt his phone vibrate mid-stretch, a notification of a new direct message on Instagram.

Opening up the app, a message from Jazmine popped up, congratulating him on today's match.

*"...Sorry I couldn't make it out today. No excuse either since I'm literally a mile from where you are 😅 Had stuff going on with the opening that's*

## Jade Olivia

*happening soon, finally! Can you believe it? I couldn't do it without your support. Sending you love."*

She included a video of herself lying on a bed with her hair pulled back into a tight bun, plump lips and fresh-faced, blowing a kiss at the camera with a playful finger wave. He hadn't seen her since Rand's party a few weeks back, after getting Clive to take her back to the airport once he offered to take Imani home. This was their first interaction since then.

In an alternate reality, DeAndre could definitely see Jazmine as his girlfriend. To be honest, she was pretty much operating as one currently, without the title. She didn't challenge him, was patient, loyal, and moved through spaces with him so pleasantly - her presence barely registering over a whisper.

Jazmine didn't demand anything from DeAndre over the years of them knowing each other, which was why he did something for her he never did with the other women in the fringes of his life - he invested in her.

In a casual conversation with her a year or so ago, Jazmine mentioned a lounge she wanted to open in Los Angeles with a business partner she met in grad school. The space was a property she saw up for sale in a newly-gentrified area, and Jazmine seemed to have the small team she assembled ready to execute plans. It wasn't much at all for DeAndre to just give her the money and he hadn't done it to get anything in return. He never loaned money out and much preferred to give it and be done with it. But, the way she made herself available to him afterwards, getting on her knees on multiple occasions to thank him, was more than appreciated.

*"Thank you, Jaz. Next time I'm free, I'll hit you up."*

Whenever he was free in whichever city or state he was in, Jazmine always had a way of getting herself there.

After a quick post-game assessment from Coach, DeAndre was more than ready to get something to eat before heading back to the hotel to get some rest. He remembered a time when he'd party the night away after a match, but the aches he'd endured over the years were starting to catch up with him. More than half of the tournaments and matches he competed in, were played while DeAndre was injured with stress fractures, hamstring strains and wrist pain. The game he played today was the first one he'd done without a bandage to stabilize his leg but he was starting to feel the sting of pain already. The feeling of invincibility he felt at his home court in the Port last week was becoming more rare – the feeling of being hyped with so much adrenaline that he couldn't even feel the pain. Yet, that was a different game and a different day because overall he was changing. His recovery time, down to the number of days required for him to rest, was different.

DeAndre watched Coach's team walk out of the room after gathering their own materials and supplies when Rand stepped in as one of them was leaving. Shoving the door open wider, he clapped his hands.

"'You know the next question, dawg, 'yo, where Dame at?'" Randall rapped, walking over to DeAndre.

"This track the Indian dance that get our rain back, 'what's up wit' you and Jay, man? Are y'all okay, man?'"

DeAndre chuckled, recognizing his cue to finish their back-and-forth with the start of Jay Z's verse on the song. He could never imagine not having his best friend on the road with him.

"Yup...I got it from here, 'Ye...damn."

They used to do this as kids – drop rap lyrics when one recognized something was off with the other, utilizing a morse code only the two of them could decipher. Neither one of them cried nor talked about feelings. There was no time for all of that in the hood. But, Rand never made DeAndre feel bad about having an off-day or feeling the weight of resistance neither.

"My ass is old, dog," DeAndre said with a chuckle after a beat.

Rand hiked an eyebrow.

"Thinkin' of putting down the racket?"

"Hell nah," DeAndre pushed his head back in offense. "Just need to take my rest more seriously. I still got more fight in me."

Pushing his head back against the wall, DeAndre let his eyes close. He'd typically do this after a game to get his mind settled for a moment, but he was feeling himself slowly drift into slumber this time. DeAndre lifted his eyes, shaking his head.

Damn. Was he ready for a nursing home already?

His phone vibrated once more, in his front pocket this time, with another Instagram message notification. He pulled it out and flipped it over, preparing himself for a potential lingerie pic from Jazmine.

But that wasn't it.

*"Hey there, can I have your number?"*

DeAndre almost jumped out of the chair he was sitting in while staring at the direct message Imani just sent. Typing his number immediately, he watched the ellipses dance across his screen.

"You good?" Rand asked, taking quick glances between DeAndre and his own phone as he too scrolled through it.

The characters on screen disappeared, no response given, before DeAndre's phone chimed with a text notification.

*"Thanks, D. I'm confirming you as a client, if you're still interested. Let me know when we can coordinate schedules to discuss details."*

DeAndre felt himself beam from the inside out, his entire mood shifting instantly.

"Bruh, I'm more than good."

~

DeAndre opened his eyes Saturday morning, sprawled across his Egyptian cotton at home, suddenly possessed with the spirit of Mr. Clean.

Even with the housekeeping staff vacuuming downstairs and the landscapers tending to the lawn outside, this feeling to tidy up crept in even before his feet touched the carpet. Once showered and dressed, he started chores in no time - wiping down the banisters, inspecting windows for fingerprints and making sure picture frames on the walls were leveled. This was Imani's first day at the house as his commissioned artist and he wanted to make sure not a thing was out of place nor a speck of dust detected.

She had obviously been to the house the night after Rand's party, but he realized that Imani hadn't seen it during the day. The night can cover a host of sins that would be more obvious under the sun's rays...everything had to be perfect. She told him today wouldn't be very long, much to his disappointment, as it was more like an official client consultation, so to speak. Imani would get a feel for his vision then she'd work on getting the supplies she needed to execute her interpretation of it. He had no real idea in mind for what he wanted and was more than willing to just follow her lead, vowing to go along with her process.

Now in the kitchen, DeAndre slid a duster along the countertops as Glinda, one of his longest-employed housekeepers, stared at him with wide eyes.

"Uh…Mr. Harrison, sir…is everything okay?"

"Yeah, yeah…just handlin' a few things myself."

As he continued, with Glinda moving much slower, observing DeAndre suspiciously, the intercom next to the refrigerator sounded off an alert.

"Lemme in," Randall said, voice muffled.

When DeAndre opened the door, with the duster and a few dishrags in hand, Randall took one glance at him and shook his head.

"Don't work up too much of a sweat," Randall said, walking past him to the living room. "Then your ass will be funky and you'll have to get dressed all over again."

"Tell me why you're here again?" DeAndre projected, wiping his forehead with the back of his hand.

"Eve dropped the rugrats at soccer practice and went out with Mel, so I got extra time to kill before I gotta pick 'em up."

DeAndre eventually filled Randall in on hiring Imani for this project and his best friend shook his head with a cynical chuckle.

*"Playin' a risky game with that girl,"* he had said.

DeAndre knew he shouldn't have been making this such a big deal and he was honestly shocked at the rise he got out of simply thinking of Imani being here. Once he left Melody's house a few nights ago, he thought she'd reject him as a client, forcing him to move on from this hold she had over him. Surprisingly she hadn't, so he was doing everything in his power to make sure she was comfortable.

Stephanie arrived an hour or so later, taking a phone call in the foyer, as DeAndre wiped the spot on the coffee table underneath Randall's sock covered feet crossed at the ankles.

"Get yo' crusty feet off my shit, man," he said, hitting Randall's feet, as Randall chewed the chips stuffed in his mouth and attempted to ignore

DeAndre as he was deeply engrossed in the Snowfall episode streaming on DeAndre's big screen.

Randall sucked his teeth.

"Damn," he stood up from the couch, straightening his T-shirt. "So sensitive in your older age."

When DeAndre turned to him, he found Randall rubbing his hand over his chest.

"You got some Tums or somethin'?" he asked, "this indigestion is kickin' my ass."

"Should be in the first bathroom down here."

Stephanie appeared in the kitchen, smiling at whatever held her attention on her phone, when she glanced at DeAndre and Rand. She did a quick survey around the room, before her eyes settled on the rags in DeAndre's hand.

"Is the president coming?" she asked.

Randall laughed.

"Nah, just a woman D payin' to do arts and crafts in the crib," he joked, "just as an excuse to get up in shawty's grill."

Stephanie perked, her eyebrows raised at his casual admission, while DeAndre's arm s collapsed at his sides. Randall said it as if he just told Stephanie the sky was blue.

"Yo!"

"What?" Randall shrugged, "might as well keep her in the loop."

He grabbed a bottle of water from the fridge. "Imani's gonna be battin' her little fairy wings up in here for a few weeks. I'm sure you're hoping to get somethin'."

Stephanie chortled, looking at DeAndre, her mouth agape.

"A woman? Here?" she asked. "Oh, this is...new."

Stephanie knew DeAndre never invited any of the women he messed with back to the home he currently resided in, preferring to keep his casualties as far away from his personal assets as possible. But, she also didn't know anything about Imani or the fact that she wasn't a woman he was just messing with. He couldn't define what she was to him, yet he took her a little more seriously than any woman ever before.

"Yup, yup," Randall folded his arms.

## A Month of Sundays

"Not gon' lie," he smirked, "girl is kinda bad, too. Got that Kelly Rowland complexion, keeps her hair super short...some Nia Long from the 90s vibes."

Stephanie, a captivated audience, nodded at his every word as DeAndre scratched the back of his neck.

"Oooohh, Nia Long from the original Best Man movie?" she asked, pointing a finger at Rand, "...or Nia Long from Fresh Prince?"

Randall's eyes narrowed as he pointed in exaggeration.

"Okay, Stephanie, you already know!" he yelled. "Fresh Prince, Will's fiancé...that Nia! Got the petite thing going on and everything."

DeAndre, not finding any of this amusing, glanced at his phone. Imani should be here in a few minutes.

"Okay!" she said before covering her mouth with her hand, angling her face at Randall. "I'm just glad she's a sista."

"Oh," Randall's brows furrowed, "always, always...c'mon, now."

The two fell into chatter like children at recess.

"A'ight...girls," DeAndre said, looking between the two of them in annoyance. "Make yourselves useful."

He looked over at Stephanie, who mentioned having to go through his upcoming monthly itinerary for travel and events, when he had a chance, and threw the remaining rags at Randall. Not even a half hour later, the bell chimed again, making DeAndre's heart race. He didn't even recognize his own anticipation, but he enjoyed this rush of exhilaration after being in a state of dormancy for so long.

This is the most DeAndre had seen Imani in person since the party and each time felt a little like Christmas. He pulled open the door without thinking twice as Imani, standing on the front step, turned around to face him.

Opting for loose-fitting jeans and a pair of Dunks, Imani tugged at her ear, both studded with a gold bar across the cartilage, as her lips ascended into the warmest smile. She was in a yellow oversized shirt unbuttoned with a tight orange crop top underneath, pulling the essence of the sun into his home. Imani's bordeaux painted lips were moving, but he couldn't hear a damn thing she was saying.

He was so captivated.

DeAndre has talked, wined, dined and sexed all kinds of women, each with many similarities and very few differences but, Imani was cut from a different cloth. With her eyes meeting his, without Michael or any other distraction nearby, DeAndre took advantage of studying her much deeper in the daylight. He also *recognized* the Kelly Rowland-esque vibes that Rand mentioned, but Imani was still very much in her own lane.

"Your house has such a different vibe during the day."

Imani's voice slowly entered DeAndre's consciousness as he acknowledged the sounds of the birds outside, the lawn being cut and the monotony of the sprinklers. Everything behind her suddenly looked a little brighter, a lot cleaner and much sharper.

"DeAndre?" she angled her head. "Are you okay?"

"Yeah," he blinked and noticed the smallest freckle just above her lip. Who knew he had even more to discover about her?

"So...can I," her smile dimmed, "come in?"

"Oh, yeah," he said, wiping his hand across the top of his head. "My bad."

DeAndre stepped aside to let her into the foyer as the soft amber scent he smelled at the wedding three years ago tickled his nostrils. The fact that he even remembered a scent from way back then was wild. She had a different scent at Randall's party that was nice, but this one held him from their first meeting. The two were now walking side by side with DeAndre leading the way into the living room.

"You smell nice," he said, as casually as he could. He had thought it for so long that he knew he had to say it.

Instead of simply thanking him for the compliment, Imani looked at him, brows furrowed, as if he were speaking another language.

"Thanks," she said, folding her arms in front of her.

*What the hell was that?* he thought. Did he offend her?

Once in the living room, he watched her attention turn to Rand who had his arms outstretched as he came into view near the television.

"Imani! What's up, girl?" Randall said. "Rollin' up in here lookin' like a Starburst. How you doin'?"

Imani chuckled, shaking her head and tugging at her ear.

"Thanks, Randall," she smirked. "Glad you finally got that shaving cream smell off of you."

## A Month of Sundays

"Okay, okay," Rand put his hands defensively, "Jokes are cool. That was cool."

While DeAndre watched Imani and Randall's banter for a few more minutes before introducing her to Stephanie shortly after, it became apparent to him how at ease he was having her here in his space. Similar to how he felt the night they were here alone together, there was no other place DeAndre would rather be.

Forget hoping that Imani would only be here for a matter of weeks. DeAndre wanted her to be in his space for as long as she could.

# Chapter 15
# Delirium

The first time Imani ever painted for someone else and bore witness to its impact was in the fifth grade, the year before everything changed.

After begging her mother for months to play with her more expensive paints, Helena finally stopped at the convenience store not too far from the apartment one day and bought Imani her own set. It was a square metal tin of 12 primary colors with a flip lid, packaged in individual squares across horizontal rows. She first tested out all of the colors, getting a feel for how the different hues looked on paper before mixing and matching them to make colors of her own.

As someone who was pretty quiet in school, Imani never felt like she could express herself through words on paper or even through music, like her father – a musician did. Her gift was that she could see anything - a feather on top of her dad's saxophone case, the perplexed facial expression of the substitute teacher assigned to her class or all of the colors in a classmate's outfit and remember every detail. From memory, Imani could draw and paint anything or bring her memory of anything to life through her art. Her voice was loud and apparent once she had paint and pencils.

Even though he was a musician, Imani's father encouraged her communication through art the most, framing each and every one of her "masterpieces," even sketches and rough drawings, everywhere in the apartment.

## A Month of Sundays

"*You gotta keep going, babygirl,*" he said, "*art breathes life into folk.*"

Helena, who Imani often looked to for validation as a fellow artist, would merely smile and nod without saying much of anything at all, as if critiquing art was somehow forbidden. So, Imani kept painting. At first, she filled up composition notebooks with sketches of interesting objects she found on the playground before transitioning to heavier notepads with stockier paper that she needed to save several allowances in advance to purchase. By the time she was sketching in the notebooks with the velvet covers, friends of her parents began taking notice of her gift.

"*You always make the prettiest little birds, Imani,*" their neighbor Judy had always said.

As one of the oldest women on Imani's block growing up, Judy had few words for anyone, but would always take the time to compliment Imani whenever she visited Helena for company.

Even at her young age, Imani always felt like Judy was lonely or at least not the happiest she could be for a woman who Helena said lived life to the fullest when she was younger, traveling the world as a flight attendant and even acting in a few plays on Broadway. Imani often wondered where that spirit went, but for whatever reason, she felt like she saw traces of it when Judy looked at her work. Like, her pieces took Judy back to a younger time she once had but never forgot.

On the evening before a big $5^{th}$ grade exam, Judy rang the doorbell. Her mother, who was in the kitchen cleaning the dishes, went over to open the door.

"Helena, hi," Judy said. "Has your daughter gone to bed?"

"Oh," Helena said. "No, she hasn't – is something wrong?"

Imani was in the living room, lying on her stomach on the carpet, peering down at her science textbook. She looked up to find Judy watching her with cautious optimism and a nervous smile. Dressed in a trench coat over a brightly colored printed dress with a purse clutched under her arm, Judy looked as if she was making a pitstop at their apartment on her way to a more important destination. Helena opened the door further, letting her inside the small open floor space. When Judy's eyes landed on Imani's, the older woman looked like she was about to burst into tears.

"Are any of your creations for sale?"

Imani looked at her mother, not sure how to even respond. She had never thought about giving her art away, neither did she understand the concept of making potential allowance money from it.

"Whatever you choose, Imani," Helena said. "Are you okay with Miss Judy seeing a few of your paintings? You can pick out a few that you think she'd like."

She turned to look back at Judy. "You wouldn't mind waiting for her to see what she has, right?"

Imani rushed back to her room, going through the disjointed piles of canvases and large papers smeared with charcoal and ink on the floor. Based on her observing Judy all this time, she had a feeling the woman wanted something in color that looked alive. Imani felt a thrill down her spine just looking at the three paintings she knew Judy would love – an acrylic painting of a fleet of doves, an oil painting of a light blue sky with the puffiest clouds and a painting of a young girl, around Imani's age, wrapped in multiple scarves and donning a large pink feathered church hat. Imani smiled at the last one, only because it was an interpretation she imagined of Judy as a younger woman, full of all the life and possibility she couldn't even imagine for herself.

Walking back into the living room with Judy and Helena now talking on the couch, Imani turned the three canvases to face the women. This was her first time opening her heart to someone besides her parents, resting the canvases against her legs. As always, Helena glanced at each piece individually, a forlorn smile on her face, yet Judy was entranced in no time. She drew closer to each one, falling onto her knees to examine every detail of them all. But, it was the last painting of the young girl - the one Imani had hoped would resonate...that made Judy fall into a trance, her mouth widening and tears filling her eyes. Placing a hand to her mouth, she allowed her eyes to collapse as she took a deep breath, nodding slowly. Judy opened her tear-filled eyes, looking over at Imani as she tucked her hand under her chin.

"Your gift is something so special. Thank you for bringing me back to myself."

Imani smiled, not exactly understanding what Judy said at the time. She was barely a preteen herself and knew absolutely nothing about her elderly

## A Month of Sundays

neighbor with the penchant for colorful attire. Imani never knew Judy's full story, but she always remembered exactly what she said.

The feeling that Judy had that day was exactly what Imani hoped DeAndre would have once she was done with his piece.

Imani had spent about six weeks on it already and fought tooth and nail to get to this point, where she was almost finished with the painting. Her struggle wasn't because she didn't have the skills to execute the concept, one in which DeAndre didn't contribute anything, or because she didn't have the supplies or time or space to do what needed to be done. She was struggling because of the time she was spending with him and around him - watching how he moved, how he interacted with his team and just his entire being. It all allowed her to pinpoint exactly what would resonate with him.

Imani knew that DeAndre needed a piece of art embodying the many iterations of who he was, confident and charismatic, while representing how far he'd come.

Imani thought her blinders would kick in as soon as she stepped into the foyer where the completed piece would be displayed, especially because DeAndre promised he wouldn't poke around her while she worked.

*"I don't need to look at the masterpiece in progress,"* he said. *"I'll be ready for it when you're ready to show me."*

He also wasn't home that often and was out of town for almost half of her time working on the project. But what she observed on the days he was in town kept distracting her and slowing down her progress.

Surprisingly, Imani saw firsthand exactly how many people demanded *something* from DeAndre - his time, his energy and, much more blatantly - his money.

She had a chance to meet his mom – Andele, for the first time and was hoping she'd never see her again. Andele stopped by with DeAndre's cousin about three weeks into Imani's commission and looked at Imani with more disdain for her than she would his housekeeping staff.

"Ma, this is my friend, Imani," DeAndre smiled warmly, "she's adding a special touch to the crib."

As Andele's eyes crawled from Imani's short hair - dyed lilac that week, down to her camouflage Crocs, Imani mustered up a small smile despite his mother's visible disdain. Imani didn't think much of what Andele thought of her. She already seemed to be a piece of work, having only been in Imani's presence for two seconds. Imani just needed to get through the next few weeks.

"Great," his mom said.

Turning her entire body back to DeAndre, Andele undoubtedly dismissed her, allowing Imani the opportunity to walk back to the canvas she was painting. As she crawled on hands and knees to paint the top corner of the canvas, Imani kept her eyes trained on her work and ears alert.

"What's up, Ty?" she overheard DeAndre say to the young man with Andele. "Congrats on everything. How's the fam?"

"It's well...uhm..good."

Before Ty could get another word in, Andele interrupted the conversation.

"DeAndre, Tyrone needs some help with getting a leg up now that he's out of school," she said. "Trying to forge his own path and everything...aren't you?"

"Yeah. I'm reselling sneakers on an app—"

"That's...on the side, Tyrone, right?" Andele asked. "What he's really doing is working on putting that accounting degree to good use. He'll be in the city for a summer internship at an accounting firm as an intern but needs some help with a few basic things like rent, food, transportation, clothes...you know, DeAndre, all those tools that you needed to prepare yourself for your career-"

"What's up with the app? I don't know why moms interrupted you like that," DeAndre said, pointedly.

Imani folded her lips, keeping herself from bursting into laughter, which would most definitely echo into the room with her Musiq Soulchild playlist in the background. She was learning that DeAndre didn't let a lot of things slide and wasn't shy about letting anyone else know it either.

"Oh, well..." Ty cleared his throat. "I've been working on it since my sophomore year and promised Mom I'd put it down when I graduated, but....I don't know...I like it."

"I got you," DeAndre said.

A silence fell among the three of them that seemed to drag for a while, Imani thought they all walked away.

"Come walk wit' me, man, talk wit' me I wanna see what you're thinking. I'll take it from here, Ma."

# A Month of Sundays

Imani was done shortly after Tyrone and Andele left. She ventured into the spacious living room overlooking the tennis court to let DeAndre know. She thought everything about his space was beautiful, but this room, complete with a domed ceiling and three stone arches, was probably her favorite - not that she had seen the entirety of his home. Even with the tour he gave her those few weeks ago, Imani knew she barely saw everything.

Stephanie was sitting across from DeAndre on one of the lush sofa seats that mirrored the larger couch, discussing whatever business needed his attention. She looked up catching Imani's eye and smiled wide, deep dimples on display. Imani liked Stephanie from the day they met and was impressed with DeAndre's decision to have a Black woman spearheading his image.

"Don't mean to interrupt," Imani glanced between the two before training her gaze on DeAndre. "I'm heading out and just wanted to let you know."

"I'll walk you out, hold up a second."

Getting up from the couch, DeAndre went over to Imani as she made her way towards the hallway leading to the front door. The two walked in stride with one another as they sauntered between the vacant walls that, while nice, Imani thought could use some much-needed color.

Imani pulled her fabric tote, filled with a few brushes and paints she no longer needed for the remainder of the job, further up her shoulder once they were at the door.

"Is there anything else you need?" DeAndre asked.

They faced each other as Imani suddenly noticed the depth of his complexion. Against the cream and gray colors of the house and the late afternoon sunlight spilling from the windows, the red undertones in his hue were amplified, making him look like a sculpture.

Whenever Imani had to open buckets of rich paint colors, like brown or red, she loved watching the pigment spread and fill the tray, like melted chocolate spilling onto a pan. It looked so delectable, like Imani could almost take her finger and taste it. Imani's heart raced as she watched him, wondering if he tasted as rich as he looked.

"Hello?"

"Sorry," she blinked, clearing her throat. "I don't need anything. Just gotta get myself home. It's been a long day."

## Jade Olivia

Imani was exhausted, which meant her delirium was just around the corner. After working on this painting for weeks on end, she was more than ready to get it done. She had work for other clients she was juggling, but no project she was working on currently took as much mental energy out of her as what she was doing for him. Imani just wanted it to be perfect and wanted him to love it as much as she did. Getting his stamp of approval would be the personal validation that she truly desired.

DeAndre looked at her with raised eyebrows.

"Hope you get some rest, then," he said. "You know Clive's got you."

"Yeah...thanks for that. I thought I'd be able to have Kaylee's car a little more consistently, so...I appreciate it."

"Yeah," he took a breath, wiping his hand over his mouth before clasping his hands behind his back. They seemed to always do this with one another. There was so much Imani wanted to say to him and learn about him. She had never felt so invested in someone she barely knew.

"So, what happened with Tyrone?"

Imani asked it so quickly she didn't realize the amount of time it took for the question to come out of her mouth from her brain. DeAndre straightened and folded his arms across his chest.

"Oh," she followed up with haste, glancing at the floor before looking up again. "That's none of my business."

DeAndre chuckled.

"I actually forgot it even happened today."

Imani nodded, her own brows raised.

"Get asked for money that much, huh?"

DeAndre gathered the top of his shirt in his hand with a chortle.

"I'm not always asked for money," he said, "and, I don't walk around giving it away like that if that's what you're thinkin'."

"Well," her eyes widened. "It was pretty easy for you to give me money."

"Yeah, well," DeAndre tilted his head quickly from one side to the other. "You're different."

He sobered, his gaze plastered on hers.

Imani folded her lips together and took a breath, feeling herself becoming warm all over, before scratching behind her ear.

# A Month of Sundays

"So, are you…helping him out?"

"Yeah," he admitted. "He only gets it one time from me, though. Now, whatever he's gonna do with it is up to him."

DeAndre shrugged, placing his hand on his neck, "…and, I told him that too. When I was his age, I blew so much on clubs, ice and everything else, so all the advice I gave him probably went in one ear and out the other…he might fall on his ass or he might not. Who knows?"

Imani looked at him, feeling exactly how she did when she met him at Melody and Hosea's wedding. There was so much she had assumed about him based on his persona in public and on the court. But, his generosity outweighed her perception of him.

"It's good that you keep your boundaries, though," Imani placed her hand on her shoulder again. "Seems like you enjoy what you have."

"Yeah, I ball out every once in a while," he scratched his beard. "I ain't gon' lie."

The two chuckled.

"But, I'm thinkin' I'd like to share it," he looked at Imani pointedly. "You know?"

Imani swallowed, shifting her gaze from his.

"I don't," she laughed.

"Anyway, see all these brushes?" she asked, shifting her tote to the side of her leg for emphasis. "They're coming back home with me. Your painting should be done this week."

"Damn. That was quick," he commented.

"Yeah," she said, smiling. "I'll be out of your way in no time."

*Thank you, Lord.*

# Chapter 16
# Masterpiece

*Something was wrong.*

"...Just so you're aware the next few weeks are going to be much more hectic. You have a few shoot campaigns that're due for Elite Athletics, a couple of charity matches and a meeting with the foundation..."

For the past half hour, Stephanie was talking to DeAndre about priorities for the next quarter, but he had been tuned in and out of their conversation for the last ten minutes. Imani had been pacing from the kitchen back to the area she was working in for several weeks. Today was the day she said the painting would be ready and, even though DeAndre had obviously prepared himself for the inevitable, it still came as a surprise that it was ending so soon.

Wasn't there a fee attached to finishing a job this early? Didn't she have to guarantee him a minimum number of weeks she'd be working on it?

But none of that mattered anyway, because Imani looked like she was either ready to leave or needed to say something.

"...We're still in talks with *Late Night Show* producers. They've been wanting you as a guest for a while, but timing was off," Stephanie continued. "They weren't sure of the angle, topic, that kind of thing...Whatever is going to come from this Elite Athletics sponsorship this year, that'll be perfect for promo time and while we're in New York..."

The day after Andele came over with Tyrone, having him all but perform acrobatics for money, she asked how long Imani had been working at the house. With her hand on her hip and eyes squinted, Andele listened to him tell her what she was hired for. She shook her head, her lips perched.

*"I'm sure you've been entertained by little Miss Tinkerbell floating around."*

Andele made the comment with a tinge of annoyance, yet Rand had also made a similar comparison of Imani, as if she was scurrying about like an untamed creature.

Yet, DeAndre didn't think Imani was like either of those things.

She reminded him of a hummingbird with a presence that was hard to pin down, as she always held his attention each time she came around. An old trainer of DeAndre's who was Native American used to always pinpoint hummingbirds near the trees by the gym, they used to frequent, as a sign of good luck.

*"Whenever you see one out, you know everything's going to be good after that,"* he'd say. *"The earth is more beautiful with them in it."*

Watching Imani over these past few weeks, DeAndre agreed that Imani encapsulated that sentiment to a T. He was learning that her beauty went beyond the physical. Her laughter and her conversation added this vibrancy to his home that he hadn't expected. She confined herself to one area for the commission, yet her energy spread all over the house.

A few weeks into the project, DeAndre sat down to eat lunch with Imani. Chef Sebastian gave them the works that day with Cajun cuisine that even had DeAndre salivating after practice. He had only been home a handful of times while she was there, and wanted to make sure they spoke when he was around. They made small talk about how the project was going, even though Imani remained extremely vague with details. The two had a brief pause in conversation as they focused on their plates.

As usual, Stephanie was sitting at a glass table nearby, pounding away on the keys of her laptop, balancing her phone at the crook of her neck, while Rand - arms extended across the back of the couch, was laughing obnoxiously at a Martin episode he saw a copious number of times.

"This is random," Imani had said, biting at the corner of her lip, "but, I actually see colors radiating off of people when I'm around them long enough."

DeAndre looked over at her, her eyes twinkling with her skin aglow. Unlike many women DeAndre came across, Imani's smile was one of genuine excitement, like she was sharing a secret just for him.

"Does that sound weird?"

He smirked, looking her over. "It does."

Imani sucked her teeth, knocking his leg with her foot under the table and smiled, her eyes landing on Stephanie.

"Like, she has a gold hue to her that I just...feel like I see when she's around me. When she walks away, I could see faint yellow smoke trailing behind her or something, like everything she touches turns to gold. She also reminds me of random pictures I've seen of women from the '70s. Yeah, she's like, solid gold, '70s fine..."

She then shifted her gaze to the couch. "Randall is definitely orange - bright, optimistic, endearing."

She smiled. "He's a fun time but is sometimes underestimated, too."

"What about me?"

When their gazes met, DeAndre felt time stand still. Everything else fell away around him, allowing him to hear the softest buzzing sound in the lowest audible frequency. Her smile dimmed as her eyes scanned his entire face before she blinked, biting down another grin. He wanted to reach over to kiss her so bad, he had to bite down on his teeth to keep them from trembling.

"I can't tell you," she said as if telling him he was ridiculous.

And, she never did. The mystery of the whole thing was stored in the back of his mind all the way up to this point. What did she see? He hoped he didn't personify some wack ass color like...seafoam green or something. Nobody ever pulled that color out of the Crayola box to use.

Stephanie continued, "...Your issue with Men's Health is coming out next month in print and online. But Men's Health wants to do a video with you as a component of the issue. Like a quick rapid fire questions kind of thing."

DeAndre took a few quick glances at Imani, who was now typing into her phone, biting on the side of her thumb before going into the kitchen to dump a cup of dirty water into the sink. She then walked back to the room for a second before walking out again, making her way toward him and Stephanie until she stopped to check her phone again, shaking her head.

"You're not listening to me at all, are you?"

## A Month of Sundays

DeAndre looked back at Stephanie who had her head tilted, eyes lifted above her planner staring at him.

"Yeah, yeah, I heard you," he said, scratching his cheek.

Imani caught DeAndre's eye and a slow smile ascended her face. As she walked closer to them this time, DeAndre straightened himself in his seat. Stephanie followed his line of vision, turning to face Imani too.

"Everything cool?" DeAndre asked. He always wanted to keep himself ready for whatever she needed from him.

"Yeah. It's fine, I'm fine," she said. "The painting is ready whenever you are…"

Despite himself, DeAndre smiled with all his teeth, feeling as giddy as a kid anticipating presents for their birthday.

"Is it cool if Michael comes here to pick me up?"

That quickly, DeAndre's smile dropped, feeling as if the cup of water Imani had earlier, now splashed on his face, instead.

"We have to head out somewhere after this and it'd make sense for him to come get me here…so, is it ok?"

*Hell no.*

He just so happened to take a glance at Rand who was shaking his head, stifling his laughter.

"…I just wanted to ask before I gave him the go ahead—"

"Yeah," DeAndre responded quickly, scratching behind his head. "Sure."

No need to give it any more energy than was necessary. He suddenly felt a creak in his neck that was like a thorn in his side. Whenever he was around Imani, talking to her and vibing with her, the very last thing on his mind was her attachment to someone else. Michael's ass always had a way of popping back up to remind him.

Imani nodded, casting her eyes down to her slim fingers decorated with various rings.

"Okay….so, whenever you're ready," she pivoted to make sure Stephanie and Rand heard her as well. "Y'all can come and check it out, too. Some of the staff propped it up against the wall, so you should get some of the effect at least…I hope you like it."

Imani was radiant today, standing with even more confidence than

DeAndre had ever seen in her. He definitely wanted to see this side of her a lot more.

"I feel so important! Seeing an artist's original work for the first time," Stephanie smiled, gathering her laptop and planner to walk ahead of the guys to follow Imani on her way to foyer. They laughed as they walked together. DeAndre followed behind them at a distance with Rand joining him halfway.

"I hope you like it," Rand mimicked a feminine laugh, batting his eyes and wiping a hand against his chest. DeAndre, void of expression, stuck up his middle finger.

Chuckling to himself, Rand patted DeAndre's back.

"You know I'm just messin' around witchu, man," he said, still smiling as DeAndre nodded, scratching the side of his neck. "I'm rootin' for both of y'all to get it together."

"Uhh huh."

"Wanted to keep you posted, though," Rand stopped walking, making DeAndre slow down. "Got a few things to take care of outta town so I won't be here for a little bit. E knows, but I didn't have a chance to tell you."

DeAndre pushed his head back, an eyebrow raised. "You straight?"

"Yeah, just know I can't scope around the crib while you're out this week. I could get Jay to come through, if you want."

DeAndre leveled a look at him as Rand referenced one of the guys who was with the crew that was at the Royal Court match a few days ago.

"You know that man don't know his ass from his elbow," he said, "might set off an alarm or somethin'..."

Rand laughed, as DeAndre led them towards the room again. "I'll figure it out."

"Oh my God, Imani..."

Stephanie let out the smallest gasp that DeAndre heard just before the painting came into view. But, once he stepped into the space, Stephanie's reaction made sense.

Propped up against the large wall between the two custom window grilles, a collage of deep blue, purple and black paint brush strokes decorated the entire canvas. It looked like a disorderly array of colors at first glance, but a further examination of the surface revealed the image of a skyline. Above the city skyline were portraits of three Black boys in hoodies and fitted hats, staring at the viewer with unyielded confidence. Each boy expressed a different emotion - joy, meditative and defiant - that rang true for DeAndre one way or another. Without any words being exchanged, Imani understood exactly who he was.

"It's blue."

Imani, who was next to him now, said it just above a whisper for only him to hear.

"That's what you represent, I think…Everyone talks so much about how regal and powerful purple is, which it is - it's true. But nothing regulates and calms things down like blue. It can make someone happy or represent something sad. It's such a familiar color…we see it all of the time, but it goes so far beyond the surface when you take a closer look. It's also really expensive…"

Imani chuckled. DeAndre managed to peel his eyes away from this creation to her. With her arms folded across her, Imani held his gaze.

"But, to me aside from black, blue is the most versatile and dominant color in the entire spectrum. Not many other colors can exist without it."

DeAndre barely thought much about how others perceived him, but Imani's entire read of him now made him feel like he instantly grew ten feet tall. This woman was beyond any other person he'd ever experienced. He couldn't even comment.

"Yo Imani," Randall said, cupping his hand over his mouth. "This is straight fire! You did all of this by yourself?"

He approached Imani, draping an arm over her shoulders, his eyes still fixed on the piece.

"Like, no elves popped up to help you or anything?"

"No," she laughed, "it was all me."

DeAndre smiled, his heart beating so fast, he just knew everyone could see it but he didn't care. There was absolutely no way he wouldn't have someone like this in his life. How could she not be?

DeAndre's phone vibrated, pulling him from the moment.

"Mr. Harrison," the front guard said when he answered. "You have a guest…Michael Johnson. Am I letting him in?"

Just to mess with dude, DeAndre thought of telling the guard he wasn't, insisting this "guest" be escorted off the grounds immediately. Imani wouldn't even have a clue but DeAndre wasn't in the business of giving her a hard time and pegged Michael as the type who'd project any offense onto his girl even if it had nothing to do with her.

"Yeah," he dragged, looking at Imani who was staring at him skeptically.

"How did you even think of something like this?" Stephanie asked her.

Imani began explaining her process, from how much she thought of Port Springs and the little she knew about DeAndre. He noticed how specific she was in referencing tidbits about him that were general information, far from some of the insight he gave her in the private conversations they had shared, even their discussions about some of the people closest to DeAndre. He was impressed even further that Imani wasn't trying to air out the intel she had about him.

In some roundabout way, she was being protective.

"It also helped that D was pretty flexible with me," Imani smirked. "So, I didn't really have to worry about missing any sort of mark or anything."

The doorbell rang a few moments later as Stephanie offered to get the door. When Imani and Rand looked over at DeAndre for any sign of...a reaction or life, he realized that he hadn't even said anything yet. He just continued staring at the painting and vaguely listening to Rand and Imani talking. He knew as much about art as he did quantum physics, which wasn't anything at all. But, he knew he was witnessing something one-of-a-kind and beyond special. If Imani did all this within a few weeks, he could only imagine what she'd do with a house that was all hers.

Noticing the sheen of the blue in the painting's backdrop, he couldn't look away at how the colors seemed to suddenly meld together, congealing in slow motion.

Wait...

Was he high? Was the painting actually moving?

"Imani," Randall started. "I think you done made this grown-ass man speechless."

"Excuse me," Stephanie said, re-entering the room. "Ummm...is it Michael? He's here for you, Imani."

## A Month of Sundays

DeAndre turned around, as any desire to drown Imani with all the praise he could express evaporated like smoke.

"Wow, this is incredible," Michael said, taking in the painting for himself with his hands on his belted waist. Similar to the party, he was dressed like he was a step away from a business event in pressed jeans, with a crisp white button-down shirt under a black suit jacket. He stood next to Stephanie who was now cutting glances between him, DeAndre and Imani. DeAndre could see his publicist's mind working overtime.

"Thank you, sweetie," Imani responded, walking past DeAndre as her amber scent...his favorite scent...lingered next to him. She approached Michael to give him a hug and a quick peck on the lips. Pulling her close with his hands on her waist, Michael's eyes met DeAndre's gaze.

"Thanks for letting me come in to get her," he beamed with a closed mouth smile.

"Yup."

Moving his eyes away from this clown, DeAndre grazed a hand across his stomach, feeling like he just got sucker punched.

"Stephanie, you're the only one who hasn't met Michael," Imani said. "This is my boyfriend."

DeAndre felt his jaw tighten this time, surprised at himself for just standing there. This dude was at his house, on his property, and the fact that he didn't kick his teeth in or break his hand was beyond his logic right now.

"Oh!" Stephanie said, her eyes cut from Michael to DeAndre in utter confusion. "Nice to meet you, Michael."

And, after Rand offered Michael a lazy head nod, the entire energy in the room shifted. A pin drop could have broken the silence.

"Well, DeAndre," Imani said with finality. "I really hope you love it. It was such a pleasure working with you and let me know if there's any other work of mine you're interested in."

He held her gaze in straight disbelief. Whatever energy and ease they had built over these past few weeks came crashing down like dominoes. Imani was now all but a customer service representative, thanking him for his loyalty. It felt like he was being dismissed. Was he being dismissed in his own house?

"My baby..." Michael said with emphasis, leaning against her, "is just so talented."

DeAndre didn't know what buddy knew or whatever hunch he had about him and Imani, but he saw the slight squint in his eye - daring DeAndre to say something. With the creak in his neck now throbbing incessantly, DeAndre was immobile, a rope of chains keeping him standing in place. A fire ignited in his system that was so strong, he thought it would spill out of his mouth if he opened it wide enough. Can't she feel what her departure was doing to him?

She's the artist - there was no way she couldn't see it.

But, Imani just stood there with Michael, looking at DeAndre, without an ounce of the desperation he felt. No matter how many jokes and intimate conversations, nor the familiarity they had shared, DeAndre was now reminded of where her loyalty had always been - with the man who claimed her just before DeAndre could. She made her choice clear, time and time again.

So, why couldn't he just leave her be?

"She's a genius, actually," he said, keeping his eyes on Michael.

*Challenge accepted, nigga.*

"A masterpiece, really," he added.

From his peripheral, DeAndre saw Rand slap his hand across his eyes, leaning his head to the side as Stephanie pulled her planner close to her chest. With the corners of her lips turned downward, Stephanie's eyes softened like she was watching the leading man in a movie pour out his emotions to his unrequited love.

Everyone in this room knew just how competitive DeAndre was, especially for what he thought...what he felt ...was rightfully his. But, DeAndre decided they needed a reminder. He suddenly could care less how he looked in front of anyone because he was nowhere finished with this woman.

## Chapter 17
# Real Recognizes Real

"'Take my heart and split it in two! Why don't you?!'"

The frantic actress in the movie Imani was watching screamed at the top of her lungs to the strangest looking alien Imani had ever seen. Curled up on the couch, Imani didn't even know the name of the flick as she fought consciousness in front of the television. Soon, everything went dark.

A ray of sunlight hit behind Imani's eyelids, stirring her awake. Taking a deep breath, she inhaled the sweet scent, allowing it to drench her insides. She let her hand graze the soft skin etched with ripples of muscle that curved under her fingers. Pulling herself up by her forearms, she opened her eyes, smiling down lazily at this beautiful man underneath her. He was still inside of her from the night before, but she didn't let him go. Imani was afraid to detach herself and feel his absence from deep within.

"You're my masterpiece," he said to her now before stroking her deep, revving her from her core all over again. "What do you have for me?"

She looked at him and smiled, knowing exactly what he meant. With a deep shout, Imani felt her heart charge up her throat then release up and out of her mouth. The wet, warm organ beat incessantly, leaving Imani in a daze as she held it, cupping it in her hands, the drips of blood spilling between her fingers.

He smiled, looking at her with such intensity in his gaze. The heart...her heartbeat...in her hands was already slowing down as the blood began to dry, leaving a cast in her palms but she could care less. She was waiting to give this to him.

Pulling her hands closer, he nodded before closing his eyes and placing the most delicate kiss onto the heart, re-igniting its relentless beating.

Finally...

Imani was so happy he wanted to cry. Instead, she pushed her heart back into her mouth, squeezing it between her cheeks before relaxing her throat. As she took her first swallow, he pushed himself back into her with a force that would be almost unbearable if it hadn't felt so...damn...good.

Imani was jolted awake out of her dream, taking rushed breaths as her eyes opened wide. With a hand on her chest, she looked around, realizing very quickly that she was on her couch and safe in her apartment. She must've dozed off while watching the SciFi movie that was still playing regardless of whether she was watching it or not. Imani was definitely home and she sure wasn't with DeAndre.

This was her third dream about him this week and the strangest one so far. They started off innocent at first, mere re-enactments of the night they met or expanded on conversations they had with each other recently. But, now that her commission was complete, her fantasies of him were much more explicit and oddly more pleasurable.

Imani wished she could kick herself for how he made her feel even in dreams. Ethel always said dreams were only subconscious manifestations of someone's deepest desires. There was no way Imani could desire him though... was there? She wasn't with him. More importantly, she was with Michael - the *actual* man of her dreams.

What she had to do was see Michael more often, and the opportunity presented itself as their pre-marital counseling sessions began. It had been about two weeks now and they had developed a routine around it. He'd pick her up after work to head to the church.

The day he picked her up from DeAndre's was a bit out of the norm since they tended to hang out later in the evening on Saturday nights, but Michael insisted on picking her up so they could grab lunch. Michael felt like they hadn't done something spontaneous in a while. Imani then asked DeAndre before she sent his address to Michael who showed up a little sooner than she thought he would.

    The last day of any commission was always either a relief to Imani or bittersweet, depending on how she felt about the client. But, leaving DeAndre's house that day was more than bittersweet for her, it was downright sad. She didn't think she'd miss being around him or his home as much as she did, but over time she had grown familiar with his friends...his team - Rand and Stephanie and was much more comfortable with DeAndre's whole...vibe. Just being around him, gave her all the energy she needed to complete the entire piece for him, which even she had to admit was a bit of overkill.

    The paints and supplies she used were all top quality and accessible for his project because of the amount he initially paid her which allowed her to use a portion of her profit to invest in the best materials needed. Prospective clients would sometimes ask Imani to perform straight up miracles, pulling inspiration from Pinterest boards or Instagram and demanding pieces that would take forever to do with supplies that cost an arm and a leg. Imani would have to let them know she could do all of that, but only at the right price. Having the materials she did for those few weeks with DeAndre, opened the door to creative freedom and was definitely something she could get used to

    But, that was a week ago. She fortunately had the experience of having a client of his caliber under her belt now and that provided endless possibilities for securing other huge clients in the future.

    Standing up from the couch, Imani went to her room to change for today's art event. It was an outdoor gallery crawl where local Port Springs artists showed their latest collections at the various galleries on a strip downtown Port Springs. The annual community event was also a gateway for Imani to scout new artists who were just under the radar and could use Artgo's stamp of approval. Getting Lauri's approval was still touch-and-go for her, but Imani wouldn't give up. She just had to find the right artist who would be a proper fit for Artgo's mission. Michael asked to tag along and she expected him to arrive to the apartment at any minute now.

    Now outfitted in jeans, wedge sandals and a tube top, Imani checked her phone just in time to get Michael's text - letting her know he was parked and on his way upstairs. She walked into her living room, stuffing her sketchpad into her tote.

"Did Michael lend you the money?"

Imani turned around to find Kaylee standing in the living room with her hands on her hips.

"No, he didn't," Imani answered, without meeting her gaze.

She wasn't avoiding telling Kaylee, per se, but she didn't feel like telling her how their rent was now paid for the next three months. Imani used part of her profit from DeAndre's commission to pay the rent up for a few weeks, ultimately getting their landlord off their backs. Kaylee knew about her commission, but Imani didn't give her an inkling of how much he gave her for it. Plus, since Kaylee hated hearing Imani using the money she'd get from client work for anything other than savings, she chose not to even share the plans she had for it.

"Trust that I'm not doing anything crazy," Imani said, pulling the back of her shoe over her ankle. "We're fine, you're fine...and neither one of us have to pinch pennies for at least twelve weeks. Should be enough time to plan for the quarter ahead, right?"

Kaylee rolled her eyes as Imani blew her a kiss, making her way out the door. No need to give any more time to a conversation she refused to have... ever.

About a half hour later, Imani and Michael were at the gallery crawl downtown, chewing on soft pretzels and sipping the hard cider that vendors offered registrants at the first participating studio. They visited about three galleries, which allowed Imani to introduce herself and talk to three new artists she had only heard about on social media. Fired up from being surrounded by all this eclectic work within the first hour of the crawl, Imani suggested she and Michael go back to the car to take a little bit of a break.

She climbed into the car as soon as Michael disengaged the locks with his keys, not even waiting for him to open the door for her. Taking a cleansing breath, Imani was too excited to even think straight. She had scheduled two more projects this month alone - a portrait for a restaurant owner who was the matriarch in her family and a live painting for a non-profit fundraiser. Preparing for them often meant she didn't allow herself time to take in work from other artists. But, the nature of her job at Artgo meant she had to make time in order to remain aware of the new artists generating buzz in the industry. It was a part of the job that Imani enjoyed and she never wanted to put herself in a position where she wasn't supporting her peers, but it sometimes made her mentally choose between her career at Artgo and her personal vision as an artist.

Michael climbed into the driver's seat but wasn't empty-handed. A large bouquet of red roses spilled over onto Imani's side, a vibrant punch of color that caught her eye immediately.

"Thank you, sweetie," Imani smiled. "They're beautiful."

Michael always gave her nice flowers, even if they were typically the same kind of flowers. It was his thoughtfulness that made it special. She hoped that wouldn't change if they got married.

"They were in the backseat," he said. "I wanted to give them to you before the night ended."

"Thank you."

Their gazes met before Imani drew close to his lips and Michael closed the gap. His clean scent was all over the car as the two pressed into the softness of each other's lips.

"How're you feeling about counseling this week?" he asked once they pulled away.

"It's good. I...didn't realize you had so many plans for your life."

"Plans with you in it," he said, holding her gaze again.

They were now in the part of the sessions where they both had to discuss the vision they had for their lives as part of a married unit. They were initially given the assignment a week prior to be worked on individually without the other knowing their answers. And, once they came together during the next session, they'd each share their respective visions with Pastor Coleman mediating. For the most part, Imani's plans pretty much mirrored her reality now - she would live in the Port Springs area, maybe even Rapid Springs once she and Michael elevated financially, continue working at Artgo, but ultimately build her business as a sustainable career for her to live as a working artist. The only thing that would truly change is she'd have a baby or two, babbling in her arms or balanced on her hip.

Michael then revealed his vision during the session, listing a few of the plans he and Imani had already discussed at least the year before. He'd continue working at the marketing firm even though during the MBA program he would ultimately be accepted in. Even with that, Michael and Imani agreed they were planning for kids immediately after the wedding, much to Imani's delight. They both knew it would be a strenuous time, especially since they'd both be working but, the two agreed to it. Hearing Michael mention all of this during the discussion didn't come as a surprise, but it was what he said afterwards that made her pause.

"Do you really want to leave the Springs?" she asked now, tilting her head to the side.

"Yeah, I mean...not immediately," Michael said. "I know we'd have to save some more and I have to see if I even get accepted into Harvard, but God willing - I will."

When he mentioned this tidbit in front of Pastor Coleman, his father hadn't even batted an eye, making Imani assume they had conversations about this before. She knew Michael wanted to go to an Ivy League school and had the diligence and resume to do so, but she didn't think he'd want to move so far from home. It took at least ten hours to drive to Harvard from Port Springs.

"You could always just go to Stevenson that's not too far from here," she said. "It's still a good school."

"And, you...could always work at the Museum of Living Things," Michael smirked, "helping the little kids build Playdough castles."

Imani leveled a look at him. "Michael..."

"See how that sounded?" he asked with a small smirk, his brow raised. "The alternative is a fine option...but it's not what you'd want."

Imani took a deep breath. "Okay. I understand what you're saying. I just want our kids to be raised in the city."

Despite the excitement of other cities, there was truly no city in the country quite like Port Springs. It was a metropolis with the feel of a small town, once a resident was connected to even one person in the community, they were entrenched for life. There was nothing like the close-knit nature of Port Springs' residents, including those who were in the wealthier area of the Rapids.

## A Month of Sundays

"And, we'll still be in a major city - Boston."

Michael assessed the reluctant expression on Imani's face.

"It'll only be temporary, honey," he said, placing his hand on top of hers under the bouquet.

Imani paused. "So, only until you're done with the program?"

"Well, no," he said. "But I don't see us living there for another ten years."

Imani pushed her head back at that statement. There was no way she was leaving her family, her aunt and best friend, here for ten years.

"As long as we're not living there for very long."

Though Imani wasn't a fan of moving in the first place, she knew she'd always follow her husband's vision for their family. She found comfort in doing so. Imani knew she could put up a fight about this, but why even go there? She'd have her family and stability in the form of a lifelong partnership. If she had to make a little compromise here and there, it wasn't a big deal in the grand scheme of things.

After a few moments in the car after their cider finally finished, Michael and Imani went to visit the remaining studios that were a part of the crawl. They met a local artisan who specialized in pottery, sculpting functional pieces in eclectic shapes and colors. Plates and bowls shaped into asymmetrical masterpieces looked like tiny sculptures on the round wood display table. The pieces were arranged on the table as if a dinner party were about to commence.

"Hello there," a Black woman with bone straight, jet black hair smiled. Dressed in an all-black linen pants set, a stark black line was etched on her face starting at the top of her hairline and disappearing at the neckline of her top.

"My name is Xena - welcome to the exhibit. Let me know if you have any questions."

Imani took in the rest of Xena's pieces when she heard someone calling her name. She turned around to find Stella in the clunkiest pair of platforms that Imani never thought she'd see on a woman her age.

"I knew that was you," she said, approaching Imani for a hug.

The two laughed as Imani pulled her gently towards Michael.

"Sweetie, this is the legend," Imani beamed, "Stella Rose. She's the artist I was telling you about who's in residency with us."

## Jade Olivia

Michael smiled, shaking Stella's hand as Stella pinched his arm gently, giving Imani's hand a playful squeeze.

"It's so good to see you, Imani. What brings you down here?"

"Just like you," she smiled, "I wanted to scope out some of the artists here this year."

"Rapid Springs is such a unique place," Stella said, "people rarely talk about the treasure trove of talent here. There's no place like it."

Imani casually looked at Michael, raising her eyebrows at him. *This is what I mean.*

"Excuse me?"

Imani peeled her attention to another woman standing next to Michael who was smiling at her sheepishly.

"Are you Imani?" she asked. "Imani Wright?"

"Um, yeah."

"Sorry," the woman said. "It's...you did a piece for my cousin's 21$^{st}$ birthday that everyone still talks about. It was like two years ago, but you look like the woman she called to the stage for her to thank. I think you had a different hair color, but I'm usually good with faces. I know you probably don't remember..."

"No - no, I do," Imani chuckled.

She typically remembered a majority of her clients, especially the earlier ones who took a chance on her, simply based on one or two Instagram posts of her work. Imani definitely remembered that 21$^{st}$ birthday party, which ended with the celebrant almost beating down a guest who wouldn't be her background singer during Karaoke.

"It was a few minutes outside of the Port, right?" Imani said, squinting. "Like, near 60$^{th}$ and First Avenue."

"Yeah," the woman beamed. "That day was crazy."

The two chuckled before the woman looked behind her at Michael and Stella.

"Sorry, I'll let you get back to your conversation," she said to Imani. "Just wanted to say hi...and wanted to let you know that you're dope."

When Imani turned around, surprisingly perked up at the random run-in, she saw Stella looking at her - frozen in place.

## A Month of Sundays

"I knew you were one of us," she said, narrowing her eyes at Imani before breaking into laughter.

"Okay, okay. You caught me."

"Why didn't you say anything when I asked you before?"

Stella pulled at the strap of her crossbody, her veiny eyes looking Imani over with renewed interest.

Imani shrugged. "I don't know...I haven't been at Artgo very long and honestly I just need insurance."

She laughed as Stella joined her.

"I understand that, young one." Stella folded her arms, shaking her head. "But you shouldn't hold this in. Does Lauri know?"

Imani's eyes widened. She was about to curse in front of this older woman, something she never did.

"No, no. She doesn't...nor...do I think I want her to know yet."

She looked at Stella pointedly, hoping she'd pick up on the hint.

"I can't promise it'll be a secret forever, but...I understand needing time," she reasoned. "Don't want to take too long, though."

Stella's warning still played in Imani's mind on an endless loop by the time she was back at her apartment from the day's outing. Now that she had confessed her secret to Stella, Imani knew it wouldn't be kept from Lauri much longer. She should just...tell her boss. What did she really have to lose? And, if Lauri didn't like her work – the weight of carrying her hidden identity around would finally be off her back.

The woman who approached Imani today, in addition to DeAndre's epic reaction to his own piece last week, were more than enough to give Imani the push she needed to tell Lauri - and maybe...to even just *look* at AirFete's exhibition guidelines. Imani knew she was talented and had chops...maybe it was time it was time for her to take herself much more seriously.

# Chapter 18
# Retreat

Imani entered the office Monday morning with a new resolve. Pulling Lauri's office door closed, Imani scrolled through her phone and looked at the various texts she missed from Michael and Kaylee as well as a few notifications from the group chats she participated in from time to time. She didn't have a chance to talk to Lauri the way she wanted to because they had been pulled into a last-minute meeting with the acquisitions department to make sure key pieces from a donor's personal art collection were arriving on time.

That check-in turned into a longer forty-five minute meeting about the overall vision for the upcoming exhibit on the Black Arts Movement of the mid-1960s. Imani loved important work like this that gave her the privilege to actually touch work and artifacts from that time period, but none of that work was hers. Feeling somewhat dejected after Lauri dismissed her without even asking Imani if she had anything on *her* agenda, Imani took a few Artgo brochures from her desk to refill with copies for museum visitors - yet *another* task that reminded her of the administrative part of her job.

"This day can't move any slower," Gloria said, approaching Imani at the copy machine.

"I can't tell if I'm an assistant or tour guide at this point."

Imani pulled the last of the stack piled at the end of the copier, tapping the edge of them on the nearby table to get them organized. The day wasn't moving fast enough. It was slowly approaching the dreaded 3pm slump when having coffee would likely keep Imani up all night, but not having anything would make her sleepy. Gloria took one of the stacks from the table as Imani wiggled her arms forward in a lazy half yawn and glanced at Gloria.

"I got dibs on the last KitKat in the machine, but we could share." Gloria said offering Imani a piece.

Imani bit down on the chocolate, already feeling the sweet rush of it on her tongue. They were standing at the vending machine nearest to the barrier overlooking the front atrium of the museum. Shoe taps and brief chatter echoed from below.

"We got downtime now," Gloria said. "Got into any of the acrylics and Modge Podge down in the basement?"

Imani leveled a look at her. Those art supplies were for Stella to use, not anyone else. She didn't say anything, just kept biting into her candy when Gloria put up her hands in mock surrender.

"I'm just saying, the deadline for submissions for the art festival is less than two months away and how many pieces have you completed for it?"

"My job is just to make sure Stella is good," Imani said, "not me."

"I know, you keep saying that. But, if former clients are showing you love out on the street in front of Stella, you don't need to be making copies for a manager who's actively scouting other artists."

Imani rolled her eyes.

"Just promise me that you'll make the time to look at the prompts for AireFete."

Imani did more than just look at the prompts. She had them memorized. The theme of the exhibit was memory and submissions had to include artistic interpretations of the theme, utilizing 3 artistic mediums.

Oil paint, acrylic and collage were Imani's favorites and she took every chance she could to experiment, getting lost for hours in memories of her childhood, her parents, and life in general. The truth was, she was constantly working on it, just hadn't figured out how to perfect the concept yet.

"I'll take a look at it, I promise."

Audible gasps and squeals echoed from downstairs this time as Gloria and Imani walked toward cubicles.

"Damn...is someone fighting?" Gloria asked.

She was nearest to the barrier and stopped for a moment to peer down at the impending commotion.

"Well, you know this area can be kinda sketchy sometimes," Imani said.

Gloria looked around briefly before she gasped herself, pulling at Imani's elbow.

"Girl, we gotta go down there."

Without a chance to protest, Imani was being pulled by the arm as Gloria led the way down the cement steps.

"What is it?"

Once they were on the first floor, she turned around and stepped closer to Imani. Her lanyard around her neck was tangled in disarray.

"Imani, DeAndre *fucking* Harrison is here!" she squealed.

Imani felt her cheeks heat and her heartbeat in succession.

*This can't be happening.*

When Imani had mentioned working here, she never thought he'd ever show up to her job. She also hadn't seen him in person in weeks. From the random pictures of him she'd seen online - with other women following behind him, of course –she was surprised he was here 'cause his travel schedule was nuts. Imani didn't even know he was home.

His celebrity status afforded him the chance to explore Artgo privately without the attention of the crowd that was now gathered with their phones trained on his every move. Yet, he chose to visit during normal business hours. A small part of Imani thought that it may not have been DeAndre, but when she observed who was around him, she noticed Trey- his bodyguard, standing like a statue a few paces behind him.

If Gloria wasn't still holding onto her, Imani would've made a run for it back to the staircase. Recollections of her dreams of him, her straddling him while his tongue was down her throat as well as the conversations they shared while she worked on his painting, had just faded from her mind. There was no way she was going to be able to stand talking to him in person right now.

DeAndre stood in the middle taking selfies and signing autographs for the wall of people that surrounded him. He was taller than everyone, ducking his head slightly for the folks who only stood as tall as his torso, looking every bit as sexy as could be. DeAndre contorted himself to accommodate his fans with ease.

Imani always thought that not seeing him for weeks or years on end would allow her attraction for him to wane, but she realized that it never did. She got lost in her thoughts looking at him now…he was so…perfect. Taking a notebook from a fan for him to sign, one of the chains around his neck glinted under the museum light as he stood in black joggers, a short sleeve shirt and a sleeveless vest, his fade glistening with a soft sheen.

Lauri then appeared from the other side of the room, walking over to him with Ed - an Artgo security guard, in tow. The staff constantly joked that Artgo guards were merely art school kids on summer vacation, not trained professionals who could take on a legitimate problem in the crowd.

Ed personified every bit of that jab right now. With wide eyes and outstretched arms, stammering in hesitation Ed called out to the crowd that was probably more manageable for someone who knew what they were doing.

"Alright, everyone. Let's give him some room," he called, with a pre-pubescent crack in his voice. At this point, Trey had single-handedly managed to keep more people from getting closer to DeAndre and Lauri's interaction.

"You think she knows him?" Gloria asked, as she and Imani watched the whole scene unfold in front of them.

Imani prayed that wasn't the case by a long shot.

"What a pleasant surprise. It's so nice to meet you, Mr. Harrison. My family and I are huge fans," Lauri said.

Imani watched Lauri turn on the professional charm that resulted in the more than 40 percent increase in funding Artgo had since she came on board. DeAndre was speaking to her, but his back was facing Imani and Gloria. Imani assumed it was something amusing as Lauri chuckled, her tan face brightening like a lightbulb by the second. The charmed meeting the charmer, for certain.

"Damn," Gloria said. "I don't even have my phone with me."

Imani turned to her colleague, who was biting on her fingernail, staring at DeAndre with all the lust she could muster.

"Why do you think he's here? You think he's trying to see the Basquiat exhibit or Carrie Weems?"

Imani swallowed, willing her face to stay neutral. Her head felt like a furnace.

"I - don't...don't know. Artgo is a big deal. People come here all the time."

Gloria held four fingers in a grip with her thumb up, giving the universal Black girl approval of a fine-ass man. She was probably undressing him with her eyes at this point.

"Let's run to my desk to get my phone so I can get a pic with him."

*Yes. Escape, please yes.*

"Sounds great," Imani said, eagerly. "I'm right behind you-"

She was tailing Gloria until she heard Lauri's high-pitched tone stop her.

"Imani, can you come here for a moment?"

She took a breath to gather her thoughts and curled her lips into a knot before turning around. She really thought she wasn't seen.

"Oh, I'm coming with *you*. Let's go," Gloria said in a harsh whisper.

She walked slightly ahead of Imani with a renewed energy, practically bouncing on her toes towards them. Imani kept took her time as she plastered a professional smile on her face.

What did she have to be nervous about anyway? He was only gonna say hi to her then probably go on his merry way, wherever he was going. The closer Imani got to DeAndre, though, the more she realized how he was openly admiring her - slowly scanning from her sneakers to her legs then up from her chest to her face. She was gonna kill him if he didn't stop undressing her with his eyes. How dare he? In a professional setting, no less! So disrespectful, so irritating...so damn DeAndre!

When his eyes finally met hers, he released the sexiest smile that made her tighten in the middle *just* above her thighs.

"I had no idea you knew someone so esteemed, Imani," Lauri said, as soon as Imani and Gloria were in front of them.

Imani pulled her eyes away from DeAndre, who continued looking at her, with his brows raised as if impressed that she *did* know someone so highly esteemed. He let his head fall to the side, without a word.

## A Month of Sundays

"Well, we have mutual friends in common who...know each other," Imani said, clearing her throat.

"What're you doing here, DeAndre?"

He scratched the side of his cheek.

"I was telling Lauri that I hadn't been here since I was a kid. Figured I'd stop by 'cause I was in the area after practice."

"We're so glad you did," Gloria chimed in, as if continuing her part of the conversation. She stuck her hand out to shake, one brow cocked, peering into his gaze - thirst on 1000.

"DeAndre, it's so nice to finally meet you," she continued, "to be in the presence of such royalty."

Imani had secondhand embarrassment at this point, watching Gloria make a show of openly looking at him from head to toe once their hands connected. It was one thing to watch Kaylee geek out at a party, but watching it play out at work was straight up awkward. He had to have known this was going to happen. He was so...cocky.

"A huge pleasure," Gloria said, her tongue peeking out the corner of her mouth.

"It's good to meet you too, sweetheart," he beamed, casually indulging a touch of her imagination. Imani chuckled to herself at the thought of how much he did this with fans in a given month, while managing to make them feel special every time.

Imani couldn't imagine having attention like this come her way at all. With her boss and colleague now a pile of mush, Imani continued observing DeAndre handle it all with grace, nonetheless, and thank them for their support.

Lauri turned back to Imani.

"Mr. Harrison is requesting a private tour of the Basquiat collection. Do you have anything else that needs to get done today?"

*Of course he would.*

Imani offered a closed lip smile.

"Nothing that can't be done tomorrow."

"Perfect."

Lauri turned back to DeAndre, grinning once more.

"Well, you're in good hands with one of our finest, Mr. Harrison. Please, don't be a stranger at Artgo, especially when you're done with the tennis season. Gloria, let's leave them to it."

She walked toward the escalator with Gloria behind her.

"Coming," she responded.

When she caught Imani's eye, she mouthed with wide eyes *'talk later'*. DeAndre had his back turned, looking at the colorful collage at the Basquiat exhibition entrance.

Imani didn't even give him a chance to formally greet her before she got started.

When she was done illustrating a point, she walked several paces ahead of him to avoid walking next to him. Imani looked like she was running at this point, considering how long her steps had to be because of his height and she looked ridiculous. Imani was determined to get through the exhibit as soon as she could. She studied Basquiat in undergrad and knew Artgo's collection like the back of her hand.

Before she knew it, they were already near the end of the exhibit, not far from the archway leading to the next one featuring Black art from the 1990s. They stopped in front of Kings of Egypt II, one of Basquiat's earliest works that illustrated his signature style. She felt herself rambling, just to avoid giving DeAndre a chance to strike up a conversation.

"I don't think I said this earlier," she continued, scratching the side of her brow. "He was born in December in 1980 in Brooklyn, NY."

"Imani."

She was facing the painting head on now, looking like a college professor talking about a math equation, writing on the board fervently, while their disinterested students looked on in confusion.

"And, did you know that he was in a car accident at a young age? His mom gave him a book on the human body and he often referenced body parts in his work."

"Imani."

He projected his voice higher...more aggressively...commanding her attention. Feeling those familiar butterflies take flight, Imani centered herself before turning around to meet his gaze, focusing on him and...no one else.

## A Month of Sundays

For the first time since beginning the tour, Imani noticed that they were alone.

Where was Trey? What time is it? Is the museum closed?

Imani blinked and folded her arms at her chest.

"What is it?"

"You're walking so far ahead of me, I can't keep up wit' what you're saying. I stink or somethin'?"

Imani's laugh sputtered despite herself and the pent-up balloon she was holding onto began to deflate. He always knew just how to loosen her up...how to encourage her to not take it so seriously.

They were friends, after all...right?

"You don't. I just have a lot on my mind, that's all."

"Like, what?"

He let his gaze fall to the paintings in the room as they continued a lazy stroll toward the archway.

*Right now, you.*

Imani squeezed her arms around herself even tighter. "You...promise you won't make it a big deal?"

"Can't say that I won't when you put it that way," he admitted. "...Tell me."

She shook her head, mindlessly touching the back of her neck.

"There's a huge art exhibition in Miami that my boss is associated with in a roundabout way and Gloria – my coworker I was with earlier, your not-so-secret admirer, she's been trying to convince me to enter."

"Why haven't you, then?"

"I don't know. It feels like such a major deal, I feel like I need to have more credentials to my name. One of the artists-in-residence here is an OG and she's entering as a last hurrah kind of thing. It's a big deal, major international judges come out - all to select one artist from Port Springs to be a part of the exhibit."

DeAndre sat on the bench once they were out of the exhibit. "How do you get these credentials you're talking about?"

She picked at her thumb.

"I gotta enter contests."

He raised his brows at her, making her feel ridiculous for answering her own question.

"Don't look at me like that, D."

She mindlessly dragged the tip of her foot against the cement ground.

"Look, I'm not tryin' to judge. I was waitin' for you to mention to everybody how you pretty much made a masterpiece in my crib within..days...but," he shrugged, "I didn't want to blow up your spot, so...just want you to pay attention to how you move, though... that's all."

"Not everyone was born confident," she said.

DeAndre pulled his head back and looked up to stare at her, eyebrows raised, pointing to himself.

"And...you think I was?"

She sighed, straightening herself over him. She was mere inches from being between his legs and, in an alternative universe - Imani saw herself moving right between them to seal her nonsense with a kiss.

"I didn't mean that." She rolled her eyes. "You work your ass off, but you also started in tennis when you were like...three."

DeAndre pushed his hands down over his mouth and pulled at his bottom lip, chuckling.

"Okay, Imani."

He shook his head and licked his lips, looking off in the distance at the other paintings. With one hand palmed at his thigh, he leaned forward with a bent arm resting on his other leg, suddenly staring as if in a trance.

"My mom was really into art."

Imani felt her eyes grow twice their size.

"Andele?"

She thought back to meeting her for a few seconds during her commission, and Imani would've lost serious money if she was in a bet.

"For real?"

She sat down next to him as he nodded his head.

"Loved it, too - she just stopped after I started competing, for real."

Imani had a thought.

"You think you had something to do with that?"

He shrugged.

"I don't like sayin' I'm responsible for grown people's decisions, but...I think she was a lot happier back then. We were strugglin,' but she was smiling every day walking around taking shots with her camera."

"She did photography?"

"Yeah, shot a lot of folks in Port Springs Park and would be out there for hours, especially in the summer...taking pictures of old men playing chess...babies...families...guys playing ball. Doing all of that for the Spring Times...and, then..."

DeAndre stopped himself from what he was going to say and took his phone out of his pocket instead.

"All I'm saying is that you need to make the most of what you love to do."

He was scrolling on his phone until he stopped to tilt it in Imani's direction. He had her Instagram profile open to a post from two months ago when Imani painted a portrait of a Black woman dancing with scarves piled on top of her head. DeAndre tapped the screen with the tip of his finger.

"This one," he started, "is dope...I don't know about painting and all of that. But, Imani, this looks like you took a photograph..."

He went back to the main page of her profile, scrolled some more, then clicked on another post.

"Then, this one... with the waves detailed in the background was fire."

He was still looking into his phone when Imani took the chance of letting her gaze creep up his face. She was looking for traces of humor just to appease, but he looked genuinely invested, eyes gleaming with fascination.

She had all this doubt swirling in her mind about sharing her work on social media, debating if the move to do so would somehow cheapen her or make her appear like some pretty girl trying to make trendy art similar to everyone else's. Meanwhile a global superstar was looking at her Instagram profile with 900 followers and posts of her work from a year and a half ago.

"Okay, DeAndre," she said, her cheeks warming. "I get it."

If she was a few shades lighter, she would be as red as a tomato.

"Just letting you know, you got skills...more than that. I didn't just hire you 'cause you fine. Your work is straight gold." DeAndre shrugged, putting his phone away.

Imani warmed at his words, floating somewhere between the clouds and heaven from his validation alone. She was working hard at not letting validation from others affect her, but she would be lying to herself if she thought she wasn't fazed.

He nodded his head toward the staircase.

"Don't y'all got a food court or somethin' in here?" he asked. "I used to eat the funnel cakes when I was a kid like my life depended on it."

Artgo was intentional on securing cuisine from chefs around the world, yet all he wanted was the most basic, cheap and sugary dish on the menu.

He was a Port dude, for sure.

Imani laughed. "I got you. Let's go before they close the kitchen."

∼

"What made you get the tatts here?"

Deandre gestured to the back of his neck, directing his question at Imani sitting across from him at a small triangular table. Imani placed her hand at the back of her neck in response, trailing her finger down the explosion of small stars that went from her neck to the top half of her shoulders.

"I thought I was being different back when I was in New York."

She chortled at her quip, knowing it unfortunately represented something else entirely. The smartest decision she made at the time she got it was having it on her back. At least she couldn't see it every day. Imani took a cautionary glance at her other tattoo, a myriad of butterflies and swirls running from her shoulder down to her wrist, feeling her nerves ease. The art on her body held many stories.

"Glad it's not some guy's name or something."

DeAndre bit into the funnel cake he was salivating over when they got to the cafe a few moments ago. Imani could tell the two employees on their shift were preparing to leave when surprise etched on their faces, upon seeing DeAndre and they pulled themselves together. They were all smiles, handing DeAndre a tray of two funnel cakes with steam wafting from the plate, as if it was 1 in the afternoon instead of quitting time - closer to 5pm.

Sitting in one place now actually made Imani more comfortable, considering that most of their time was occupied with eating the cakes on their own plates. Imani had watched him get comfortable in the thin wire seat that was along the lines of the artsy, modern furniture decor of the museum. Wherever he went, he looked like he owned the place, never wavering, legs spread apart and taking up space.

"How come you don't have tattoos?" she asked.

DeAndre shook his head in mock disgust and opened his jacket as if announcing himself.

"You ever put a bumper sticker on a Bentley?"

Imani shaped a tiny ball of foil and tossed it in his direction, laughing at his arrogance.

"How humble of you!"

She shook her head, but hated to admit that she loved unfiltered comments like these from him. It wasn't like he was lying.

"I guess I'm a troll, then."

She rubbed the tips of her fingers together, shaking the dust from the funnel cake.

"Nah, never." He dipped his forehead. "They look incredible on you…just not something I'd be into for me."

"Ooohhhh, ok."

She smirked, taking a sip of soda before imitating the sound of a clucking chicken.

"Didn't realize the great King DeAndre had fears."

He shook his head, laughing in jest.

"You gonna have me tellin' you all my secrets."

He bit into his cake again as he held eye contact, his smile melting away. A chill ran down Imani's spine as she took a longer sip of her drink.

A moment later, Imani's eyes landed on Julio, one of Artgo's janitors, walking to the table next to theirs with a broom and dustpan in hand. She waved once he saw her and DeAndre followed her line of vision. Seeing him reminded Imani just how late it was, which only furthered her imminent anxiety of getting out of here with all of her clothes still on.

*No! All of my clothes will stay on. Am I sweating in front of him right now in these clothes?*

"¿Qué pasó?" DeAndre asked Julio. He gestured, pointing between him and Imani.

"Nosotros estamos interrumpiendo tu horario?"

Julio waved at DeAndre, with a gleaming smile, that Imani didn't even know he was capable of, spread across his hazelnut features.

"No, no. Habla el tiempo necesario," Julio answered. "Ella es especial ahí mismo."

"Lo sé, Lo sé...la quiero ahora, pero ella está jugando."

The two men shared a laugh as Julio leaned against the broomstick with the palms of his hands planted at the top. It was as if they had inside jokes for years. Julio shook his head, gold tooth glistening, before cleaning underneath another table further away.

DeAndre turned his attention back to his plate, gathering the bits of powdered sugar with his fork.

Then, nothing.

Imani was thankful she had managed to pick her mouth up from the floor before he turned back to her. He acted as if he hadn't just spoken Spanish as natural as someone of Spanish descent.

*What isn't this man good at?*

"Didn't know you took Duo-lingo courses on the side?"

DeAndre coughed before he let out a laugh, revealing his brilliant white teeth. He held a fist in front of his mouth and forced himself to be serious.

"Smartass," he shook his head. "I spent a lot of time in Madrid in the beginning of my career and was tired of being the nigga who didn't know what was being said in rooms I was in. Also, I have to talk to everyone around me, have some sort of basic knowledge, so..."

Imani kept her face neutral, appearing as unimpressed as she could, when in actuality she was getting more impressed with him by the minute.

"That's pretty..."

"Surprising?"

Before she could answer, DeAndre pushed up from his chair, gathering his plate covered with remnants of sugar and walked to the trash bin. Imani stood up, speeding up slightly before joining him at the trash bin.

"I wasn't gonna say that...it's not like you're not smart or something."

DeAndre took Imani's plate, looking at her pointedly. Her heart raced when his hand grazed hers.

## A Month of Sundays

"I get it. People only see what I let 'em...plus, they don't really air too many of the post-game interviews with international reporters in the states, so it's cool."

"Just didn't know that about you."

"There's a lot you don't know about me."

The two then began their journey back to the front of the museum, the stark white walls in contrast to their brown complexions, and Imani was grateful that her nerves weren't completely spread on the resin flooring. Trey was at the entrance - a burly statue about as tall as the archway he stood underneath.

She turned to look at DeAndre and folded her arms. Trying to avoid too much eye contact, she cast her gaze outside at the setting sun emanating a yellow hue over the tree-filled sidewalks. It had to have been a little after 6 and Imani knew Kaylee had probably already texted her to let her know she was on the way.

"How're you getting home?"

"Kaylee is picking me up for us to go to dinner."

"A'ight, well," DeAndre flushed his hands in his pockets and did a brief visual survey around the museum foyer. He took a breath before his gaze landed on Imani again.

"Thank you for today. This was cool."

Imani noticed him rock slightly from one side to the other when she herself swayed too.

"Next time you think about showing up, please let me know first."

He looked at her with renewed interest.

"To make sure security is here," she followed. "It's cool since this isn't peak season, but otherwise ya' know - you being here is a lot."

He held her gaze as if he wanted to say something before releasing a chuckle as an afterthought.

"Later, Imani."

He walked a few paces ahead with a nonchalant gait when he turned back to her.

"I gotta ask you...."

The pull at her stomach gripped her as she awaited his words. He was now closer to Imani than he'd ever been today and a light whiff of the Bergamot concoction from earlier spread up her nose.

"You good to house sit for me?"

Imani's eyebrows dipped.

"What?"

"I know it's random, but I'll be away for a week for this next match and Rand's gonna be MIA. He's usually the one who pokes his head in every few days when I'm not around."

*If* she belonged to him, she would've grabbed him by the front of his vest, thrown her arms over him and kissed him with all the pent-up excitement his request just ignited. His home was amazing, even from the little she saw during her tour, and it would be a welcome change to the monotony of the tiny, two-bedroom walkup she shared with Kaylee. She still wasn't convinced she needed to be there, though.

"Don't you have an entire staff on payroll for that?" she asked.

He shrugged.

"Yeah, but I don't trust 'em to be up in there after a certain hour."

They laughed.

"Sebastian will drop off some grub for you to eat when you're there and the landscapers will do their thing," he said, scratching his neck.

"But, it'll just be you at the end of the day. Could use the quiet as a...what do you artists call it? A reprieve?"

Imani smiled, tickled at DeAndre's attempt to relate.

"You mean a retreat," she said, folding her arms with a smirk.

He snapped his fingers.

"Yup, that....a makeshift retreat...I know the crib will be fine, but...you telling me about this application," he shrugged. "...seems like you might need it."

Imani assessed the option. It was not only an opportunity for full access to a beautiful space *with* free food, but she'd have two of an artist's most covetous assets - space and time.

She pressed her lips together, blowing out her cheeks. She *could* take the chance of spending some time alone in his house to kick up her creative mojo.

"Okay," she said, watching him place a hand at his chest in gratitude. He gently pressed a bent finger to her nose.

"A Godsend, you are," he said.

Patting himself at his pockets, DeAndre pulled out his keys, sliding one against a ring to take it out of the cluster.

Imani couldn't believe it. She blinked, folding her arms again at his audacity.

"So, you just knew I was gonna agree to this?"

He looked up at her, keeping his eyes on her as he released the sexiest, most devious smile and placed the key in her hand.

"Friends, right? How many of us got 'em?"

Imani folded her mouth, turning her head to the side to keep from breaking out into a full smile. This guy was really something else.

"How're you even gonna open your door?" Imani asked, with a raised eyebrow.

"It's the emergency key."

*Of course.*

He had given Imani the key like it was so typical for them, like a usual day. Imani's heart worked overtime, feeling the weight of their entire exchange. Was he even aware how much access he was giving her?

"And, when I said I trust you, I meant it. But, if you're gonna party in my shit…at least send me some pictures," he winked.

Imani rolled her eyes, fighting a smile. "Whatever, DeAndre."

His phone vibrated, pulling his gaze away from her and he answered it, keeping it a distance away from him at first.

"I'll hit you up later to let you know what you need."

He walked out the door with Trey trailing beside him, finally giving Imani the chance to take the breath she felt like she'd been holding since he had arrived. Imani raked her fingers across her short-fluffed curls.

"What are you doing, girl?" she thought to herself, shaking her head.

# Chapter 19
# On The Hotline

Imani filled in the eyes of the woman in the portrait, careful to make sure the paint she was using wouldn't look muddy against the canvas. This project, due in another few days, was for a client presenting it to her grandmother during her centenarian birthday celebration, which meant the tiniest details were the most important. Imani used her finest brushes to make sure every wrinkle, mark and vein was just right, making the portrait worthy of the royal giftee's honor. She personally loved doing commissions like this, but this specific one was more of a procrastination project than anything.

Hearing the sharp sound of the electric kettle in DeAndre's kitchen, Imani wiped her hands on the rag lying on the small tray that sat next to her on the couch before getting up to pour herself some tea. She was in the living room painting this time, opting to switch up where she was working just because she could. Imani had been at DeAndre's house since the late afternoon, not really doing any "housesitting" as her day consisted of mostly eating, painting, walking around the tennis court for a break, then doing it all over again. Rinse and repeat.

When she first arrived, she placed her overnight bag in the guest bedroom on the first floor, claiming this room as the one she'd stay in overnight. No room was off-limits, according to DeAndre, though.

"*Get comfortable and do your thing,*" he said to her over the phone yester-

## A Month of Sundays

day. They spoke briefly during the day as Imani quickly packed her bag while alone in her apartment. Kaylee was at work, thank God, which meant she wouldn't have to go through any questioning by her.

Imani arrived, thinking she wouldn't have any interest in the rest of the property. That is, before she was on the property for hours by herself. She was growing much more curious by the hour, especially as time was moving and no progress was being made on her AireFete submission. Pouring the hot water over the bag of loose Chamomile and Lavender tea leaves, Imani placed one socked foot on top of the other, dunking the bag in her mug to let it steep.

Imani classified DeAndre's home as the one from slasher films in which the female lead had to fend for her life, thinking of creative ways to outsmart her captor. But, she chuckled at the wild thought, without an ounce of fear in her because she felt safe, warm and protected here. Even without him physically being here, she felt DeAndre all around her.

She didn't tell Michael she was staying at DeAndre's place, only because it wasn't a big deal. Imani felt like her stay here was equivalent to a 24-hour stay at a hotel. No need to bring it up, especially since DeAndre wasn't even here anyway.

Imani took a breath, pulling out her phone to respond to Michael's text from earlier in the day, letting her know he'd call her later on if he wasn't back too late from preparing for Kid's Day at Port Springs Park tomorrow. Michael was out of town for the weekend as well - with his father at a ministerial conference.

*"Can't wait to see you tomorrow, bear."*

She typed, chuckling at the nickname she gave him that she hadn't used since the earlier days of their relationship.

Why'd she stop calling him that?

*"Not that name, again...Lol. Can't wait to see you too, honey."*

Imani's face fell. If only she was that dismissive over the "honey" he gave her every chance he could...

With her tea in hand, she returned to her canvas to put the finishing touches on her piece. About a half hour later, Imani took her phone out again to take a picture of it for her client, Sandra.

*Special delivery! Looking forward to getting this in your hands next week* 😊

Gazing around the living room once the portrait was complete, Imani made her way to the restroom she was familiar with from working here for weeks. When she stepped in now, she thankfully saw that the toilet paper ran out without an extra one waiting in the wings - not in the closet or under the sink. She then walked through the different rooms on the first floor, including DeAndre's office, to see if there was another bathroom. But, no bathroom nor toilet paper was in sight.

Walking to the foyer, Imani turned around to take in the dark brown staircase leading to the second floor. She wasn't sure why she stole a glance behind her, but she did, before ascending the steps one at a time. As soon as she got to the carpeted landing, Imani pulled off her socks, a thrill rushing through her as her toes sunk into the plush gray carpet. She just so happened to look up and ahead of her to find a door halfway open.

Imani pulled at her lips, her mind screaming at her to start her search in another room, but she couldn't resist. Pushing the door open slowly, she placed her phone in her back pocket, and realized very quickly that she had stumbled into DeAndre's room.

Unsurprisingly, the room was massive - complete with coffered ceilings, a King-size bed, a fireplace below a large screen television and glass doors leading to a porch off to the side. Imani stepped further into the space, taking inventory of the area.

Before getting to know him from the commission, Imani assumed DeAndre was surrounded by flash everywhere he went and that the pinnacle of his vanity seeped into his bedroom. But, observing his space now, the room reflected more of his interior nature that Imani was picking up on as she got to know him better – calm and resolute. It didn't take long for her to find the door of the ensuite.

The bright lights of the bathroom illuminated the marble floor tiling when Imani stepped in, cooling her feet. Imani used the restroom as intended and went to one of the sinks to wash her hands as her eyes fell to the grouping of small glass decanters, vials and spray bottles on a square glass tray in the corner.

*What was that cologne he wore last week?*

Imani hadn't been able to get his scent, when he was at Artgo out of her head and she just knew if she took even the tiniest whiff, it would satisfy her itch. She made quick but careful movements, picking up bottles in the front - Chanel, Maison Margiela, Creed - to make sure she wasn't accidentally flinging an empty bottle across the sink. Then she went through each scent, raising almost every bottle to her nose, until she found it and released the heaviest sigh. The depth of the scent wrapped around her entire body, like one of his hugs - warm, alluring and satisfying. They hadn't touched each other since his match weeks ago, but Imani pictured his entire frame under her fingertips just from being this intimate with his scent. With her eyes closed, Imani felt a twinge thunder through her from the top of her head down to her middle, biting at her bottom lip.

*I gotta get outta here.*

She opened her eyes, placing the bottle back onto the tray and leaving the ensuite, making sure to close the door behind her. The summer evening was another warm one, but Imani felt a soft breeze at her ankles, coming from the porch. She turned to find the door half-open, and next to it, a brown square table with a small box in the middle, in front of a leather sofa chair.

*Gonna just...see what this is and then, I can leave.*

Walking to the table quickly, Imani noticed a puzzle halfway done at the top and a disarray of pieces towards the table's edge. She could tell the completed puzzle was of a city landscape. Gliding a finger across the random pieces, Imani imagined DeAndre looking over it with intense focus for a few before stepping out on his porch for a break. His stare when focusing may have been intimidating for others, especially his opponents on the court, but Imani enjoyed watching him actively think.

Imani joined a piece with another one that configured to the edges perfectly before looking behind her. Another door was halfway open, beckoning Imani yet again. She never quite learned how to let things be.

Pushing the sliding door fully open, Imani stepped into an entire walk-in closet, complete with multiple shelves of sneakers sitting next to each other at equal distances apart. Below the shelving were all of his clothes, organized by color, sleeve length and item category. Imani couldn't think of a time when her own *life* reflected this level of coherence.

She walked to a section of white shirts, brightened to perfection, wondering if they were as comfortable as they looked. No matter how much washing she did to her own white shirts, Imani could never get her scent out of them and, they typically were the most loved and worn, allowing Imani to tie-dye them or cut them up just right to give them another life. She picked up a shirt by its hanger, running her fingers through the fabric gently, feeling its weight, before taking it off its hanger and gripping it hard in her hands.

*Why am I here? Why am I here?!*

Imani blinked a few times as her heart raced, her mind shouting.

*Why aren't you here?!*

Taking a burning breath, Imani took off her loose top, unhooked her bra and pushed her arms through his shirt, pulling it down her entire frame. Just as she knew, his scent was threaded in the seams.

She walked out of the closet, her top in hand with her breath still shallow as her eyes settled on the bed. It *did* look like the most comfortable one she'd seen in the house, which made sense, considering that it was his alone.

Like a woman possessed, Imani walked over and, once at the head of the bed, took her phone out of her pants pocket and placed it on the nightstand. She pushed her pants down, toeing out of them before pulling back the heavy comforter and sheets. The coolness of them hit her as soon as she tucked herself in between the sheets and the mattress. It felt like he had never been under these sheets. She wondered when last he had slept in this bed at all.

*Would you be in this bed with me right now, if you could?*

Imani felt herself pulse at the thought, folding her lips and taking a breath. She closed her eyes shut tight, seeing herself in this bed, indulging in something she never thought possible.

She looked up at the ceiling, staring at the soft shadows from the room's mellow lighting. Imani hadn't spoken to DeAndre all day. He had to have been wondering whether she was even here or not.

Sitting up on the bed against the frame, Imani grabbed her phone and called him. They had to discuss this…trust he gave to her so willingly. This was crazy. Was he doing something like this all the time? Just giving people keys to his house so they could go through everything and–

"Imani?"

The bass in his voice made her forget everything she wanted to say.

"Imani? Hello?"

## A Month of Sundays

She blinked, clearing her throat.

"DeAndre. Hi."

He chortled.

"Hi. Is everything okay? You straight?"

It didn't *sound* like he was occupied or like she may have been interrupting him. It was just his voice - loud, clear, and *concerned* in her ear.

"Yeah, yeah," her brows furrowed. "You just hadn't...called, and I thought you'd want to know I was safe."

"Ah, Imani. I'm sorry. I saw you come in and just assumed you got in your zone. Didn't want to distract you."

She heated all over, prepared to hop out of the bed this instant.

"You...can see me?"

He chuckled.

"Just from outside. You were takin' a few laps around the court, huh?"

She laughed with a small sigh of relief.

*Thank God.*

"Oh, yeah," she took a breath. "Had to give myself a little break."

"I hear that. Feeling relaxed?"

The beat of her own heart was so loud, she couldn't even hear him breathing over the phone.

"Um. Yeah," she said. "I'm getting there. So, how...was your day?"

"It was good. Just busy with interviews, meetings, stuff like that."

"Have you eaten?"

DeAndre chortled.

"Yeah. I have. Need me to order somethin' else for you?"

"No," she chuckled. "I didn't...I mean...I don't know why I asked that."

Imani realized she was doing anything in her power to keep him on this phone. It was pathetic.

"It's cool. You enjoyin' the food Sebastian whipped up?"

She thought back to the food - an impeccable feast contained in individual glass Tupperware containers organized by size in the fridge. Lobster bisque soup, fresh salad, glazed salmon and steamed balsamic Brussel sprouts were only the appetizers that Imani managed to eat before becoming overly stuffed.

She hadn't even touched the grilled chicken, Spanish rice and mashed sweet potatoes yet.

"It was amazing. Didn't realize he'd give me a nine-course meal."

He laughed.

"Yeah, I think he wanted to flex a little when I told him he was cooking for a woman besides Stephanie and my mom. I can't blame him one bit."

"Has he done this before?" Imani's eyebrow hitched. "Cooked for a woman...outside of the two of them?"

DeAndre paused, taking a breath.

"Nah, you're the first."

Imani pushed her head against the frame, moving her hand from the top of the covers to her stomach under his shirt.

"Where are you?" she asked, placing a finger at her nipple and twirling it.

"In my room for the night," he breathed. "I *was* watching Martin before you interrupted me."

She felt the chuckle in his voice rumble in her own chest, as if he could've been right here underneath her, skin to skin.

"I'm sorry, DeAndre," she said, his name coming out in the smallest bit of a moan. *Did he catch that?*

"I never want to interrupt you."

Her nipples began to harden, her breath shallowing as she bit her bottom lip. All he had to do was keep talking and she'd get *exactly* what she wanted.

"You never will."

"Okay," she let out, a sharpness laced in her tone.

"Imani?" he asked again, this time much more gently, a caress.

"Where are you?"

Imani let out a shaky breath.

"I'm...in your house, DeAndre."

He let out his own breath, with a hint of a chuckle.

"And, what're you wearing in my house, Imani?"

This would've been the time for her to just end the call without a word or at least to come to grips with herself.

*Who am I right now?* she thought.

She could've easily blamed all of this on being engrossed in a long art session and just needing a way to get her mind off her lack of inspiration. Imani, apologetic by default, would express regret profusely, vowing to never put them through something like this ever again.

But she was here now...in a T-shirt and in between bed sheets - both belonging to a man who didn't belong to her.

All the running Imani had been doing...away from what she desired... what she was so curious about - had finally caught up to her. She took a breath, choosing to take what she planned to do right now, directly to the grave. The coolness she felt in his bed was replaced by the most intrinsic heat.

"A shirt I found...here."

He chuckled softly.

"You wearin' anything under that?"

"No," she bit her lip. "I wasn't...didn't know I would even do this. I–"

"It's okay, it's okay. When I told you I got you, this is also what I meant. I'm always gonna catch every single, last thing you're willing to give me. Believe that."

Imani let her eyes collapse as her hand trailed up and down her thigh.

"But, you gotta do somethin' for me," he said, "'cause you're in my space, baby...you get that, right?"

As if clouds suddenly cleared, Imani opened her eyes to DeAndre's massive room again like she was taking it in for the first time. Tree leaves brushing against the windows, from the gusts of wind, she didn't hear until now, were all Imani heard as she realized her breath had stilled.

Sinking herself further into DeAndre's bed, Imani pulled his burgundy comforter further up her body, letting it warm her all over. It didn't take long for her to get comfortable now that her guard was down. Biting down on a corner of her bottom lip, her chest fell slowly.

"I get it."

She eased a hand under his shirt, placing it on her stomach before smoothing it down the length of her. She finally reached the middle of her folds, already drenched in anticipation.

"I want to hear you...I need to hear you."

Imani was hypnotized by his demands in no time, all logic and hesitance went out the door. Her breath came and went in shallow exhales, coaxing him to keep talking.

"Baby, you gotta let me know that you're wit' me since I can't see you. Unless you want me to?" I do have cameras in the bedrooms...wanted to give you privacy, but I could just turn 'em on—"

"No!" her eyes fluttered. "No. I want...want it like this."

"A'ight," he acquiesced.

She swallowed, her breathing seeping through the phone much heavier now with more intention.

"If I was there right now with you," he started, "you know what I'd do? I'd wrap your legs around my waist, right? Just so I could see all of you...a full view."

Imani felt like her soul was going to leave her body, grow legs and walk out of this house to head straight to him.

"I'd wanna see everything...how you touch yourself, the faces you make when you do it, the spots you like...'cause you know your body better than I do, right?"

Imani released all the air in her lungs, twirling and tugging her bud until she couldn't keep track of *what* she was doing.

"So, I'd learn all of that...all these quick tricks, right? Then, once I got a handle on 'em, you know...when I really feel like I know…"

He paused.

Imani was at the peak of a roller coaster on a lift hill, waiting for gravity to propel her forward. DeAndre sounded so sure, like he just knew the hold he had on her.

"I'd toss all that shit out and do whatever the hell I wanna do wit' you anyway."

All the energy Imani had, spilled out of her in a frantic wave of an orgasm.

Imani's eyes collapsed as her fingers nearly slipped out of her, a waterfall of moisture dripping down the sides of her hand.

"Damn," his tone was laced in mock disappointment. "You soaked all my sheets, didn't you, baby?"

Suddenly feeling her cheeks warm, Imani wasn't sure if she was embarrassed or reignited. She realized it was definitely a little bit of both.

## A Month of Sundays

She let out another breath, pulling her knees closer to her stomach.

"Yea...yeah."

"It's a'ight...I just know you look so beautiful right now. Damn...you don't even know what you do to me, do you?"

Suddenly, Imani heard the thread of control DeAndre just had, unfurling.

"Making me sit and wait? Like, you ain't already...mine?"

His own breath over the phone began sounding erratic, not out of pleasure, but out of distress. Imani's eyes shifted to the ceiling where the shadows of twigs from the tree outside his bedroom window danced above her, putting on a show for her eyes only. Everything in DeAndre's place tonight was for her to enjoy. She smiled to herself as she dragged her hand from her thigh up to her stomach and over her breast.

"I can be patient," he continued, "...at times, I can be...for you...I can be."

She let him speak, not saying a word herself, while he said everything she had only imagined in her wildest dreams. He sounded so beautiful and a little tortured. Imani knew she'd never bring this up again if he didn't. She could keep it between the two of them. Placing a finger in her mouth, Imani sucked on it slowly, her own sweet tang hitting her tongue. She would've never known how good she tasted if it wasn't for him.

"But baby, I can't do this forever...you know? I see you...I feel you everywhere on me. Shit...Imani."

Placing two fingers back into her this time, she pushed to her familiar spot and twirled her finger in semi-circles.

"...Baby...why do you do this to me?"

Imani was encased in her own pleasure, engulfed in the dips and valleys of it, while DeAndre was trying his hardest to break through her cage to no avail.

"...Especially because I'm already in you...right now...right now I'm in you and I haven't even touched you."

Suddenly, the floor was swept from under her, making Imani completely undone. She let out a cry that came from the depths of her - guttural and instinctual.

"With everything I got...I'm still a fool for you."

Imani felt her heart slow its pace as her cries petered out. She felt more satisfied and relaxed then she'd ever been. Like an internal light had been switched on. The peacefulness of his bedroom settled back into her consciousness as the two stayed on the phone in silence.

Should she say something, first? She should say something.

"DeAndre–"

Her phone rang in the background, forcing Imani to pull it away from her cheek. Michael's name flashed across her screen, causing heat to rise to her ears. Her phone was now taunting her, double daring her to pick up while she was like this.

"Imani–"

"I gotta go," she said, voice smothered in guilt. "Don't call me back. I'm sorry."

Before she could hear him say anything further, Imani clicked over to Michael's waiting call, leaping out of DeAndre's bed like she was escaping the flame of a furnace. She swallowed, her eyes darting everywhere in the room, breathing frantically.

*What am I doing? WHAT am I doing? What am I DOING?*

"Hey...hey baby," Imani folded her lips into a ball. All she had to do was get out of here and go back to the guest room she deemed as such when she first arrived. She could leave this all behind her, then.

"Hey, sweetheart," Michael said.

"How...how was your day?" she asked, feeling DeAndre's bedroom carpet meld between her toes as soon as they touched the ground.

"It was good, just a regular one. Are you...okay?"

Imani's heart leaped.

"Yeah, why?"

"Nothing really. Just sounds like you're running."

*I absolutely am*, she thought.

Imani hadn't conceptualized exactly how large DeAndre's room was until she forced herself to run out of it. It felt like she had miles to go to get to the other side of his custom doors.

Finally closing them behind her, Imani slowed her pace, smoothing her semi-damp hand on the sides of DeAndre's shirt.

"Just had to move something," she said with a chuckle. "What're you...up to now? How late is it again?"

## A Month of Sundays

Imani swallowed, reminding herself to shut up. She sounded guiltier the more she kept talking.

"I got a little after 9 on my clock," he said. "I know you're probably hammering away at another portrait and got a little caught up…"

Imani heard him smile, imagining her so fondly, doing exactly what he trusted she'd be doing. She ran a hand over the top of her coils, feeling the texture graze her fingertips. All her emotions of pleasure evaporated into thin air as the cloud of guilt grew larger.

"…anyway," he said. "I just wanted to hear your voice before you turned in for the night, since I hadn't heard it all day. Can't wait to see you at Kid's Day tomorrow."

Tears prickled Imani's eyes as she placed a hand to her mouth, her entire body shaking.

*How could I do this to you? I'm so sorry I betrayed you.*

Taking the quietest, heaviest inhale, Imani counted to five to calm herself down. Whatever she did, she couldn't allow him to hear her hesitation.

"Thank…you," she said, swallowing the emotion lodged in her throat. "You're too good to me…"

She loved Michael.

She cared for him so deeply and was taking the proper steps to marry him.

But did she truly deserve him after all?

# Chapter 20
# The Brightest Light From That Day

DeAndre wasn't sure what made him more upset - losing by the skin of his teeth to an opponent who was a tennis enthusiast at best or agreeing to not up and leave when said opponent gloated about his victory in front of him.

Michael - who he was playing against at an outdoor tennis court, approached the net, extending his arm for DeAndre to shake. Their tennis match was all a part of the United Way Church's Kid's Day - the event he told Kaylee he'd participate in months ago. Imani had ultimately put Kaylee in touch with Stephanie, who laid out the itinerary for the day to him beforehand. He was fine playing in the little tennis match planned at Rapid Springs Park, even though he had no clue who he'd be competing with and assumed they'd be an amateur. DeAndre kept his promise to show up, ultimately for Imani, but that was well before the evening they just had.

"Gotta admit it, DeAndre," Michael beamed, smiling with that wide grin of his, "We both played a fair game. Neither one of us is a winner or a loser. I'm just honored to have played with one of the greats."

This dude was acting like DeAndre was about to hang it up for good. He was still *the* greatest playing the game right now. He was just off kilter today.

"Right," he said, shaking Michael's hand more aggressively just to get the

# A Month of Sundays

gesture over with. This event was for kids of various ages at Imani's church and in Port Springs, and DeAndre was *really* trying to be on his best behavior, displaying corny-ass sportsmanship and whatnot.

The teens watched in amazement as the two of played, which sparked a bit of joy on DeAndre's part. All that came tumbling down, once he saw how puffed up Michael got from scoring repeatedly in front of Imani. DeAndre thought he had shown the epitome of strong will for not punching Michael in the jaw, when he said all that nonsense in his crib, while picking Imani up weeks ago. But, seeing him now with all his people, comfortable in his element, Michael truly had the upper hand. He had his crew and his woman.

DeAndre was in Miami just before making it back to Port Springs in time for this event. He was both anxious and excited about being here today as he'd finally be able to see Imani's face, especially after her surprising him with that phone call last night. DeAndre could tell she felt a way about it after it was all said and done. She was probably drowning in guilt or embarrassment, but it changed none of what he felt or how he thought of her.

If anything, it made him realize how much he loved her.

The love that now beat nonstop for her hit him like lightning, when he least expected it, while they were on the phone. Her call last night was unhinged from the start and DeAndre could tell it wasn't premeditated on her part - the sheer spontaneity of the moment made it even more real. Imani was pure in every sense of the word. She couldn't even take the one or two things he managed to say to her without succumbing to the quickest release DeAndre probably ever heard yet, he didn't hold it against her one bit. He hadn't even recognized some of his own sentiments, feeling like he cut his chest open to lay his heart on a table. She had been so quiet through his confessions which only turned him on more and made his feelings even more raw. Last night had nothing to do with him and all to do with her pleasure and he'd do it all over multiple times in a heartbeat. DeAndre just wanted to see her face to face, all for the excitement of knowing the secret they now shared.

When he arrived at Rapid Springs Park this morning, he approached the group of children sitting on the park's court whose faces lit up after he was introduced as the surprise guest. The genuine love from them gave him the extra boost of energy he needed. DeAndre thoroughly enjoyed giving back with his time moreso than with his money and wanted to make an effort to seek out opportunities like this regularly. When his eyes fell on Imani, who was behind the group arranging cups and plates on the picnic tables, he felt like he was on cloud 9. She gave him a faint smile before dropping her gaze first.

He wanted to see her face-to-face just because, but he also wanted to tell her to make a choice. Why was she always going back to this dude? She clearly didn't want to be with Michael and he needed her to tell him why she couldn't just be with him.

He had been thinking about it for a while - how this flirty dance, the two of them were in these past few months, was getting harder to maintain. DeAndre knew exactly what he wanted, but Imani kept claiming her loyalty was elsewhere while flirting with him the next moment. He was getting tired of this back-and-forth. She had to admit the feelings he knew she had for him.

There was no way this was one-sided.

Although it was only the middle of the year, DeAndre's schedule was already on the upswing, especially now that he was resuming his tennis regimen, before it really mattered, for next year's SW Tournament. The point was that soon he wasn't going to physically be in Rapid Springs or home for as long as he was now. His routine was reverting back to what it had always been, but he wanted Imani to be a part of all of it.

He just wasn't entirely sure how.

The group of kids in attendance for DeAndre and Michael's faux trophy presentation were now squealing and beside themselves with laughter. When DeAndre looked up again, he found Michael and Imani kissing, lips locked and eyes closed with Imani's frame dipped near his side, garnering even more claps and chuckles.

His blood boiled, watching them all loved up on one another. DeAndre turned to head back to the park's building facility. He needed to change and get the hell outta there. He would head back home with Trey and Clive who were waiting for him.

There was no way in hell he wanted to wait to talk to Imani after seeing that bullshit.

## A Month of Sundays

~

From her peripheral, with Michael's arms still around her waist, Imani saw DeAndre push open the park's office doors before they slammed behind him. She should've let him be and left him alone, especially since she could barely manage to say a word to him once he arrived today. After a quick wave from across the park, Imani left Michael and DeAndre to the competition that they agreed to, which the kids had been more than excited to witness on Kid's Day. Michael was already popular enough in the church, but to see him compete against a legend? It was a no-brainer for everyone, including the adult volunteers.

The match was fine for the first few minutes, with both DeAndre and Michael scoring, up until the two were in a tie. Imani could tell that DeAndre wasn't expecting Michael to play as well as he did, which prolonged the game. DeAndre was decent, but Michael ended up breaking the tie first, winning the game and securing his bragging rights for the day. After the score was called, Imani had never seen Michael so elated - pumping his fists and doing a little dance up and down the court. Feeling a scowl crawl up her face, she was suddenly turned off by the whole thing because it was so outside of Michael's character. He had beginner's luck on his side, but it wasn't like he just beat DeAndre in a tournament.

And, when he pulled her into his chest, giving her a dip for the audience to see, Imani couldn't get away fast enough.

"Hey, sweetie," she said to Michael, the hottest commodity in the church group right now. "Michael, I have to check something in the locker rooms. I'll be back."

Imani thought she'd caught up to DeAndre once she was in the long hallway but out of the corner of her eye she noticed another door closed on her left hand side. She ran over and opened it to find him with his back facing her, pulling his shirt over his head. The muscular cuts and curvature of his back were beyond sculpted and, once he turned around, his long, toned torso was on full display. His form was deepened to perfection to the point where Imani wasn't sure he was real. She knew he worked out, but she didn't realize his results yielded Greek-like proportions.

## Jade Olivia

Once her eyes shot up to his face, she was smacked right back into reality by the harsh scowl etched on his face.

"D, why'd you walk out like that? A kid's game shouldn't be this deep."

He laughed, sarcasm laced throughout his tone. "You know it's not about a game."

"I thought you wanted to be a part of this."

"You know this is the third time that Steph Curry lookin-ass is messin' wit' me and now I gotta see him do it in front of his little church posse?"

Imani's jaw dropped. "Excuse me?"

DeAndre pulled another shirt over his head, finally covering Imani's weakness. She was happy to get her focus back as he went to throw the contents in his gym bag.

"It's enough that nigga already has you then he has to...show off..."

"Showing off?!" Imani scoffed. "D, we're in a relationship!"

"Oh right...until you need to get yourself off then you think about me?"

Imani's heart plummeted to her feet.

"What?"

"It's amazing how you play so innocent," he said, eyes narrowing and focused on her, "when it's not just me. I wasn't the one who called last night. YOU did."

Imani's eyes shifted around the room, sweat sliding down her back. She knew that seeing him today would come down to this. There was no way to avoid it.

"I...didn't mean to...I'm sorry," she said, barely above a whisper.

"Sorry about what you did or about not doing it again?"

DeAndre approached Imani, then, not letting her escape that easily. He continued walking, backing her against the wall next to the lockers.

"'Cause the next time I'd do it," he said, "I'd be a full-on participant, in-person."

With the chill of the wall against her back, Imani felt shallow breaths escape her as DeAndre draped his arms above her head encaging her so she couldn't move. She felt herself yielding to him in no time, her nipples hardening and stomach tightening. His scent invaded her, tickling every cell and fiber of her being. Her body shook like a volcano about to erupt while

## A Month of Sundays

DeAndre looked so calm, dominating their entire exchange without even touching her.

"Why you keep insisting on not being where you wanna be?" he asked.

Imani took another shaky breath, which surprisingly helped her to build up some resolve.

"DeAndre...I'm where...I need to be."

His eyes slid slowly from her face over her frame, down to her exposed legs. With the lightest stroke of his fingertips, he grazed her inner thighs, lighting up the quickest fire between her legs. Imani forced herself *not* to watch him, but her body had a mind of its own, as her leg pushed even further into his hand. DeAndre's gaze shot back up to hers, a silent confirmation in his eyes.

"That's straight bullshit, baby."

Imani pulled herself away from the wall, finding an opening through his arms.

"Why do you care so much about where I wanna be?"

"...because I want you," he said, pushing his arms away from the wall now, turning around to fully face her again.

"...I fuckin' love you."

Imani blinked, her eyes watering and her mouth going dry as she swallowed hard. It felt so *good* to hear those words from him, but there was no way she could take them to heart... she couldn't.

"You...do not...love me."

"You refuse to see this shit," he said, his eyes darting up to the ceiling in frustration.

Imani took a shaky breath.

"You...DeAndre, you - have a harem of women following you everywhere - at your games, going with you to parties, all over social media..."

He balled his hand into a fist.

"Shit...Okay, Imani but if I'm single, I'm gonna be single!"

"As it should be," she said. "You are single! I'm not! And a gaggle of women is something I'd never have to worry about with Michael! Something I DON'T worry about, actually."

Imani's temples pulsed.

"That wouldn't even be a factor if you were wit' me," DeAndre insisted, "all of that would be deaded and what drives me so...fuckin'...crazy is the fact that I'm always trying to screw you out of my system and no matter what, I can't! No matter who I'm wit'...I'm not even giving them...a fraction...of what I'd give to you!"

His voice continued to echo like they were in a chamber, his stare piercing into her core. The two were literally raging with their eyes glued on each other, chests rising and falling in sync as if they had just worked out together...the air was thick with tension.

"I'm not doing this," Imani said, peeling her gaze away from him as she willed herself to walk away.

She had to get out of here she was falling apart - the more she let herself stay...the more she fell apart. It was ridiculous to have an argument with a guy who wasn't even hers. Imani couldn't even recall having a passionate argument like this with Michael.

"Right," he said. "Just like you hung up, you can walk out."

DeAndre's voice followed her down the hallway as Imani charged closer to the entrance. The park was visible outside through the slim cut out window on the door. She just had to reach it before he said another word.

"Do you remember that night?"

The question stopped her dead in her tracks like a boulder. Her heart raced as her mind was transported back all those years ago to that night. Of course, she remembered every detail of that night...how his breath kissed her neck before they walked down the aisle...how his touch felt on her waist when they danced...how they almost had a real kiss. Her lips parted with a tremble as memories flooded her mind.

"It plays in my head so much," DeAndre said, "so much that I keep asking myself if it was real."

Imani turned around, watching him through blurred vision now, her heart doing somersaults.

"It was real," she said, not even recognizing her own voice. She knew she shouldn't get caught up in the past, but this was the first time they'd mentioned that night to each other.

DeAndre used Imani's hesitation to shorten the distance between them again.

## A Month of Sundays

"Then be with me."

His stare was unwavering, shooting straight through her. She was on the edge of a cliff that she knew she had to escape. Imani shook her head just as he went to cup her chin in his hand.

"No, no, no, no...God," she said, "That night...DeAndre, that moment we met I was in the midst of so many dark days."

She hated revisiting the past, never envisioned really going back there... because meeting him was her brightest point, the brightest light from that day. It was such a messed-up time in her life.

She stepped around him again, facing the front door once more, and took a breath.

"I had just come back to Port Springs with my tail between my legs a year before since my art career hadn't worked out in New York. I fell for this guy, who felt just like you...oh God..."

Imani shook her head, still seeing a millisecond of his face flash across her mind.

"I felt like he had such a pulse on living – ya' know? He convinced me of so many things, even convinced me that I could live with him since he was helping me with my career. And, then...he just..."

Imani looked at DeAndre before casting her eyes to the floor again. There was no need to get caught up telling him anything that had nothing to do with him or with her life now.

She swallowed.

"I just had to leave New York...once I got back to Port Springs, I begged my aunt to take me in for a little while, just so I could figure things out. She was cool with it, but I had to follow her rules. Everything was safe when I followed her rules. She hired me to help her part-time and I got really involved in her church. Not too long after, I met Michael."

Imani noticed that the fire in DeAndre's eyes dimmed.

"He wasn't just a nice guy, but he showed me what happens when you live a life of temperance, patience, thinking about what you should do before you just step out and do it. He's so kind to me and helped me to follow a path that's more stable. He made me feel safe."

Gathering her strength, she let her shoulders relax.

## Jade Olivia

"DeAndre, he eventually wants a future with me," she said. "I can't be with someone who won't see me in their future."

He looked at her with his forehead creased, visibly assessing her words as Imani stole a glance outside. One of the volunteers was walking towards the door they were behind as Imani's heart pounded. She had to think quickly. There was no way she wanted anyone to see her alone with him because if Michael found out...

"DeAndre, I'm so sorry I was selfish with you. In so many ways, I'm so sorry."

She shook her head, words falling out of her mouth like a stream. DeAndre's eyes went wild, like he was watching sand spill from his fingers.

"Imani."

For the first time ever, she witnessed him looking defeated. If she didn't leave now, she'd be a puddle of tears herself.

"You don't have to forgive me," she said, "but you gotta...just let it go. Okay?"

She pushed a hand to his chest once more before rushing past him, leaving all of her feelings behind.

Imani felt her heart pounding with each step she took toward the outdoor table where Michael was sitting. He was talking to a few of the young church ministers when he looked up, meeting Imani's eyes.

"Hey, sweetheart," he said, once he got close enough to her. He smiled at her with so much admiration but unfortunately it couldn't extinguish any of her guilt.

"Yeah, I...uh...had to make sure we had enough garbage bags inside to clean everything up."

"Babe, you're not lifting a finger. You don't have to worry about that." He regarded her with pure pride.

"You're always so considerate," he continued. "It's wild that you're even mine sometimes."

Imani locked eyes with him, on the verge of crying.

"You know that trip you have out of town, I wouldn't mind going."

He pulled his head back in surprise. "Really? You're gonna be cooped up in the hotel all day, though."

## A Month of Sundays

She smiled. "Yeah, but Cincinnati is somewhere I've never been, so I wouldn't mind exploring. I can always request a few remote days now," she chuckled.

He pulled her into a hug. "My girl is gonna be with me this time. I'm sure I can sneak out of one of my meetings for us to grab a bite."

Imani fell into his hug. She had a man standing in front of her who's been about her, from the beginning. Why would she mess this up?

# Chapter 21
# Break Up

"This is all they had?"

"They didn't have what you wanted, so I wanted to at least give you an alternative."

"But, I never paint with that brand, you know that..."

"Actually, Imani, I don't...I barely know anything you do really at all."

"What do you mean by that?"

Imani looked at Michael, sitting in front of her at Willow's, a soul food restaurant that took Michael months to grab reservations for. This spot was on Imani's list as one of the restaurants she had to try before the year was out and Michael willingly made that happen. The only problem was, neither one of them could even get through their highly anticipated southern cuisine. She and Michael were arguing again. It was becoming a more common occurrence, especially now they were back home from Michael's work conference.

Michael shook his head before looking up at Imani again, exasperated.

"I don't want to argue with you, sweetie," he said, his eyes pleading. "Especially over something that's not even that serious. Are we really about to fight over a pack of paintbrushes?"

He looked down at his plate, gathering his suit jacket before picking up his fork.

"Why don't we just enjoy this...crazy expensive meal you wanted."

## A Month of Sundays

"Now it's a meal that only *I* wanted," she said, narrowing her eyes at him.

Imani folded her arms, feeling the same prickle of annoyance she felt all last week. At this point, they really were about to fight over paint brushes, especially because of how dismissive Michael was about picking them up today. Imani had to get last minute supplies for another client project this week and asked Michael to pick up a specific brand of brushes she relied on to do some of her best work. She went through brushes in a similar way that small children went through box crayons - there were never enough in her disposal. And, Imani, knowing that Michael had purchased items on her behalf before, assumed he knew the brand to buy. He didn't, though, and ended up purchasing a cheaper store brand that was too stiff for Imani's liking. If Michael had owned up to the mistake, she wouldn't have thought his error was too much of a big deal. Yet, Michael barely apologized for it at all and didn't even offer to correct it when she first brought it up.

Ever since the two of them had gotten back from his work trip in Cincinnati, little incidences like this were piling on top of each other. On the surface, they were tiny inconveniences that weren't earth shattering, but the bickering that resulted was starting to get on Imani's nerves.

This argument alone felt like the culmination of all the words they exchanged in Cincinnati.

It turns out that Michael hadn't been exaggerating when he said the work conference would mostly have her stuck in a hotel room. And, the first two days, Imani didn't mind it. She had more than enough work to do for Artgo - holding virtual meetings with artists, checking in on the status of deliveries at the museum and following up with vendors about the banquet - that zapped all of her energy by the time Michael was even finished with his day. But, by the third day, she had a feeling that he hadn't even carved out a half hour for them to explore the area. Unlike many work conferences that were sometimes located in the middle of nowhere, the hotel in Cincinnati where they were staying was in a city with small shops, restaurants, bistros and even a movie theater - all walking distance from the hotel. So, instead of waiting for him, Imani went out to explore by herself. But, when she returned, Michael gave her a stoic greeting and barely looked her in the eye.

"Rough workday?" she asked, placing her small bag of incense and essential oils on the table next to the single bed she was sleeping on.

"I didn't realize you were gonna take so long," he said, letting out an annoyed breath. "I would've ordered food for myself a lot earlier."

"I texted you that I'd be back in less than a half hour."

"It was more like 45 minutes, but...who's counting?"

Imani gave him a cautionary glance before ultimately letting the entire conversation go. Even with the weird tone Michael had with her in that moment, they managed to get past it once they both ate and settled in for the evening. And, Imani thought they'd continue with the week, smooth sailing. But, then Michael started making little comments that had Imani feeling... funny.

Whenever conversation about Imani's job was brought up, Michael would always offer himself as a listening ear even though he truly had no idea of the intricacies of the art industry. But, he'd actively engage with Imani, asking her questions on acquisitions, cataloging and any of her other tasks that she may have wanted to vent about. Imani wouldn't bring up her job to him to get any specific answers, but she always appreciated that he was willing to listen and encourage her. But, during this trip, when Imani made a point to discuss her other job - her true vocation - as a freelancer, Michael all but dismissed it and tried to redirect the conversation back to Artgo.

"But, I'm not talking about what I'm doing for Lauri right now," she said, slightly annoyed. "I want to take on this client in the next few weeks, but I'm wondering if I could dip out of town. This season is so nuts for us at Artgo."

Michael shrugged.

"I'm sure you'll make a decision that works for your clients," he said with an edge in his tone.

Imani placed a hand on his arm.

"Hey, do you have an issue you want to discuss that I don't know about?"

"You're spending a lot more time on a side hustle than the job that's going to help set you up for true success."

Imani had been sitting on the couch with her legs crossed but stood up just then.

## A Month of Sundays

"Didn't think you'd ever say that my art business is just a side hustle," she said. "It isn't, by the way."

As if realizing what he just said, Michael took a breath and sat down on the couch himself. Rubbing his hand over his eyes, he rested his forearms on his knees and looked up at Imani again.

"I'm...I didn't mean to even...honey, I'm sorry. I don't want to start nitpicking with you."

Imani chose to let it go after his half-hearted apology and didn't bring it up again, even when they returned home. But, now being here at Willow's with Michael and thinking of what he said about her "side hustle," Imani couldn't just let it go anymore.

"Michael, do you support me?" Imani asked, balancing her fork between the tip of her index finger and her thumb.

"I do. You can't be doubting that because of some stuff that can be returned, are you?"

Imani shook her head, still annoyed.

"I'm not even talking about the brushes anymore. It just feels like ever since these last few commissions, you've been throwing these shots at me...calling my work a side hustle and cutting me off when I try to talk about clients - "

"You're still not over Cincinnati?"

Imani pulled at her silver hoop earring. "I'm not, if I'm being honest."

Michael took an exaggerated breath.

"We're not even married yet and you're already deeming my life's work as a side hustle, like you don't take it seriously or you don't want me to do this or - "

"No, Imani," he said with finality in his tone. "I'm neither of those things. I want you to make sure you keep your main goal in mind. You have such a great opportunity with Artgo that you don't know...what other opportunities could come...when we're in Massachusetts."

She looked up at him from her plate, staring at him in shock. All the pieces in Imani's mind that were once scattered everywhere were now coming together in spades.

"So, you want me to stay at Artgo because you think I'll be primed to just... what...get ready to move away from home," Imani said, placing her hands down on both sides of the plate. "And, move from one corporate job to the next to... meet your expectations, is that it? Will that make you happy?"

"We have to be realistic, honey," he said. "Neither one of us can just be out here, living only off of dreams we had at 9."

"But, you're living yours. Going into ministry, climbing this corporate ladder. You're already living your dream."

"I'm not saying you can't have them, but life is a constant push and pull."

"So, you push me...away from my family and...I pull away from the plans I have for myself?"

"What plans do you even have for yourself, Imani?"

She looked him over, suddenly feeling her heart race. Up until this point, Imani was willing to work with Michael's vision, especially because she didn't feel she had one that was too rigid or required too much compromise. But, what Imani wasn't going to do was bend into another version of herself that didn't speak to her. She didn't want to be a First Lady or the corporate wunderkind that Michael thinks would take her corporate job seriously. Imani wanted to wake up every morning, feeling a zeal to live, and she most definitely wanted to feel that way with her partner. There was a time in her life when she didn't think she'd ever have a mutually beneficial relationship that *didn't* terrify her every second of the day. Imani refused to return to that.

"You gotta get serious, Imani," Michael said, pulling her out of her trance.

Imani chuckled, scathingly.

"I can't even believe you're talking to me like this right now...like I'm a kid."

"Well..." Michael raised his brows, placing his napkin next to his plate.

Imani stared at him, shell-shocked.

"Wow. I can't believe how easy it is for me to walk out on you right now."

As if a light switched on, Michael froze.

"What're you saying right now?" he asked, as if she was speaking of something outrageous.

But, Imani wasn't being funny or ridiculous. She needed him to hear her clearly.

"I don't...want to marry you, Michael."

Instead of hearing her words and pleading for understanding, Michael started laughing.

## A Month of Sundays

"C'mon, Imani," he said. "We'll get out of here soon and enjoy the rest of our night. I think we're both going down a road neither of us mean to."

"I know exactly what I'm saying right now," Imani said, void of emotion.

Imani and Michael started their evening as a couple on a typical date night with neither one of them knowing it would be their last.

∼

DeAndre walked into the brightly lit room that was in complete contrast to the dimmed lights of the stadium, without saying a word. Nine times out of ten, he hated post-game interviews, especially after games he lost. They were such great experiences for him when he was first starting out, moving up in rankings and building a rapport with reporters across the country, but between rude questions he'd been asked over the years about sportsmanship and behavior on the court, both he and the reporters handled the whole thing as one of contractual obligation.

Taking a seat at the chair positioned in the middle of the long rectangular table, DeAndre pulled himself closer to the mic, resting forward on both elbows, his head sagged slightly between his shoulders and his eyes cast down – he focused on a large, colossal camera lens in front of him, belonging to a photographer kneeling down near the first row of reporters. Their gazes met and DeAndre could see the unyielded anticipation on his face, waiting for any sudden outburst. It's happened more times than DeAndre could count and, honestly, he was a stone's throw away from one today.

He rubbed the back of his neck with his hand before placing it back on the table. Looking up and ahead of him, he nodded to the sea of barracudas.

"DeAndre. Hi, Robert Kins, from AP Sports...That was a tough match out there for you today. I don't think we've seen you perform like that in a long time. How're you feeling right now?"

"Not good," he said, flatly with a shrug. "One person gotta lose and I guess that was me, so...no excuse for it, but it happened."

He scratched behind his ear, already counting the minutes in his head of how soon he could get out and move on with the rest of his day.

"James Townson. ESPN," another reporter started. "Was there anything about Phillip's game that surprised you or threw you off? What made you check out?"

DeAndre paused and stared at James, taking in his horrible tweed suit that was about four sizes too big for him in the shoulders. Resting his chin on his hands, he stared at the clock in the back of the room - a stark black and white circle against a cream wall. DeAndre was checked out long before he even stepped foot on the court today and only one person was on his mind.

*"You don't have to forgive me. But, you gotta...just let it go. Okay?"*

What Imani said to him reverberated in his ear so loud during the match, just when he went to return a serve that he thought she was right next to him saying it to him all over again. It was like the ball had a mind of its own when it moved further to the left, making DeAndre miss it by only a few feet at the baseline.

Why was he so screwed up over this girl?

He couldn't believe she was able to run away from him so quickly that day. DeAndre was surprised when she came to the locker room and was instantly heated when she acted as if his frustration was over losing some silly park game. All she was doing at first was denying her feelings, trying to make him seem like the stupid lovestruck one.

But, once DeAndre brought up the night they met, the night where the stars aligned, it was like they were both transported back there. She couldn't shake their connection, either, which meant he wasn't losing his mind. Her feelings were there all along. He had her right at the tip of the mountain with him until he didn't.

*"I can't be with someone who won't secure me in their future."*

DeAndre was acutely aware of the decisions he made - some good, some bad and some downright reckless. When he felt good about something, he'd hold on to it for dear life, taking it by any means necessary. But, DeAndre didn't see Imani as this conquest for him to take for the sake of having it. The love he had for her was real and very much secure. He didn't want her only in his future. He wanted her in the present.

But, none of that shit mattered now.

A ripple of camera flashes shook DeAndre out of his thoughts, making him pinch the corners of his eyes. "What was the question again?"

## A Month of Sundays

Stephanie had been asking him for the past month to work on his patience with the press and keep himself quiet in general, if only for her sake. But, with Imani now removing herself from his life, DeAndre spent the past few weeks without a care in the world for what anyone else wanted. He'd been in LA for the past few weeks after their emotional exchange, without her and without Rand, acting like the badass kid whose parents weren't home. He hung out with a few friends of his who he hadn't really messed with in a while, hitting up multiple clubs, lounges and random homes just to do something.

LA was the kind of city where he could always get into something...or someone - which he did...multiple times throughout the week. There was the makeup artist from the Men's Health Magazine shoot, an Instagram model in VIP at one of the nameless clubs he stumbled into the night after and, of course, Jazmine.

She was always good at giving him a soft place to land. They had been hanging out a lot more than normal, to the point that even she noticed.

"Trying to move in with me or something?" she joked one night, laying with the hotel bed covers twisted around her chest. He chuckled but didn't say anything after that, something he was doing a lot lately. DeAndre would just let people say whatever they wanted around him, letting it go in one ear and right out of the other.

He just couldn't shake the unease he felt of Imani's instruction. But, if she could give up their connection so easily, he definitely would have to... eventually.

# Chapter 22
# Departure

Standing up from the bronze metal stools, Imani and Lauri followed Xena to the front door of her loft where she pulled it open, extending a hand for each of them to shake.

"I'm so happy you've seen a few things you liked," she said, beaming from ear to ear. The loose yellow sleeves of her top moved as she gestured to Imani who met her hand first.

"We're happy this could work out as well," Imani said. "I knew when I saw those pieces at the crawl, I had to let Lauri know. I've seen some of your work floating around online for a while...but, you have so much you haven't shown."

Xena smiled, her signature look – an artistic black line tattoo down the middle of her face slightly stretched. "Well, it's all about timing, you know?"

She then rolled her eyes in mock exasperation, "Guess I don't have to dance on TikTok to get my work seen, right?"

The three laughed as Lauri and Imani gave Xena a few instructions on getting her small sculptures transported to Artgo for an exhibit showcasing her work. Artgo would sometimes host joint exhibits for contemporary artists on the rise who may not have had enough work to have an entire exhibit to themselves, so they could still have their pieces showcased. Xena would be one of three artists featured for three months in a group exhibit featuring her abstract

## A Month of Sundays

kitchen and housewares tying in both her African American and Mexican heritage.

After Imani texted pictures of Xena's work from the gallery crawl to Lauri, her boss merely signed off on them with a thumbs-up emoji. But, during a quick meeting with Lauri in which she was halfway listening to Imani, Lauri brought Xena up again, requesting that they visit her studio to view her work in person.

"Imani will make sure the deliveries are coordinated and that your pieces will be well taken care of," Lauri said. "We'll be in touch, Xena."

In an Uber heading back to the office, Imani suddenly felt a small wave of restlessness and turned to Lauri, finally ready to talk about her art. Something about seeing Xena in her element and space reignited Imani's desire to share her own work. But, as she turned to her, Lauri was in the midst of a phone conversation and Imani could tell it wasn't going to be quick.

"Yes, Sam...the proofs look phenomenal. Let's go over some of the specifics," she said, settling into her seat for the already short ride.

Although Imani couldn't find the right time to tell Lauri about her own work, she knew that managing to tell her about Xena was ironic. That night of her last date with Michael already felt like five dog years, had passed - it was so long ago. But, Imani was keeping herself busy, trying not to harp on the gloom she felt being on her own for the first time in a long time.

She had anticipated seeing Michael at church, but hadn't since their breakup, which she assumed was on purpose. He had probably convinced his father to keep him busy with matters either before or after service that kept him from being physically present. A few church members who Imani only knew loosely had gone out of their way to ask her about Michael, eying her suspiciously.

"He's been so busy with work, but he'll be back soon," is all she'd say to keep them from asking any more questions.

Meanwhile, Imani was also keeping herself busy, too. Kaylee started dragging her to several Pilates classes during the week after work or on weekends when she wasn't meeting with clients. Imani actually felt the difference after only a matter of weeks. She just so happened to pass her standing mirror in her room getting ready today and almost didn't recognize herself - the prominent curve in her waist and the cut in her arms from several weeks of workout sessions were apparent. She might be crying herself to sleep at night, but she was in great shape. Even though the pace of work was picking up again, Imani kept herself booked with art clients and occasional styling gigs from Melody who promised not to eat up too much of her already limited time.

After Lauri and Imani got back to Artgo and settled back at their respective workspaces, Imani wrapped up a few emails and attended a quick meeting with coworkers before climbing into an Uber to Melody's house. She had asked Imani to style her for The Webbies, a livestream award show, where Melody was walking the red carpet and presenting an award. Several pieces from various designers were arranged on a rolling rack by Melody's assistant in her living room. Though, Melody was no stranger to the bevy of gifts she'd often receive from designers, waiting for her to make a public appearance in one of them, Imani always found it amusing how overwhelmed she was with it all.

"I need you," Melody said over the phone a week ago. *"I've been looking at this shit for so long, everything's starting to look exactly the same."*

Once at the house, Imani took inventory of everything on the rack, from long avant-garde gowns to couture boots attached to pants and she spent a few hours arranging the pieces into several outfits that Melody tried on. The two managed to put aside three options by the evening, which soothed Melody's superfluous anxiety.

Imani was in the living room, gathering her bag and seamstress kit, preparing to head out when Melody called out to her from the kitchen.

"I'm bored and hungry as a horse," she sighed, patting her still taut stomach. "I'm gonna whip something up. Wanna stay for a little bit?"

In addition to being dramatic, Melody was also an exceptional cook who tended to go over-the-top by cooking too much food. She now had her husband and three mouths to feed, but the amount of food she made yielded a feast with leftovers that Hosea often ended up donating to soup kitchens. He wasn't home yet, which meant it was just Imani and the little ones home with Melody.

"You convinced me with the grub," Imani joked, watching Melody clap her hands.

"Caleb has toys we could get into, right?"

Within the next hour, Caleb and Imani were playing with blocks and Legos he had dragged from his room to the living room with a bright green wagon.

## A Month of Sundays

The smell of hamburgers along with sweet potato fries sizzling on the kitchen stove enveloped the air as Imani helped Caleb stack his Lego pieces by color to complete his small Lego Island.

"...We need one more red piece to finish the roof of the house. Can you find one?"

Before he could pick another piece from the pile, a sudden shatter of dishes, followed by a piercing scream, startled the two of them.

"Caleb, stay here, sweetie..."

Imani shot up and power walked into the kitchen, finding Melody on her knees, bent over leaning against the kitchen island.

"Oh my God, Melody!"

Imani ran to her, her heart racing as she pulled her up from the floor. Gripping her phone against her cheek, Melody was frozen in a puddle of tears, not saying a word with her mouth agape.

"What is it?" Imani asked, before placing a hand at Melody's waist below her stomach. "Is it the baby? Melody?"

The question seemed to jolt her consciousness as Melody shook her head vigorously, sobbing.

"No...no. We have to get to the hospital. Let's get the kids ready. We gotta go."

As Melody snapped out of it and called her driver. Imani got the children together and they all rushed outside to the awaiting vehicle. About fifteen minutes later, Melody, Imani and the kids arrived at Frontway Memorial Hospital, Hosea rushed over as they entered the first set of doors just before they made it into the lobby, a gust of air-conditioned wind hitting their faces. Melody barreled into him, breaking down in another round of tears as Imani stood in shock, rocking a sleeping Judea against her shoulder and holding Caleb's hand.

"Mel...," Hosea said, pulling away from her but holding on to her arms. His eyes were bloodshot. "I'm gonna need you to pull yourself together before you walk in there, okay?"

Hearing the crack in Hosea's voice, Imani dropped Caleb's hand and covered her mouth, tears pooling over her fingers.

"Why're we crying, Daddy?"

## Jade Olivia

Hosea nodded at Imani and knelt to speak to his son, who was rubbing his eyes amidst the late hour.

The five of them were just before the clear automatic doors of the hospital, clear of the sensors that would open to the lobby. This all happened so quickly but Hosea was right, they had to hold it together.

Beyond the doors, Imani saw Eve sitting down, staring off in a catatonic daze.

"Where're the boys?"

Imani heard Melody ask in between her sobs.

"They were all over at her mom's house, so they're good," Hosea responded.

Imani couldn't take her eyes off of Eve. She'd never seen her so drained of energy or without a smile on her face.

"Who called her?" Imani asked.

"He wasn't by himself," Hosea said, taking a breath. "One of the guys he hangs out with from time to time was with him when it all went down and hit her up after the cops were called...but, I'm lookin' at all those jokers crazy right now...their asses all need to be questioned."

Imani thought back to the group of men who were with Rand at the tennis match all those months ago. Had he been with one of them?

"She didn't even know he was back in town. He's been dipping in and out of the Springs for weeks now."

"What was he even doing over in that area?" Melody asked.

Hosea shook his head, rubbing a hand across his forehead.

"I couldn't stomach even asking her that question right now," he said, his eyes pained.

"This is so crazy," Melody said, sounding as drained as Imani felt. "Why... what the hell?"

"Yeah. We're waiting for the doctor's update now. Let's get in there."

As soon as they all piled into the lobby, Eve turned to them and jumped out of her seat to hug Melody.

"I'm so sorry, Mel," she pleaded, her eyes wide in shock. "I didn't even know who to call. I tried getting in touch with DeAndre, but he didn't pick up and I just kept scrolling through my contacts then I saw Hosea's name. I didn't know who to call—"

## A Month of Sundays

Melody shook her head, wrapping her arm around Eve's neck, pulling her close.

"Stop apologizing right now," she said, sternly with her voice shaking. "Okay? Stop apologizing. Do you hear me?"

Releasing herself from Melody's embrace, Eve turned to grip Imani's hand. "You're here?"

Eve didn't have one tear in her eye, she was so shell shocked. Imani could see she was on the cusp of breaking, depending on the news to come.

Nodding her head, Imani willed herself to stand in place, despite her heart galloping in her chest. The familiar hollowness in her stomach she hadn't felt in years, decades even, came back to her. She was only thirteen years old the last time she had this feeling, this numbness, but Imani had to shake it off. This entire situation had absolutely nothing to do with her.

When Melody pulled Judea from Imani's arms, Imani enveloped Eve in a deep embrace.

"Yeah, I'm here."

Another hour passed as they waited in the lobby when Imani looked up, seeing two doctors approaching the front desk. Eve was leaning against Imani's shoulder, semi-awake, when Imani tapped her on the arm with a shaky hand before turning behind her to grab Hosea and Melody's attention. Hosea then stood up, pulling his phone out of his back pocket. Looking at his screen, he blew a harsh breath puffing out his cheeks before looking back at Melody.

"Lemme take this outside, it's DeAndre."

As Hosea left the lobby, one of the doctors, taking off his glasses, walked to Eve who stood up from her seat slowly.

"Mrs. Thomas," he paused, looking away from her for a moment to glance at Imani, Melody and Hosea.

"I'm so sorry."

Melody gasped, bursting into more sobs immediately. As Imani's eyes collapsed – she gripped Eve's hand.

"We really did all that we could do," the doctor continued. "And…we were so shocked by, well, everything."

Imani opened her eyes and blinked, looking up at the physician who had his own face dipped in consternation. As if knowing how confused he sounded, he took a breath.

"See, where the bullet hit Randall...it wasn't fatal," he said. "But, your husband had a lot of underlying issues...breathing issues and heart blockages that were preventable for someone his age. The impact of the bullet just exacerbated what was already there."

Pulling Eve closer, Imani held onto her as she felt Eve fall further into her embrace.

"Dammit, Rand," she said, before finally breaking down into her own set of tears, screaming against the hospital walls.

## Chapter 23
# Mind Numbing

If circumstances were different, Imani would've most definitely complimented Eve for the patience, grace and poise she was displaying today. But, if today was different, it wouldn't be her husband's funeral.

Imani sat in the den of Eve and Randall's single-family home, positioned next to the backyard. Relatives and friends of the couple milled about, transporting closed aluminum pans of food from the kitchen to parked cars and carrying opulent displays of floral bouquets and greenery from said cars to the house. Imani sat on the couch with Eve and Randall's twin boys, suited in black and white tuxes, and helped them color in the lines of their respective coloring books. They weren't much older than Caleb, which meant they could only sense commotion around them instead of senseless tragedy.

She looked up and found Eve in the living room, frozen in place on a chair as everyone's activity buzzed around her. With her hands in her lap, she was a carbon copy from last week at the hospital, with the same distant look on her face. Imani tucked her crayon pencil in the spine of the childrens' coloring book before standing up to walk over to her. Eve had called Imani a few days after the hospital emergency, asking her to come over the morning of the funeral. She and Imani weren't close at all, but Imani figured that was the point - sometimes, being intimate with the nearest stranger was all someone needed to feel a semblance of normalcy.

She placed a hand on Eve's shoulder once she was at her side, pulling Eve out of her trance.

"Need a minute?"

Eve blinked at Imani with a forlorn smile. "Yeah."

Imani looked around, prepared to sit in her seat to allow Eve to gather herself privately but, Eve turned to her, taking shallow breaths.

"Can you come with me?"

Imani followed her upstairs into her bedroom. The space was a little smaller than Imani expected, but with its light blue walls and beige accent pieces, it was still comfortable and now...eerily quiet. She could only imagine the pain these four walls had been holding over the past few days.

Imani walked over to the chair of the vanity as Eve closed the door behind her, resting her back against it. Eve then marched over to the only window in the space with such urgency that Imani stood up herself, walking over to her with a spike of anxiety. Eve pulled up the window, leaning forward with her hands resting on the ledge and stopped. She closed her eyes and inhaled, letting the wind blow her caramel curls. Feeling her heart settle, Imani sat back on the chair and waited.

Eve always had such a calm energy to Imani, so it shouldn't have surprised her that Eve's demeanor wouldn't change. That was one of the things that guests and strangers said to Imani at her parents' funeral.

*"You're doing so well with...all of this,"* an older guest had noted, placing a cold hand at Imani's wrist, as if she scored well on a test. Imani didn't even know who the woman was at the time, assuming she came to the public funeral either by her aunt's invitation or after hearing about it on the news.

But, Imani learned that day how much people *didn't* know what to say to those experiencing loss. It's such a common experience that Imani assumed the appropriate words would be much more...common. But, they almost always never were.

Eve turned around and walked to her bed, taking a seat at the edge of it. "I wish everyone would just leave me alone...it's mind numbing."

She closed her eyes and tilted her head back before opening her eyes and staring back at her bedroom window.

"I begged Rand for months to get out of that gambling mess...he'd either get himself hurt or us. He kept insisting that he had it under control and nothing would ever make it to our doorstep...always trying to better his chances at getting a higher return..."

Imani's eyebrows dipped in the middle. She never knew what Rand actually did for a living, but she assumed DeAndre at least offered his friend a job at some point. They seemed that close, almost like brothers.

"Did he ever work for D?"

Eve nodded, smoothing her hands down her thighs covered in stockings.

"He does...I mean, he did...but...RJ has been needing help developmentally for a while now. At first, it seemed like everything was under control. But, then the costs of the support he needed just became too much. We dove headfirst into debt, maxing out credit cards, getting loans, owing everybody and barely seeing a dime come into the house."

Imani didn't even know what to say to Eve right now.

"I kept telling Rand to just talk to DeAndre, just to see if he could loan him the money, at least. We'd work on paying it back. But, he never wanted to ask him for anything...shut down the entire idea of asking him."

Eve shook her head, chuckling to herself. "And, guess what D ended up doing anyway?"

Imani shrugged.

"Paid for all these arrangements...and gave me something to move me and the kids to another home. Imani, what he gave me is more than enough and it wiped off all the debt we had."

"Now, why did it have to take Rand putting himself in harm's way for that to happen?"

Dropping her head to her lap, Eve sobbed, visibly shaking.

"Eve," Imani said, kneeling by the bed and placing her hands on top of Eve's hand. "I'm...so sorry. Does DeAndre know about this? Did you tell him?"

Eve looked up at Imani, suddenly, tears streaked against her cheeks.

"No," she said, "I couldn't...it's no use to say anything now. I'm good. The kids will be fine. Please don't say anything to him at this point, Imani."

Imani shook her head. She hadn't spoken to DeAndre in weeks, especially not since Rand passed. Anything she could say to him either wouldn't matter or would be an iteration of what he's probably already heard. Having a flashback of DeAndre's face that day at the park before she ran off, Imani thought the way things...ended wasn't exactly on the best terms.

"You don't have to worry about that at all," she said as Eve gave her a cautionary glance.

It didn't mean Imani still didn't think of him as soon as it happened, though. Or think of him every day, multiple times a day.

"Is he here? In town?" Imani asked.

"Yeah," Eve said, clearing her throat. She turned around and glanced at the clock on the bedside table. "He should be here in a few..."

Despite herself, Imani's heart ballooned.

"Haven't even spoken to him in a week," Eve continued, "but, he said he'll be here."

She took another breath.

"I never heard him sound so formal," she said. "He lost his best friend, so...I can't even guess what he's feeling."

"And, you lost your husband," she said, "don't take on what anyone else *could* be feeling. We love doing that as women."

Eve dragged her tired eyes to meet Imani's and nodded.

"So," Imani sighed. "You're gonna be moving out of this house soon, it sounds like?"

"I have to," Eve said, shaking her head. "But...we won't be far. Gotta figure this all out, but I'll be in touch."

Imani smiled. They hadn't known each other for long and only met being at Melody's events, but Imani always felt like Eve would be someone she could build a friendship with whenever Eve was ready.

"Looking forward to it," Imani said.

Eve's smile fell slowly.

"I can't believe I have to do this."

Imani gripped her hand reassuringly before they both stood up.

"Let's get back downstairs," Eve said, sniffling. "I gotta get the boys ready."

Imani walked down the carpeted steps first, noticing how quiet the space suddenly was in comparison to mere minutes ago. As soon as she turned the corner, heading back in the living room, she saw why.

DeAndre stood near the foyer with his hands in the pockets of a slim all-

## A Month of Sundays

black suit painted on his lean frame. He was talking to someone next to him who Imani assumed was the one who initiated conversation by DeAndre's reserved expression. Imani's skin tingled as she watched him now, feeling a rising heat travel from the top of her head down to her feet.

*I miss you. I love you.*

The thought came to her so quickly, with such force, that she thought she said it out loud. Rubbing his finger against his bottom lip, DeAndre nodded to the man speaking, his honey brown eyes creeping over to her as if in direct response.

Did he hear her? He wouldn't have heard her if she did, right?

"DeAndre," Eve said, walking past Imani and approaching him with a hug. The two embraced before DeAndre gave her his full attention, consoling her as silent tears emerged again. Before they finished, Imani looked around the living room, searching for a task to keep herself occupied.

Yes, she was single and, yes, she was still very much attracted to him. But, there was no room for her to entertain anyone right now, especially someone she lost a semblance of control with. DeAndre wasn't someone to get serious with, no matter the amount of care she had for him.

Coming up short with what to do with herself, Imani approached the two of them, feeling DeAndre's gaze searing through her. She had to pull herself all the way together if she was going to make it through the day. Imani prayed that she wouldn't be sitting next to him at the funeral.

"Eve, I don't see RJ and Rico around here," she said. "I'll find them and get them ready to go."

"Right, yeah thanks," Eve said, as if remembering her initial intention for coming downstairs. "Definitely. Um...we need to head to the church in a few minutes."

She turned back to DeAndre.

"You sure you don't want to ride with us?"

Eve was riding to the funeral in a large, premium Escalade with her sons, parents, and in-laws, mentioning to Imani how overwhelmed she was about riding with all of them in one vehicle.

DeAndre cleared his throat and scratched behind his ear.

"Nah, I'll see you at the church."

## Jade Olivia

Eve stepped away to greet relatives as Imani went to tend to the chore she volunteered for just to avoid DeAndre. But, before she was out of his sight, he tugged at her arm gently, igniting a flurry of nerves.

"Can you ride with me?" he asked, his eyes worn either from fatigue, worry or a bit of both. Just moments ago, Imani had assumed DeAndre was maintaining himself well since Rand's passing, but seeing him up close now, she realized that he wasn't as pulled together as he appeared.

Imani hesitated.

"I need you with me right now."

Imani's heart accelerated and it took everything in her not to just walk off with him right then and there.

He had never said *that* to her before.

Taking a breath, Imani pulled her gaze away, seeing Eve's sons just beyond the foyer, their mother nowhere in sight.

"Let me just get the twins ready for Eve and then I'll come with you."

Instead of walking towards the door, however, DeAndre remained in front of her, his eyebrows dipped in concern. Imani folded her arms, tilting her head.

"What is it?"

"Just...don't run away, a'ight?"

The question pulled Imani back to DeAndre's emotional proclamation at the park where their feelings were laid out in the open. Before Imani could respond, DeAndre stepped away from her, getting the last word this time.

# Chapter 24
# Jumping Over Fire

Now sitting in an SUV in the middle of traffic, Imani watched Robert inch his way closer to the church. DeAndre was sitting next to her, quieter than she'd ever seen him, even after making it clear he needed her here. He told her that Robert was a substitute for his usual driver - Clive, who wasn't available. But, DeAndre hadn't said a word to her since.

She wasn't sure what she expected him to say - he was mourning his best friend, after all - so she focused on making sure she gave him the space to feel however he wanted to, just like she did for Eve.

It was something Imani had learned that from her therapist who helped her cope with her parents' death. It was something they used to say that before the first few sessions.

*This is space for whatever comes up for you. This is your time.*

Imani never thought she'd be in a position to actually say that to someone and mean it, but here she was. Imani shifted in her cinched black dress, smoothing the bottom of it over stocking-covered knees. She stole a glance at her black pointy stilettos with two bejeweled gold bows attached to the front, a tiny bright spot during such a terrible day. The bows reminded her of the black flats she wore to her own parents' funeral as a kid. They had bows as well - two red ones that Imani spent the entire day looking at, instead of the two caskets descending at a snail's pace into the earth.

## Jade Olivia

Traffic was still jam packed, but what made it worse was the crowd forming outside that now closed in on the SUV like a mob. Word must have gotten out that DeAndre was here to pay his respects. He hadn't made a formal announcement but it didn't take much for fans to know his whereabouts when he was in town. Robert inched his way further down the street, careful not to hit anyone ahead of him. He pulled up closer to the dashboard as if he was scanning the area ahead for bugs.

"Ah, this is crazy," Robert said. "These people can't get out the damn way?"

Imani had only driven with Clive once before, but Robert was definitely more aggressive on the road. He pushed on the gas before making a sudden brake, jolting them forward in their seats. Imani held a hand in front of her to keep from shoving into the back of the passenger seat as DeAndre reached over, resting a hand on her knee. He scowled at Robert in the rearview.

"Yo, man, you good?"

"Sorry, folks," Robert said, his eyes apologetic in the rearview mirror. He managed to get out of traffic, rounding into an alley near the cathedral where the crowd was nowhere to be found. Once parked, Robert turned his body to them, resting a hand against the passenger seat headrest.

"Lemme check what the protocol is and I'll come back. No one will bother you guys here."

As soon as Robert slammed his door shut, Imani continued looking at DeAndre's hand still resting on her knee. Imani knew she was small in stature, barely over 5'5" and, seeing his hand cover hers, the gentle weight of it sending shockwaves up her thighs - made her feel enveloped in protection. She wanted his hand to move further up her leg until it was no longer visible, so all her attraction that burned for him could *finally* be felt without guilt attached. The quiet enclosure of the car reverberated in her ears as she imagined an invisible wave cascading down her body.

"I missed you," he said, piercing through the quiet with his baritone. His eyes stared out the window on his side. "I never heard from you."

"What was I gonna say to you?" she asked.

"Why didn't you call me?"

"Where have you been?" they asked in unison, their gazes crashing into each other.

## A Month of Sundays

DeAndre's hurt eyes narrowed as he pulled his hand away from her, turning his head towards the window on his side again. Imani turned to her own window in silence, grabbing at her elbows. Neither of them had an obligation to tell the other anything. Imani was finally a single woman and DeAndre was still very much single himself on top of losing his best friend.

*The man is grieving, Imani, get a grip. He doesn't need anyone asking what he's been doing.*

"I've never felt this way before," he said. "Have you?"

Imani stayed still for a moment, looking at the brick wall next to the alley outside. She was always on the tip of exploding whenever he was close to her. But, she thought concentrating on breathing would help until she turned to look at him.

With his nostrils slightly flared, DeAndre had so much pain in his eyes, staring at Imani like he needed her to take all of it away. There were still remnants of the look he gave her when they first met, a combination of surprise and fascination, but it had intensified into a gaze that held slight desperation. Imani grazed her tongue with her lips and swallowed.

"Yeah, I...I have," Imani finally said. "Losing someone you love, especially when it's unexpected...hurts like you couldn't imagine, but every day you'll get closer to a new normal that makes this hurt more manageable. It'll get easier."

Seemingly satisfied, he turned his head forward again, placing a hand on his chin and resting his elbow on the car door. Imani thought back to his visit to Artgo that day he surprised her, when he looked just as pensive as he did now. A phantom of a smile passed across her face.

"What about my love for you? " he asked in sharp rasp. "Will that get any easier to manage on my own?"

Imani's stomach did a somersault as her eyes shot up, colliding into his.

"Do you know how much I love you?"

Imani felt her heart deep dive to a level that she didn't know existed. She didn't say anything for what felt like forever and his gaze held her hostage.

"DeAndre..." she said it quieter than she meant to, with much less resistance than she wanted.

"I don't want to lose someone else who's important to me," he said.

"DeAndre," she tried to control her breathing to no avail. "You won't lose me as a friend, I'll be here for you as much as I can be-"

"Bullshit."

Imani's forehead dipped.

"What?"

"This friend charade shit that you're trying to pull with me is stupid," he said, an edge in his tone.

"We're not kids, Imani."

He reached over to her again, grabbing her by the crook of her elbow.

"I got what you said to me. But, you can't tell me you don't feel anything."

Of course, Imani felt *it*. She just kept herself from naming it. There was no point in acting on it now, especially after that night at his place. She had never gotten over that, either. As much as she prayed and journaled and wrote and painted and meditated, all of his words from that night were etched across her body like one of her tattoos.

Imani gently pulled her hand out of his grasp, straightening herself in her seat before putting up both hands as if handling someone with care.

"You're just grieving right now D," she swallowed. "It's a lot going on and you just need to slow down for a minute."

"Tell me to my face that you don't love me...and I'll leave you the hell alone."

Imani felt her breath hitch as she swallowed again, letting her eyes fall out the window. Not a cloud in the sky was present today and they were still the only two people here - no friends, no partners, no ambiguous associations...just them. She turned to find him without a trace of a smile on his face.

"I...just..."

Of course she did, with every cell in her body she knew she did. Imani had been thinking about him for months, wondering where he was or who he was with, praying that he was well. But, admitting all of that right now would be, for what? Imani closed her eyes, taking a deep breath, only to open them just as quickly.

"I promise you," he said, his gaze unwavering, "I'll leave you alone."

She trembled, sweat gathering at her spine.

## A Month of Sundays

"DeAndre–"

Robert knocked twice on DeAndre's side, jolting her, but not phasing him at all. Imani felt like she was going to burst out of her skin while he kept staring at her, unbothered by an entire wake in progress.

"Alright, we got 5 minutes here before y'all need to take seats," Robert said.

She felt more than enough pressure from him to say something. She had to say it now. But, Imani had to be logical about this and own up to her side of the matter at this point.

"Yes," Imani said, her voice resolute. "I...love you...I do. But, there's so much I shouldn't have done with you, DeAndre."

Placing her fingers at her temples, Imani took another breath. She couldn't believe they were having this conversation just before a funeral, for God's sake. There was no way he knew what he was saying. DeAndre represented everything she left behind years ago. There was no room in her life for someone so... impulsive, especially not now. She always knew he was a flirt, something he did with her for years, but these past few months, invisible boundaries had been crossed and as much as she tried to bring them back, they were all falling apart, one by one.

"But, did you want to? Do all of that with me?" He turned his body fully toward her, letting his hands fall to the headrest in the front and backseat.

"Whatever you feel bad about has nothing to do with how I feel about you. Anything you did with me, I'm not holding it against you because I was right there with you."

Hearing his words made Imani feel vindicated of all the guilt she'd been holding for weeks. She didn't regret breaking up with Michael, but she regretted what she did while being with him, letting her emotions drive her so far ahead of herself. Imani didn't feel like harping on that.

"I was in a relationship when all of that happened, and I literally just got out of it-"

"Which means you can be in this one with me."

Imani squinted.

"A relationship–? DeAndre..."

Imani looked beyond him out the window, shaking her head. She had gotten out of her relationship with Michael in order to figure herself out, to see how life would be when she wasn't tied to someone and their expectations. Now, what? She was supposed to get into another situation with someone else who presumably had even *more* expectations in their life?

"This isn't something I need right now."

"But, is it what you want?" he asked.

"What?"

"I don't need to be what you *need*," DeAndre said, staring her in the eye. "That's it right there...we'd be choosing each other because of what we want."

She just looked at him, stunned.

"Listen, I'm not telling you that I have this whole thing figured out," he continued, "but, I want to figure all this shit out with you."

Imani stammered as if trying to solve a riddle.

"DeAndre...What is there to figure out?"

Another tap on the door from Robert, this time with much more force.

"Okay, time to get inside, guys," he said. "You ready?"

Still unbothered by the disruption, DeAndre's gaze bore into hers, opening his jacket to reach into his breast pocket.

Imani's eyes widened as realization slowly seeped its way into her mind. Suddenly shaking, Imani felt sweat pooling at her fingertips as her stomach dropped in her lap.

"What?"

She hadn't realized there was enough room in the backseat to move forward, but that's what DeAndre did. He bent down on his knee - crisp black suit and all - and took her hand. There wasn't much space, so his head would almost be cradled in her lap if he had made a sudden turn.

Imani wanted to cry and run all at the same time.

"I want to give my all to you. Imani. This isn't me just telling you I want you in my future. I'm promising it all to you right now."

Still holding eye contact, DeAndre pulled a small black box out of his pocket.

"Please say yes," he said, his voice strained, before pulling his eyes away to open the box.

## A Month of Sundays

Imani was gasping, her heart racing a mile a minute, and placed the hand he wasn't holding onto her stomach, trying to gather her bearings. She felt light-headed, but her feet were firmly planted on the ground.

"DeAndre...what?"

The sun was at its brightest in the sky today, but nothing compared to the clarity and glow of the solitaire diamond - a long angular rock that was tapered at the ends - facing outward in the box. Imani never had specifics for the kind of ring she wanted, but the ones she did see - on Pinterest or Instagram and online, all looked similar in shape, cut and style, no matter the price tag. But, this ring looked like it was extracted from the deepest ends of the earth, merely shined and polished, before being placed on the prongs of a simple band. The imperfectly sharp edges of the ring made it stand out in more ways than one, a testament to a disjointed journey.

"Be my wife, baby."

Imani held her breath, placing her hand to her mouth as the glare of the ring blurred her vision from tears pooling under her eyes.

"Rand kept telling me...he kept telling me that you wanted commitment," he said. "And, I refused to see it...then once you told me what you wanted, it was the easiest thing I could give to you. How could I not give this to you?"

DeAndre looked at her, staring at her, damn near pleading with her.

When she sat there with him, releasing her breath, she thought over every interaction, every conversation of theirs, forming in her mind like the rough sketches she toiled away at endlessly - scribbling, erasing, adding onto them before they came together in one fleshed-out piece. It all added up to this. A moment that felt so liberating. On top of that, Imani always knew in her heart she'd marry only when it felt right, not by some default loyalty to a specific time frame or number of years of being in a relationship.

Robert suddenly knocked on the door, this time - four times.

"Are we ready? Are we ready? Are we ready? " he asked, patience extinguished from his tone.

Imani curled her lips and released them. In her heart, she knew exactly what she was agreeing to, yet her mind was in disarray...

She was still going for it, though.

Imani was making yet another leap, just through the fire. *You runnin' straight through that fire, girl,* her aunt used to say. Imani always danced with uncertainty, skirting the line between what she *knew* was right and what was much riskier.

So, what stopped her from doing that now?

*This is insane. I'm insane.*

"Okay..."

Imani felt her heart galloping in full speed, bursting.

"Okay," she nodded, meeting his eye. "DeAndre, yes...I'll be your wife."

He didn't move at first, assessing her with reluctance before a smile slowly spread across his handsome face in shocked relief. DeAndre pulled the ring out of the box and slid it gently down Imani's finger. There was slight resistance, but the ring eventually fit, secured on her hand like it was meant for her. Imani paused to look at it for a beat, marveling at the new weight she felt on a previously naked, bare hand.

DeAndre then slid one hand to the back of her head, drawing her close before letting his lips descend onto hers. This kiss, their first kiss, started with gentle pecking and prodding before they settled into a languid rhythm that made Imani quiver from her head down to her toes. His scent was so potent that it felt like a coat was wrapped around them. Everything could've easily gotten deeper in the car, but Imani managed to pull herself away.

She knew, then and there, that she wanted to play in fire with him every single day.

"Mine," DeAndre said, voice strained, his chest rising and falling.

She nodded mechanically, planting her hands all over him, from his hair to the sides of his cheeks to the rough texture of his beard to his soft lips, to make sure she wasn't dreaming. Her ring sparkled as her hand rested against his mahogany face - a luminous diamond over chocolate bronze. He chuckled, the white of his teeth visible, looking at her now with a mixture of both admiration and concern.

Imani bit down on her lip, still holding his face.

"Are we really doing this?" she asked, barely a whisper.

His cheeks fell slowly, narrowing out his face as he nodded.

"Yeah...and soon."

## A Month of Sundays

He stared at her with this vein of unspoken finality that Imani hadn't seen from him before.

She nodded, just as serious, just as committed, knowing that her life was beginning to change at this exact moment.

"Okay."

# Chapter 25
# Guess Who's Coming to Brunch?

Imani fiddled with her ring, gazing at the magnificent view from a table on the balcony of Houston 324, one of the most exclusive restaurants in Rapid Springs. She glanced down at the menu in front of her with options that were fairly limited before gazing at DeAndre, scrolling away on his phone without a care in the world.

The two had officially been engaged for a month now, set to marry in less than three, but had never gotten around to telling his mother. Kaylee and Aunt Ethel knew, so Andele was the only one still in the dark. They were finally meeting her for brunch today to share their plans with her and Imani was a ball of nerves, trying to find something to release her pent-up anxiety.

"Know what you're gettin'?" he asked, placing his phone next to him before looking at the menu himself.

"I don't know…"

Imani bit the side of her finger before putting her hand down on her lap, trying not to look any more nervous.

"Mind ordering for the both of us?"

He looked at her before leaning forward, elbows on the table with his hands folded.

"You know we're not asking for her permission, right? Whatever she says isn't gonna change anything."

## A Month of Sundays

Andele had been out of town for over a month now, so Imani hadn't seen her since the first time they met, especially since she and DeAndre weren't living together. Imani chose not to move in with him before they were married, even though he asked for her to move in not even two days after he proposed. It would've been the easiest thing for her to do, especially when he made it so tempting.

*Everything will already be set up just how you like before the wedding and you could...just be right here with me, hummingbird,* he had said to her, tantalizing her with soft kisses behind her ear. Imani absolutely melted over this nickname he had for her and felt like he'd only break it out when he *really* wanted something.

But, despite some of the choices she'd made up to this point, there were some things she decided well before DeAndre, even before Michael, that she wasn't willing to compromise on. She believed he respected her, no matter what she chose, but Imani wanted to keep a standard for herself, too. He didn't push once she made her decision, either.

"Yeah, but I don't want this to be an ambush. I was there when you invited her to brunch, but you left out a lot, D. You didn't tell her I'd be here. I mean, did you even tell her you were gonna propose?"

DeAndre rubbed his chin, moving himself back into his seat.

"Nah, I didn't. But, she knows how I feel about you."

"And, what did she say?"

"Does it matter?" He looked at her straight on for a moment until Imani caught his eyes shift with hesitance. A waiter appeared with a carafe of water to fill their glasses.

"I'm not just your hired help at the house anymore," she continued. "I'm gonna be your wife in a matter of weeks."

"Yo first off, on the real," DeAndre started. "You were never *hired help,* so let's get that out the way."

However DeAndre may have felt, Andele made it clear that she wasn't a fan of Imani when she was introduced as a friend all those months ago. And, to be fair, Imani hadn't thought much about it at the time - she figured she'd never see her again. But, now that Imani was going to officially be in the family, the circumstances were much different. She wasn't sure what Andele would say.

Hearing a few of the conversations DeAndre had with her over the phone, Imani knew that Andele spoke her mind much like her son, which meant she was preparing herself for the worst.

Patting the back of her neck, Imani straightened her shoulders and looked down at the cream cotton stretch dress she decided to wear today at the last minute.

Yeah, yeah.

Wearing cream and white mere weeks from the wedding wasn't exactly original, but Imani couldn't help how giddy she felt about marrying this man. She was either wearing this or DeAndre's face on a T-shirt and that would've just been...a little too much.

"How do I look?"

Imani pulled her mouth into a grimace, dragging her tongue across her front teeth as

DeAndre chuckled.

"Like the woman I want to marry tomorrow," he said, smiling at her now, his eyes soft.

Imani looked down at her empty plate, warmed by his words, before looking up at him again.

"Which we technically could..." he said, reaching for her left hand. He pushed his fingers in between the crevices of hers, shifting her ring slightly.

"You really want a wedding, though."

"You right," he said as the two of them laughed, "and, if I gotta drop a few M's to see you in wedding white every year, I'll do it."

Imani crossed her eyes, playfully. She couldn't deny how what he said to her made her smile from the inside out, no matter how dramatic it was sometimes.

Her man loved talking.

"I'm not gonna let anything go sideways, a'ight?"

She took a breath, and nodded, allowing herself to calm down. He was right...she was safe and they were finally committing to each other - fully and wholeheartedly. That's all that mattered.

Imani settled into his touch, feeling the warmth of his hand engulf hers. In moments like this, Imani would have to pinch herself to make sure all of this

## A Month of Sundays

was real. Not even three months ago, she was daydreaming about him, imagining what it'd be like to wrap her arms around him. Now, they were both doing just that, freely. It seemed like the minute she said yes, it opened the floodgates of PDA - his arm draped over her shoulders, walking up behind her to pull at her waist and sneaking all the kisses he could. From being in a previous relationship that was much more subtle in affection, to now being with someone who had no qualms about showing his feelings was an adjustment. It was all a little heady for her.

"Got somethin' to show you," he smiled, releasing his hand from hers to pull a small felt bag out of his pocket.

Imani tucked her hand under her chin, brows dipped in curiosity. He pulled a square black box out of the bag, not as small as a ring box, but larger in dimension. He pulled the top open, placing the box on the table before rubbing his hands together in adulation.

"This shit right here? Tell me it ain't fire."

He turned the box to Imani, revealing two diamond encrusted grills stacked on top of each other cushioned in the felt grooves at the corners of the box. A horizontal bar held together two shiny fangs on opposite sides.

"Are you for real, right now?" Imani laughed. "Baby, '05 called and they need their stuff back."

She sipped her water as he took them out the box, affixing both of them to the top and bottom of his teeth. Once secured, he made a show of pulling at the corners of his mouth with his pinkies.

"Now, we got the matchin' drip."

Against his deep brown complexion, the diamonds glistened.

"You are..."

Imani meant to say...something, but quickly got lost in how sexy he looked. She stretched her fingers to touch his mahogany face, tugging down at his bottom lip to get a better look at the other set.

"See?" he said, "My baby always passes the vibe check."

He bit down on the bottom corner of his lip, lust on his face like he was a second away from throwing her on top of the table, devouring her from the inside out *and* licking the rim. The movement of his mouth shifted her fingers from his lips to his goatee as her own diamond, positioned just underneath, caught the light, complimenting the glint of his grill perfectly. DeAndre held his mouth open again and picked his phone up to snap a selfie of their moment.

"...so crazy," she said, taking her hand away. She was drenched with need that urgently, her heart racing by the second. Imani rubbed her thighs together in her seat.

*Good God, could two and a half months come any faster?*

"Can you even chew on your food with those things on?" she asked, with a playful scowl.

Just as he took the bottom front out of his mouth, Andele appeared walking over to their table, her arm hooked with the restaurant host. She looked every bit like a woman bored with most of what anyone had to say and unbothered by what they thought. Imani never felt maternal energy from her, considering how beautiful she was with a complexion as deep as DeAndre's and the same semi-slanted eyes. Dressed in a linen tunic with cream capris, Andele's eyes were covered with wide-rimmed circular sunglasses above a resting scowl etched across her face.

They both stood to greet her with DeAndre giving her a kiss on the cheek as she patted the side of his face. He pulled out a chair for her, which she sat down in immediately, leaving Imani standing there awkwardly for a moment before she cleared her throat and sat back down.

"Good morning, my son," she said jubilantly, picking up her cloth napkin to lay on her lap. She turned to regard Imani next to him with a short smile, not even taking off her sunglasses before doing so.

"Imani," she said, speaking in the weirdest accent - a mix between American and a faux British one. "I saw your completed piece."

Imani straightened her neck slightly, perking up a bit. She stole a quick glance at DeAndre for assurance, but he was completely unaware, thanking the waiter for the coffee he was pouring creamer in.

"Nice. What'd you think?" she asked, placing her hands on her lap.

Andele took off her shades, folding them with exaggerated delicacy before resting them on the table beside her.

"It was all..."

She spoke with her hands, fingers polished the lightest shade of pink, twirling them about, like she was envisioning something she couldn't comprehend.

"Very dark."

Imani scratched behind her knee, pulling another breath in.

"In what way?"

The waiter returned to fill Andele's water glass to the brim.

"I just assumed that any artwork DeAndre commissioned would add more...light to his home," she said, pulling the glass to her lips. "The boys in that portrait made me think of those...streets we left so far behind."

Although Imani never got caught up caring what people thought of her work, especially when they weren't her clients, she was always mindful of the message she hoped to convey. She'd usually get direction of that message from who she was working with but considering how DeAndre let her run free with it, the painting was birthed from her own interpretation. He loved it, though, so Imani tried not to let Andele get to her.

"Oh, well," Imani said. She cleared her throat, pulling her cloth napkin from the table onto her lap.

"I hoped it would've brought back...fond memories."

"It did."

Imani turned to DeAndre, who had finally inserted himself in the conversation, giving her a smile that felt like a hug to her heart.

"Right," Andele said with an edge to her tone, "Memories of when I was... broke, tired and fat..."

She looked at Imani, her brow hiked.

"Beautiful memories," she said.

Imani blinked, giving her attention to the coffee and basket of artisan breads that appeared at their table, seemingly out of nowhere. The waiter returned a few seconds later to take their orders and break up the awkward energy that was like a dark cloud above the table now. Imani observed as Andele spoke with DeAndre - surprisingly like an employee more than her son - about his upcoming matches, the start of the new season and upcoming events he was committed to attend as a member of the International Tennis League. Once their food arrived, any acknowledgement Imani thought Andele would give her never happened, as Andele treated her as all but a figment of her imagination.

"It's about to be another wild season," DeAndre said, nodding, "on the road a lot these next few months."

He reached for Imani's hand, pulling it next to him on the table.

"Which is why we're getting married before it starts back up," he said.

If any music was playing in the background at the restaurant, Imani could no longer hear it.

Andele paused for a moment, her fork in hand. She then placed the food slowly in her mouth, taking her sweet precious time chewing what was on that fork. But, Imani noticed the subtle chink in her armor - the twitch in her eye. Andele then looked at Imani openly this time, letting her gaze fall languidly from Imani's ring, now visible on the table, back up to her face again.

"Is that so?" she asked, once her food was well into the pit of her stomach, probably in the throes of digestion as she spoke.

"Yeah in October," DeAndre said, "in Paris."

He wasn't even looking at Imani but held onto her for dear life. Andele's brow hitched.

"This October?" she said. "That's not...even three months from now."

"We know," he said with a smile.

Andele let out a deep sigh, fixing her attention on her plate while she stared as if in a trance. Rubbing the tips of her thumb and index finger together, she shifted her gaze up to Imani again without moving her head.

"Are you pregnant?"

Imani's heart accelerated. It shouldn't have come as a surprise that Andele would think she was trapping him. She barely knew Imani and the little she did know was probably all assumptions.

"No," Imani said.

Andele blinked, tilting her head.

"You are...a citizen of this country, right?"

"A'ight, Ma," DeAndre interrupted, giving her a look of indifference.

Andele placed a palm on her chest.

"My apologies," she said, with a slight nod to her son.

## A Month of Sundays

"But..." she hesitated, rubbing her chest now like she had heartburn. "Why....why are you getting married, then?"

Andele literally looked like the definition of confusion, staring between the two of them. Imani didn't sense disrespect behind it, though. It was a question she asked herself but had yet to even ask DeAndre out loud.

*Why are you marrying me?* she had thought.

She didn't think countering whatever he'd say with a proclamation of her love for him felt like enough. Imani took a breath, preparing to justify her case.

"Because she's my family, Ma."

Imani had never been to outerspace, but she felt like she was ascending close enough to it. This moment had to encapsulate what that felt like.

She watched Andele glance between the two of them once more before her forehead relaxed, opening to the revelation that this was all really happening. Andele took another breath, the corners of her lips curled up, a reluctant mother accepting her adult child's decision.

"I guess there's the rest of *the* family," she said, pointedly, "that I have to let know..."

Imani then watched Andele re-calibrate like a robot on autopilot, ticking off the tasks that were now at hand due to this new development. Imani's eyes wandered for a moment before landing on DeAndre's as he took another sip of his coffee. With his eyes above the rim of the mug, he threw her a wink.

"...I have to make sure Carol knows," Andele continued her diatribe, "Since she'll let everyone know on the west coast...and all of the cousins...did we settle on a planner?"

DeAndre swallowed the sip of his coffee. "Stephanie's taking care of all that."

Andele blinked, as if DeAndre just knocked the wind out of her.

"Well...okay," she said. "So, it seems like everything is set."

DeAndre looked at her for a moment, a half-smile hiking up his cheek. "Pretty much," he said.

In terms of the wedding day, Imani chose to remain hands off for most of the process. The only two requests she had were to be in total control of designing her wedding gown with the designer of her choice and selecting the number of people in their bridal party. Clearly, Imani missed the boat in girlhood priming her to obsess over her "dream wedding" with every detail well-crafted in her mind. But, DeAndre gladly took up the baton, talking with Stephanie about everything from the guest count to the venue to the color scheme to choosing desserts.

The two of them were even having a meeting with Stephanie today after brunch to go over a few more details and Imani assumed it was the showman in him that wanted to make sure everything was in order. She trusted it would be. Her focus, however, was actually settling into the marriage part, not one day that would come and go in a blur.

After a few moments of the three of them eating in silence, DeAndre cleared his throat, pushing himself up and out of his seat.

"I'mma head to the restroom real quick," he said. "Be back."

Imani rested her eyes back on the woman who would be her mother-in-law in less than three months' time, taking another breath before biting into a slice of bacon, the only food she didn't pick over. Andele perused the menu, not bothering to look up at Imani even though they were now alone.

"I know this is gonna be an adjustment," Imani said. "But, I truly hope we can have a chance to grow…a nice bond."

She offered her brightest smile to which Andele looked up, offering a blank stare.

"Let's…not get ahead of ourselves." Andele tacked on a lackadaisical smile before looking down at the menu again.

*Fabulous*, Imani thought, sarcastically.

She placed her hands on either side of her plate before grabbing her lemonade to take a sip that was watered down with all the ice melted.

"Do you maybe have any sort of advice?" Imani cleared her throat. "You know DeAndre more than anyone."

"I do," Andele perked up. "My one and only child."

She looked up with such nostalgia, a fondness in Andele's tone that Imani hadn't heard from her before.

"He's very competitive, which sometimes means he makes decisions just to keep himself from losing out on something he *thinks* he wants."

### A Month of Sundays

Imani's smile faltered.
"I suggest you get very comfortable with your own company..."
Andele smiled as if telling her good news.
"You'll need her."

# Chapter 26
# Maybe, Baby

"We need to talk."

DeAndre felt Imani's soft hand on his leg as the two sat on the couch in his living room. Even feeling her near him redirected DeAndre's focus - it had become so natural for him to give her his full attention. They returned to his house from brunch, with Imani watching reruns of *Living Single* on the big screen while he watched match footage on his phone, waiting for Stephanie's arrival for their meeting.

The meeting that DeAndre had set up just days after the engagement was to discuss matters surrounding the wedding and the overall vision for how Imani would fit into his "brand narrative," if she really wanted to be a part of it at all. For all the very casual dating he did over the years, DeAndre was never officially confirmed to be in a committed relationship with anyone. Imani was the first for him in that regard, but her being a part of his "brand" was never a consideration for him. He was just going to continue doing what he did naturally and he wanted her right there with him. Stephanie was the one who brought this to his attention, and just when he was going to shut down the possibility of them doing some media blitz bullshit, she made a point.

*She has a career, too, DeAndre. Imani being connected to you publicly could grant her access when you're not even in the room,* she had said. *Why don't we at least see what she has to say?*

## A Month of Sundays

So, he said he would. No matter what Imani wanted to do, he was willing to put every effort to support her as she saw fit. Now, since returning home though, DeAndre had grown a bit antsy, anticipating Imani overthinking their relationship, on some women's intuition mess.

"What's up?" he asked.

"Brunch with your mom was...interesting, huh?"

DeAndre held her gaze.

"I guess," he said.

Once they bid Andele a farewell, DeAndre didn't even think about her afterwards. His mom acted exactly like he knew she would - annoyed but accepting since it wasn't messing with the life built for her. DeAndre could tell his mother didn't see Imani as much of a threat, but moreso as one of the many people in his life she had to tolerate. He didn't care, though. As long as she didn't take it any further than that.

"I don't think we ever talked about this before," she said, searching his eyes as if trying to find an answer. Her ebony features glowed from the mid-afternoon sun seeping into the window behind her and he could see flecks of bronze in her hair, which she recently dyed a pink rose gold. Looking at her like this, when she wasn't even trying, took his breath away almost every time.

"Talked about what?"

"Having children."

DeAndre was thankful he wasn't drinking anything that could have easily been spit into his beautiful fiancé's face right now. He scratched the back of his head, training his face on a neutral expression.

"Right," he said. "We haven't."

"I'm not sure how many you want," she said, without blinking. Her gaze on him was so intense that he felt like he couldn't say much outside of what she might already be thinking.

Looking from her hand on his thigh back up to her face, he tried to think of what to say, then gave her a half smile. Coming up short, he decided to just ask her.

"How many..." DeAndre heard the strain in his voice. "Do you want to give to me?"

"We could do two," she said, quicker than expected. He thought the question would make her hesitate a little, but instead, it perpetuated her response even faster.

"...a few months apart but, I can do three..."

DeAndre shook his head, feeling like he was on a rollercoaster he didn't sign up for.

"...I mean, four is a maybe," she smiled, "but I wouldn't be against it."

"Whoa...wow," he let out a huff, shifting on the couch. "Baby, okay....You tryna keep up with Mel and Hosea?" he asked in jest, but she just continued staring at him.

DeAndre spoke with Hosea earlier in the week to ask him to be in the wedding, when Hosea let him know he and Melody were expecting again - adding yet another child to DeAndre's growing list of godchildren.

"Do you..." Imani hesitated, as if the thought was impossible. "...not want to have kids? You're always so sweet to Judea and Caleb...I just figured..."

"No...I mean...yeah," he said, giving her knee a rub. "I want them. I was just wanting you to myself for a little bit, ya' know?"

*More like a lotta bit.*

Imani smiled at him, but her eyes were wide with hesitation.

"And you will," she said. "I'm on birth control to keep myself regulated... but, not for *prevention*. I just assumed since neither of us are getting any younger, we'd be able to get started."

"You plan to stay on it, though - right?"

Imani's expression faltered.

"At least for a while?" He might as well get every bit of what he was saying out as fast as he could.

"I mean, yeah. I can. I'm open to talking to you about *not* being on it anymore, but...I mean, it is *my* body."

"Yeah, absolutely." DeAndre nodded, wiping his hand over his mouth before pulling at his bottom lip. This was all going left very quickly. Why was it so damn hot in here all of a sudden?

"But don't you want to put more stock in your career, Hummingbird?" he asked. "Your art? I can imagine that takes time to...ya' know..."

DeAndre was now picking at a scarce pile of straws.

## A Month of Sundays

"Do."

"I can *do* both, D."

"Yeah, yeah," he said, eyes scanning around him haphazardly. "I know you can."

Just when Imani was going to respond, the doorbell rang.

*Saved by the fucking bell*, he thought.

Without blinking, he held Imani's gaze. "Let's talk about this later...cool?"

Imani looked at him and smiled, nodding her head reluctantly. "Yeah, baby."

He stood up from the couch, walking towards the foyer, when he finally let out the longest sigh of relief.

DeAndre was telling her the truth - he did want kids. He wouldn't have asked to marry her if he didn't think it was a strong possibility of it happening. But he didn't already have them for a reason.

There were still a few goals he had for his own career and he knew Imani wasn't done growing as an artist - she said that herself multiple times. There'd be no way for them to even fit in the demands of a kid right now, let alone two. As much as DeAndre loved his friends' children and the kids he often volunteered with for the League, they also weren't *his* kids.

He remembered when Randall filled him in on the wild emotional ride Eve had gone through after she had their twins, a revelation they found out about during Eve's last OBGYN visit. Rand loved her without a shadow of a doubt, but he even admitted that having children changed the entire dynamic of their marriage in a way they never quite recovered from.

Plus, DeAndre's own parents weren't exactly docile grandparent material. It's not like the number to David's prison facility could be used on an emergency contact list and Andele probably didn't have a maternal bone in her body left, outside of shopping for kid's clothes in an effort to morph her grandchildren into her own image. DeAndre couldn't even remember the last time he felt his parents actually be *parents* to him in the first place. He couldn't imagine bringing up a kid in all of that right now.

DeAndre opened the door for Stephanie, leading them back to the living room where she and Imani hugged each other like they were girlfriends who hadn't seen each other in a while. Stephanie would come to the house when Imani was at work, so this was technically the first time they had seen each other since the proposal.

"Congratulations, Imani!" Stephanie beamed, bending slightly to Imani's height for a hug.

DeAndre watched them push away from each other, talking while holding each other's hands like women tend to do. He never expected his fiancé and his publicist to be so cool with one another, but he also didn't think he'd ever get married.

Life was a funny thing.

"I've been waiting forever to see this ring," Stephanie said. She was trying her best to remain professional, but she even let out a squeal once Imani, taking a loving glance at him, extended her manicured hand to proudly show it off. She had her nails done in an array of intricate designs about every week at this point, elated to see how her ring looked with different colors, nail lengths and textures.

His baby was so damn creative.

"Okay, DeAndre," Stephanie said, throwing a smirk his way. "You make sure Trey is out with her when she has that thing on."

He and Imani never talked about his proposal or the impression she had of him based on how he asked her. He just hoped she wasn't in her head, overthinking a decision they were both going into with their eyes wide open. DeAndre knew they were both getting to know each other. He and Imani just so happened to be doing that with a commitment attached. He didn't think they'd ever actually stop getting to know one another, which intrigued him. Randall was always telling DeAndre something that Eve said or did that was unprecedented.

"Aye, I've been with E for 10 years and shawty still throws me for a loop," he had said.

DeAndre couldn't pinpoint the exact feeling when he thought of what Rand said, but he knew he was looking forward to that feeling over and over again.

"What're you smiling about?" Imani asked, pulling him out of his thoughts.

## A Month of Sundays

The three of them were now sitting at the table in the den, Imani's painting serving as the backdrop. She was sitting next to him in a separate chair - too far away from him for his liking, while Stephanie set up her laptop.

"Nothin,'" he said.

He tacked on a reassuring smile and extended his arm across her chair, pulling her closer. DeAndre was working on keeping some things to himself and not becoming a complete cornball over her.

"Alright, you two," Stephanie started. "I have a few more meetings to get to today, so let's dive in."

∽

Imani took a breath, taking in all of what Stephanie had to say about the wedding. From the logistics of the actual day to the many vendors who were making last minute changes to their schedule just to accommodate a wedding abroad, it was clear to Imani that their wedding would be the complete opposite of Melody's laidback nuptials years ago.

She didn't have any issue with it, but Imani was more than ready to move on from this entire day, including brunch this morning, and go to her Aunt Ethel's house for their much needed catch up. They hadn't spoken to each other since Imani broke up with Michael nor had Imani been to church since the proposal.

Yeah, she was dodging it all in the worst way.

"...so, Imani, I just want to make sure we're clear about a few things," Stephanie said. Imani noticed her quick cautionary glance at DeAndre.

"How do you feel about the wedding being reported? People Magazine is already requesting exclusivity on the pictures, but I wanted to go over that with you, first."

Imani wasn't oblivious to the attention and curiosity she had suddenly gotten now that she was with one of the biggest athletes in the world. DeAndre posted her on his Instagram a few weeks ago - a blurry selfie of them laughing with Imani covering half of her face with her left hand and her follower count skyrocketed within days, even without him tagging her. She was still trying to reconcile her own identity as an artist with her soon-to-be identity as a wife to such a public figure.

Imani scrunched up her face.

"No, I don't want bloggers or reporters or anybody to get that," she said. "I mean, whatever's on the 'gram I don't mind, but I don't want to see my short-self plastered around on a cover somewhere."

Imani and Stephanie chuckled, but DeAndre looked at her with a seriousness she didn't expect.

"Of course not," Stephanie said. "And, with that, do you want to do interviews with those who might be interested...like, if you have an art show to promote?"

Imani blinked, pushing her head back in surprise.

"Stephanie..." she hesitated, "Don't you handle DeAndre's publicity?"

"Yeah," Stephanie smiled. "But...he's my client and anyone who's associated with my client the way you are, can get those privileges, too."

Imani's eyes widened as she nodded, settling into her feelings over what Stephanie just said. Imani felt like a magician had just waved her into a new reality without any of the struggles with gaining exposure that she had in the past. But, the artist in Imani depended on that struggle to do some of her best work. The struggle of not being known enough or feeling like you're not good enough as an artist was constant.

Imani thrived on it, if she really thought about it...hell, the art she produced for DeAndre partially manifested from the struggle of denying her feelings for him. She spilled her resistance into her art and there was no way she was ready to give that up completely.

"You know, what?" Imani said, "I don't think I want to...take any questions about him or anything. If it's gonna bring too much attention, I don't even wanna be at his matches."

DeAndre cast her a look of surprise that Stephanie mirrored. He had passed on competing in several games for weeks now, wanting to give Imani as much time as he could when he wasn't traveling out of town for other responsibilities. But, once the season started, he had upwards of 10 matches to play within a given month.

"You not tryna come to my matches?" he asked.

## A Month of Sundays

Imani swallowed and took a beat before turning to him.

"It's not that I don't want to...but you even mentioned how much of a distraction I could be for you."

DeAndre narrowed his gaze. He had joked with her when she was at a match of his out of town just last week, her first one as his fiancé, that she couldn't hold a poker face to save her life, meaning she'd have him knowing exactly how a game would end if he looked at her in the Players' box.

"Okay, but that wasn't for you to stop comin' altogether."

Before Imani could get another word in, Stephanie interrupted.

"How about you two talk about this privately, hmmm?" she asked with a softness in her voice. "It's an adjustment for both of you and I want to make sure *both* of you are in agreement."

The three of them continued discussing some of DeAndre's upcoming events and meetings out of town including his meeting coming up in a few months with Elite Athletics - a lifestyle brand that wanted to potentially collaborate with him on a new collection. It was going to be an intense few months for him after the wedding so everything had to be streamlined for him to the finest detail.

When Stephanie left about an hour later, DeAndre grabbed the keys to his Porsche and handed it to Imani as they walked out the front door.

"You know the ride is yours already, right?" DeAndre asked. "We don't have to keep doing this thing where you drop it off here when you don't think you need it."

Imani gave him a lazy smile, shoving him playfully.

"I love that you want to give it to me," she said. "But I'm not gonna have it sitting across the street from an apartment for days on end."

Since they were engaged, DeAndre had given Imani access to all his cars for her to choose from on any given day. She didn't live that far from his house, but he wanted to give her the convenience of having them just because.

Standing on the limestone of the front yard steps, Imani wrapped her arms around his neck, looking up at his brown eyes. His arms embraced her in no time, allowing herself to fall into his frame.

"I really *am* excited about our big day," she beamed up at him. "Can't wait to see you show off your wedding planning expertise."

He gave her a smirk, but it didn't reach his eyes. Imani paused.

"What is it?"

Still holding onto Imani, DeAndre continued his focus on her with a tilt of his head.

"You don't wanna be seen wit' me?"

Imani anticipated his laughter but it wasn't forthcoming. He was extremely serious. She tried not to laugh in his face at the undeniable irony of it all.

"Baby...yes...I do!" she said, pulling herself away from his grasp. *Where was this coming from?*

"What - is this about earlier?"

DeAndre put one hand in his pocket and rested the other one at the back of his neck. Imani let out a deep sigh.

"D, of course I want to be seen with you," she said. "I just...want to make sure I'm not throwing myself to the wolves so soon... and all. You respect that, right? At least I'm not trying to use your name to promote...a...a mixtape or something."

"Yeah, 'cause I don't know if I could even sell *that* voice," DeAndre said in amusement.

"I'm not even gonna make a comment on my misunderstood gift," she retorted, folding her arms across her chest. Imani looked down at her heeled snakeskin booties before looking up at him again - all humor out of the way.

"I just want to take my time with all the attention coming my way."

This entire conversation was veering into awkward territory for Imani, but there was no other way to put it. There was DeAndre - the incredible man she was agreeing to spend the rest of her life with, and then there was "DeAndre Harrison" - the manufactured machine behind him. The two were never the same for her, but they'd both be a part of her life.

"But, you're not in it alone," he said, hooking a finger into one of her front cargo pockets, pulling her closer. "I never want you hidin' behind me, I want you walkin' beside me."

Imani felt her heart gallop at warp speed.

*She could just give it to him right now. God would forgive her since they're getting married anyway, right?*

She turned to take in the view from the front porch, where you could see the sun wasn't as high in the sky, but the birds were still chirping. The weather was slowly transitioning, giving hints of the Fall season. Their wedding season was coming up...steadily approaching. Imani held her arms together, biting at her bottom lip while tapping her foot. She didn't need to make a mountain out of a molehill. She could compromise as long as they had a handle on their own public narrative.

"I'll go to one match a month," Imani said, meeting his gaze squarely in the eye, "as my schedule permits. I can probably work out going to a few out of town, but I'm not sure if I could always go out of the country on a whim."

Imani still had a whole full-time job and clients she to tend to, so there was no way she'd be able to suddenly drop everything to jetset for weeks on end. Yet, she knew she had to make an effort to show up for him. Wasn't showing up what most of her friends complained about their men *not* doing?

DeAndre smiled, laying a kiss on her lips that she didn't even have a chance to prepare for. His scent enveloped Imani to the point of delirium and she had to shake off the shock of electricity when he finally released her. Their kisses weren't as deep as their first one - even chaste, to be fair - but she felt such a pull that she could only imagine what it'd be like once they were on the other side of matrimony.

They walked over to DeAndre's car, and he opened the driver's side door for her. When he closed it, she turned the car on, opening the windows. He bent halfway down the driver's side, resting his sculpted arms on the roof.

"Lemme know when you're back from your Aunt's...Gotta figure out what we gon' do tomorrow before I head out again."

She nodded and blinked, letting herself get lost in the sharp angles of his mahogany face, biting down on the inside of her cheek. He was so damn fine, just looking at him hard enough was going to get her pregnant...for sure.

"I didn't know you had bars, by the way," Imani said, throwing him a grin.

His brows furrowed.

"The whole," she deepened her voice, "'hidin' behind me, walkin' beside me.'"

"You need to stop pressin' me," she said, smiling wide before putting on her seatbelt.

## Jade Olivia

He looked at her, taking in all her teasing with a smile and a shake of his head.

"I should," he asked, "shouldn't I?"

When she looked at him, he looked like he wanted to say something to her...like he couldn't quite figure out *what* he wanted to say. Instead, he stood to his full height and tapped the car roof, letting her pull off the property driveway.

## Chapter 27
## A Ring In the Big City

The first time Imani stepped foot into her Aunt Ethel's house, she barely knew who her father's sister even was. She heard about her a few times in passing conversation and saw her maybe twice while her parents were alive, but Ethel wasn't etched into her mind as the doting aunt who she spent time with on the weekends.

The day her parents passed away, Imani wouldn't have had a clue it happened had it not been for Ethel coming to her school that day. Principal Smith called Imani into his office over the intercom just before lunch, a rare occurrence for a quiet student like her. Once she arrived, Mr. Smith gave Imani a small smile, but looked like he had either been crying or was just on the verge of tears.

"Um, Imani," he said. "Someone is here to see you."

Mr. Smith stepped aside to allow her to see a woman, sitting on the bench next to the office door. Imani guessed she was around her mother's age, more or less, but dressed much more conservatively. Outfitted in brown slacks, ankle boots and a form fitting brown turtleneck, Ethel's honey brown skin was the exact color match of her attire and the only item that stood out was her bright red paisley scarf. The scarf around her neck caught Imani's attention, allowing her eyes to trail up her face. The older woman smiled as well, revealing an appearance that looked so strange, but reassuringly familiar.

"Hi, Imani," she said with a swallow. The woman moved herself over, making even more room on an otherwise empty bench, and patted lightly on the surface.

"Whenever you're comfortable, you can have a seat. But, I'm pretty sure you'd like to know who I am first? Haven't seen you since you were a baby."

Imani blinked before setting her gaze back on Mr. Smith.

"Am I in trouble?" she asked.

Mr. Smith took a breath, closing his eyes in disbelief that she'd even ask that question. But, now she knew that the sympathy was all over his face as well. She really had no clue what was going on or that her life was about to change drastically.

"Not at all, Imani," he said. "Not at all."

Aunt Ethel let about a month of the summer go by with Imani living in her home for the first time before she started enforcing rules on her niece without much explanation. During the remaining three years of middle school, her Aunt's rules didn't faze her much. But, it wasn't until she got into high school that some of them - especially her asinine curfew of 8pm - weren't adding up. While a few of Imani's classmates were going out on dates, going to the movies and hanging out at the mall, Imani was relegated to her Aunt's one-family home. She was only allowed to watch Hallmark movies and listen to gospel music like Kirk Franklin and the Winans Family, if she wanted a little rhythm with her blues.

Imani didn't want to break rules because she was boy crazy or ready to sneak off to follow friends at a house party. According to Aunt Ethel, it was worse than that.

"You gotta learn to stop following people around, Imani," her aunt complained to her one day, shaking her head with a hand on her hip. "If a friend told you to jump off a cliff, would you do it?"

And, to Imani's detriment, back then anyway, she most certainly would have.

All because she at least had a friend who did the convincing. Especially after her parents died, Imani craved people, often maneuvering in and out of friend groups just for the thought of belonging to someone or something that superseded her grief. And, she was good at maneuvering, too, mainly because

# A Month of Sundays

she was more of a listener than a talker. Girls at school would spill their guts out to her, revealing the boy they lost their virginity to or the exam they cheated on to get the grade they did, and boys toggled between both liking and resenting her quiet nature. But, Imani wouldn't divulge anyone's secrets thus she was a physical trove for everyone's confessions. And, all those secrets went into her art, of course. She could communicate the deepest secrets in her art without many people knowing the exact meaning of her work at all. Art was her secret weapon whereas words were the tools she didn't have much of a handle on.

Imani recognized that words were what got her caught up with DeAndre in the first place. His words played in her head like a song, especially because they felt so honest, true and good to hear. Forget coffee...once she heard his voice in the morning, it kept her vibrant for at least the first half of her day.

But right now, Imani barely had any words to say to Ethel, who looked up at her from across the kitchen table. The two had just finished praying over Ethel's makeshift Italian feast of angel hair spaghetti with ground turkey meatballs and garlic bread. The salad tossed in the ceramic bowl at the middle of the table was for dietary balance.

"You've missed church for the past month," Ethel said, shaking her head, "and you didn't answer any of my phone calls until last week when you decided to tell me you're engaged to someone I had no idea you even knew. Now..."

She chuckled, sarcastically. "Isn't that somethin'?"

Imani closed her eyes, huffing with annoyance. Everything her Aunt couldn't tell her over the phone, Imani knew she was going to hear that and more once she saw her.

Ethel gestured to Imani's hand with a fork.

"Why would he even get you a ring that big? You work in the city for God's sake. Unless you've quit that too?"

"No, Auntie, I haven't."

Imani looked down at her hand, cradling it protectively. "I don't even...wear it to work, just when I'm with him."

"You plan on returning to church? You've already let a breakup and this man keep you distracted from your source...Is he even saved?"

"Auntie," Imani sighed, looking at her with an exasperated expression.

They had never discussed what attending church would be like once they were married nor did Imani want him to feel any pressure to go along with it just because of her. Imani made it clear to him that God and her prayer life were important to her but, whatever DeAndre decided about God would be his personal decision.

"I'm coming back," she started. "I just...gotta get a few things sorted out... and, him coming with me isn't completely off the table."

"Oh, okay. Hope you told him there's no special section for visitors. He has to sit in the pews like everyone else."

Imani rolled her eyes. "He's not like that."

"So, enlighten me. What is he like? I'm not talking about what he *looks* like or what he *has* either."

Imani thought back to the past month they'd spent betrothed. She was still learning so much about him - his likes, his ticks and what drove him to have this force that Imani had never experienced with anyone else she'd ever met. He had so much going on around him ...so much he acquired yet, he still made her feel like this prize he was so grateful to actually have within his grasp. Like he knew at any moment, she could walk away from this entire thing - a thought she couldn't fathom neither though he didn't seem to realize that, so he savored every new moment with her that he could. Imani wasn't sure if this kind of admiration for her would end and was aware of the ebbs and flows in any relationship, but each day he was with her felt like he was seeing her anew all over again.

As usual, Imani couldn't put what she thought of him into words.

"You're just like your father," Ethel said after Imani didn't say anything. "Always chasing another thrill."

Ethel shook her head, cutting into one of her meatballs.

Imani rubbed her hand over forearm, casting her eyes down on Ethel's wood floors.

"He's not just a thrill, Auntie. I really love him."

Ethel scoffed, taking her glasses off to wipe the lens with the corner of her sleeve. Imani knew she sounded like a teenager trying to convince her parents about the boy blasting love songs with his boombox beneath her bedroom window, but she truly was that far gone for DeAndre. Once Imani succumbed to her feelings, there was no turning back as she ran headfirst with open arms, straight to him. Besides, it felt so right. Imani never knew she could feel so empowered simply by loving someone.

"You don't love him, Imani," Ethel said. "You don't even know him...GAH-lee...just falling into another trap of your own lust, just like you did with–"

"If you say his name," she said, her eyes affixed on Ethel, "I swear I'll leave immediately."

The fire in Ethel's eyes subdued, softening only slightly.

"This...love that you think you have, Imani, is on sinking sand. There's nothing of substance in this and the fact that you're doing all of this...wedding...in a matter of weeks...for his schedule?"

"He didn't tie my hands behind my back, forcing me to marry him, Auntie. I'm a grown woman, making my own decisions."

Imani inhaled, sounding ten times more confident than she actually felt. She knew how soon the wedding was and had her own minor doubts. She just kept reminding herself that it felt right. There wasn't much of a courtship, similar to the relationship she had with Michael. Then again, look at how that turned out with all the time that passed.

Plus, she trusted DeAndre. There were couples she knew through Ethel and at church who said they dated for a few years and still wound up separated or divorced - all under the guise that trust wasn't there from the beginning. Imani knew the timing of being together was irrelevant when it came to the success of marriage.

"I can't even believe you're being such a fool in all of this."

Imani looked at her, feeling like Ethel just cut her with a knife.

"What did you just say to me?"

"I spent more than fifteen years trying to keep you focused on making the right choices for your life. You had such a sure, reliable, steadfast husband-to-be in Michael. He was kind to you, respectful of you despite your past, and he wanted to honor you properly. Yet, you willingly drop that because of..."

Ethel raised her hands.

"A guy from Port Springs...with some money and a little bit of flash. It's not real, Imani. Wake up."

Imani stared mournfully; her eyes narrowed at her Aunt's venom.

"I don't know...who hurt you, Auntie. I'm so sorry that you can't be happy for me, and for your information, DeAndre is all those things to me now. You really think I would run to someone who didn't have at least a baseline of respect for me?"

"You did somethin' similar before," Ethel said, taking a bite.

Imani's teeth clenched. This was now Ethel's second time making reference to him in conversation and Imani wasn't staying to give her a third chance either. She slammed her fork down before standing up, the chair legs scraping against the floor.

Ethel cut her eyes at Imani's plate.

"I know you're not about to waste this food..."

"I'm not gonna sit up here and allow you to talk to me like this. I thought I'd be able to invite you to the wedding—"

Ethel pushed her chin to her neck, looking at Imani over her glasses.

"Invite me to the wedding? I wouldn't pay to be a witness to a mockery of God's institution, no matter how much money is thrown at it. I'm not going to that."

"Okay, Auntie I hear you loud and clear... please, don't say that you're not coming to the wedding."

But, Ethel wasn't smiling, folding her arms in front of her. Imani blinked at her incredulously before confusion laced her features.

"Wait, are you...serious?" she asked.

This entire conversation went to hell in a hand-basket quickly, but Imani didn't think her Aunt - her only family left - would refuse to come to her wedding.

"When have I ever not been?"

The two held eye contact, neither one of them turning away.

"Auntie," she croaked, her eyes suddenly filling with tears. Her knees buckled, making her reach for the back of the chair she just sat in.

"Who's gonna be there...for my day...for me?"

"You should've thought of that before you made such a selfish decision."

Imani took a shaky breath, turning her back to the woman who was the closest thing to a mom for her. She couldn't believe she was actually making her choose.

## A Month of Sundays

"I'll always need you, Auntie," she said, wiping under her eyes.

Without another word, Imani grabbed her jacket and headed out, letting the steel metal door slam behind her.

# Chapter 28
# Never Hiding

Imani wouldn't describe herself as much of a crier, but she was an entire blabbering ball of tears parked up at her apartment with DeAndre on FaceTime in the car. She planned on just shooting him a quick text once she returned home from Ethel's, but the seeds of doubt her Aunt planted and the venom of hurt she spilled all over her carpet for Imani to see wouldn't go away. Over the years she lived with Ethel, even when she came back almost five years ago, Imani never felt her Aunt's righteous anger.

"I've never seen her so pissed before," she said to DeAndre, in between her tears. "It was like I was a stranger to her. She looked at me like the devil's spawn, telling me off about not coming to church and being with you. Baby... she said...she...she isn't coming to our wedding. She's not coming, your mom can barely have a conversation with me no matter how hard I try. DeAndre, is anyone on our side?"

With his head leaning on the back of his hand, DeAndre assessed Imani so hard she thought the call dropped because of a glitch in reception. But, it was only when he took a breath and blinked, his eyes falling in empathy, that Imani realized he was listening to her. He wasn't trying to give her a solution or say something that would make her feelings go away. Imani wasn't sure what she wanted him to say, but she appreciated him just being in this moment with her.

"I'm on our side," he said, after another pause. "I'll always be."

## A Month of Sundays

Imani calmed herself, nodding. "I'll always be on our side, too."

No matter how unsettled Ethel was about Imani's decision, Imani was clear about her choice of being with him. Nothing was going to change that.

"Can't say I know how you feel, baby," he said, placing a hand at the back of his neck. "But, I'm sorry it all went down like that for you."

Sitting in DeAndre's car, Imani looked out the window at the late afternoon. It was now after 5pm, but it was still early enough for a few people in the neighborhood to walk their dogs, jog and take a casual stroll in the area. Imani cast her gaze back at her phone, shaking her head with a chuckle.

"Yeah, me too."

"Gimme a few and I'll be over there," DeAndre said.

Imani's eyebrow dipped. "You don't have to–"

"I know, but I wanna see you. This time next year, I'm not gonna be able to just see you when I want to...so," he said, "just like you insist on *thanking* me, lemme insist on seeing you."

Imani smiled feeling the pang of his comment. Just like at brunch, the mention of his schedule always put her on edge. She wasn't oblivious to the demands of DeAndre's career nor was she upset with him over it. She just wasn't looking forward to the days when she'd miss him...there was no use in ever bringing that up, as it was inevitable. She either accepted all of him or not, and that aspect of his life was yet another thing she chose to accept.

Closing the door behind her, Imani called out to Kaylee, letting her know she was home and DeAndre would be over in a few minutes.

"Yeah, okay," Kaylee projected lazily, not stepping out of her room at all.

Imani had waited a few days after DeAndre proposed before dropping the news to Kaylee, as she – herself needed to process the fact that they were getting married. When Imani finally told her, though, her best friend's response was quieter than she had anticipated. Kaylee was far from the jealous type. She was always proclaiming opportunities that came Imani's way even before she knew of them standing behind her 100%. But the night Imani laid it out there, Kaylee had just smiled at her bedazzled finger, nodding with a weak "Oh, wow," before offering the shakiest "congratulations." They hadn't talked about the engagement or that night since.

After taking a much-needed shower to get herself recentered, Imani chose a simple black shirt with leggings and a lime green kimono that fell to her ankles. She examined herself in the mirror, chuckling at the absentminded thought of putting on lip gloss or adding blush to her cheeks.

*Girl, stop. This is not your wedding night.*

All she really wanted to do was sleep, but she would keep it cute just like this for her fiancé. DeAndre arrived shortly after and the two settled near the small square table that Imani found at someone's front yard sale when she first moved here. Kaylee always said she could find gold in a pile of trash, no matter how small. And, seeing DeAndre sit at the table now, Imani understood just how miniature her cherished find really was.

"...You shouldn't be lettin' anyone keep you from what's most important to you," he said, his gaze steady on Imani.

They were still talking about her visit with Ethel earlier and even though DeAndre understood Imani's hurt, he did agree with Ethel's observation of hiding behind her decisions. So what if she made a choice that had people talking? They were always going to do that anyway, doesn't mean she had to stay away from her priority...her faith.

Imani let her head hang to the side, reaching her hand across the table to stroke the side of his cheek.

"What if clown school was important to me?" she smirked. She didn't want to keep harping on Ethel or the upsetting mood the entire visit placed her in.

"Then...we makin' sure you're registered for every session...with the flyest clown suit, and those big ass shoes."

Imani laughed so hard tears were forming in her eyes.

"...have you pushin' a tricked out clown wagon and everything," he said.

Even though Imani and DeAndre had their fair share of differences, Imani always found that he rallied behind her, ready and willing to convince her to go with what was in her heart.

"You know what?" he asked, stretching out his arms in front of him before folding them again. "I'd like to go tomorrow."

"You? To church?" she asked, her eyebrows lifting.

He chuckled, placing a hand at his chest.

"Damn baby, tell me how you really feel?"

## A Month of Sundays

"No! I mean..." Imani breathed. "You never mentioned wanting to before and I don't want you to think you have to go only for me."

"I got you," he shrugged. "I don't know - I'm curious...Think my heathen ass needs that good Word anyway."

"Don't claim that."

If she was being honest, Imani thought DeAndre displayed more Christ-like qualities in a matter of weeks than many self-proclaimed Christians did on a Sunday after service.

Looking down at their interlaced fingers on the table, Imani stroked his finger on top of hers before the two engaged in a silly thumb war. A few moments later, they got up from the small square table before he pulled her closer to him. When she stood between him and the table, DeAndre rested two hands on it, caging her in as he seemed to love to do.

"Lemme get out of here, then," he said, stealing a quick glance at her lips, "You a'ight?"

She smiled and nodded, his familiar scent warming her insides. He looked down at her with his eyes squinted and a smirk that made her heart accelerate. All this man had to do was say "jump" and she'd start hopping on one foot, hitting her head against the ceiling fan, risking a concussion like an idiot.

"I am now," she said, pulling the strings of his hoodie.

Slippers were heard dragging against the hardwood floor before they stopped. Placing her hands on DeAndre's arms, Imani turned around to find Kaylee meeting her gaze.

"Oh, sorry," she said. "Am I interrupting?"

She pulled her long cardigan closer to her frame as Imani faced Kaylee head on with DeAndre now at her right side and his hand on her lower back.

"No, not at all," Imani smiled.

"Yo Kaylee," DeAndre said. "I'm picking up Imani for church tomorrow. Open invitation if you want to ride with us?"

Kaylee stood for a moment, eyes widening as round as her curls.

"Oh wow," saying her now famous phrase, "Uh...yeah. Ok, I'll go with you guys."

She looked between the two of them before looking at DeAndre again, face serious.

"Thank you."

DeAndre's cheeks lifted. "No problem."

Imani walked DeAndre to the door a second later. Leaning his hand against the doorway, he snuck a kiss on Imani's cheek before playfully biting into it.

"See you tomorrow," she said.

Imani turned from the closed door to find Kaylee still standing in the same place, quickly averting her gaze. She was clearly observing them and Imani was getting impatient with this shift in her energy.

"Kaylee," she sighed, her head tilted with her hands on her hips. "I know this is all...surprising–"

"No...no...Imani," she shook her head. "It's fine. It's okay."

"It's not, though, I really don't want or need this to become an issue between us. You haven't said anything to me about any of this."

The two best friends held each other's gaze before Kaylee sighed, shoulders dropping.

"'Mani, okay look," she started. "You're all the way grown. So, you can just tell me to mind my business. It's just...I...don't want to see you get hurt."

"I know," Imani nodded.

"I mean, the last time I saw him - the first time I met him was at the party not even six months ago."

"I know."

"It's just...so sudden," Kaylee scratched the top of her curls. "Like, were y'all seeing each other while you were with Michael? For real...no judgment, either."

Imani blinked.

"No. Well," biting at her bottom lip, "would you believe me if I said it was complicated? I always had feelings for DeAndre. I just wasn't honest with myself. And..."

"Your heart couldn't let him go," Kaylee stated.

Imani nodded, warming to the exact idea she wasn't even able to articulate out loud. When she ended things with Michael, she had honestly felt relieved, which made her feel guilty that it was that easy to just let go of over four years of a relationship. But, the feeling she felt saying "yes" to DeAndre was unimaginable. She had never felt so at ease.

## A Month of Sundays

Kaylee smiled at her, before settling her gaze around their apartment. With her lips still twisted into a smile, she put her own hands on her hips.

"He is...really, really fine," she said.

Imani chuckled, rolling her eyes.

"Yeah, he is," she said, before growing serious. "But, he's more than that too...ya' know?"

Kaylee's eyes met hers. "I know."

The two rushed towards each other at the same time, embracing in the tightest hug that burst the bubble of tension that had lingered between them for weeks. Imani didn't have much family, but Kaylee was easily her sister, perfectly connected by God himself.

"I'll always have your back Mani," Kaylee said.

A tear fell against Imani's cheek as the two pulled away from each other. Kaylee was a puddle of tears at this point, wiping underneath her eyes with her knuckles.

"Are our periods synced? Jesus," she laughed. "We're such girls."

Imani chuckled, patting under her eyes as well until Kaylee pulled her left hand to her face.

"But this ring!" her eyes, widening. "Forget Pinterest. I didn't even know this cut existed."

The two examined the intricacies of the diamond as Imani finally rested in the fact that her sister – her Maid of Honor, if Kaylee accepted - was one of the few people she considered family who'd be there for her wedding day and in life.

Kaylee looked up from ogling Imani's hand and sighed.

"Hopefully, it doesn't take me forever to get a new roomie who isn't crazy," she smirked. "It took forever to get you. Though, you're irreplaceable."

Imani stayed silent, thinking about the conversation she had with DeAndre about making sure Kaylee wouldn't be left to shoulder the rest of the lease on her own. She initially asked if he could help pay up until the end of the lease. But the check Imani gave to Luis last week from DeAndre covered until the end of the current agreement and an additional year.

"*Kinda messed up that I'm stealing you in the middle of a lease. I'd hate me, too,*" he'd said.

"You know how many applications I went through before finding you?" Kaylee laughed.

"It was actually terrifying. People are nuts, 'Mani."

"I'll help you out where I can," she smiled, pinching Kaylee's cheeks playfully. "You'll be fine."

Kaylee nodded, running her fingers through her curls.

"Sis?!" Kaylee yelled suddenly, taking her hands out of her hair and holding onto Imani's shoulders. Chuckling to herself, Imani kept her body loose as Kaylee jerked her from side to side, making her dizzy.

"You're getting married!"

∽

Imani used to think there was nothing more distracting than trying to hear Pastor Coleman's sermon while people behind her were chatting away in their seats, until she showed up to service with her fiancé for the very first time.

DeAndre arrived at the apartment this morning at the exact time he said he would - punctual, as usual. Imani was far from prompt and took much longer than normal to get ready, annoyed at how indecisive she was with everything from what she was wearing to her lip color to her shoes. She was a ball of nerves, still jolted by her Aunt's words last night and even more anxious about the elephant in the room - Michael.

Part of Imani not going to church for the past few weeks was to avoid seeing her Aunt – true, but she was equally as mortified to see her ex-boyfriend, his family, and all of the many mutual acquaintances who'd bet every dollar they tithed, on the divine success of Imani and Michael's relationship. Michael's inner circle and most of the church knew about their breakup by now, she was sure. But, the only thing Michael may not know about was who Imani moved on to and just how quickly. Michael wasn't on social media so he wouldn't have seen the few blurry pictures that DeAndre had posted of Imani on his Instagram.

The bottom line was that she was willingly stepping back into church, the

## A Month of Sundays

lion's den, with a ring and the man who gave it to her. Without taking another glance in the mirror, Imani walked out of her room with as much confidence as she could pull together. She fought to stay calm once she was in eyeshot of the kitchen, where DeAndre was sitting on one of the bar stools. Kaylee, who had let him inside, looked at Imani with brows raised and the corners of her mouth turned downward, giving her best friend a telepathic high-five.

Dressed in a dark blue suit that shielded his broad shoulders and slim frame, DeAndre looked nothing short of delectable and left very little to Imani's very vivid imagination. He was covered from head to toe, but Imani realized she'd never grow tired of seeing him fill out a suit. Not today...not when he proposed...probably not ever. This was just a regular Sunday - Lord knows how good he would look on their wedding day.

"You shinin' bright, baby," he complimented, stepping out of his seat to give Imani a hug and a quick kiss on the lips. The compliment made her suddenly aware of her own outfit, a form-fitting black and purple midi dress that she felt good in. It wasn't as if she was walking out the door looking like she was going to the grocery store, for God's sake.

"Ready to go?"

On the ride to church while Kaylee talked DeAndre's ear off, Imani did multiple rounds of mental gymnastics, her mind concocting all the scenarios that could potentially play out once they showed up. Kid's Day was one thing, but no public figure as prominent as DeAndre had made an appearance at the actual church for years. The last person to even raise an eyebrow was a Clark sister, and she visited to perform on behalf of one of The Coleman's family friends. Having him at a New Life service was bound to be a totally different set of circumstances.

As she walked through the church lobby with DeAndre holding her hand and Trey trailing behind, Imani saw the lights of recognition twinkle across members' faces as soon as they laid eyes on him. Peers of Imani's who hadn't spoken to her since she first visited the church were openly smiling and waving at her as if they knew each other. Older members who Imani admired for their unshakable resolve in Christ, openly scanned DeAndre from head to toe, looking at him like a seared piece of meat as they waved their paper-thin fans across their chests. The vestibule was known to be busy just before service, but today all of the talking and chattering echoed through the chambers with much more zeal.

DeAndre took it all in stride, keeping most of his attention ahead of him and offering the occasional hint of a smile to those who made their ogling more obvious. Something Imani admired about DeAndre, even before he showed up to Artgo all those months ago, garnering a much smaller dose of attention, was that he wasn't a prisoner of his own notoriety. Instead of opting to stay inside or expecting special treatment when they went out, he'd just bring Trey and go with the flow, aware of the hoopla his presence could bring but not preventing himself from living his life. In some of their first conversations since they were engaged, DeAndre told Imani he was ready to do all of his living with her.

Once the four stepped through the church doors, an usher who Imani never saw crack a smile was now beaming from ear to ear, escorting them to the middle section of the church. Imani chose not to sit at the front of the church, but they also wouldn't be totally out of sight, neither. The usher finally stopped, gesturing his hand to four vacant seats in the middle of a row. Praise and worship commenced after a few minutes, followed by Pastor Coleman's encouraging sermon.

Service moved quickly after that.

With the congregation now clapping after Pastor Coleman's benediction, Imani was pulled out of her thoughts. She hadn't learned not one lesson from his sermon today but released a sigh of relief that they had survived it without any awkward run-ins with her ex or her Aunt. Everyone in their row stood, gathering their belongings to talk to friends and fellow churchgoers. Imani, got up from her seat and placing her Bible in her tote, glanced at DeAndre who was still seated. His eyes were cast down at the chair in front of him, looking as if he was mentally on another planet.

"Are you okay?" Imani asked, placing a hand on his knee, sitting back down again.

He looked over at her, solemn at first before pulling up a corner of his mouth.

"I'm just thinkin' that's all."

## A Month of Sundays

She chuckled, assessing how quiet he suddenly seemed.

"Well, alright," her eyebrows wrinkled. "Are you thinking of anything specific?"

"Are you happy?" he asked, his stare unwavering.

Imani's face relaxed.

"Absolutely. You don't think I am?"

"I do," he took a breath. "I don't want you to keep yourself from this...from growing here because of me. It's a vibe."

"Yeah," Imani smiled. "It is."

Pulling her gaze away from his, Imani just so happened to look ahead of her, meeting Aunt Ethel's squinted eyes. She was in the front row, talking with her girlfriends while simultaneously spewing curses under her breath, Imani assumed. Ethel never hid her emotions from anyone, so what made Imani ever think she'd do that now, even with all of her niece's cards on the table?

"This is gonna be worse if I don't go and talk to her," Imani said.

"I'm going with you," he said, wiping his shoulder haphazardly.

"D, baby-"

"I'm already cool with your sister," he gestured to Kaylee who was trying to get a laugh out of Trey. "...I can't meet my Aunt?"

Despite the assumptions Ethel made about DeAndre mere hours ago, Imani realized they were literally just that. The two hadn't met each other before and there wasn't a more opportune time for formal introductions.

Imani narrowed her own gaze at him before releasing a smile she couldn't help. The mention of Kaylee as her sister, a title they bestowed on each other, was special to her regardless of the array of siblings Kaylee had.

"Okay, you can," she said. "Your charm can be disarming sometimes, you know that?"

DeAndre smiled.

"You disarm me a *lot* of times," he admitted, inching his head behind Imani, giving her a more than generous once over.

Biting the bottom corner of her lip, Imani rolled her eyes, praying over her thoughts on him, thankful that he was hers now.

She walked towards Ethel immediately upon leaving their aisle, but it wasn't until she was mere inches from her that DeAndre pulled her gently toward him.

"I'll introduce myself."

Stepping to his side, Imani looked at Aunt Ethel's friends, settling their attention on Imani and DeAndre, as they arrived at the first row of the church. Ethel was sitting down still, her hands folded over her prayer cloth and legs crossed at the ankles.

"Hi Sister Pearl, Sister Reed, Ms. Louise," Imani nodded to each of them with a smile before looking at Ethel.

"Did you enjoy service, Auntie?"

"I always do...in the household of God. Praise the Lord. Glad you finally decided to join us."

*Here we go.* Imani smiled, to keep from rolling her eyes, when she felt DeAndre move himself forward.

"How you doin,' Ms. Ethel?" he asked, smiling so wide that his forehead creased. With his long arms outstretched, he shifted forward for a hug, giving her a cordial kiss on the cheek. DeAndre then sat next to her, not breaking his gaze on her.

"It's so good to meet you," he continued. "I want to tell you that anyone who's as special to Imani as you are will always be important to me."

Looking at the expression of dismay slowly melting off of Aunt Ethel's face in real time, Imani was reminded of the effect DeAndre had on pretty much everyone.

*I get it Auntie,* she smirked.

"Amen," Ethel said, giving him an inquisitive side eye. "I hope you were blessed by the message, young man, since you'll be...leading a family in the next few months."

"It was a blessing," DeAndre nodded before looking at Imani, "and, I'm just honored she's choosing me to do it."

Imani stared at him, all but ready to climb on his lap and tongue him down right in front of her aunt and her Bingo buddies.

"DeAndre," she said, gesturing to the church doors. "We should go. Kaylee wants to order takeout from this restaurant that gets packed around this time."

"You can start heading out. I'll catch up in a little bit," he said.

## A Month of Sundays

DeAndre stood up and gave Imani a kiss on the cheek before pulling his attention back to Ethel, sitting down next to her again. Her friends stared, eyes wide, at the entire interaction as Imani went to give her aunt a hug.

Ethel, with her arms still in place, was a block of stone staring up at her.

"Be good," Ethel said in her ear. Imani thought she had finally convinced her to maybe give DeAndre a chance, especially since she just saw how in tune he was with her. He obviously wanted to make a good impression.

But, when Imani straightened herself, Ethel's face was still serious.

"I love you, girl," she whispered, a hint of sadness in her eyes.

Imani walked out of the church doors, finding Kaylee talking in the lobby with a friend of hers from the choir.

"'Mani," Kaylee said, gesturing her over, "Brittany needs someone to do a portrait for her son's fifth birthday and I thought of you."

Imani was making her way over to them when she heard commotion from behind her.

"Let me say something to her!"

She turned, placing her hand on her chest, when she saw Michael marching towards her after two other church members tried holding him back. DeAndre and Trey were suddenly nearby and they stepped in front of Imani protectively, blocking him from getting any closer.

"This is what you've been busy with?" Michael asked, his gaze shifting from Imani to DeAndre then to her hand, her diamond suddenly feeling as heavy as stone.

"Yo, if you got an issue," DeAndre said, pointing his way, "You could most definitely say it to me."

Michael laughed sardonically, shaking his head but staying in place.

"Shouldn't even be surprised."

He looked ahead of DeAndre and Trey, staring directly at Imani. "Hope it was worth it to you."

Before she could respond, she watched Michael turn in the opposite direction, pushing open the doors that led to the church leadership offices.

On their way back to the apartment with bags of to-go brunch food in tow, Imani couldn't get the last image of Michael out of her mind. She knew he'd still be hurt – seems like they had just started premarital classes before Imani called it quits. She didn't expect how drastically it would affect him within a matter of weeks. His lightheartedness, and the hope that once dominated his eyes was now all but gone and replaced with a weary gaze like that of a zombie.

Looking at Michael reminded Imani, yet again, that she was the villain in someone else's story.

# Chapter 29
# A Line Drawn in the Sand

"So, you like it?"

DeAndre asked, glancing from his laptop back to Imani, who was assessing his screen with her elbows on his desk. They were in his office looking at mock-ups of the limited-edition sneaker, he collaborated with Elite Athletics on, that would make its debut sometime next year. It was part of the first round of several meetings he had to get done with the company, but DeAndre was glad that, just like this process, everything in his life was moving forward.

After the emotional few weeks they had, informing their respective relatives about the wedding - now just shy of a week away, their days were even busier. Imani was balancing her job and putting the finishing touches on projects for a handful of clients she wanted to take on just before the wedding, while DeAndre was dealing with several meetings with the Tennis League and brands for sponsorships.

Imani was here at the house, taking a break from her soon-to-be-old apartment where she was packing up her belongings. It was a task DeAndre reminded her wouldn't be as stressful once she let the organizers and movers he hired do their job. But, Imani insisted on packing everything herself, placing her precious art supplies and equipment a certain way, in specific boxes before letting the movers handle the physical labor.

"These are cool," she said, pointing to the sneakers with the green and black color-ways. "The texture adds a nice touch."

Imani was completely casual today in green Crocs, oversized jeans with large holes taking up half the pants leg, a cropped tie-dyed t-shirt with Beyoncé's album cover on it and oversized thin-rimmed frames which Imani called her "personality glasses." DeAndre was always confused as to why women wore glasses meant for prescription lenses, but his fiancé still looked fly as shit.

"These look good," she nodded, the laptop screen reflected in both lenses.

There was a beat of silence afterwards that persisted longer than needed and it wasn't the first time today that Imani seemed *too* quiet. When she first arrived with a few more of her art supplies, Imani greeted him with a half-ass hug and kiss. He figured the move was starting to weigh on her, and opted to leave her be unless she needed any sort of help but, a few hours had passed.

"That's it?" he asked.

He wasn't sure what kind of reaction he was expecting from her, but DeAndre learned early on that Imani didn't hold back her excitement for those she cared about.

Something wasn't adding up.

"Yeah, I mean," she said. "It seems like a lot has gone into the color-ways and logo placement and everything," she said. "You should be proud, baby."

She pecked him on the cheek as she headed out his office. She had completely shut down and checked out.

"Yo," he said, halting her. "Baby, what's up?"

She turned, looking at him like she was trying to decide if she wanted to say something or not.

"Nothing's up."

One of the things that DeAndre couldn't stand was being around people who weren't honest with him. Blatant dishonesty was one thing, but subtle omission of the truth was like paper cuts. If anyone had been harboring any issues, he'd prefer for them to just say it for it to be resolved. There was a resolution for everything. He was going to let Imani slide right now and figured she'd get comfortable in due time.

"I can't read your mind," he chose to say.

Imani pushed her head up to the ceiling in exasperation.

## A Month of Sundays

"When do you want me to sign your pre-nup?"

That was unexpected.

"What?"

"Your pre-nup? The document that protects both parties' assets–"

"Nah, I know what it is, Imani…"

He shook his head, dazed in disbelief. Had he mentioned it? He knows he didn't say anything to her about it…did he?

"Where's this coming from?"

He leaned closer in his seat, this time giving her his full attention. Of course he had thought about a pre-nup. What logical person in his position wouldn't?

As soon as he told his team about their engagement, the dust hadn't even settled before they called him and his lawyers into a meeting to discuss the very "assets" that Imani had been referring to now. They broke it down to him chart by chart, line by line about the properties, multiple streams of income and overall estate he was protecting…just in case things in their marriage went "left," just to protect what he was already coming into the marriage with. But, despite all of that, all of the figures, projections, legal language fine-tuned to the smallest detail, something about it didn't sit right with him.

DeAndre didn't fail at anything. So, why would he agree to sign something that, by his standards, already alluded to the demise of his marriage?

"I don't know," she said, brushing her hand over her short pink curls. "I just…got to thinking about what'd be best business-wise and it just makes sense."

DeAndre sat back, placing his hands on his thighs.

"Is it something you want to sign?"

"I would," she said, looking at him, eyes wide.

His eyes narrowed, watching her take a breath.

"We can't just live off of emotions," she continued. "At some point, we gotta think this through and take counsel."

"Have you spoken to anyone?"

Imani folded her arms and pursed her lips.

"Not exactly, but I heard your mom–"

That was all he needed to hear.

Before he could even think, DeAndre pushed himself up from his seat and bolted past Imani, out of the office, across the hall, down the stairs, and through the living room. He couldn't even hear anything else, not even tracking if Imani was following behind him or not. Once he got to the den, he saw Andele and his aunt sharing cocktails at one of the tables, dressed in expensive basic-ass clothes that were probably bought on his dime, one way or another. It was time to set shit straight once and for all.

"Aye, Andele," he said. This wasn't a confrontation between a mom and his son, he had to deal with her as his *former* publicist.

Andele and his aunt stopped all conversation, looking over at DeAndre who pulled up a chair, sat down and leaned over the table with his hands folded.

"Let's get this straight right here, right now..."

Whatever Andele had said about pre-nups more than likely didn't take Imani's best interest into consideration and shielded DeAndre's assets from any digging Andele thought she could get away with, without one. For what it was worth, DeAndre didn't throw all caution to the wind. In the smallest chance things didn't work out he'd be fine, but Imani would be more than taken care of, even without popping out a kid, to the point that someone would advise her to marry him just *to* divorce him.

"I know you have an opinion of Imani, and frankly I don't give a damn what it is. But, what you're not gonna do is put doubt in her head about issues that have nothing to do with you."

He just so happened to glance ahead, noticing Imani standing closest to the yard's entrance, looking like she wanted to stick her entire body into the nearest hole.

"Imani, who's always considered *you,* is gonna be *my* wife...your daughter-in-law, in less than a week. I'm not gettin' into what kinda relationship you two could have 'cause that ain't got nothin' to do with me. But, she's the woman of this house which means you will respect her, especially when I'm up in here. So, whatever you gotta do to get yourself together about that, do it.... A'ight?"

This woman didn't even have his last name yet, but the earnestness he felt for Imani seemed to make up for the nonchalance he had with every woman he was with before her. When it came to Imani, it was getting harder and harder for DeAndre to let anything slide. First, it was not being able to say much of anything when Michael's weasel-ass came at her a few Sundays back. Then, there was the tension she felt from her aunt - an area he knew wasn't really in his place to address.

But, anyone that was on his side of the aisle had to be clear – he would make sure of it.

Andele looked at him, shooting daggers into his eyes like any Black mother would. In the deep recesses of his mind, he knew he was talking to her crazy, but Andele would never bite the hand that fed her. That was something she taught him.

Her head barely moved before she took another sip of her cocktail, but her eyes acquiesced. Satisfied enough, DeAndre walked out of the den, confident he'd never have to bring this up ever again.

~

Imani stood in the den, frozen from what she had just witnessed. Although she hadn't been given the privilege to spend a lot of time with her own parents, she knew to never challenge what they had to say, even if she didn't agree. So witnessing DeAndre just tear his mother a new one like she was a child herself was shocking.

"Andele..." Imani started, walking towards her.

Both Andele and DeAndre's aunt stood from the table when Andele raised her hand, closing her eyes for a moment to halt any further discussion. Without a word, the two walked past Imani, throwing daggers of fire at her with their eyes.

She wasn't going to say anything to DeAndre about what she overheard, mainly because she was willing to bring up the whole pre-nuptial agreement herself. The wedding was in a week and DeAndre hadn't said anything about it. But, something about the way Andele discussed Imani signing a pre-nup felt like she was betting on their divorce.

*"I think the girl will do all she can to keep the peace,"* she had said. *"She's quiet enough, but so are most of those women...all I know is, that pre-nup better be signed and delivered, for her own sake."*

Imani wasn't surprised by Andele's doubt about her and her relationship with her son. She understood that all his mom wanted to do was make sure DeAndre's estate, that he had worked so hard for was protected, as any mother would. That had to be it. But, even Imani had to admit that Andele's comment had an effect on her. She was ready to sign the pre-nup if she had to, but she couldn't ignore the doubt in her mind that was growing, which already stemmed from the speed with which their relationship had advanced in the first place. DeAndre was the most passionate man she'd ever been with, even without sex, but all passion eventually fizzled out. She knew that firsthand. Would he eventually get bored, look elsewhere and decide it wasn't going to work anymore?

If he did, realistically, he'd be fine while Imani would be the blemish on his life that would take time to remove.

Imani went through her fair share of heartbreak in her life and knew that a heartbreak from him was one she didn't think she'd fully recover from.

Walking through the dining room, Imani spotted DeAndre leaning on the kitchen island, eyes on his phone as the chef chopped produce for the week's meals. She stopped in front of him with her arms folded, waiting for him to acknowledge her.

"You didn't have to curse your mom out of a job, D."

As his shoulders sagged, DeAndre pinched the inner corners of his eyes and chuckled.

"Yeah, that was just the final straw after a lot of other things." He stretched his arms before folding them, his forearms flexed.

Imani's gaze fell to Sebastian chopping onions with the precision of a samurai.

"I just want to make sure we have each other's best interest in mind for the future."

"And, you don't think I have your future interest in mind?" he asked.

Imani watched him, letting the words that he didn't say sink in. If she didn't think he did, then why was she marrying him?

"For real," DeAndre continued. "We can sign the pre-nup if it makes you comfortable. I could get Rick to send it over and arrange representation for you. No harm, no foul."

## A Month of Sundays

Imani remembered helping her church with community service one day when she and Sister Linda, one of the soloists in the choir, had a conversation. She wasn't sure how the topic shifted to marriage, but Sister Linda was a recent divorcee who returned to the church shortly after it was finalized.

*"Sister Imani, my ex had become, like a shell of himself. It was like all love had vanished after 25 years. He said, 'Even if I'm single, at least I'm not broke.' David always saw divorce as an option where I chose to not even entertain the possibility."*

Imani had never forgotten Sister Linda's words for the sheer fact that she agreed with her. Just like everyone, Imani wasn't oblivious to divorce, but she genuinely didn't think of it as an option once she got married. But did DeAndre?

"You never told me what you thought about it," she said, examining his handsome mahogany features closer..

"I can't predict the future," he said, "but, I sure as hell don't want to step into it with doubt. Those agreements…just…spell out doubt to me."

"I agree," she said.

DeAndre grabbed Imani's hands, placing them together, then pulled them to his lips.

"Plus, doesn't God want you to be one with your spouse or somethin' like that?" he asked. "I don't want to feel separated from you because you got yours and I got mine…when I'm supposed to be married to you, you know?"

"I know."

From DeAndre's reflective gaze, Imani could tell he was still trying to work out a way to justify why they most definitely weren't signing a pre-nuptial agreement. She smiled, already resolved in her mind that no other option was needed.

# Chapter 30
# A Union

Imani held in her breath for a second before releasing it, feeling her heart rise and fall in her chest.

"Okay, my beautiful bride...This is your moment. Open your eyes when you're ready."

Taking in Victoria's words, Imani didn't open her eyes right away, thinking of all she'd experienced this weekend so far, a stark difference from the tension she felt on all sides for weeks.

From the eight-hour flight to Paris to the gorgeous hotel that she, Melody and Kaylee were staying in up until today, Imani felt like she was in a dream. The opulent interior of the historic Parisian opera house that was today's venue which, from the quick glances Stephanie allowed her to see, included a grand staircase, several crystal chandeliers and a painting on the ceiling that Imani had only seen replicas of in a museum. Imani couldn't possibly imagine what else was in store for her today...her wedding day. She surmised that even her wildest dreams couldn't compare to DeAndre's vision.

Imani smelled the sweet aroma of white roses surrounding the perimeter of the room. DeAndre's face flashed across her mind, garnering a smile. They hadn't seen each other all week, not even via FaceTime, after Imani jokingly posed it as a challenge he wouldn't win. But, neither one of them caved and that only charged the anticipation she had of seeing her soon-to-be-husband. She couldn't believe she was going to see him for the first time at the altar, but she had to see herself first.

Standing on a circular platform in front of a 3-way mirror, Imani's eyes fluttered open. Her breath hitched at the sight of the long-sleeve French lace mermaid gown practically painted on her mahogany skin. With a flared train at the end, the gown completely covered her from head to toe, her waist accentuated with a thin diamond belt. Imani gasped, placing her hands in front of her mouth as the ends of her long sleeves cascaded to the ground, in waves of premium silk. Her veil, attached to a diamond encrusted hair comb tucked at the back of her short honey blonde hair, spilled over the platform and spread a few feet behind her, well past where Kaylee and Imani were standing. The drawings and rough sketches of this gown that Imani had discussed with Victoria over Zoom and virtual calls for weeks, didn't prepare her for seeing this creation...her creation...come to life.

Imani didn't quite feel like herself...her entire life up until this point flashed before her eyes - everything until this very real-life transition. Even with the number of times she was included in weddings as a bridesmaid or a guest, nothing compared to this moment that she spent so long thinking about - first with someone else and now with someone she still felt like her mind conjured up.

Was she *really* going through with this?

Imani turned around, facing her two bridesmaids dressed in black gowns, beaming with pride and tearing up beside her.

Kaylee, her large brown curls pinned up in a voluptuous bouffant, let out the first gasp.

"You look positively stunning, Imani," she said, mesmerized.

"Girl, no notes!" Melody snapped her fingers, her straight brunette bob moving just above her shoulders. "Beautiful, iconic, incredible! If DeAndre acts a fool, hell, I'll marry you."

Imani examined every angle of herself in the mirror, feeling just as beautiful as everyone said she looked. Everything was perfect, down to the wrap style black gowns Kaylee and Melody wore - uniquely styled for each of them.

Kaylee's was tied in a grecian style while Melody's was wrapped as a halter gown.

Yet she still felt so weird.

Placing a hand on her midsection, Imani felt her stomach boiling from the inside out as she fluffed the bottom of her dress behind her. She turned to her two gorgeous friends, not even realizing how much she needed them until now.

"Do you think I'm crazy for marrying this man I barely know?"

Imani's question came out of her in a flurry, halting everyone's movement.

She watched Melody and Kaylee pause and glance at each other, exchanging expressions of unease and hesitance.

"Oh my," Kaylee said, biting into the cuticle of her thumb. Her eyes searched Melody's for reassurance.

"Don't look at me," Melody responded, defensively. "I HAPPILY let Hosea get the milk for free before walking down the aisle to him as his SECOND baby mama...I can't judge you, sis."

"Yeah, but you and Sé were together for at least a year," Imani countered, staring down at the lace that covered the outside of her hands before plopping herself down on an upholstered chair to have a seat.

Victoria, the utmost professional, pressed her palms together in front of her, approaching Imani cautiously.

"Peace and many blessings to you, Imani," she said, simply. "I need to get out of here to catch my flight back but today...will be an overflow of blessings for you. Don't worry."

Imani offered her a smile as she, Kaylee and Melody bid their farewells.

As soon as the door closed, Kaylee sighed then nodded, clearing her throat and placing a hand on her chest.

"'Mani, crazy is so subjective," she said, staring at her through brown smokey eyes.

"I mean, my grandparents...who I'm always talking about, they've been together for like 50 years. They met and got married within two weeks of knowing each other..."

"It was also probably 1925," Melody said, her voice dropped a few octaves, "so I'd take that with a grain of salt."

Imani shook her head, gathering herself in her arms. She didn't need to be getting cold feet, especially not now. She loved this man, craved him to the fullest and felt so good being with him. Her heart was finally where it wanted to be and she knew that.

But would that be enough? Was this all too good to be true?

"Okay - okay, let's just take a minute y'all," Melody announced, raising both hands in surrender.

"Imani, do you like DeAndre?"

A sardonic chuckle spilled from Imani's peach tinted lips. "Mel, I wouldn't be here, if I didn't."

Melody shook her head.

"No, I'm not being funny," she said, sitting down beside Imani. "Take away all that he gives you - gifts, money, even all of the 'I love you's…can you look at him and say, 'I think I can actually…grocery shop with you'?"

Imani and DeAndre had never exactly been to the grocery store together, especially since they didn't live with each other yet. He'd likely insist on getting it delivered anyway.

She did remember being at his house one day when something occurred that was so trivial, so intimate, that it shook her a little.

She was painting mindlessly one weekend in the sunroom when the thought of doing her hair struck her like a light switched on. Imani was restless in that sense - she'd spend weeks not feeling like doing much, then suddenly have a burst of energy, ready to change her look, change her environment, switch everything up. The change, that day, had to start with her hair.

She first called Kaylee who typically helped her making sure she didn't miss coating parts of her hair in the back. She was prepared to meet Kaylee at their apartment when Kaylee let her know she had plans.

*"Sorry, girl,"* she said. *"This midterm is like half of my grade in this course and I really have to buckle down and study."*

Preparing herself to return to her spot but without help, Imani walked towards DeAndre's office to say goodbye when he was already at the front door, heading out himself.

"I thought you were sleeping," he said, motioning towards the room Imani had just came out of. "Didn't want to disturb you, but I was gonna dip out to pick us up somethin' to eat real quick. You need anything?"

## Jade Olivia

Imani was about to answer him, but something stopped her. The thought of actually admitting what she wanted to do, but would need assistance on, made her hesitate. It wasn't like she was a teenager asking her boyfriend to pick up menstrual pads. But, for some reason, this request still felt like she was propelling them into another level of their relationship.

"It's not that important..." she said. "I was gonna dye my hair and pick up some supplies to do it, but I'll figure it out later."

"Oh," he said, raising a brow. "You still tryna do it? You got somewhere to be tonight?"

Imani looked at him for a beat, trying to gauge whether or not he was going to make light of something so minor – 'girly shit'- but also something she really wanted to do.

She shook her head.

"I don't have anywhere to be," she said. "But...I...uh...I usually ask Kaylee to help me out with...with...umm..."

Why was she so nervous? She was mere months from marrying him and she was hesitating over some damn hair? She was in for a personal slice of hell if she was so concerned about a little thing like this.

"...with helping me dye...my hair since sometimes I miss little parts in the back." She scratched the back of her neck, suddenly feeling embarrassed.

DeAndre looked at her, moving his head to each side, assessing her. "Soooo...you need help...I'm assuming?"

Imani's eyes shifted slightly, but she met his gaze again.

"Yeah, I do."

He shrugged.

"Well, just gimme the list of what you need and I'll run and get it," he said, matter-of-factly. "At the beauty supply store, right?"

He might as well have seen her naked right then and there from how close this entire exchange felt. Imani texted him what she needed, including developer, bleach, color *and* purple shampoo, and he returned about an hour later, ready to report for duty. Once they were situated in one of his bathrooms, with Imani's full-on assembly line of hair products on top of the sink, she was glued to the mirror in no time - watching herself paint the front of her hair with the liquid bleach mixture while DeAndre - with his own silicone brush in hand, painted much more slowly in the back. Imani marveled at how precise and exacting he was with the whole job, taking the small level of instruction Imani provided beforehand much more seriously than she thought he would.

In the grand scheme of things, he could've brushed this off as personal maintenance that he could easily offer to pay for, saving them both time and resources. But he never complained how crazy this was or settled into a state of careless confusion, annoyed that he agreed to do this. The fact that he was so willing to humble himself just to go with it and be in the trenches with her, in this extremely trivial and lighthearted way, spoke volumes to her.

"A'ight," he said, pulling off his black latex gloves, "so, how long you gotta leave all this on?"

He did a full survey of her entire head, angling himself up, down and reviewing both sides.

"Umm...for a little bit, but I'm good now. I got it from here."

"You sure?" he asked, with kindness in his voice. He wasn't being condescending, arrogant or even sexual, but it genuinely felt like he cared.

Her heart always swelled with the love she had for him, but this time she really thought over how much she truly *liked* him.

Feeling Melody's hand cover hers, Imani was pulled back from the bathroom that day to the confines of the room in which she was preparing for her wedding day.

"Yeah, I can," she said, her voice coated in emotion.

She was truly marrying her friend.

"Then, girl," Melody said, giving her hand resting on top of Imani's a small shake. "That's more than half of what you need to succeed in marriage right there."

Stephanie arrived a few minutes later, in her own black off-the-shoulder gown, showering Imani with unadulterated praise, letting Melody and Kaylee know they were needed downstairs. After a tight hug from Kaylee and two air kisses from Melody, Imani watched her small bridal party walk out before Melody closed the door behind them. Stephanie, typing on her phone briefly, looked up at Imani and released her own sigh.

"Cold feet?" she asked with a smirk.

Imani scoffed, dropping her head to the floor before looking up again.

"I don't know. I'm just ready to see him."

Stephanie's pleasant expression slowly fell into slight concern.

"Do you want to?"

"No."

Despite herself, Imani clutched her stomach again, feeling her chest tighten. Looking to each corner of the room, she suddenly felt like they were caving in on her.

"Imani," Stephanie said, grabbing her hand. "Are you alright?"

"Can I just talk to him?"

Stephanie, on alert, nodded, pulling a bottle of water out of her tote bag. She handed it to her and marched to the door.

"Tell him not to come in, though. I'll leave the door cracked."

With the door now open, a thought struck.

"Stephanie? Please don't tell him I'm like - barely breathing right now. I just need–"

"I get it," she said, knowingly. "It's okay."

Finally alone, Imani took a deeper breath, closing her eyes again as she took slow sips of water. Was she legitimately having a panic attack right now? She had absolutely nothing to worry about. Why was she overthinking this?

Out of nowhere, Imani thought of her parents - her father's kisses and her mother's patient stare - and Aunt Ethel, hearing her laugh reverberate in her ear. She had been overthinking all of this, doubting herself because none of them were here. This was the first major decision Imani was making outside of pressure or expectations others had of her, a decision that was solely hers.

Could she trust it?

"Imani? Baby?"

Hearing DeAndre's smooth voice followed by a knock on the door nudged Imani out of her musing. Before the door was pushed further, Imani ran to it, holding on to the doorknob to keep it from moving.

DeAndre chuckled.

"Calm down, baby, I'm not comin' in. I just want to make sure you're good?"

Looking at the ornate white framing of the door in front of her, Imani swallowed. Her entire heart lunged in her chest, while this man sounded like he was about to pick up a cup of coffee and needed her order.

God, why hadn't some of his confidence rubbed off on her yet? What part of the relationship was that supposed to happen in?

"I'm a little off," Imani admitted, her voice shaking. She turned around and leaned back against the door, sliding to the ground, her dress billowing around her. With her knees at her chest, Imani pushed her hand up and behind her, feeling the cool air of the hallway.

"Can you hold my hand?"

Hearing DeAndre shift behind the door, she felt the warmth of his hand in hers a second later. Her nerves calmed instantly.

"Only you could have me sittin' on the floor in Tom Ford, baby," he joked, making them both chuckle.

Imani laughed once more before choking back silent tears. She pushed her head back against the wall.

"D, I'm so scared," she said. "Not because I don't love you. I'm usually okay with being by myself, but I'm totally on my own in this. I miss my parents…I miss my aunt…soooo much."

Imani sniffled, patting softly under her eyes.

"This is just all hitting me…at once right now."

The two held onto each other's hands in silence for a moment, the faint chords of a violin playing softly downstairs.

"You wanna know somethin'?" DeAndre asked.

"Yeah."

"This is the most scared I've ever been in my life."

Imani blinked, looking around the salon with wide eyes.

"What?"

"Yeah," he chuckled. "I am. Yo Imani…I'm not walking in doubt. I'm not letting fear dictate what I already know I want. I know I don't want to be without you. You're not on your own in this. When you move, I move. That's all for me forever."

A fresh wave of tears overtook her, falling down her cheeks.

"I can't believe I tried to force myself to believe I didn't love you for so long," Imani said, " when I always did."

"I love you, too," he said, giving her hand a squeeze.

Imani sighed, suddenly feeling like the weight of another human being had just been taken away.

"So, you cool wit' moving this conversation away from a wall so I can marry you?"

A smile burst onto Imani's face as a laugh spilled over.

"Yes."

DeAndre left the vicinity shortly afterwards - both still unseen by the other - before Stephanie returned to the room. She patted down Imani's face gently with tissues, thankfully the makeup setting spray was top tier, and escorted her down to the foyer. Standing just after one of the columns next to the door leading to the opera house, Hosea, with his hands in his pockets, waited for Imani.

"I'll be at the door when you're ready," Stephanie whispered to her with a smile.

Imani continued walking towards Hosea, thinking back to the day she asked him to walk her down the aisle. It was over at his house in the living room while Melody sat on one of their chairs in the kitchen, ready to post a selfie. When Imani asked him, Melody heard her and ran over to them with tears in her eyes, agreeing to it a second after Hosea did.

Imani didn't have a father to do the job and didn't know of any other relatives on her mother's side. But, when she thought about Hosea, she knew his gentle nature would be comforting during such an emotional day. In front of him now, she was glad she went with her gut.

Hearing her heels against the marble, Hosea looked up, his caramel face brightening.

"Wow...Imani, just beautiful. Look at you..." he smiled. As she stopped in front of him, he gathered her hands as if she was a China doll.

Imani smiled, feeling herself tear up again.

"Thank you."

She took a moment to size him up and realized she hadn't seen him this dressed up since his own wedding day. With four pristine cornrows against a gradient fade, Hosea - in a classic black and white suit, was handsome in the rugged kind of way that was right up Melody's alley.

## A Month of Sundays

He straightened his jacket, his tattooed hand fixing his lapel, before placing Imani's hand at the crook of his arm. They stood in front of the tall wood doors, below a multi-tiered crystal chandelier, leading into the opera house. Stephanie stood, waiting for her cue.

"Just so you know," he said, turning his frame toward her, "Mel and I got y'all back. Marriage ain't no cakewalk and somebody always got something to say, tryna tell you that you're better without it. Tune all that out. Deal?"

Imani nodded, her lashes brushing against her cheeks.

"Wow," he said again with a chuckle. "This dude..."

"I remember not even a week into my honeymoon, you know he called up my wife, cursing her out over you."

Imani laughed, surprised that she never even heard this story from Melody.

"Are you serious?"

"Am I?" his hazel eyes widened. "I had to tell him to fall back. Asking her how she never introduced you to him after all this time, hounding her for your number. And, you know Mel didn't give it to him..."

He shook his head. "She was trying to let him know about your...situation at the time."

Imani knew he wanted to tread lightly referencing Michael.

"But he didn't wanna hear it...and he wouldn't let it go, not like 'alright, I get it'....nah, he made it clear he wanted you from jump."

Imani let Hosea's words soothe her. Words he didn't even know she needed to hear.

"Y'all are gonna be alright," he said. "Plus, D needs somebody to humble his ass every now and then."

Imani smiled.

"Thank you," she whispered to him, placing her head on his shoulder temporarily.

Imani held her head up, took a breath and glanced over at Stephanie. She was more than ready to see him now, to finally be his wife.

Once Stephanie opened the tall cathedral doors, the cool air - drifting with the faintest scent of lavender, sent goosebumps up Imani's silk covered arms. Walking to the base of the staircase, she looked over the large crowd with their heads tilted up at her. They were all seated in a semicircle until the minister announced her entrance, asking them to stand. Melody and Kaylee stood a short distance from the percussionists playing the opening strings of "Spend My Life With You." As Hosea led her down the marble steps, Imani felt like she was on top of a cloud, looking at the balcony seats above decorated with purple, blue and white flowers wrapped around the banisters. There wasn't a window in sight, but the bright light from the chandeliers of various sizes cascaded above the guests dressed in all-black, just like he had specifically requested.

"*You need to be the only one in color, hummingbird. They gotta see the rose among the thorns.*"

She chuckled when he said it a week ago, joking that white was technically a shade not a color. But, seeing the effect of it now was devastatingly breathtaking. Imani was truly the light in the center of the room.

Her eyes fell to a few guests in the crowd, some who she was familiar with and others she hadn't been introduced to yet, still managing to smile and keep her composure. It wasn't until her eyes fell to the altar that she felt her knees almost buckle.

DeAndre looked like the man of her dreams, standing even taller than usual in an all-black three-piece suit with a hint of white from his shirt peeking out. He and Hosea were comparable in height, but DeAndre's frame was leaner with long muscular arms. Imani fell in love with him all over again, her heart beating incessantly, and was reminded that she'd follow him anywhere. Hosea stopped a few feet away from the altar, halting Imani's own ascension.

Stepping ahead to close the distance, DeAndre slapped hands with Hosea, smiling as the two embraced. He then grabbed her hand, pulling her with him to the officiant who led them in prayer shortly afterwards. The entire ceremony, including the exchange of vows, went much faster than she expected. And, before she knew it, they faced the crowd that cheered once they were formally announced. Imani's gaze then fell to the front row, finding Andele clapping before wiping away a tear that threatened to break her otherwise unreadable facial expression. She didn't look happy nor disappointed, just somber.

"You ready?" DeAndre asked her, before squeezing her hand again.

Looking up at her husband now, she quickly realized they were on a level playing field for the first time. They were both new at this. Neither one of them were ever married before... never committed to anyone like this before...and they both had to just figure it out. That thought alone gave Imani confidence.

Imani nodded, a wide smile on her face before caressing his cheek and he glanced down at her lovingly as she met his gaze and their lips united in the deepest kiss.

## Chapter 31
# Different

Once outside the opera house, DeAndre climbed into the Escalade after ensuring Imani was settled in and the two collapsed into each other as soon as Clive closed the door behind them. DeAndre never thought he'd be as tired as he was after the wedding, but he realized that all the pent-up energy he had today - all week - if he was being honest, was released as soon as it was all over.

He couldn't recall how many people he actually spoke to or laughed with tonight, especially because all he anticipated was finally being alone with his wife. He tried his best to preserve his energy, choosing not to indulge in too much alcohol, so he was as present and alert as he could be for Imani. Though exhausted, DeAndre was relaxed while Imani was biting down on her cuticle, looking like she was plagued with every worry under the sun.

DeAndre had anticipated her feeling this way but chose not to harp on it. He just wanted tonight to unfold as naturally as it could.

Pulling up to the hotel only a few minutes later, the two walked across the quiet lobby with gold ornate finishes, to the elevator bank. The hotel's restaurant was on their right and Imani's eyes searched for any sign of life. At this hour, the kitchen was probably closed. But she recalled Stephanie mentioning when she booked the rooms they'd likely stay open for an extra hour or two for them after the wedding.

## A Month of Sundays

"I could have something else to eat," Imani said, eyes still scanning.

"We could order room service," he said.

Imani smirked.

"As long as it's not red velvet cake."

DeAndre stopped, staring at his wife.

"That was the cake we just had two hours ago."

"Correction...that was the cake *you* had two hours ago," she chuckled before rolling her eyes. "I'm so glad you didn't insist on that cake smash thing people do sometimes."

Imani waved her hand. "I actually can't stand red velvet."

DeAndre turned as if he heard a record scratch, looking behind him on both sides.

"You playin' wit' me, right?" he asked. "Awww, baby. I don't want to have to annul this marriage before it even gets started."

He squinted at her as she laughed - her sweet giggle playing in his ears. Imani shrugged, looking at the ceiling in jest.

"Sorry to break it to you, now that it's too late."

The conversation was all in fun but DeAndre still looked at her for a moment, surprised that she hadn't made that tidbit known beforehand. She really hadn't said anything about what she wouldn't want at all - he just realized Imani did from time-to-time. But, if she didn't make a big deal about it, he wouldn't.

"It's too late, huh?"

Pulling her by her waist, DeAndre watched her nostrils flare slightly as he smoothed his hands over her ass, giving it a firm squeeze, before covering her mouth with his. Imani caressed the sides of his face, as he backed her up against the closed elevator doors, kissing her fervently while reaching to press the elevator button. They lost themselves in each other until the elevator dinged and the doors slid open, causing Imani to slightly lose her balance but DeAndre wasn't gonna let his wife fall. She giggled as they tumbled back into the empty elevator. Imani relaxed her mouth further to deepen the kiss. Her amber fragrance, that had been teasing him all day, heightened his desire even more as he stooped down, running his hands down the back of her thighs to pick her up off the ground. Imani, hooked her arms around his neck and wrapped her legs around his waist. Shoving her pussy against him, she cupped his impending erection. DeAndre wasn't expecting her boldness in this moment at all. Her curiosity must have gotten the best of her.

*Was her first time really gonna be in an elevator? It was one in Paris, but still...*

The thought crossed his mind as he pecked along her jawline down to the skin peeking just above her mock neck dress. The jerk of the elevator descending made him lose his footing for a second, and they both dipped. Imani burst into laughter, but DeAndre was not entertained. She pushed her head down between them, giggling before looking up at him, her eyes glazed in humor. The elevator stopped, opening up at the basement level.

"How did we end up here?" she asked.

"Don't look at me," DeAndre smirked, "you had me too busy to press our floor."

Imani hit his shoulder playfully as he punched the button for their floor and the elevator doors closed.

He leaned against the back of the elevator and pulled her closer, resuming their kiss. Suddenly she placed her palms on his chest, slightly turning her head to gaze at him. Her face grew serious.

"Can we slow down...I'd like to be a little more comfortable," Imani purred, ultimately placing the ball back in his court. She was saying she *preferred* to be more comfortable upstairs.

He looked at her and nodded, sucking her bottom lip. From the way she was looking at him, her legs still gripping his waist, he could tell she wasn't fully against giving it to him right then and there...in a moving elevator with all romantic wedding night expectations thrown out the window.

DeAndre took a deep breath, gently resting her down. If he was being honest, he really didn't want to taint this experience for his wife. His impression of Imani from the very beginning never wavered. She was different, which meant he wanted to be different with her. He wanted to step in with a little more patience, instead of going in for the kill - calculating and strategizing like his life depended on it as he had in the past. DeAndre chased after his career, his ambitions, and Imani - strategically, like his life depended on it. But, now that she was his wife, he wanted to savor her slowly... for as long as he could.

## A Month of Sundays

Imani went against every rule in his book, the number one being to never...ever...be a virgin's first. But that was then.

Now, he was actively looking forward to handling his wife properly and much more gently. Her hand massaged his shoulder as they stood side by side leaning on the elevator wall. During the reception, she had changed from an impeccable wedding gown that made his heart stop, into a shorter lace cocktail dress that stopped just above her knees. All night long, DeAndre had been staring at her sexy legs, imagining them hanging from his shoulders, as he watched her hips and perched ass moving rhythmically to the music. He watched her all night for any sign - a nudge on his shoulder, a glance from across the room, hell...even a thunderous blatant interruption during conversation – that she wanted to leave.

But they stayed, mingling and dancing with as many guests as they could.

The elevator finally pinged at their floor before the doors opened, DeAndre motioned for Imani to walk out first. Keeping a short distance between them, he continued watching her move with that feminine grace that he loved. However she was feeling right now, Imani still managed to look present in herself, never awkward or clumsy.

She stopped midway down the hall and turned around, crossing her legs and dropping her hands folded in front.

"I guess it'd make sense if I knew the room we were staying in."

Once in front of her, he noticed the slight glisten of sweat along her hairline even though her makeup looked just as perfect as it did hours ago. DeAndre swore women used straight alchemy to pull themselves together.

She was really nervous, though.

"Almost there," he said, before pulling her hand to lead her three doors down to their room.

With the key in hand, DeAndre was going to scan it over the lock of their door until Imani tugged his arm. She didn't say anything when he turned around but her eyes danced between him and the closed door.

"Oh," he smiled, "How could I forget?"

They had watched a movie one date night in which a groom carried his new bride across the threshold. She never told him explicitly it was her heart's desire, but Imani was a puddle of tears watching the scene next to him.

Bending halfway at the knees now, DeAndre lifted Imani with ease, her legs crossed at the ankles as her arms fell around his neck effortlessly. She held his gaze once at his eye level, giving him a small smile. He moved closer to the lock again when Imani gently squeezed his neck.

"This is cute but no...can you put me down now?"

He froze immediately.

*Okay...* he thought suspiciously.

Placing her on the ground, he straightened up, scratching the back of his neck as she pulled her dress down.

"And can I have the key please?"

DeAndre squinted, but gave it to her cautiously, suddenly not knowing what the hell was happening or why.

She smiled before disengaging the lock, opening the door to reveal their suite, aglow with dim amber lights and an array of candles on the window ledge, the coffee table in the living room and even on the bedside tables in their room. The sweet smell of vanilla and jasmine permeated the air as small flames danced in glass jars of various sizes and shapes. Transfixed at this production, DeAndre stood looking at this peaceful oasis he had absolutely no part in planning.

"I didn't let Stephanie tell me anything about today," she said, standing beside him. "But, I did ask her to add some candles wherever we were staying for the night."

Imani stood in front of him, twirling her fingers.

"Since we're not doing a honeymoon yet with your travel and all, I thought I could..." she shrugged. "I don't know...add some romance here tonight."

Imani turned back to the gorgeous presentation as DeAndre looked at her, not even sure where to start. He typically hated surprises and was more than willing, and much more comfortable, being the giver of them. Imani had thrown him for a loop, once again. Being romanced, not even a full day into his marriage, was not on his Bingo Card of Life at all.

"This is really, really nice," he said.

Imani smiled wide like a student acing an exam.

"Good. I'm glad you like it," she sighed with relief.

## A Month of Sundays

Imani placed a hand on DeAndre's arm for balance while taking off her shoes.

"Um...you can go ahead and freshen up," she said, standing up straight. In heels, she was as tall as his shoulder but now on bare feet, her height reached his elbow.

"You wanna come with me?"

"No," she said, without hesitation.

He blinked.

"Sorry...I mean...I put some thought into tonight and I want us to relax. You sort of helped me refocus in the elevator," she laughed, sheepishly.

Scanning her for a minute, DeAndre suddenly felt a slight pull at his chest as he grew harder by the millisecond. Was this how women felt when shit like this was done for them?

"I know it's kinda corny..."

DeAndre snapped out of his revere, suddenly well aware of his voice again.

"Okay," he said, shaking his head. "I don't want you to do that."

She blinked, visibly confused with her head pushed back defensively.

DeAndre took another breath, re-assessing his approach. He could've said that more tactfully.

"I need you to know...Imani, you're my reflection. When I see you, I see myself. And, what I ain't ever gonna do is belittle myself or what I'm doin.'"

His head tilted. "You get what I mean?"

Imani stared at him, her expression softening in understanding.

"Yeah, I do."

Just like he did moments before their ceremony, DeAndre wanted her to see what he always did. She really was his equal and he wanted her to start accepting it.

Looking up at him again, Imani took a breath, raising her chin slightly.

"So, take your shower then I'll take my own and...we'll see," she smirked. "Okay?"

DeAndre nodded slowly, in disbelief that he truly didn't know what was happening next. But, so far, he was enjoying surrendering a little bit of control.

In the shower, DeAndre was fully relaxed for the first time in a while as the hot water ran down his back, shoulders and legs. He sat on the shower bench, resting himself against the marble wall before shutting his eyes for a moment, letting his mind wander to Imani again. He definitely wanted to take his time tonight, but he couldn't help thinking how damn good she looked today, during the reception and right now...barefoot in their wedding suite.

Opening his eyes quickly, he realized he had to get out of this damn shower.

Once dried off, he grabbed the robe hanging behind the door, draping it over his frame before pausing. DeAndre had every right to walk out butt ass naked, dick swinging without even batting an eye, a move that would likely throw Imani all the way off. If she wanted to play the surprise game, he could make it an entire competition. Somehow, his curiosity outweighed his instinctual defiance. She wanted to spearhead tonight, so he'd let her...for now.

DeAndre stepped out of the bathroom, his robe tied loosely at the waist, to find Imani looking at him with her eyes wide in wonderment. The thought of her enjoying just looking at him made him feel invincible.

"I'll only be a few minutes," she said, walking to the bathroom with urgency and closing the door behind her.

After changing into an undershirt with sweats, DeAndre lay on the bed, scanning through Netflix and Hulu before deciding on an ole school Eddie Murphy movie. He figured it'd help him pass the time, but his eyes began fading more than halfway into it, the movie waning in and out of his consciousness.

"Enjoying yourself?"

Opening his eyes wider at her voice, DeAndre's gaze shifted once before taking a second glance.

Standing a short distance from the bathroom, Imani had on a white halter lace bodysuit with cutouts on the sides, raising and accentuating her chest while showcasing the curves of her waist. She completed the look with a sheer white long-sleeve robe, decorated with white polka dots, that cascaded to the floor.

Imani didn't present herself with her hands up touching the sides of the door like a showgirl nor did she stand there looking like a deer caught in headlights, wide-eyed and petrified. She appeared only a tad nervous, yet assured, meeting his eyes in a direct gaze as she leaned seductively against the doorway.

In an instant, DeAndre knew there was absolutely no way God wasn't real.

## A Month of Sundays

He turned off the television, sitting up on the bed as Imani approached him. He reached out for her hands before his feet hit the floor. Taking notice of everything down to her nail design with flecks of blue glitter, he was fully alert, admiring every sexy inch of her from her short hair to her perfect manicure this time lost in his own wonderment.

"You're beyond stunning. It's just me and you, you know that right?"

"Thank you, baby," she whispered, a small smile on her face. As she approached, DeAndre could see her breathing rapidly.

Now, it was his turn.

Pulling her hands to his lips, DeAndre closed his eyes and kissed them gently. His eyes met hers, with a smile.

"I want you to tell me how you felt about our wedding."

Imani blinked, her eyes shifting in confusion. DeAndre assumed her mind was in overdrive right now, not expecting him to say anything like that. He was genuinely curious of what she had to say right now...for the most part.

"Umm...well," she stammered. "It was..."

Placing his hands on her waist again, DeAndre gently pulled her down onto the bed with him, noticing everything about her. Her eyes were bare of the black liner she had on earlier, her lips covered with a light gloss, her rounded breasts cupped in the lace fabric, her nipples were visibly peeking through and the curve of her hips that he was certain enclosed the sweetest honey. He was willing to bet all his cash this was going to be the best he'd ever indulged in.

"It was beautiful, and, um...everyone looked great..."

Watching her chest rise and fall in anticipation, DeAndre wasn't sure where to start. It was like finally gaining access to the finest cuisine, all plated delectably in front of him, only to not know what to try first.

"I loved the floral arrangements. I don't think I've ever seen peony flowers arranged to cascade like that before. They were gorgeous."

"They're just pretty...you're gorgeous."

He kissed her with gentle pecks at first before drawing out longer, passionate ones that had them gulping for air.

DeAndre wasn't much of a kisser before Imani. He often felt like it was more of an obligatory sendoff. For some reason it was different with Imani, he enjoyed kissing her from the very beginning, especially because it was the only thing she allowed him to do when they were engaged. Surprisingly, each kiss deepened their intimate connection to an extent that DeAndre never had with anyone before.

Imani drew him closer to her chest as he dragged the straps of her lingerie down with his teeth, revealing her smooth rounded breasts. Massaging her gently as his hand roamed up the middle of her chest, DeAndre cupped one breast, caressing the fullness gathered in his palm, while gently flicking the deep brown nipple of the other one. He watched her eyes draw closed then open again, as she gasped.

"Is that it?" he asked. "What else did you like?"

Moving forward, DeAndre lay Imani down, still massaging one breast before circling her nipple with just the tip of his finger. He then folded his free arm at his elbow, leaning his head against his hand. Screw a movie, DeAndre was about to enjoy every last minute of this.

"I...liked...ugh."

Imani turned her head, resting her cheek against the comforter, a battle of wills etched across her face from this torture. She was so soft in every possible way that whatever he imagined, based on their phone sex, all those months ago was nothing in comparison to this.

"The...space...the venue..."

He looked at her squirming with anticipation as he grazed his fingers down the middle of her chest, trailing a cursive tattoo in between her breasts. Half of her bodysuit was gathered at her stomach, and he dragged it past her hips before it fell to her ankles.

"When I was thinkin' about where to have the wedding, I really wanted to find a place that felt like you..."

Straightening his arm to push himself up, DeAndre traced his hand up the soft inside of her thigh, allowing his thumb to gently graze her clit. Imani's panting was much faster now as he rubbed it in the smallest circles.

"...somewhere that looked like you belonged there."

Imani's face was filled with desire, as he kissed the lower half of stomach, twirling his finger around her clit one more time before easing it into her. He gently inched into her, just until he could get to...

"Oh my God...oh my God," she said, arching her back while gripping the sheets. Imani's walls loosened, allowing him to inch another finger inside. Hearing her whimpers and soft moans was enough to get him rock hard in an instant.

Playing with her soft, thin flesh inside, he pulled down his sweats before joining her on the bed. Damn this priceless exquisite being is his wife. He had to remind himself that this wasn't a dream.

This was the reality he manifested.

"Anywhere you go, you belong," he said. "Everywhere you are, you bring beauty."

Imani blinked in succession, her eyes rolling with each earth-shattering sensation caused by his fingers. He soon felt her fingers grip the center of his back.

"DeAndre...baby..."

"I've waited so long to be with you," he whispered. "To love you like this... Do you feel it too?"

He felt Imani's wetness soaking on his fingers, her slickness making it much easier for him to stimulate her...

"I...think I'm..."

Pulling his fingers out of her gently, DeAndre watched Imani close her eyes, anticipating a sensation she never felt before.

"Remember I always got you a'ight?"

She opened her eyes as he brushed her lips before their tongues rolled together. He eased his dick into her with measured force, feeling her wetness along with a tight cushioned fit. Her body tensed...

*Fuck.*

DeAndre didn't move at all, but stayed still, closing his eyes and allowing himself to savor the feeling of this treasure trove, Being with someone untouched like this was so refreshing, DeAndre questioned all of his experiences up to this point. He thought he had reached a peak at the mountaintop a few times, only to realize there was another uncharted level.

He opened his eyes again, finding Imani's wide with trepidation. Her delicate handheld caution at his chest.

"Am I...?" she winced.

"Everything," he nodded, "you are."

With tears welling up in her eyes, Imani nodded, biting the corner of her bottom lip.

Placing Imani's hands, one after the other, behind his neck, DeAndre pulled out slightly before stroking her a bit deeper. Her rigidity eventually loosened, her entire body unfolding and releasing underneath him in the most pliable way. His own release followed, a bullet shooting through his system much more powerfully than he anticipated.

He pulled out, hugging her from behind. Imani unfurled herself and sat up gently, moving her knees to her chest. With her lips slightly plump, Imani stared at him, teary-eyed with a small smile on her face.

"You good?" he rasped, cradling her cheek with his hand. She nodded, holding a soft gaze as his eyes went down to the sheets, in between Imani's legs. DeAndre kissed her before rising from the bed. He went to the bathroom, returning a moment later and gently pressed her stomach with his hand.

"This feels so...perfect, baby," her eyes descended in relief as her hand fell to cover his, while he gently pressed a warm damp cloth where she ached, to soothe her pain.

He watched her relax as her plump lips fell open languidly. It was the most sensual he'd ever seen of her before.

After that moment, Imani turned over to her side again to curl up into the fetal position. DeAndre lay behind her, pulling her back into his chest, right where he always thought she needed to be. He knew he wanted this woman in his life for the long haul and tonight had only confirmed what he vowed to himself long before the engagement, well before the wedding and weeks before Paris...he'd never let her go.

Pressing soft, sporadic kisses at her neck that trailed up the side of her face, DeAndre imprinted promises of forever on Imani until they drifted off to sleep.

# Chapter 32
# Precious

With a reputation that often preceded him, Imani's new husband was allegedly the ultimate ladies' man when he was single - taking women down, left and right - without much effort before they even knew their panties were off. Some men had to exert a lot to get women, but, for DeAndre, just being in the room was more than enough.

So, why, for the life of her, was Imani so bored?

It was now a few weeks after Paris and their amazing wedding day, and Imani was officially someone's wife - a role she fell into right away. It felt good to have a partner in life, knowing that she wouldn't have to weather these trials and tribulations alone. It had been so easy for her to trust DeAndre, but what was she also trusting him with? She trusted him to lead her to new unimaginable sexual heights.

Before the wedding, they hadn't spoken much further about Imani's virginity other than that it wouldn't change until their wedding night. DeAndre was surprisingly patient before the wedding and had been as gentle and sweet as could be that night, top-tier husband material. But Imani had assumed that sooner rather than later, they'd be jacking each other off like rabbits with her hanging from the chandeliers.

Yet, none of that was happening...like, at all. Now that she had a taste of how good sex felt slow, she felt even more ready, willing and able to have it rough.

"Baby...do you enjoy having sex with me?" she asked at the breakfast table. It was the morning after yet another night of tender kisses, sweet rubs and innocent spooning. Imani felt like she was stuck in the 1950s.

DeAndre looked up at her from his phone, his plate of eggs, ham and grits still untouched.

"Of course," he said without a trace of hesitation, giving her his full attention. The look on his face was that of someone who was suffocating in love. Even when he was focused on business or his game, DeAndre never looked as if Imani was interrupting him. He had always been attentive, but now being married to him, it was as if he turned it up a notch.

"Do you not...like it?" he chuckled with the smallest dip of his brow.

"I do," she said, keeping her gaze on him. Visions of him pushing their plates, utensils and glasses away from the table, letting them shatter on the floor as he pulled her waist for her to straddle him, penetrated her mind. Visions that were all fantasy at this point.

"I love when you kiss my neck," she said.

*Even though you could squeeze it. Hard.*

"I love when you kiss my chest."

*A bite or two of my nipples wouldn't hurt.*

"I just...love how...soft you are with me."

*I want to feel your dick rat-a-tat-tatting on my bladder.*

Imani chewed her eggs, swallowing down all the inner thoughts that wreaked havoc.

DeAndre grinned at her, narrowing his gaze.

"Okay..." he said.

"You know, sometimes..." she said. "I don't want sex to be soooooo...."

Imani's eyes widened.

"Loving," she said.

He grabbed the glass of orange juice next to his plate, bringing it to his lips to drink, looking at Imani with a smile. Placing his glass back on the table, DeAndre's eyes sparkled with admiration. He scratched his neck and shook his head.

## A Month of Sundays

"Nah..." he said. "I love you. There's no other way I'd want to treat you. You want me to not *adore* you?"

Imani smiled, warmed by his words.

"I'd much rather ease into whatever sex is gonna be like for us..." he shrugged. "Not like we don't got time."

Imani nodded, drinking her own juice.

"Yeah..."

"Baby..." he held her gaze. "You're like my...."

*God, please don't call me cute.*

"My precious...flower..." DeAndre looked off in the distance for a moment before looking at her again. The sun gleamed in his chestnut eyes. "Ya' know?"

Imani smiled, his comparison of her even worse than she thought. He basically called her everything but a child bride.

*No, I don't.*

She placed her glass down with a louder thud than anticipated.

"Not another woman just hanging on my arm...though, you look good as hell there, too."

He winked at Imani, but what he said rang in her head long after they finished eating. Wait...was he holding back because she was his *wife*? Imani never thought she'd have to beg her husband to basically whore her out, all because he thought she was some fragile, unscathed Black Madonna?

What in the respectability politics was this?

Imani was about to bring up his previous statement when Stephanie walked into the kitchen, greeting the house staff with a radiant smile. Imani knew what that meant - they were getting down to business right away.

"Hey, beautiful family," she said, approaching Imani at the table to give her a kiss on the cheek.

"Ready for our catch-up?" she asked Deandre, her professional tone taking over.

Instead of answering Stephanie right away, DeAndre looked at Imani for confirmation - yet another thing he often did to signal that the small tasks of his life could wait, if needed. He *did* really love her - this matter wasn't the end of the world.

"Yeah," she smiled, looking at DeAndre. "Go ahead. We can talk about it later."

The sex may have been a little too mild for her liking, but why complain about something that was bound to ebb-and-flow over time, as he suggested? Besides, what woman wouldn't want her man to be soft with her?

But, the conversation they had at breakfast already felt like ions ago and Imani was growing more restless. He was away for a while, beginning this week, giving Imani more than enough time to think about her next angle. She had to figure out how to suggest spicing things up in the bedroom, at least for her sanity. Having a direct conversation about it wasn't going to cut it, she had to *show* him exactly what she meant.

∽

Scanning the street across from a row of small local Port Springs shops, Imani parked in an available spot. She walked into Pins & Needles and heard the bell ring once inside, allowing the familiar smell of ink and disinfectant to soothe her. This was the first time in about a year that Imani was back at the shop to see Shiya in order to get some of her tatts filled in and touched-up. She rarely had a plan when she was in her chair, but she knew she wanted to walk out with something different, something that would catch DeAndre's attention.

Shiya happened to be at the front desk, scribbling in a notebook, when she saw Imani.

"Well, helllooo, Mrs. Harrison," she said, with a wide-tooth smile, a silver labret ring pressed in the middle of her bottom lip.

"Heyyyy," Imani waved.

Shiya was one of the first artists Imani actually bonded with when she returned to Port Springs from being in New York. Great tattooers were a dime-a-dozen in the city, but not many of them were Black and a majority of them weren't women. When Imani found Shiya, an artist who was talented *and* had the warmest energy to match, Imani kept her on speed dial. She had done more than half of the tattoos on Imani's body.

Once Shiya gave Imani a hug, she glanced over Imani's shoulder, with a raised eyebrow.

# A Month of Sundays

"Oh, that's you?" she asked, pushing her chin up towards Imani's car outside.

Imani nodded, with a reluctant sigh.

"Yeah, you somebody's wife now," Shiya said, "pushing a Bentley in the hood...at least this block's gentrified."

Scribbling her signature in the appointment book, Imani rolled her eyes playfully, not even trying to think about the car she was stuck with today. The Range she typically chose was in the shop this week and believe it or not the Bentley was the least flashy out of all their cars. Plus, she didn't feel as bad about having bags of blank canvases, paint tubes and supplies in its spacious backseat, which was now a little cluttered.

"You ready for me?" Imani asked.

Not even a half hour later, Imani heard the buzzing of Shiya's needle, coaxing her awake from a nap she didn't even know she needed.

"Welcome back, sleeping beauty," Shiya chuckled, dipping the needle in a small pot of black ink. Her locs were a pile of intricately woven vines on top of her head as she leaned against Imani's arm to continue filling in the ink on her wrist.

"Was hoping you'd be awake so you could give me *some* of the tea. You know you can't step foot in this shop and leave me high and dry."

Imani laughed, careful not to move too much, though it was always difficult holding still when she was in Shiya's chair. The woman was a comedian in some other life.

"If you must know, the wedding was stunning, the food was great and my dress was actually a lot more comfortable than it might've looked."

Imani hadn't thought much about what she was going to say to people in her life when they asked about the wedding or her husband, but neither she nor DeAndre were secretive about being together. They also trusted that the other wouldn't say anything that would breach their privacy.

"I mean...you looked incredible," Shiya said, "That dress was killing it at every angle, in every shot."

Imani shook her head, still processing the idea that her wedding was plastered everywhere on social media. She didn't mind and was thankful for it since she didn't remember taking pictures that day. It had flown by so quickly.

"Soooooo...I don't want to pry too much, but you gotta tell me...what's the most surprising thing you've learned about him since marrying him?"

"The most surprising?" she asked, biting her bottom lip.

Imani pushed her head back at the question, impressed with the thoughtfulness it required to answer.

With DeAndre's schedule, he wasn't home too often, which meant the subtle nuances she observed were like tiny pieces of a puzzle scattered everywhere. But, they were there and the little he gave her made Imani work overtime to fit the pieces together.

For one, she hadn't realized his insatiable need for perfection in all aspects of his life. She very quickly realized how fastidious DeAndre was about keeping the house clean. As an artist, Imani was the quintessential stereotype - untidy and chaotically organized. She typically had small piles of sketchpad papers, palettes and tools scattered around her studio, but she always knew exactly where everything was.

Imani had purposely migrated one of those piles to the living room near the bookshelf one day, knowing she'd come back to it after painting. Not even fifteen minutes passed before DeAndre knocked on the door, a small smile on his face and her pile cradled in his hands.

*"One of these days, one of us is gon' bust our ass,"* he said, making a bit of a show of placing the pile in his hand next to another one in her art studio. DeAndre then backed up to observe what he did before he spent the next twenty minutes lining up each pile by height. Turning to face Imani once this chore was complete, he pointed to his recreation of Mount Rushmore.

*"This cool right here withchu?"* he asked, scratching the inside of his cheek.

Imani blinked, folding her arms across her chest. Knowing how damn near perfect and in control he was with his tennis game, she shouldn't have been surprised by this, but again - it was one of those subtle things.

"There's just...little stuff, ya' know?" Imani said to Shiya, halfway listening as the needle scraped against her skin.

"I gotta think for a sec," she chuckled, shaking her head.

On the flip side, Imani realized he was one of the most sensitive people she had ever met who was constantly gauging her reaction, asking for it immediately, without giving her much time to process. His brain seemed to move a mile a minute, from one point to the next – the total opposite of Imani's own mental processing that could be summed up as a Leon Bridges harmony playing on loop in her head.

During a recent date night they decided would be at home, DeAndre focused on every single detail of it and kept asking Imani if it was perfect - not good or nice, but perfect. Imani wasn't involved with the fine details of their wedding planning, so experiencing all of this in real time took a bit of adjustment. She hadn't even taken three bites of the salmon he made with Chef Sebastian when he asked her to give a ten-point critique on taste, texture and seasoning.

*"But, would you have it again?* he asked, his eyes plastered to hers. *"Baby, would you eat this ever again if I made it?"*

This trait of his could've made her anxious, but Imani saw it as his unfulfilled need for validation, like he missed out on someone he cared about telling him how proud they were of him outside of his career.

On top of that, his need for physical touch outside of sex went beyond a hug or a few kisses. As soon as he was within proximity of her, DeAndre was a baby who wanted to hold on - onto her hips with his head cradling her middle when he napped, onto her shoulders with his weight partially on her, or onto her stomach when they were sleeping at night. Imani didn't anticipate how much mental weight she'd have to carry with him as his wife. While DeAndre didn't press her about domestic matters, Imani barely knew how to boil rice properly, carrying both of their expectations was enough to wear her out before he was away on travel again.

Imani was never going to say any of this out loud to Shiya, though. Not only was that extremely unnecessary, but what good would that have done? What would Imani gain spilling her husband's quirks all over Shiya's leather chair?

She decided to go with something more relevant.

"Ya' know...he's not a big fan of tattoos," she said, throwing in a contrived mischievous grin like she was giving Shiya the *real* inside.

"Noooooooo," Shiya said, eyes wide, taking the drill away from Imani's skin. "Well...now that I think about it, I don't think I've noticed any tatts on him on TV or anything."

Imani laughed.

"But, does he know who he's married to? You're getting a refresh and another one today, right?"

"Yeah, but he's cool with them on me. He likes my level of crazy."

"Okay, girl," Shiya said, an eyebrow spiked. "I see you. So, how crazy you tryna get, then?"

Imani pulled her attention to the rest of Shiya's private parlor. They were in a small room just behind the reception area covered with wall-to-wall vintage Blaxploitation movie posters, portraits of clientele with their completed tattoos and drawings of work from the other artists who Shiya employed.

Imani's eyes then caught the small glass display case in the corner behind Shiya's chair that held two shelves of shimmering body jewelry.

She followed Imani's line of sight and chuckled.

"Oooooo," she asked, wiggling her eyebrows. "We're reconsidering now, aren't we?"

When Imani first started coming more consistently, she'd periodically mention the idea of getting her nipples pierced, asking about pain level, how long it'd take to get and even how she'd switch out the jewelry if she grew tired of them. And, as soon as Shiya would take a few of the delicate jewels out of the case for her to examine, Imani would freeze up, almost anticipating the level of anguish just getting them. The juice just wasn't worth the squeeze...until now.

She didn't step foot into Shiya's shop thinking she'd get any piercings today. But, she couldn't let go of the conversation she had with DeAndre at breakfast earlier in the week. Imani was flying out to California tomorrow to see him at another game before heading back home the following day. If she was going through with this, she knew she needed ample healing time, which meant stalling on sex, something that was hard for either one of them to do when they were in the same room for too long.

*But, imagine the look on his face when he sees these?* she smirked. *Precious flower, my ass.*

She was most definitely going through with this.

"Hhhmmm," Imani cut her eyes back at Shiya, "Let's do it."

The two laughed as Shiya rubbed her hands together.

"That's my girl!"

# Chapter 33
# Headlights

For years, whenever DeAndre took a glance at the crowd after a match, he'd only register faceless onlookers with pops of camera flashes interspersed through the dark stadium. Today shouldn't have felt any different, but it did.

"DeAndre, we're thrilled to have you here tonight as we celebrate your 26th Matrix Slam title."

Jack Smith, the tournament director, smiled behind the mic on the makeshift podium as the applause from the crowd rang at an all-time high in DeAndre's ear. He stood on the podium with Jack, sports journalist Marsha Campbell, and his opponent during the match - Liam Henry, waiting to be presented with the Matrix Slam trophy for his win. Playing out in California was always a mixed bag, especially when DeAndre was competing against someone who had more of a fan base on the West Coast. Liam, who he won against today, was one of them. But, the crowd surprisingly showed him much more approval than he thought they would.

*"You have more appeal being married,"* Stephanie said to him out-of-the-blue a few weeks ago. *"Like, the refined bad boy who's been tamed. Your name is in so many conversations now."*

DeAndre never took into consideration what being married would mean for his reputation nor did he see Imani as a business move, like many of his peers did in their own contractual relationships. He saw his wife as his confidant, his safety and his best friend - a moniker he didn't think he'd ever use again.

"This has been a truly incredible tournament this year, and like every year, we know we couldn't do this without all of you - the fans," Jack continued. "You all make the Matrix Slam one of the best sporting events in the world..."

The crowd cheered as DeAndre and Liam applauded, and the mic was passed to Marsha.

"Thank you, Jack," she smiled. "Let's take a moment to celebrate our finalist..."

As Marsha went through a short introduction of Liam that highlighted many of his previous wins, DeAndre covered his mouth to keep a laugh from escaping. Rand used to hate sitting through the start of these ceremonies because he thought presenting the runner-up with anything aside from a pat on the back was a complete sucker move.

*"See, that's the problem wit' your sport, man, everybody's a winner,"* he'd say, shaking his head. *"I don't deserve no plate or vase for my crib if I didn't win."*

But, even with his qualms over the politics of the sport, many points of reluctance that DeAndre - himself had about it...Randall was there for him through it all - the highs, the lows and all of the unnecessary mess in between. But, there was no need to get bent out of shape about that now, especially since his love was here. With his hands folded behind his back, DeAndre looked up and found Imani staring directly at him with a smile, her hands clasped in front with her head tilted.

Just as she promised before the wedding, Imani had religiously attended at least one game every month and would even catch a red-eye flight every so often to attend a second one. She was here now, staying with him for the night before heading back home the next day just in time for work. He didn't like not being able to return with her, but there were multiple games he was set to play out of town all month long, including a match he was waiting to see if he had to compete in to qualify for the SW Tournament.

## A Month of Sundays

DeAndre gave her a side smile as he thought back to when they were beating around the bush about their true feelings mere months ago. He swore he could hear all of her thoughts when their eyes met back then, like she was beckoning him to grab and hold onto her in some way. He was thankful he didn't stumble on Imani when he was younger, during a time when he couldn't imagine being with a woman who held onto his every word. But, now, he loved having his wife as his primary listener. There was nothing he wanted to keep away from her.

"On behalf of the Professional Tennis League, Jack, would you present Liam with the finalist trophy?"

Liam turned to DeAndre to shake his hand before walking over to Jack who handed him a reflective silver plate. The crowd cheered as Liam stepped to the front of the podium, while photographers at the photo pit near the baseline snapped shots of him holding up the symbolic token. Once Liam stepped back in line, DeAndre walked forward to Marsha who announced him to a raucous crowd during his own introduction.

"Congratulations," Marsha smiled. "DeAndre, hearing all of those stats... you've achieved so much in your career. The great Althea Gibson once said, 'if you have a purpose in which you can believe, there's no end to the amount of things you can accomplish.' What have your accomplishments meant to you?"

"Aww, man, a lot. I'm just amazed at how much this game has given me. You know...I'm thankful for all the hardships, all the sacrifice. I put everything on the court, so I'm thankful to get it back tenfold..."

"But, with all due respect to my fans, who I appreciate for their support, my wife changed my life..."

He shifted his gaze to Imani, whose smile was brighter than the camera flashes, before facing the crowd who erupted in cheers.

"So, I wanna thank her...and my team, my staff, and associates. It's all love. Thank y'all so much."

After lifting the large steel cup above his shoulders for the crowd and photographers to capture, DeAndre was back in the holding area a few moments later with his team and training staff who congratulated him before leading him into a post-game stretch session. He still felt a few of the aches and pains from competing mere minutes ago, but he wasn't about to complain about that in front of Imani. He wasn't showing weakness in front of her.

"Where do you want to put this one?" Imani asked now, raising his winner's trophy only an inch above the table it sat on before placing it back down gently, grimacing at its weight.

DeAndre pulled himself up from the mat after extending his arms forward over his legs, taking a cleansing breath. He walked over to her, taking her by the hands before taking a seat on a bench against the wall.

"I don't know," he smirked. "Think you got room in your studio?"

The glass shelf enclosure he had in his office had been overcrowded for years and Imani was helping him clear out some of his current trophies, little by little. The majority of them were replicas of the ones presented during the ceremonies, but some, like this one and the trophy he was banking on winning during the SW Tournament, were special and original.

Imani rolled her eyes with a smile.

"Unless you want paintbrushes in it, then no."

DeAndre took a beat to watch her for a moment, an activity he relished in just to see her melt from his stare. She laughed, her eyes dancing around the room, as he drew in closer to kiss her pouty lips lined with a chestnut color that brought out her cupid's bow. She let him give her a peck but stopped him when he wanted to deepen the kiss. He always wanted kisses with her to last much longer.

"Baby..." her brows dipped in amusement, pushing him back slightly with her hand on his chest. "You gotta shower."

When Imani brought up sex to him a week or so ago, he was shocked that she assumed he didn't enjoy it with her. DeAndre loved every second of it, especially because it was the total opposite of what he was used to. Women he was with before her would pull out all the stops to perform for him during sex with the wildest outfits, the freakiest tricks and the most salacious words they could conjure up in the moment. DeAndre, though having no complaints about any of it, started to wonder if they held a national convention just to compare notes.

He appreciated that sex with Imani was refreshing. He didn't feel like she was performing for him, she was simply being herself. For the first time, he was catering to someone else's desires.

"I'll be here when you freshen up," she said, giving his beard a playful scratch with her nails. "Go ahead, so we can leave."

Imani walked over to Trey and Coach Williams who were waiting for DeAndre to signal everyone's exit. He watched the natural sway of her hips, up to her perky ass in straight-leg jeans. DeAndre never thought there'd be a time when a woman telling him to leave would cause him to react with such urgency.

After freshening up after the match, DeAndre was walking from the changing rooms, down the hallway and back to the holding area with Trey as journalists, fans with backstage access and Tennis League executives greeted him with waves, handshakes and cheers. He was mere feet from the front door when he saw a familiar face on the opposite side.

"Hey, you," Jazmine said, her signature dimples on full display.

DeAndre took in Jazmine's brand, new appearance in front of him, shifting from the vivacious bombshell she presented herself as when she was rolling with him - from jumpsuits, miniskirts and heels to baggy denim overalls, sweaters and sneakers. Even her makeup was much simpler than he remembered and her braids were wrapped in a top knot. DeAndre picked up on this Erykah Badu, Earth-woman vibe she had going on.

"How you doin'?" he smiled, offering a half hug. "Whatchu doin' out here?"

"My cousin is a friend of Liam's, I think you know her?" she asked, her head tilted in question.

He didn't.

"Hmmmm."

"She asked me to come today, so we're heading out in a little bit. How've you been?"

Despite himself, DeAndre let out a sardonic chuckle, scratching the back of his neck. Jazmine caught herself, chuckling at her own question.

"I mean, I *know* how you've been. You just won," she laughed. "Duh."

"Nah, it's all good. Yeah, I'm fine," he said. "Just getting ready to head out with the team, my wife, you know, the crew."

Jazmine perked up, her eyebrows raised knowingly.

"Oh, yes. I did congratulate you on that. It's Imani, right?"

He nodded.

"She's beautiful," she smiled. "I remember meeting her at that party and she was the sweetest."

DeAndre held her gaze for a moment, assessing her, but didn't pick up on any awkward undercurrent.

"She is."

"Jaz...girl, we gotta go," a woman called out. When DeAndre turned to the voice it belonged to, he realized he...did know her.

"Oh, shit, Raquel?" he said, cupping his hand around his mouth.

"Hey, DeAndre," she said, smiling hard before chuckling. He extended his arms as she walked into his embrace.

"You look good!"

"Thank you, thank you," he beamed before splitting his attention between her and Jazmine. "Y'all are cousins?"

Raquel rolled her eyes.

"Unfortunately," she joked. "And, not for play, play...our mothers are sisters."

"Wow..."

DeAndre blinked, in slight disbelief that his previous social media manager, before Stephanie took on the responsibility, was directly related to a woman he messed with.

"Small world."

"Exactly," Raquel said. "Anyway, I'm supposed to be shooting these reels, and Liam's trying to head out to this party."

She looked down at her phone before looking up again, in slight frustration.

"Y'all mind being filmed for a reel? My boss wants me to capture more BTS shots of Liam and the match festivities for social."

DeAndre nodded.

"No doubt," he said.

He looked at Jazmine, still in front of him with a smile, before looking back at Raquel, expectantly.

"So, what I gotta do?"

## A Month of Sundays

The three of them chuckled.

"Nothing," Raquel said, with a wave of her hand. "Just act like I'm not here. I was interrupting your conversation anyway. I'm not recording any sound, so y'all are fine."

Jazmine nodded to her cousin in jest with an eye roll before turning to DeAndre again, her smile dimming slightly.

"But, how're you feeling?" she said, quieter. "Must be kinda weird playing without Randall around."

DeAndre's eyes shifted, feeling the hair on his arms stand up just hearing her say Rand's name.

"Yeah, it's…different. But, life moves on - right?"

Jazmine smiled, placing a hand at his forearm.

"I wish you well, DeAndre."

He wasn't sure if it was her braids or her empathetic gaze or the mere mention of his best friend he had thought about back on the court, but DeAndre gave her another hug. It was a quick one that he wouldn't have even registered if he wasn't the one doing it, but it was enough.

"Thanks."

"Got it!" Raquel beamed. "Thank you, DeAndre! Jaz, let's dip."

He watched the two of them walk down the opposite end of the hallway, still in a bit of a daze at the random occurrence. And, when he turned back around, he found Imani standing at the door, staring at him like a deer in headlights.

"Who was that?"

DeAndre continued walking to her, releasing a breath.

"Jazmine and Raquel," he chortled, with a raise of an eyebrow, tilting his head back in their direction. "Her cousin used to work wit' me. Crazy how that happened."

Imani nodded, her forehead creased in the middle as she crossed her arms.

"How'd she get back here?"

"Raquel is doing social media for the game, so Jazmine tagged along."

Grabbing her hand, DeAndre led her back into the holding room, where the team was now packed up with everything they needed. Everyone piled into the sprinter van that took them to the Continental Hotel, a few minutes away from the stadium. Imani and DeAndre took the elevator up to their room. She opened the door first, marching inside with haste. The move caught DeAndre's attention, making him look up from his phone, watching her as she stood at the floor-to-ceiling room window with her back facing him with her leg bouncing slightly.

"What's on your mind?"

*Please just tell me so we can move on.*

He noticed her mood shift when they were in the van, but he chose to ignore it. Imani turned around to face him, her eyes filled with doubt.

"So, any other groupies I should know about that you failed to send the group text to?" she started, pulling the corners of her lips downward, "...letting them know their services were no longer needed?"

DeAndre pulled back defensively, his eyebrows wrinkled. Her comment would've been hilarious if he wasn't on the receiving end of it.

"Not sure Imani, wanna have a fireside chat on how you broke up with Michael's sorry ass before I fill you in?"

Folding her arms in front of her, Imani blinked.

"You and Jazmine *were* together?"

"No."

Imani squinted, assessing him for a moment before relaxing the tension in her face, releasing the grip she held in her arms.

"I'm sorry. Your past is your past. That was petty...I just...was surprised to see her there today."

DeAndre shrugged.

"She can get a ticket to a match just like everyone else if she wants."

Yeah, he was a little surprised to see her, too. But, he wasn't fazed by any of it. This conversation was a total waste of time.

Imani looked up at him, pointedly.

"If you're in the same room with her, you need to leave."

DeAndre chortled.

"Baby, what?" he sucked his teeth. "You're for real right now?"

But Imani continued looking at him, unamused, not moving a muscle.

"I can't guarantee that I'll always be able to leave a room if she's in it..." DeAndre scratched behind his head. "I'm not even peepin' her like that."

## A Month of Sundays

Imani rolled her eyes, shaking her head as DeAndre pulled her closer.

"I'm here wit' you, no matter how far I am, a'ight?"

Turning her around, DeAndre wrapped his hand around her waist, swaying her from side to side under his arms.

"Worryin' about worker bees when you're the queen."

"They can always kill the queen, though," she said coldly.

DeAndre paused at her tone and angled her face to his by touching her chin. Her expression was already in a half-smile.

"You actually finished that documentary?" she asked.

The other night, the two started one of those nature documentaries on Netflix over FaceTime with Imani asleep not even a half hour into it.

"You be hatin,' but they're better than anything else on TV right now."

Imani laughed.

"I only have you until tomorrow morning," he said, in mock sadness. "Gotta milk tonight for all it's worth."

He started kissing behind her ear, already hypnotized from the softness of her skin and feeling the previous tension falling away like bags being dumped. All of that nonsense from a second ago was irrelevant and there's no way he was going to let it mess up the limited time they had together.

Imani unfurled from his grasp gently, turning to face him with a small smile on her face.

"Can we just rest tonight when we come back from dinner?" she asked. "I'm just really out of it and I know you had a long day on the court."

DeAndre released a breath, a hand hooked at the nape of his shirt.

He couldn't believe she was gonna do him like *this*.

In his previous life, DeAndre would be making plans by now to head out to the club in a few hours. Winning a match was all the pregaming he needed. But, he looked at his wife now, hearing a flash of her orgasmic scream, music to his ears he was looking forward to hearing tonight, and pushed a hand down the top of his fade.

With a grimace of a smile, he nodded at a glacial pace to her innocent smile.

"Okay."

Imani chuckled.

"We're seeing each other again in less than a week," she said.

"Yeah."

"Don't worry, I'll wear a garbage bag, all attraction gone to keep the torture at bay," she laughed, as she walked toward the bedroom.

Even if she wore a full-on garbage bag suit, losing attraction to his wife would never be the case. But - again, he was more than willing to follow her lead now and then, even if it was hard as hell to do sometimes.

# Chapter 34
# Support

While Imani was adjusting to her new life she started noticing certain things with a newfound perspective. For instance, something that she had never paid attention to before today were Lauri's diamond stud earrings.

Although she was fairly certain that her boss had worn them before, Imani noticed the intricate design of the tiny gold palm tree earrings with shards of crystals on the ends in Lauri's ears.

Thanks to her husband, Imani now had an interest in jewelry that she never knew she possessed. She found herself attracted to unique pieces and had jewelry trays, glass cups and velvet boxes with a variety of diamond bangles, bracelets, earrings and necklaces in every shape, size, color and clarity - all within a matter of weeks. When he was in town overnight or for a day or two, he'd give her thoughtful pieces at the most random moments - while waiting for their meal at a restaurant, on the way to the airport or the most unusual one - right after sex. When DeAndre had first done it, clasping a dazzling tennis bracelet on each wrist with a kiss, Imani shook out of sexual satiation immediately, her eyes widening. . Transactions were never something she was comfortable with in her relationships anymore, especially not in her marriage. Years ago in New York, she swore the man she thought loved her would abandon her if she didn't keep up her end of the deal in their twisted excuse of a relationship.

Seeing her reaction, DeAndre would often laugh.

"Don't overthink it," he said. "I never gave diamonds to anyone before, and I love how they look on you. Remember the coins you got at arcades back in the day? I always thought I used them all, but I'd find a few still in my pocket, like keepsakes. Think of them like that."

Well, DeAndre gave her a lot of keepsakes, then. So much so that any diamonds she saw on others or while she was out somewhere would have Imani in a mental tailspin of who the diamonds were from, what they represented to the person wearing them and why they wore them in the first place. DeAndre would always remind Imani that diamonds only held as much quality as the person wearing them.

"You see these niggas out here with the biggest ice, not worth a damn. Most of the time, they ain't worth even half of what they paid for it. Diamonds ain't ever gonna be cheap, people just make 'em that way."

Thankfully, Lauri wasn't one of those people. She was a minimalist, opting for simple touches that made her stand out without looking like she was trying.

It had been weeks since she and Lauri were in the same room together, let alone the same state, since Lauri spent the last two weeks in Portugal - visiting local museums and native artists in their studios. Plus, Imani got married. They were now in one of the last round of meetings about the upcoming Black Architecture banquet that was less than two months away.

"Thanks for being patient, Imani," Lauri said. Taking off her glasses, her palm trees waved just above her shoulders. "This trip was so worth it, but God, the work I come back to afterwards…"

She took a breath, shaking her head. "…it never ends. Weeks like these I wish I was still an MFA student."

Imani smiled. Even with Lauri being about fifteen or so years older than her, Imani knew all too well what she meant.

"The ramen days…"

"The ramen days," Lauri repeated with a smile. "Yes, yes."

Pausing to look at Imani for a moment, Lauri folded her hands together.

"I know we haven't seen each other in a few weeks, and I don't like to harp too much on my colleague's personal lives, but I'd be remiss if I didn't congratulate you on your recent nuptials."

"Oh," Imani beamed. "Thank you."

The meeting moved forward after that, with Imani checking off tasks that still had to be done - donors she still had to contact and confirming the photographer for the event. DeAndre had told Imani, over FaceTime after a game one night, that he'd like to be her plus one at one of Artgo's banquets one day. He teased that he'd follow her around to take pictures of her all night as her personal photographer.

"This all sounds really good, Imani," Lauri said. "We at least have most of what we need to pull this all together. At a certain point, we just have to be okay with what this banquet will be."

"So, shifting gears..." she continued. "I know you've been supporting Stella on-and-off for a little bit while taking care of your own responsibilities. How's that going?"

Stella and Gloria were the first colleagues Imani had seen after the wedding. Between the two of them - their utter shock and the number of questions thrown Imani's way wasn't a surprise at all. At a coffee shop during one of Stella's self-proclaimed "meditative breaks" from studio work, it didn't take long for Stella to allude to the fact that DeAndre wasn't the same man she had seen Imani with months prior.

"*Glad you didn't let your boyfriend keep you from the love of your life,*" she said, laughing like a hyena, in her wide-rimmed red glasses. Imani cast her eyes down then, feeling horrible, but folding her lips to keep her own laughter from escaping.

Gloria, on the other hand, was much more straightforward.

"*So, you're gonna quit, right?*" she asked, after a team meeting. "*You know you could go to like... Dubai on a whim and just stay contracted for small projects when you get bored.*"

But, as much as Imani contemplated leaving her job, especially because she was in the position for it to be an option, she decided not to. DeAndre didn't mention her *not* working and Imani wasn't trying to leave her job to be a housewife, at least not before having children. With more money came more options, but Imani never wanted to not have the option of being with people, being in community and being a resource. It's how she stayed inspired and creatively motivated. Besides, having the opportunity to do all of that with Lauri's support was the cherry on top.

"It's been great," she said, chuckling to herself. "Stella is a character, but I'm learning so much from her."

"Good," Lauri nodded. "Hopefully, one of those things is promoting your own work."

The professional smile Imani had all throughout the meeting faltered. Stella had warned her little secret wouldn't be one for long.

"Imani, why didn't you tell me?"

Looking at Lauri's expression, which was both a mixture of surprise and a touch of disappointment, Imani was reminded of the many delusions in her own mind.

"It's not like I didn't want to. I just…know that you're very selective of the talent presented here and I didn't want to make it seem like I was taking advantage."

"But I know now so I can introduce you to so many people who could help you."

Imani blinked. "Yeah, I know…"

She cocked a brow, widening her eyes. "…because I have potential, right?"

Lauri's own eyes narrowed as Imani's words seemed to sink in.

"You used the oldest trick in the book," she said, folding her arms. "I should've never believed you paid anyone for a mock-up of anything."

The two chuckled.

"Amazing," Lauri said, shaking her head. "I didn't know an artist could hide in plain sight."

Little did she know, Imani had learned to do that very well.

"Are you considering applying for AireFete?"

Imani grimaced.

"Honestly, I'm trying to figure out if I have the chops to even compete."

"You do, despite everything you see me say about other artists… you really do, Imani. You need to cultivate that. I'm open to at least help. Why don't you bring me some photos of your work and we can figure out what to do from there?"

## A Month of Sundays

"Wait, really?"

Lauri nodded and chuckled.

"Yes. I'm not on the judicial panel of the festival, but I know a few of the judges this year. One, in particular, is even pickier than me…"

She arched her brow.

"But we don't have to worry about that. Let's make sure the submission you present is worthy of consideration."

With a sigh of relief, Imani smiled, filled with a boost of confidence she didn't imagine feeling today.

"Thank you so much, Lauri."

∽

Imani collapsed on top of the large blue, orange, black-and-white striped plush pillows arranged on the couch in the living room. She sat on the couch drinking a warm mug of lemon tea after stripping out of her work clothes and into her silk pajama shorts set. After her meeting with Lauri, Imani was done in the office for the day and spent the rest of it at home. She FaceTimed DeAndre when she got settled, but he didn't answer, which would've been a big deal if they hadn't spoken this morning. They'd likely still talk tonight well after the Zoom call she had scheduled with Stella in another few minutes. Pulling up the Zoom link, Imani greeted her mentor with her eyes narrowed.

"You could've at least held our secret for another month," she said.

"It's my gift to you," Stella said, smiling. "It truly is."

The first few minutes of the call, Stella spoke about her own AireFete submission. In contrast to her signature lighthearted abstract pieces that were popular for decades, Stella was taking a different approach with her work for the festival.

"I'm at a point where I'm tired of doing what's expected of me," she said. "Even at my age, I want to break out and work on something that has a little more gravity, you know what I mean?"

Imani nodded, knowing exactly how Stella felt, especially now that so much in her life had changed. Most of Imani's pieces were much darker and felt more reflective but even Imani was starting to feel a distance from that vision. Nothing in her life right now was dark...finally, and the personal pieces that were works in progress well before her wedding, felt like such a chore.

"You've had so much success, though," Imani said. "I'm pretty sure whatever you do, we'll love it."

Stella smiled. "The question of 'what next?' never goes away Imani, no matter where you are in life."

Shortly after their wedding, she and DeAndre discussed all of the travel plans and upcoming professional commitments he had that were swiftly approaching. He had Imani added to his digital calendar from the time they were engaged but, Imani hadn't paid much attention to his schedule until now. As they toggled through the color-coordinated schedule blocks on the calendar, Imani suddenly felt this odd pang of sadness.

*Did he really need to do all of this?*

The question percolated in her mind over the last few months of Imani being back in his life. DeAndre, for all intents and purposes, was at the highest he could go in his career. There was no record in his sport he hadn't broken nor any trophy or title he hadn't won. But, like Stella mentioned, there would always be a "what's next?" floating in the deepest crevices of the mind, no matter how much you'd achieved in pursuit of your passion.

So, Imani chose to not bring it up to him at all, knowing what it was like to be driven by an insatiable passion like she kept having to reconcile with herself.

"I'm ready to go in a different direction too, believe it or not," she said. "I want my work to reflect my vision now, not the past."

"Well, you do have the luxury of resources," Stella said, her tight curls springing in multiple directions on the top of her head as usual, forming a makeshift halo around her face on camera. "Just continue following the muse and you'll know where you need to be."

"What does being inspired by your muse feel like?"

Stella looked above her screen and closed her eyes, her chin resting on the back of her hand.

"That's a very good question," she said. "It varies, really. It can feel like the smallest voice in the loudest room...or it could just..." she clapped her hands together, "smack you in the face like a car crash."

Imani laughed, thinking about how being with DeAndre pretty much felt like the latter. She was fully present and aware when she finally let him in and it was such a relief, almost like releasing pressure from a wound. What she wasn't expecting was how everything about him would spread all over her so quickly.

Things moved so quickly she couldn't even absorb everything he poured into her fast enough.

"Enjoy the rest of your week, my dear," Stella said as they wrapped up the call a few minutes later. "Many kisses and blessings to you."

Offering a virtual wave, Imani logged off and closed her laptop. She looked around the spacious living room, now painted a sangria red that Imani wasn't too sure DeAndre would even like. Though he insisted he did, granting Imani free reign to do whatever she wanted in their space. So far, Imani was working on transforming everything, from choosing and hanging artwork to setting up gallery walls in several rooms, and even installing sculptures of various sizes - both in and outside of their home. Imani wanted to transform their place into a living, breathing personal museum. In her eyes, no work of art was off limits.

For one of their first dates as a married couple, they had a private dinner at Maxwell's - an auction house that Imani mentioned to DeAndre was a major fixture in the art world. Some women got a thrill out of their men offering shopping sprees on clothes and jewelry, which Imani thought was nice. For her it was different, she damn near lost her mind when DeAndre picked up the tab for every piece of art she liked at an auction, including a 30-foot sculpture from a public art installation that was once in Europe before making its way to the States.

When it arrived at their home a week later, coincidentally on a day when DeAndre was in town, even Imani was shocked at its height.

"That's a big-ass paper clip."

DeAndre, with his hands in his pockets, observed the installation ahead of them. They were standing next to each other on the front porch, staring at this giant red paper clip being installed in the front yard, next to the circular driveway.

"It is," Imani said, "but, it's more than that, baby. It's really a commentary on the everyday items that could be extinct from our lives in a heartbeat…"

Noticing the technicians placing it too far near the driveway, Imani called out to him.

"Can you make sure to just inch it a little bit to the right? Thank you!"

She turned back to DeAndre.

"Like, one day, there might not be a need for this mundane item anymore because we will be such a digitally-driven society. This is the type of art we need to appreciate. It reminds us all of what we take for granted."

Imani paused, deep in thought, wound up from her emphatic rant, before looking at DeAndre again, who just stood there nodding and scratching his chin.

"Okay, I believe you. It's still a big-ass paper clip."

All eclectic art purchases aside, Imani still felt the most at peace in her art studio - a gift that DeAndre presented to her the day they got back from Paris after the wedding.

With her mug in hand, she walked into the open space, turning on the recessive lights to the dimmest setting.

The day they returned, the bright afternoon sun greeted Imani when she stepped into the foyer, heading toward the living room when DeAndre took her hand, pulling her into a small hallway on the right side.

"A'ight I really want you to like this."

He wrapped his arms around her waist, nuzzling her neck while peppering her neck with tantalizing kisses.

"You have a pretty decent track record, so I wouldn't be too nervous," she teased.

Before shutting her eyes as he requested, already mushy from his featherlike kisses, Imani watched him turn the glass knob, pushing the door open to reveal a spacious white room, one she never noticed was back here. The morning light spilled through a stain glass window with a kaleidoscope of colors across from where they were standing. The light showered over everything Imani needed to create her art and toil away to her heart's content - easels, canvases of various sizes, stools, long drafting tables and even a ceramic kiln for pottery.

Imani covered her mouth with her hands, tears pooling in her eyes. She never thought or gave herself permission to even imagine something like this.

## A Month of Sundays

With his arms still wrapped around her waist, DeAndre pulled her into him, kissing her from her shoulder up to her ear.

"I want you to dream in here. Those masterpieces in that beautiful mind of yours need someplace to land, right?"

Imani thought back to that moment almost every time she came in here now, making her feel like she was in a dream that DeAndre granted her permission to fall into.

She walked over to the large table parallel to the stain glass window. She gathered a few paintbrushes and turned on the water from the sink. After filling up a metallic canister with water, she sat on her stool where a work-in-progress was propped on an easel. She popped open the new tray of watercolors, recently shipped to the house and color tested several options in her palette, allowing herself to experiment with all of the possibilities.

A Neo-soul playlist, featuring Jill Scott's infectious proclamation of taking a long walk with her love and Erykah Badu's pleas for wanting to be left without anyone near, floated through the room surround sound system as Imani fell into the flow of painting. It was an ongoing meditation where she felt her full body engaged, from the bend of her index finger on the tip of the brush to the pressure she placed on the canvas in spurts. She couldn't believe there was a time in her life when she was going to give up on this passion of hers…this love, that pulled her through even her darkest moments. Imani loved DeAndre so much, but the love she had for her art saved her from herself…she'd never let anyone pull her away from that love again.

# Chapter 35
# On Fire

The sun was peeking in and out behind the clouds today, but it made for the perfect temperature for the practice match that DeAndre attended on behalf of the Tennis Alliance. He was at the Royal Court playing a charity game against a younger player, which meant the rules of engagement were much less formal and more laid back than a tournament match.

This was the first weekend DeAndre was back in town , after being away for a few weeks and Imani was bursting with excitement. She'd finally have him all to herself for at least a week and she was ready to take full advantage of it.

Sitting in the players' box with DeAndre's team, Imani watched him serve the ball countless times, with each hit more fluid than the next. The game was only for fun, so he wasn't competing as intensely as when she first saw him play months ago, but he was just as dominant. She loved seeing him reach, run, and pound the ball against his racket with sheer determination and wished, yet again, that his intensity and aggression translated in the bedroom.

She thought back to her day at Pins and Needles and the spontaneous nipple piercings from that visit that had been sensitive to the touch for weeks on end. She couldn't wear a majority of her wire bras, thankful that it was still somewhat cool enough to have on a layer or two of clothing. Her nipples had finally healed, adding twinkles of light to her deep brown areolas. Imani hoped

## A Month of Sundays

DeAndre finally seeing them would send a direct signal that she was ready for the kiddie gloves to finally come off.

She rode with Clive this morning to pick him up when his jet landed in Port Springs. And, when they hugged in front of the open backseat door, Imani felt a tingle in her spine just from his chest, covered in a warm hoodie, brushing against hers.

"*What's up, baby?*" he smiled, covering a yawn with his arm as it escaped his lips.

DeAndre didn't have a clue, just anticipating his reaction to this little secret she'd been holding for weeks made her feel excited, more feminine and hornier than hell. Imani was looking forward to reuniting with him since he'd been away for two weeks but hearing him now on the court was a completely different sensation.

His grunts and groans with each pound of the ball made her damn near wiggle in her seat. If she didn't have her legs crossed, she'd be thrusting her hips in his direction like a horny sociopath. With her delicate piercings now freshly healed, her nipples hardened, waking up this need in her that had to be satisfied...right now! After a break was called for a set, DeAndre stood alone stretching each arm across his body in front of him, elongating his muscles.

*This man...*

"DeAndre," projecting her voice just shy of a moan, with much more urgency than the event called for. She gripped the metal bar in front of her, on the verge of standing up.

The few who were around gave Imani a cautionary glance while DeAndre looked at her with much more scrutiny. He strolled over to her, jogging up the few steps - a beacon of nonchalance and masculine confidence - swiping a finger across his chin.

Once at her seat, DeAndre bent down to Imani's level, quickly glancing to his right side. His profile offered her a glimpse of his angular jaw, plump lips and high cheekbones before he turned to face her, waiting silently.

Imani wrapped her arms around his neck, drawing him close to look him square in the eye.

"I cannot wait until you beat this pussy tonight with as much force as you hit that ball. I'm so glad you're home."

DeAndre, suddenly punch-drunk, unwrapped Imani's arms from his neck and stood up. DeAndre jogged back down the steps then turned to look at Imani, walking backwards on the court, staring at her in a state of bewilderment like he'd just seen a ghost.

The entire match seemed to go as fast as the speed of light after that, with DeAndre serving forehands with an aggression much more reserved for a game with a cash prize at the end. Once the game was done and the score called, DeAndre threw his racket down before speed-walking, damn near sprinting, back to Imani. He grabbed her hand and pulled her up, dragging her through the row of seats, beyond the double doors of the court and through the tunnel to the locker rooms.

"Wha...wha...what about the press conference?" Imani asked, now winded. Each match, especially one done for charity, had post-game press conferences with sports reporters that players were required to attend and would often get fined if they didn't. From Imani's vantage point, he definitely wasn't going to attend.

Feeling the wind against her face, Imani felt her polka dot shift dress clinging to her on all sides, as they continued. She wobbled in her 3-inch ankle booties, smiling like a maniac behind him, trying to keep up with his pace.

He suddenly turned, pushing open a heavy metal door to the holding room he was often in before a match. Before she knew it, DeAndre pulled her in front of him, grabbed her butt, and lifted her legs to his waist with her back pressed against the wall. The bottom of her dress bunched up, and Imani heard fabric rip before feeling the head of his dick then his shaft plummet straight into her without warning.

Her head fell back to the wall from a pain that had her seeing stars. Imani's eyes crossed for a moment with her breathing shallow as DeAndre stood there, looking her over with a grin of his own.

"I tried taking it slow witchu..." he said, his voice buried in passion. "I didn't need...you like this...with me so soon."

Staring in her face like a parent scolding a child, DeAndre pushed into Imani again, her mouth gaping open this time.

"Ooo...mmmm..."

She was already wet from earlier, but now she was basically drowning, feeling her pussy settle into him, sculpting itself around him, without him doing a damn thing.

"Is this...what you want?"

After another thrust that felt like he had reached a kidney, DeAndre pulled out inch by inch without taking himself all the way out. Imani felt the rush of their skin-to-skin contact much quicker than she'd ever felt and was more sore than she thought she'd be. But, she wanted more - her heart fell apart into tiny pieces in her chest - already deflated from him leaving her. DeAndre followed it up with another thrust into her, though, before rolling his hips slowly.

"Oh...my...Oh...my Deeeeee," Imani said. "Waaa...wait."

DeAndre stopped, openly assessing her.

"No...I...no...I mean, yes," she said, stumbling. "Yes...I just..."

He smirked.

"I know you ain't actin' shy after saying all that shit out there."

She smiled at him, keeping her gaze steady, as she pulled her dress over her head. Imani felt the coolness of the room on her nipples immediately, not used to having them exposed outside of their bedroom. When DeAndre's eyes locked onto them - the precious jewels, he tilted his head, his eyes widening.

"Shit, baby..."

He immediately kissed her left breast right next to her piercing, making her knees buckle. DeAndre pulled his head back, still looking at her.

"Oh, you down for it, for real?"

With a smirk playing on her lips, Imani felt exactly the thrill she had wanted for weeks. Within seconds DeAndre pummeled into her again, kissing down the side of her neck, and she screamed loudly in pure elation.

∽

DeAndre stepped back into their bedroom, pulling down his shirt and checking the few messages on his phone he'd missed since being back home. He was home for another week until he had to head back out of town for the TL1000 tournament as part of the International Tennis League Tour and he was happy to actually wake up in the same time zone as his wife.

He walked to the bed and sat on the edge, glancing at Imani now, hugging a pillow as she lay underneath the sheets wrapped around her waist. DeAndre wished there was a way to quit this entire day and stare at her like this all day long. The early morning sun that spilled across her face and shoulders illuminated her to the highest degree, offering her a glow that even had DeAndre considering if they should move out the country and live on a beach somewhere. He couldn't always put into words how stunning Imani was to him, but he was learning his wife was more inclined to use her words with much more intention.

Yesterday at the charity match, DeAndre was caught off guard, to say the least. When she called him to the benches, he assumed she was going to ask when the match would be over or if they had lunch plans afterwards. But, no, she was anticipating something a little different.

*"I cannot wait until you beat this pussy tonight with as much force as you hit that ball."*

DeAndre thought someone had kidnapped his wife and replaced her with a clone. But, she was there in the stadium with him, her arms wrapped around his neck, her chestnut brown eyes brazen with unmitigated lust. There was no way he could deny that nor did he want to deny her any further than necessary. Her words lit a match in him that hadn't been ignited for months, a reckless sexual energy he was honestly working hard to keep down for a little longer, at least for her sake.

But, Imani's words made him bring it out in full force, baiting him not to hold back. Seeing her writhing underneath him, taking all of him in even with a little discomfort, thrilled him. And, once she pulled off her dress revealing the most delicate diamond barbells pierced through her nipples, DeAndre went straight feverish. He had to literally pace himself to keep from releasing in her so damn early. Imani may not have had any experience sexually before him, but just her curiosity and willingness to go over the edge put her well ahead of the class.

Peeling his gaze away from her on the bed, DeAndre went to his Instagram feed that refreshed with new posts. Most of them were a random mix of sports talk, a few athletes and peers who were casual friends and productivity gurus who swore they had the best tips to make it "your best year yet." But, in the bevy of his scrolling, he came across a photo of Jazmine, her head tilted towards a cloudless sky, smiling with her eyes closed. Her golden curls from months ago were now intertwined in long thin blonde braids that were gathered in front of her chest.

*Blossoming into a new season with a new breakthrough.*

DeAndre pushed his head back at the caption, careful not to laugh out loud to stir Imani awake. Even though DeAndre wasn't pressed about his own image, he knew enough to know when someone was "rebranding" themselves for clout. Seeing her the other day in California made him realize that something must be on the horizon for her to want to switch from selfies in the club with her girlfriends to photos of her out in an open field with sunflowers in her hair. Shaking his head, he mindlessly double tapped the image before looking back up at Imani.

From where DeAndre was sitting, Imani resembled a model in one of the many paintings in her studio that she told him were never complete, but always "in progress." She looked so serene with her head bent forward just enough to see her profile and the light purple in her hair forming a halo around her head.

He had to capture her at this angle, just like this. After snapping two photos, he chose the second one to upload and caption.

*The black Mona Lisa with better features.*

His profile mostly consisted of professional action shots of him on the court that Stephanie uploaded herself after a game. But, DeAndre started personally posting random pictures of him and Imani out and about whenever they spent the weekends together - some at home, but mostly when they were just hanging out. Without all the professional images to break up his personal ones, his Instagram could easily be a digital shrine for his wife.

DeAndre dropped his phone in his pocket, inching closer to Imani - still reclined in peace. Placing his hand on her cheek, he kissed her forehead, stirring her awake. DeAndre thoroughly enjoyed adjusting to suit her needs, but always wanted to make room for being gentle with his woman too.

Shaking her head, she opened her eyes slowly, adjusting to the sunlight.

"What time is it?" she asked, her voice drenched in sleep.

"High time for you to get up, baby. C'mon, what you got goin' on today?"

Stretching her arms out wide, Imani rested her chin on the pillow, looking at him with a smile.

"Playing hooky."

DeAndre cut his eyes at her.

"What that mean?"

She laughed.

"It means...I don't have any meetings or deadlines today. So, I could either sleep here like I was doing or I could spend the day with you?"

DeAndre put a hand at his chest.

"You wanna spend the day with little ol' me?"

She shook her head, pulling him forward by his shirt.

"I haven't seen you do anything besides play a match."

"Yo, but that's a top-dollar experience you seein' for free, baby. I'm sayin'..."

"Yeah, yeah," Imani pulled him even closer, planting a kiss on his lips. "But, I wanna see what else you got goin' on. I'll be a quiet observer of your ordinary day."

DeAndre raised an eyebrow.

"A'ight, you can roll wit' me. I told Aiden I'd see him play this season and haven't gotten around to it. Down for a basketball game after my brand meeting with Elite?"

Imani nodded, her eyes shining brightly. If she said she was going to be a quiet observer, DeAndre believed her. He didn't *always* want her to be that way, though. He pulled his phone back out of his pocket to let Trey and two of his friends know Imani would be joining them.

"So, do we have extra time for something before we go?"

He looked up at her, instinctively shoving his phone out of the way. He absolutely had time for anything she wanted to do.

As if knowing what he was thinking, Imani shook her head, putting her hands up.

"Not that, DeAndre," she said, laughing before biting the corner of her lip. "You owe me something else."

∼

Loosening his grip on his racket's handle, DeAndre swung at the tennis balls coming his way from the service machine, watching them bounce into center court on the opposite side. He had done a few stretches just to get himself limber but stopped himself from going through his usual lengthy warm-up routine. He wasn't preparing himself for a match, and promised Imani he wouldn't exert too much energy on her. He'd go easy for now.

"I'm ready, Mr. Harrison."

DeAndre turned towards Imani's playful voice as she strutted from the patio to the court, sticking her chest out and waving. With his hand at the back of his neck, he watched her with a smile, shaking his head.

She was lucky as hell to be who she was in his life because he never entertained the thought of giving lessons to anyone, not even his closest relatives. Helping a group every once-in-a-while for charity was one thing, but coaching someone one-on-one required a different level of patience that he didn't have. No matter how many offers he received from organizations and even previous coaches offering to train him to do it when he retired, DeAndre couldn't stand to even play an opponent off their game. What would it look like for him to *train* someone who didn't know what the hell they were doing in the first place? When he was talking mess in front of Michael all those months ago, DeAndre was only being funny. Apparently, Imani didn't forget what he said.

Watching her approach the court in sneakers with a short, cream pleated tennis skirt and a matching tight sleeveless lycra top that hugged her from the waist up, the imprint of her nipples pressing into the fabric as if trying to escape bondage, Imani must've had this in her memory bank of fantasies.

Despite himself, he dropped his head, laughing, in disbelief of how Imani could turn the mundane into something far more entertaining and, still look sexy as hell while doing it too.

Imani planted herself in front of him, making eye contact.

"A'ight, we don't have much time," he said, his tone laced with laughter. "So, we'll go light."

"I thought we talked about not going light on me all the time. I can adjust," she winked.

DeAndre pulled a hand down his face, in an attempt to hide his grin.

"Imani..."

"Okay, okay. I'm listening. I'll be good."

She straightened herself with a smirk, fluttering her eyes up at him like he was the best thing since sliced bread. Her submission to him in the most subtle ways, outside of sex, was a little overwhelming at times.

After guiding Imani through a series of stretches, surprisingly without any innuendos, they stood at the baseline where DeAndre pointed further up the court.

"Let's go up to the service line. We're gonna start closer to the net."

Grabbing another racket before following Imani, he handed it to her once he stood next to her.

"So, put your thumb around the bottom of the racket. It should be next to your middle finger."

Following his instructions, Imani held the racket so tight, he could see the white of her knuckles. DeAndre smiled, settling into how much of an honest beginner she was at this. He placed his hand over hers.

"Free your hold on it a little, baby. It's not goin' anywhere."

His comment seemed to relax her a little as she chuckled.

"You've really never played before?"

It was something so natural for DeAndre that he couldn't imagine anyone not being exposed to it. Imani shook her head.

"My athletic career stopped when I got hit upside the head with a volleyball in the second grade," she shrugged. "So, no, I didn't actively pursue an opportunity to get tennis balls thrown my way."

DeAndre laughed, picking up the two tennis balls next to him on the court.

"A'ight. I'm gonna just bounce this ball in front of you and you're just gonna practice swinging at it."

"When you swing, the back of your hand has to end up at your cheek, with your elbow pointing forward, like this..."

DeAndre bounced the ball and demonstrated, angling his body to twist in the direction the ball needed to go.

"Where your racket goes, your body's gotta follow, a'ight?"

Imani looked at him with her eyes agape, clearly taking all of this in.

"Oh well, that looks easy enough."

But, when DeAndre bounced the ball in front of her this time, Imani missed it, swinging the racket and spinning her body backwards. She looked up at him.

## A Month of Sundays

"How long do we have again?"

DeAndre shook his head, chuckling at her.

"Nah, I'm not letting you quit just like that. C'mon, let's go."

It took a little more time for Imani to get the hang of her swing, but she did eventually. Before he knew it, DeAndre was on the opposite side of the court serving her, the two falling into a casual rally. Even though he had sworn he'd never coach anyone, DeAndre wouldn't mind helping Imani who had the potential of being decent – he'd do anything for her.

After a few minutes, DeAndre took his phone out of his pocket and checked the few messages that came in from Trey, letting him know he was on the way. Imani served the ball, which he saw bounce away from him on his right side.

Imani yelped in triumph.

"Did I just score against the king?"

She cupped her hand around her mouth, walking closer to the net.

"The Kaaaang of Tennis?" she shouted.

DeAndre peeled his gaze away from his phone, looking at Imani like she lost her damn mind.

"Chill out," he said, walking over to her. "That ain't count at all. Let's get ready to get outta here." Once at the net, DeAndre picked her up off the ground. She wrapped her legs around his waist and showered him with kisses.

"I think I could use some weekly lessons from you," she said.

"Weekly?" he asked, raising a brow. "That's serious."

He walked them back into the living room, placing her down at the end of their L-shaped couch. She sat, with her arms still around his neck, before placing her hands on the sides of his face. Imani stared at him with such enthrallment, her eyes sparkling.

"Yeah, so I could get really good," she said, smiling with a hint of mischief. "Then, I could really beat you."

DeAndre smiled, admiring the bronzed glow of her skin, already thinking of the many ways he could have her right now. Enjoying Imani was something that he didn't think he'd ever get tired or bored with, especially because he felt something new with her every time.

As Imani pulled his head towards her, she reclined her body even further on the couch, her already short skirt rising well above her thighs. DeAndre placed a kiss on her lips that she responded to passionately, as he danced his fingers up her chocolate legs until it disappeared underneath the pleated fabric. He soon felt the wet depths of her dripping almost instantly as he caught her, observing him, while propping herself up on her elbows.

"You ain't ever beatin' me."

"Ever?" Imani said, "Why can't I?"

Pulling his finger out of her, DeAndre sucked on it, closing his eyes with a smile. A coffee first thing in the morning, doctored up to perfection couldn't even beat his wife's sweetness…couldn't even come close. When he opened his eyes, he found her staring up at him grinning, as she parted her thighs even further. DeAndre dragged her towards the edge of the couch and wrapped her legs around him, allowing Imani to cross her ankles at his back. Without any panties on, Imani's scent engulfed all his senses, making him lose all sense of time and space.

"I'm tellin' you," he said, looking up at her again. "That ain't happenin' ever.'"

Before she managed to say anything further, DeAndre began placing the softest kisses on her stomach as he made his way down to fully indulge in her sweetness, her screams echoing up to their high ceilings.

## Chapter 36
# Boss Barbie, Reporting for Duty

After taking one last glance at her work emails that finalized the banquet plans, Imani pushed her laptop closed once and for all before walking over to her and DeAndre's closet. She had just gotten out of the shower and was peeling off the 5-minute face mask at the sink. Looking at her phone, she knew DeAndre was waiting on her slow self. She had to get a move on.

Imani chuckled, thinking about the look of slight dread on DeAndre's face after she asked for that private tennis lesson a few minutes ago. She could tell he only agreed to it because *she* was the one who asked him and was glad that by the time he saw her in that ridiculous tennis outfit she picked out, all hints of aggrievement were gone.

Imani vowed to herself that she'd do what she could to make the moments with him surprising, sexy and a little bit ridiculous, if possible, since the time they spent together overall would be limited due to his schedule. Teasing him at tennis matches and egging him on for silly lessons were the tip of the iceberg. Imani wanted to make the time they spent with each other count, no matter how tired she was from her own responsibilities. She wasn't kidding when she said she could sleep all day in that bed of theirs. It was getting more difficult to get out of it as the months grew chillier in the mornings. But, when he stirred her awake this morning, Imani was instantly reminded of how damn fine he was...his deep smooth skin just close enough for her to touch. So, she became much more interested in whatever plans he had going on than going to work.

Pushing the long sliding door of their closet, Imani walked to her side of it, which honestly had just as many clothes as DeAndre's side. Silk, linen and chiffon took up the majority of her space, along with multiple rows of shoes that were either old favorites or recent purchases within the short time she and DeAndre had been together. Just as they discussed, the two weren't going on a honeymoon until late next year, right after the tennis season. Even though Imani understood and didn't make a big deal about it, DeAndre still booked them a weekend stay at 30 Montaigne in Paris the day after the wedding. Imani wasn't sure how much he spent, but the number of Dior packages she had to unbox and sort through proved to be a delightful house project that took her an entire week to finish.

Staring at the array of colorful, textured fabric spilling over the rack and onto the beige carpet, she realized if she didn't start wearing some of these pieces now, they'd likely just sit in her closet untouched for a year. It didn't take long for her eyes to land on a nude chiffon baby doll dress with puff sleeves that was one of the last items she picked out at Dior. It was the only one DeAndre hadn't seen on her and was more of an impulsive choice based on how close the nude was to her own complexion.

Tying up the straps of her gold sandals, Imani accessed her look, complete with the dress, in the mirror. She's never shied away from dressing exactly how she felt and today was no exception. Being with DeAndre and being loved by him brought out a more adventurous side of her that she never expected. It felt like she was above cloud 9, at the peak of frenetic energy. Colors appeared more vivid and her creative output was the highest it had ever been. She had been working on the pieces for the exhibition application off and on, but thought she might go in a different direction artistically. Right now, all of her pieces were abstract homages to the love that was brewing in her...in both of them. She couldn't just ignore what was becoming so instinctual.

Picking up her mini lime green Brandon Blackwood purse that held absolutely nothing of necessity besides a lip gloss and a pack of gum, Imani sauntered down the steps. Her hand grazed the iron banister, with pink, green and yellow diamond tennis bracelets hanging from her wrists. Once she got to the

## A Month of Sundays

living room where DeAndre, Trey, Will and Malik were waiting, Imani took one glance at all the men dressed down in jeans, sneakers and hats, and laughed at herself for wearing an outfit that was about as rational as a Barbie doll costume. But she didn't care, as long as DeAndre didn't mind.

He had been sitting on the couch, going through his phone, when he glanced up and saw her, devouring every inch of her. Imani always felt like DeAndre observed her intensely, but there were moments like this where he gazed at her with yearning like a kid unwrapping toys on Christmas Day.

"Beautiful."

He walked over, took her hand and lifted it above their heads for Imani to do a slow spin. When she was facing him again, his gaze seared into her, making her squirm and her nipples harden. If they were by themselves, Imani would've undid his belt and jumped right on him, right then and there, from the way he was looking at her. He turned back to his crew, who were watching TV and scrolling through their own phones, pants sagging and wearing multiple chains of ice.

"Y'all definitely ain't ridin' with us."

Once they arrived at Elite Athletics headquarters in Rapid Springs, the five of them followed the receptionist into the spacious conference room, complete with a wall of mock-ups next to a view of Rapid Springs, 100 feet above ground. The square glass boardroom table on the left side of the room had jet black folders placed in front of each white rolling chair. Imani sat down, only to realize how much of her skirt was spilling over the chair, looking like she was drowning in a puddle of tulle. If she thought she stood out here, she knew she was going to stick out like a sore thumb courtside at a game. She shifted in her seat twice, sliding her hands underneath her, to no avail. Placing her tiny purse on the desk next to her folder, she might as well be a kid among adults. When DeAndre sat next to her, she noticed amusement dancing in his eyes.

"You good?"

"I wasn't being very realistic with this outfit, that's all." Imani shifted again.

He sat with his arms on the table, affection lacing his features and shrugged.

"Realistic is boring, baby."

A small group of executives dressed in corporate casual attire filed inside, each of them greeting everyone individually and congratulating DeAndre and Imani on their recent nuptials. A few moments later, they presented DeAndre and the group with mock-ups of his sneakers that would be released for a limited run. Imani watched the entire presentation, complete with conceptual interactive graphics displayed on a large screen television and couldn't help but be stunned...by the pretentiousness of it all.

Imani remembered talking to DeAndre about today and how excited he was to be offered the opportunity to release a line on the heels of so many other greats before him. How he'd tell Rand and anyone who'd listen to him that they'd be rocking his shoes one day. He wasn't too impressed with much of anything anymore, so far into his career, but this was the one milestone he was looking forward to the most. Imani couldn't help but swell with pride. But now, she wanted this ostentatious show to end.

"...we want nothing but the best colorways to represent each facet of your legacy," an executive was saying. "From your first major Grand Slam as a teen to where you are now, competing at the highest global level any player has achieved thus far. Your story started in Port Springs, and it never left."

The laughter that spilled out of Imani's mouth penetrated the quiet in the room, unexpectedly. She hadn't said a word the entire time they were there and everyone looked at her, including DeAndre, his forehead creased in confusion.

"Sorry," Imani said, sarcasm still at the tip of her tongue.

"What's up?"

She shook her head, tugging on the jewel pendant on her necklace.

"Don't mind me," Imani said, not wanting to draw any more attention to herself but DeAndre was still looking at her like they were the only two in the room.

"What's on your mind?"

"It's just..." Imani looked at the executives - all White men in navy, brown and black suits, telling four Black men from Port Springs what representing their neighborhood looked like.

"The idea of y'all dropping a shoe at a price point higher than what some Port Springs residents make in a month is kind of...tone deaf."

The executive speaking looked between Imani and DeAndre, pushing his glasses up on his nose. His face washed red in an instant.

## A Month of Sundays

"Oh well," he said, clearing his throat. "Mrs. Harrison, we, at Elite Athletics, always want to offer products of quality...which means that could reflect in higher pricing."

"Right," Imani said. "It's just you're specifically putting this out in the middle of Port Springs. I know it seems like everyone there now has it because of all the new development going on, but the street you're having the pop up on is directly opposite the poorest middle school in the area."

A pin drop could have been heard in the room.

Trey, who was sitting next to Imani, shook his head with his teeth pulled into a grimace. Malik, sitting next to Trey, let out a chuckle, pulling up his hat to scratch the top of his head, all while DeAndre looked at her, taking in her words.

"We could always look at other options for location," another executive chimed in.

"Nah, we need to scratch this and get another mock-up design," DeAndre said. "I was buggin.' Nothing I got my name on needs to be inaccessible."

The suits all looked at each other flustered at the unexpected direction of the meeting. A pang of guilt hit Imani. The achievement of DeAndre being chosen was enough. His presence...making decisions in a room like this, with people like this, was enough. She should've just kept her mouth shut.

"Sure, Mr. Harrison," the first executive said. The sigh he let out didn't go unnoticed. "Do you have any other concerns?"

"I can't tell you any concerns," DeAndre said, "if you haven't applied what's been said in the first place."

Imani had no idea she could be turned on by her husband any more than she had been. But yeah...it was possible.

"Fair enough," the executive said. "I'll be sure to give you updates within the next few weeks. We really want to make sure this is a mutually beneficial collaboration."

After shaking hands with everyone, DeAndre, Imani and the rest of the crew left the headquarters to find Clive waiting with the Escalade idling. Everyone climbed in, making room for each other in the back seat as DeAndre sat next to Imani. When she looked up once she was settled, she found him staring at her, his face obscure.

"What's wrong?" she asked.

He shook his head, placing his focus back on his phone.

"Nothin'."

Imani felt the energy between them shift slightly and it hadn't gone away by the time they pulled up to the basketball game. In the few months Imani had really gotten to know DeAndre as intimate as they were now, she'd noticed how good he was at acting like he was normal, placing his hand on her thigh or draping his arm over her shoulders. However, subtle shifts in his gaze when she tried to catch his attention during the game let her know that something was on his mind.

During halftime, as the dancers performed their routine with pom-poms, gyrated thrusts and long hair flying about, Trey tapped Imani on the shoulder. She was moving slightly to the rhythm of the music in the stadium, so she stopped sipping her Coke and turned to Trey.

"Imani, you lookin' fresh off the runway today," he smiled. "This is a good look for you."

"Oh Trey, I just threw this together," she chuckled nervously. "It's not a big deal."

She faced the court again, feeling DeAndre's stare as he sat next to her. Taking a quick glance his way, Imani watched him shake his head slightly, lifting his eyes in disbelief. She didn't understand why, so she just shrugged it off.

Once the game ended, Clive drove Imani and DeAndre home first before dropping off the rest of his crew. The two walked inside with DeAndre following behind her up the stairs to their bedroom. She stopped midway, playfully bumping him on his head with her ass in all that tulle. He placed his hand on her backside, gripping it.

"C'mon, stop playin.'"

Imani still heard a tinge of humor in his voice, letting her know that tonight didn't have to be a total bust. The way she wanted him all on top of her and through her was criminal.

Once in the bedroom, she went straight to their closet, taking off her jewelry and placing them back onto the trays on her vanity. She wiggled her feet out of her heels and put them back on the second shelf before turning to

## A Month of Sundays

find DeAndre standing there, leaning against the doorway. His arms were folded across his chest, he was still fully dressed, looking at her in the same way he had earlier.

"Hi." Imani raised her eyebrow. "Is there a reason you're looking at me like I killed your cat or something?"

"Do you know what happens when you're in a room?"

The question came out of DeAndre's mouth much lower than she expected, making Imani pause.

"What?" she sighed, clueless as to where this was going.

"Do you know how much attention you command just by being yourself?"

"And...I take it you're mad at that?"

DeAndre shook his head. "No, I'm not."

He went to his side of the closet, taking off his own chain and wedding band, then turned back to her.

"I don't know what got you actin' like you're not confident, but it's starting to get annoying."

Imani put her hands on her hips and paused from undressing to focus on him.

"First of all, who says I'm not confident? Were you at the same charity match that I was at? Or...was that not real?"

"At the meeting today," DeAndre continued, "You clammed up on me, then at the game - Trey throws you a compliment and you do that deflecting shit."

"Okay." Imani tried to gather her thoughts on how to respond. "I told you how I felt at that meeting."

"Yeah, after I had to ply it out of you."

"D, I tagged along to a meeting that I had no say in. This is a huge step in your career that was in the process of happening long before I entered the picture."

"But, you're here now and you're my wife. Wherever I go - you do too and you need to start owning that. I told you I don't want you shrinkin' behind me. I need you to call shit out to me when no one else does. Those jokers could care less about the way my shit is sold in the 'hood, as long as it's sellin.' But *you* care. *We* care."

Imani looked at DeAndre, speechless. She didn't know whether to be pissed that he was picking a fight or turned on by how he upheld her in his life.

"I don't even know why we're fighting right now."

She attempted to push past him out of the closet when DeAndre pulled her backward into his chest by the waist.

"Nobody's fightin'," he said, his tone much gentler. He planted a kiss on her neck, making her tingle. "My tone ain't that great. I'm sorry…but, I want you to see what I see…in you."

He turned them around to the standing mirror where Imani saw the two of them linked together. Imani never had an issue with her looks or what she brought to the table, yet something prevented her from feeling like she belonged in DeAndre's world. There were so many moving parts to it that she'd often become overwhelmed just trying to keep up with the whole operation, never realizing it was hers for the taking. She needed to learn to take now and ask for forgiveness later.

"What do you see?" she asked.

"I see…my heart."

Imani, feeling her pulse race, turned towards DeAndre and pressed her lips against his cheek. He met her lips in a long languid kiss that Imani felt pulse throughout her body. With her arms wrapped around his neck, she was about to jump to his waist, when he pulled both of her arms down gently.

She opened her eyes, disappointment settling in, only to find DeAndre looking at her, neither with annoyance nor lust, but more like curiosity.

"You sayin' you confident?" he asked in that sexy low, deep tone of his.

DeAndre pulled away from her, but held onto her hands, leading them to the chair next to the standing mirror. He sat down, leaning against the back of the seat with his legs naturally spreading open. Imani stood in front of him, clueless as to what he was even thinking. He didn't say a word… just sat there looking at her. Though Imani still had her dress on, she felt naked under his gaze. It was always so startling for her.

"What is it, D?" she sighed, feeling her heart in her throat at this point. The anticipation was making her crazy.

"You said you're confident and I want you to prove it," he said. "I want you to touch yourself in front of me."

# A Month of Sundays

Imani's breath grew shallow as she sputtered out a laugh.

"What?"

"We already know what you sound like, but I want you to see it."

Her eyes fluttered excessively as she blushed.

"What is doing that gonna prove?" she asked.

"It's gonna either prove the confidence you already have or give you just what you need to finally have it," he said. "Either way, once we're done, you're gonna be screaming your own name when I'm deep inside you."

Imani laughed even harder at how absolutely insane DeAndre sounded. He never ceased to amaze her and she searched his eyes for any sign of humor, finding none. He was dead serious.

"What're you gonna to be doing?" Imani pointed at him, trying to show a level of debate.

"I'm just gonna watch you."

Imani felt herself throb with urgency despite her mind telling her to shut it down. She thought back to when she was housesitting this very home, throwing all caution to the wind and how she had not envisioned how that one moment could change everything. Now they were married, obviously having sex, but it never crossed her mind to have him *watch* her pleasure herself. What was in it for him? She couldn't fathom being focused enough to see it all the way through.

But now, with her eyes locked into his in a war of wills, Imani felt like she had a sudden urge to go against any sort of logical reasoning she possessed. If this was what it took for them to get it in tonight, so be it.

She dropped her sleeves from her shoulders, letting the dress fall to her ankles, before stepping out of it. With only a thong and pasties on, the air felt cool against her bare skin as she saw the faintest smile on DeAndre's lips.

Her eyes grazed over her reflection in the mirror, allowing her to fully observe her shape, the tattoos filled with memories of her past and hints at her future …the dips of her figure. Rubbing a hand on her stomach, she moved in closer for a better view, trailing her hand from her waist to the edge of her breasts, her pasties peeled off slowly as she started rubbing her nipples… one by one before pulling at them together already feeling her nub swell.

She then smoothed her hand down the middle of her chest, between her breasts, feeling herself as her hand ventured lower to her sweet spot. As she rubbed her clit lightly before alternating between pinching and pulling on it with much more pressure, her eyes focused on the mirror, sinking deeper into a hypnosis of her own doing, forgetting DeAndre was even there. Familiar moans escaped her lips, sounding foreign as viewing her facial expressions increased the intensity her self-stimulation evoked. Falling to her knees, she drove her fingers deeper into herself, faster then slower, before settling into a successive rhythm of hip thrusts guided by her own touch.

Her entire life was handed to her in a way that familiarized her with being alone...by herself, even when she was in a crowd of people. But, she never felt the potential of its power...never felt like she could truly let go even behind closed doors because she always felt like she had to keep it together to prevent falling all the way apart. For the first time she realized there was so much beauty in doing just that...so much beauty in accepting all of the fallen parts for what they were.

She lazily glanced at her reflection on her knees, chocolate tone aglow and she collapsed backwards to the floor as moisture of dynamic proportions spilled out of her.

"Aahhhhhhhhhhhh," she moaned. She closed her eyes, letting her orgasm wash over her in waves over her entire body.

DeAndre's woodsy smell ignited all of Imani's senses as she felt him kissing her neck. She opened her eyes to find him staring at her with a mix of pride and lust.

"How does it feel to own your shit?"

Staring up at him with a renewed flame, Imani smiled, wrapping her arms around his neck to pull him close without saying a word.

# Chapter 37
# Countdown

What DeAndre loved the most about being with his wife was how supple she seemed to be anytime he was inside her. Now that they knew each other physically for a few months, Imani no longer had an issue with switching things up. She made it abundantly clear that she was more than ready for variety, so the fact that he delivered variety in every form imaginable was apparent in sex between them very quickly.

They went fast...they went slow...they made love in bed...in the kitchen on countertops and even in the pantry doing their best to time their sessions around the staff's schedule. DeAndre even suspended Imani in mid-air once, giving her head in the living room with her cocoa brown legs hanging from his shoulders and her back against the windows facing the tennis court.

Even with their urgency for one another, DeAndre noticed early on that Imani loved having sex in the dark, enjoying the suspense of not knowing where their hands would land or when he'd actually penetrate her. He liked that part of it, too. DeAndre definitely preferred, and was obsessed with, seeing his wife in the light. He loved having a clear view of every inch of her body.

Just like now as they lay in their hotel bedroom, with the moonlight streaming over them as he admired her body. He dropped kisses all over her as she lay beneath him in bed, smiling lazily and looking at him through half-lidded eyes dazed from post-coital pleasure. Their eyes held for a moment until

Imani looked away first, biting the corner of her bottom lip. Her smile suddenly vanished.

"What's on your mind?"

Imani's flight back home was set to leave in a few short hours and, even though she wouldn't say it, DeAndre picked up on a shift in Imani's mood whenever either of them had to leave the other. She'd be cool for the first half of the week - fully present, jovial and lighthearted with him when they'd go out for date nights or out to breakfast. But, by the night before or the day of his flight, she'd become distant, detaching herself slightly as she anticipated his departure mere hours later. At that point, DeAndre developed a habit of taking it upon himself, to pull out all stops to show his affection, not because he was guilty but for her to know that he missed her too when he was away and, no amount of distance between them would keep him from feeling it.

"Just thinking about what I need to do at work this week," she sighed, biting the side of a fingernail she drew to her mouth. "My clients and my boss...the usual."

He knew she was blatantly lying, but he wasn't quite sure he wanted to open himself up to receive her true feelings in this case. Talking about his career and the sacrifices that came along with it was a slippery slope for him - a touch point he wanted to keep off-limits for as long as he could.

DeAndre watched Imani for a beat. Her eyes were affixed to the room's high ceilings in a trance as she kept biting on her nail. He lay on top of her, his legs sprawled, his arms resting on both sides of her and he could feel the rise and fall of her abdomen. He could stay in this exact position with her all day.

But, another thing he loved doing to his wife? Surprising her.

"You know..." he started, "You have this curiosity that I've picked up on."

Imani's eyes shifted back to him.

"Huh?"

"Well, you tend to bring up your concerns about other women before you..."

Imani's eyes narrowed, physically tightening herself underneath him.

"Are you curious about what I did with them?"

Imani pushed her head back slightly, eyebrows dipped in offense, her mouth ready for battle as it curved into an 'O.'

"Just...listen to my question."

He placed a soft hand at her breast with just enough force to slow down her thoughts.

The fire in Imani's eyes slowly settled as she closed her lips, his words sinking in. She didn't answer the question. But, her eyes probed, waiting for him to continue. DeAndre eased himself into her softness and positioned himself to go deeper again. And, without a smile in sight, Imani allowed him to, opening her legs a little wider just for him.

"I ain't gonna lie, I've done my fair share with women, sometimes...with more than one at the same time."

Imani blinked as a flash of surprise and intrigue flooded her face. DeAndre felt her quake in the middle.

"Oh, that got you curious?" he chuckled. "You wanna know how it went down?"

Her eyes blinked a mile a minute before she looked up again, her mouth slightly agape.

"I'll spare you the details, but...I gotta say, the women who I was with..."

He nodded.

"...would've loved you..."

Within seconds, Imani's wetness began to fill all around him.

"Would've been affirming you, sayin' all these sweet things to you, all that...and I'd have to watch them do it 'cause they'd be so caught up wit' you. Like, I didn't deal with women who got down like that and didn't *like* other women. What sense would that make?"

Imani continued staring, with the smallest smirk gracing her lips.

"Though somethin' I learned about myself since bein' with you is...I get jealous. I'm getting to know you too well, baby. Pussy's top notch on the shelf - no comparison. I ain't sharin' you with anyone."

DeAndre pushed himself further into her suddenly, causing Imani to release a sharp breath.

"I know you just came. But...but....you really think that's all you have to give me?"

Imani still didn't answer, but an even wider smile crept over her face. He dropped small kisses across her collar bone before planting an even deeper one at her neck, inhaling her amber scent. He circled his fingers around her nipples, her diamond piercings pushing against his fingertips.

"Oooohhh," she let out.

After one stroke, DeAndre felt her explode all over again, moisture releasing the bits of friction they had between them a moment ago. Imani's eyes crossed as he glided into her languidly before picking up speed, only to rock into her slowly all over again.

"Baby...I'm gonna..." she muttered. Just before an impending orgasm, Imani would be rendered speechless or stop speaking mid-sentence but, he wasn't done with her just yet.

"You gonna...what?" he asked, in mock confusion. "You gonna cum for me?"

Imani placed a hand on his chest, gripping his pecs, as if she wanted him to stop it all and take a breath. She pressed her pelvis towards him as the wave of her orgasm took over. Catching her breath after releasing a drawn-out scream, it took some strength for DeAndre not to meet her orgasm with his own. He stilled himself in the depths of her.

"That was...amazing," he said. "But, I...I don't know. You could give me more...I'm thinkin' I could get it outta you."

Imani sighed, rolling her eyes.

"DeAndre..." she whined.

"Well...a'ight."

Raising a brow with a sigh, he pulled out of her slowly until she damn near yelped, placing her hands at his back, forcing him forward again.

"No, no...don't," she looked up at him, this time batting her honey-colored eyes, almost bashful.

He looked at her, tilting his head to the side, her beauty plummeting him in the face.

"You givin' me another, right?"

Imani nodded before releasing a nervous laugh. He felt everything in her now and thought, *how long would it take for her to cum again? Could he predict that?*

He knew he was good, but was he *that* damn good?

"Don't worry, baby, I gotchu," he said. "I'll count you down."

## A Month of Sundays

She blinked, her forehead dipping in confusion. Before she could question or respond, he resumed stroking his way into her thoughts, pushing into her to the hilt, so that all thoughts vanished from her mind...except him. Imani's eyes fluttered as her nostrils flared.

"What're you...how do you," she stammered.

"Now, lemme see...lemme...lemme think," he said, drawing close to her ear. "You wanna start with a number or should I?"

Imani let out a harried breath, shaking her head in agony. She held onto him with her arms around his neck, letting her body following his lead.

"Let's start with 10," he said. Then, he thought about it, taking a pause, ceasing all movement. Imani's eyes widened in response, alarmed at the abrupt halt in his pleasurable motion.

DeAndre smiled, chuckling.

"Nahhhh...let's start with 7...I like that number." Her response let him know she was almost there, that quickly, again.

"So, when I count down to 1," he whispered in her ear, "I wanna hear you scream so damn loud for me that you pull an orgasm outta me."

Imani's lips trembled as he continued thrusting in quick, rhythmic movements.

"7...."

Imani moaned, making his heart race even faster. If he knew he was gonna have this much fun being married, DeAndre would've dragged her ass to the Justice of the Peace the night he met her.

"6..."

"Oh myyyyyyy...oh my God."

"5..."

Imani wrapped her legs around his waist tightly, giving him even more of her.

"4..."

"I...I.."

"3..."

"Pleassssseee, DeAndre...uhhhhh..."

"2..."

He felt her entire body soften under him as she stilled herself. DeAndre stopped for a second, pulling himself up slightly to peer into her face. There was no way in hell he could ever not be with this woman. With a hint of a smile, he moved to her ear again - her body doing exactly what he thought it would under his command.

"I."

# Chapter 38
# Vegas Nights

"Ahhhhhhhhh! I absolutely love it! You hear me screaming right now? If you don't, I'll do it again…"

Imani chuckled at the dramatics of her latest client, Nina, who she was on FaceTime with while sitting on one of her wood stools in her studio. Nina was a young singer just signed under Stephanie's PR client roster. Nina's record label was looking for artists to design the cover for her debut album, the first project she'd be releasing with them, and Stephanie had called Imani personally to make the request. Through FaceTime now, Nina stared at the portrait with a broad smile and wide eyes, ogling at Imani's creative interpretation of her chestnut brown face with her large head of curls dipped in foils of glitter.

"When am I going to get this in my hands? " Nina asked, wiggling her fingers playfully. "Please tell me I'm getting this tomorrow?"

Imani chuckled.

"We'll do what we can," she said, taking a quick glance at Carl with an eyebrow raise. He was one of DeAndre's employees responsible for shipping the piece to Nina, which meant that it'd likely make it at the time she said she wanted it.

"I'm so glad you love it."

"I do. This had to take you forever and a day to do. Like, I can't get over the detailing."

It didn't take Imani forever and a day to start it, but it sure took her months to actually finish it, mainly because she didn't feel she had the time. Between quick one-off trips to see DeAndre at matches, work for Artgo and finishing her AireFete submission that was due for Lauri's review, Imani could barely make the time. She had fortunately started working on the cover a few days after Stephanie asked her, but she only finished it tonight, shortly after her workday at Artgo, her first day back at the office after her little rendezvous with DeAndre at a hotel room in LA.

They had seen each other the week prior when he was back home for meetings, but that night had been so good, Imani had to run it back a second time. It had been so good, she called in sick and canceled meetings the following week, all to book a first-class flight to meet him where he was. Imani never thought she'd chase dick around the world whether it was her husband's or not.

Nina took another loving glance at her portrait before Carl wrapped it with the utmost care, covering it with soft cloth for its voyage to the opposite coast. After hanging up with Nina and escorting Carl out the door, Imani was by herself and in her studio shortly afterwards.

She dipped into the orange and yellow acrylic paint mix with her thin pencil-like brush and applied small strokes onto the canvas. With Lucky Daye crooning in the background through surround sound speakers, she took a breath, thankfully feeling the day melt away from her. Her first day back at the office was also the Monday after the banquet, which meant the majority of Imani's day was spent in a debrief meeting with Lauri. They talked extensively about what worked during the event, what didn't and, of course, what to avoid for next year's banquet. Although Imani spent most of the meeting listening and offering light feedback, all she kept thinking about was how she truly didn't want to be at the museum this time next year. She truly wanted to work on her art, full-time, with her man here and her baby cooing and crawling in her studio behind her. But, Imani wasn't going to bring that up to DeAndre now.

Even sexually satisfied, she was still salty with him.

Imani had knowledge prior to her meetup with him that he wasn't going to make it to the Artgo banquet that he initially promised to attend months ago.

## A Month of Sundays

He wasn't going to make it because he had to play a match...that wasn't even a requirement for eligibility in this SW Tournament he had been talking about for months. From his explanation, DeAndre was basically taking on an extra credit assignment that would bump up his grade only by a couple of points. Imani never bothered to pay attention to DeAndre's rankings or position, but she was more than certain that he didn't need any help in that category. He was still undefeated.

"Hummingbird, all the points I got last year don't count this year. I just need this match to keep up with them."

The deeper they got in conversation about it, the more confused she got with his explanation and stopped him from talking about it anymore than he needed to. Just before they managed to tell each other goodbye, Imani's phone died and she didn't bother hooking it up to her charger, deciding to head to the banquet even with her slight annoyance and crappy mood. And, just when Imani had all but forgotten about it, pushing it into the recesses of her mind just enough to have a decent time mingling with guests, Lauri thanked her for their generous donation, bringing the subject up again. Imani was glad her boss didn't make a huge deal about it, but something about the gesture made it feel like DeAndre knew he really wasn't going to show up all along, well before he told her. Even though her husband was impulsive in some ways, DeAndre also didn't spend his money for the sake of just doing it. It was more than likely planned. Too bad Imani didn't have a clue about that plan at all.

But, Imani chose to let it go, dig up a hole in the soil and bury it underground. As she continued layering the colors on the canvas, eyeballing the amount of color she was adding, Imani heard her phone ring on the stool next to her with Kaylee's smiling photo flashed across the screen. Kaylee appeared when she answered, the exact same smile on her face, if not a little wider.

"Hey, you," Imani said, with a smirk.

"What's up, buttercup?"

"Just getting some painting done before I call it a night."

Imani dropped her brush in the cup next to her, wiping her hand on her jeans. She blinked at the phone, as Kaylee stepped out of wherever she was into the late evening, her curls blowing in the wind under a hat and a scarf tied around her neck.

"Where're you?"

Kaylee, still smiling from ear to ear at Imani on the phone, was now walking.

"Just hanging out here near your front door, about to knock."

Imani rolled her eyes, shaking her head with a chuckle. She got up and left the studio, walking back down the long hallway to the door. Disengaging the alarm system, Imani pulled open one of the arched iron doors as Kaylee went into her with a bear hug, taking Imani's breath away.

"Girl...," she chuckled against her shoulder before giving Kaylee a slight shove to assess how she looked. She stood in front of Imani with her hat, scarf and jacket over a hip-hugging purple midi dress Imani swore she'd seen before.

"Um, hello," she said, before narrowing her gaze. That dress definitely looked familiar and one she probably left in the midst of moving.

"Is that mine?" Imani pointed. Kaylee cackled before grabbing Imani's hand and pulling her back inside.

"Don't look too close 'cause it doesn't matter," Kaylee said.

She led Imani down the hallway and through the house with a confidence like it was her own.

"What're you doing?" Imani asked.

"Where's your bedroom again?"

Kaylee had only been to their home a handful of times since the wedding, and both of those times were mostly spent in the living room or in their backyard. But, as soon as Imani instructed where to go, Kaylee dragged her up to the room and pushed open the sliding door of their closet as Imani followed her inside.

Kaylee dragged clothes hanging on the rack, taking quick scans of Imani's extensive selection of silky blouses, airy dresses, and asymmetrical jackets, a small fraction of the exhaustive closet space.

"Dang, girl. Do you even have basics anymore?"

Imani folded her arms. "I can't believe I'm just standing here watching you go through my stuff like this is normal."

Kaylee didn't even flinch at Imani's comment as she actively searched for something unbeknownst to Imani.

"Guess I'll ask a second time. What're you doing?"

## A Month of Sundays

Kaylee was now at one of Imani's drawers, when she smiled at her new discovery. Pulling out a long sleeve shirt and chocolate brown hoodie, Kaylee tossed the pairing in her direction, striking a déjà vu moment for Imani. Times really have changed from the days Imani spent in her tiny, unkept apartment closet.

"Put those on and you might want to change into some stretch pants," Kaylee said, casting a glance at Imani's paint-splatted jeans.

"We're catching a flight."

Imani rested her hands on her hips, waiting for even further explanation.

"So, you're not gonna tell me where we're going? Just hopping on a plane on a Tuesday night? Don't you have work tomorrow?"

"The answer to your first question is 'no.'"

Kaylee huffed as she shoved clothes back into Imani's drawers and straightened herself before walking past her back into the bedroom.

"The answer to the second question is 'yes' and the third answer is 'yes,' but, like you, I don't have to be back until tomorrow evening, which we will be. Now, get your pants on."

Kaylee took her phone out of her pocket to take a quick glance.

"We only have, like 10 minutes to get out of here."

"Kay..." Imani placed two hands at her temples, massaging them. "Is this an emergency? What's wrong?"

She looked around her closet at the shoes and bags above her armoire for an overnight bag or maybe a suitcase? Will she need it? Did she need a heavier coat?

"What am I even packing?"

Kaylee nodded as if hurrying her along.

"This analysis by paralysis is giving me a headache," Kaylee yelled. "Just bring a jacket with you and let's go," she left the room and rushed downstairs ahead of Imani.

Not even five minutes later, Imani skirted down the stairs to the living room as Kaylee stood up from the couch, typing away on her phone. She glanced at Imani, smiling from ear to ear.

"Clive is outside," Kaylee said, pushing Imani towards the door.

Imani stopped and turned around, zipping up her jacket.

"Clive? What is Clive---"

She looked at Kaylee, her shoulders sagging, her eyes cut in slow realization.

"Did DeAndre put you up to something?"

Kaylee pursed her lips.

"Set your alarm, lock these doors and let's skedaddle," she projected louder, hitting Imani on the butt and walking back out into the chilly evening air to a waiting Escalade in the driveway. Imani saw Clive gesture a nod towards them, opening the back door with a smile.

Imani rolled her eyes but couldn't help but feel the small smirk traveling up the side of her face. She still had no idea what was happening, but she knew if this was all DeAndre's doing, she wouldn't be bored.

～

"'Maniiiiiii....'Mani....Imani!"

Imani's eyes burst open, her heart plummeting to her stomach as she placed her left hand at her chest. Adjusting the leather plane seat from the side, she looked over at Kaylee, her eyes dancing and hands clasped in front of her.

"We're here!" she chimed.

Patricia, the flight attendant on staff tonight, walked over to them and turned her attention to Imani.

"Mrs. Harrison, welcome to Las Vegas," she said, her bright cherry red lips plastered in a flawless smile. "Do either of you need anything before we deplane?"

Imani stretched her arms and legs in front of her before turning to the small square window next to her, the decadent lights of the Vegas strip illuminating her view.

"No thank you, Patricia," she smiled, rubbing her eyes.

"The fact that you managed to sleep for this entire ride is beyond me," Kaylee said, walking over to the small table across from them that was in between two reclined seats. Wiggling her fingers above the tray of donuts, Kaylee grabbed a glazed one and popped it in her mouth.

"My best friend is truly a Real Housewife."

# A Month of Sundays

Imani swallowed, taking a beat to look at Kaylee who looked around DeAndre's private jet in awe. She remembered feeling the exact same way Kaylee looked now, during her wedding weekend just five months ago, in total awe of the opulence that was at her husband's fingertips. Imani had to admit that all of it had her just as awestruck but only until she realized that access to just him wasn't always as easy.

Hearing the plane's engine finally turn off, Imani unbuckled her seatbelt and walked to the plane door, shaking hands with the pilot and giving Patricia a hug before walking down the narrow steps onto the tarmac. Another Escalade was ready for them to climb into and drove them to the grounds of a hotel that featured a swirling water fountain in the middle of the circular entrance.

In the lobby, Imani allowed Kaylee, who was handling this random surprise, to check them in as she took out her phone to FaceTime DeAndre. They hadn't spoken to each other all day, something that was a bit unlike them, and it was putting her on edge. With her face on screen, the call eventually stopped ringing, deeming him unavailable. Imani pushed her phone back into her pocket with a little more force than necessary and folded her lips with her nostrils flared. She felt a surge of frustration before shaking it off. He had a match earlier today and was probably taking some much-needed rest. She needed to get over herself. Plus, there was no excuse to act like a spoiled brat after coming from 30,000 feet in the air on a private jet.

Turning on the heels of her Jordans to look over at the guests, from corporate executives in suits to those decked out in party attire, scattered across the marble-floored lobby, Imani stood near the couches observing some checking in and others checking out of the grand hotel with cups of coffee in hand.

"Ok, let's get this night started," Kaylee said, walking up to her. "We're on the 20$^{th}$ floor."

She grabbed the crook of Imani's arm, escorting both of them to the bank of bright gold elevators.

Once they made it to their floor, Imani sighed as they walked to their room.

"Now I know where we're at. Can you tell me what we're doing here?"

Kaylee looked at her friend with a head tilt.

"Why don't you just enjoy the time?" she asked. "It's Valentine's Day week, 'Mani. Embrace the love."

Imani gathered her lips to one side, nodding at the brief reminder. She had never been pressed about Valentine's Day, not because she thought it was corrupt or anything, but simply because it felt like an ordinary day. Michael never made a big deal about it nor did she pressure him to, but Imani couldn't deny feeling an extra ounce of love every year around the 14th and made the time to send cheesy cards and chocolate to Kaylee and Ethel. But, for some reason, she had forgotten about it this year, a year of so much surprise and unpredictability.

As soon as they stepped into the suite, Imani couldn't help how wide her eyes got when she scanned the room, which looked like a small apartment, complete with a carpeted living room featuring a large screen television, mini fridge and two spacious L-shaped couches. Two crystal chandeliers sparkled above the coffee table with three candles lit in the middle.

Kaylee turned behind her to look at Imani with her mouth agape.

"Okay, this is nuts," she laughed.

Kaylee grabbed the small remote on the coffee table, pointing it to the window drapes that glided apart with the touch of a button. The entire Las Vegas strip was right in front of them - towering hotels lit up in gold, green and neon lights, fountains erupting into the night sky and structures that imitated Egyptian pyramids and Venetian canals. Imani took a breath before biting down on her bottom lip, wishing that DeAndre was here with her right now. But, she didn't stay in the feeling for long and opted to make the absolute best of tonight and the surprise that was in store. She was with her sister, after all, which was the next best thing.

Leaving Kaylee to check out the rest of the suite for herself, Imani walked into the bedroom on the right side of the front door and went to the closet just to check for any extra goodies the hotel may have provided. When she opened it, an assortment of cocktail dresses, jumpsuits, blazers and blouses hung in front of her as boots of various heel heights, colorful strappy sandals, platforms, and stilettos were lined along the closet's edge. Imani smirked and shook her head, swept away by his charm once again, as she thumbed through the clothes with various textures, fabrics and designer tags affixed to the back. No matter how far away they were from each other, DeAndre always managed to supply her every need without her having to think about it.

## A Month of Sundays

Kaylee rushed to the room, wiggling her shoulders and clapping.

"We're getting this party started! It's way too quiet in here."

With another tap on the remote, Kaylee looked up at the ceiling, a mischievous grin across her face, as the opening bass of a Beyoncé track filtered through the suite's sound system. And, when the beat dropped, Kaylee put her hands on her knees, pushing herself up against Imani's thighs. Imani folded her lips before falling into a fit of giggles, joining in Kaylee's silly gestures.

Her phone vibrated a few minutes later, shoulders perked until she saw who it was.

"Melody, hey," Imani mustered, wiping a hand across her head.

*Where the hell was he?*

"Okay girl, I know you're here," Melody said, narrowing her kohl-lined eyes. She was flawless with barrel curls framing her face with a soft glow, highlighting shimmery cheekbones and a subtle contour that chiseled her face. She topped off the look with a classic glossy brown lip, clearly ready for an evening out.

Imani gave her a head tilt and chuckled.

"I guess you mean Vegas, which I am, but I have no idea why."

"Sensational," Melody smiled. "So, you're gonna pick out your outfit in ten minutes, then come to my room to get your makeup done, then we'll be out."

"What about me?" Kaylee asked, already mixing and matching blouses and pants, laying them against herself.

"Yeah, yeah, yeah," Melody wiggled stiletto-sharp nails on the screen. "Make sure both your asses are in here. You're on the clock. Bye!"

"Mel, what's your room number—"

She hung up before Imani could even get her question answered and Kaylee rushed over, grabbing her phone out of her hand.

"I got all the info. Tonight is all about us not worrying about a thing. How long has it even been since we had a girls' night? We've been crazy busy and each time we try to hang, either you're not here or I'm at work."

Imani leveled a look at her. Over the past few months, Imani was out of town once a month to go to DeAndre's matches and would turn around and head home the same day. But, once she was home, her schedule with clients and Artgo remained busy. She barely even had time to work on her AireFete submission.

"You're right."

"I know," Kaylee smiled.

"Now, show me your ways, oh fabulous one. I don't even know where to start. Just laying stuff out without any direction."

It didn't take long for them to get some semblance of order with outfits splayed across the bed and on the floor. But, exactly five minutes later, the two of them were dressed to the nines - Kaylee fastened the second to last button of a snakeskin blouse with brown leather pants while Imani straightened her forest green blazer dress, six gold buttons lined up by two on the front. Sliding her feet into black Brother Vellies Feather pumps, Imani grabbed two rings from the small assortment of jewelry Kaylee brought with her before turning around.

"All of the yes," Kaylee said, smiling from ear-to-ear at Imani's entire look.

"Thank you, but that snakeskin gives," she smirked, and grabbed a black chrome clutch she was putting her phone in tonight.

"Let's go before Mel screams at us."

Walking to the elevator, Kaylee raised her phone to her face, making sure Imani was included in the shot.

"We cute! We cute!" she said, making kissy faces at the camera. Imani smiled, stopping to rock her hips, sticking up two peace signs in the video.

They got on the elevator and Kaylee's head was still down in her phone, probably posting their video to her Stories before it slipped her mind. Imani was always impressed with how good she was with that kind of thing. She chose to live in the moment most of the time. Imani was learning just how important it was to document special occasions.

"What's on tonight's agenda?" Imani asked, placing a hand on her hip.

Kaylee rolled her eyes. "We're going out."

The elevator chimed as the doors opened to Melody's floor. Kaylee stepped out first, rushing ahead of her to the second room on the left. Knocking on the door aggressively, Kaylee placed her attention back to her phone as Imani caught up with her.

"So, you're just not gonna tell me anything?" she squinted.

## A Month of Sundays

The door opened, revealing Melody in all of her glammed-up glory - a red skin-tight midi dress stretched over her slight pregnancy pudge with cutouts down the sides of her thighs and spiky YSL heels. Before even stepping into the room, Imani had to adjust her eyes to the ring light beaming behind Melody and she already smelled the makeup, perfume and hair sprays in the air.

"You birds ready to see Usher?"

Imani clapped a hand across her mouth, laughing hysterically as Kaylee chided Melody for ruining the surprise. Once inside, Imani took in Melody's suite that included tons of activity. With a mix of Usher's hits blasting in the background, Melody introduced Kaylee and Imani to three of her friends that were tagging along with them for the night. Imani instantly recognized one of them, Shanice - Melody's co-star on her previous reality show, and remembered she was fresh off the heels of her divorce from an ex-basketball player. It was an entire pile of mess aired out for months on social media.

Imani sat in Melody's makeup artist's chair a few minutes later, and Shanice walked over to her, languidly, wine swirling in a glass in her left hand.

"You know, I saw your exact dress at Neiman's a few months ago," she said, her small eyes scanning Imani's entire frame from head to toe. "Didn't know it was gonna look like that."

Imani's outfit was semi-covered with an apron to keep the blushes, sprays and bronzers from ruining it, but Shanice had already zoomed in on her fit when Melody introduced them.

"Guess everything can't look good on everyone, huh?" Imani asked, a dry laugh falling out of her lips as her eyes rolled with ease.

Shanice blinked at her twice, placing the rim of her wine glass at her lips to take another sip, before walking away.

Imani was a girl's girl through and through but couldn't stand mingling with women like this if she could help it. She had only been DeAndre's wife for a matter of weeks when she surmised that she likely wouldn't get along with a majority of the girlfriends, wives, or ex-wives in this case, of other athletes. She attended one of the weekly brunches hosted in Rapid Springs and even a dinner with a group of them after one of DeAndre's out-of-town games, opting to take a later flight back home to make it. But, she barely got through any of their surface-level conversations that seemed to all center on the husbands -

their net worth, their lucrative deals and the many material items they purchased for their spouses' enjoyment. Imani enjoyed everything that came along with being DeAndre's wife, but yapping about it for three hours would never be something she wanted to do. Imani had a whole career and life outside of DeAndre she'd much rather discuss...she just had to make it a priority again.

After both Imani and Kaylee's makeup for the evening was complete, the five of them went down to the Mediterranean restaurant that was just a floor above the theatre. Dinner went smoothly, especially since the drinks started flowing and Melody ordered shots for the table, letting everyone know there were a few bottles of Dom Perignon on ice next to their seats for the show. The women each fell into separate conversations with each other, as Catina - Melody's other girlfriend, spoke with Shanice about her upcoming vacation and Melody spoke with Rita about the amount of planning involved just to be here for the week.

"I love my husband but the man acts like he can't function with two kids on his own," she said. "I'm always like, "you make production schedules for a living!' How do you fail to get Caleb out the house on time, even with the nanny taking care of Judea?!"

Imani listened while scrolling through her Instagram Stories, mindlessly tapping away at quick videos of everyone getting ready for their own evening parties and festivities. For the first time in a long time, Imani was one of those people, hanging out with her girlfriends and enjoying great food and even better entertainment. She was growing anxious to tell DeAndre about it all and thank him for orchestrating it with what she assumed was Stephanie's help. But, before she could make another attempt at calling him, Melody placed a hand on her arm.

"How's your submission with that art festival going? Let me know when we gotta be in Miami to make sure me and Hosea aren't shooting around that time."

Imani smirked, thankful for Melody's confidence in her.

"Well, I haven't been selected yet," she said, "and, the submission...well it's going."

Melody gave her a side eye.

"Going as in...you're making progress on it? Or going as in...time is going as the work remains untouched?" She sipped her soda in a wine glass, eyes glued to Imani.

"I think I have a block or something...I don't know. The work will get done, though. It always does."

"Yeah, but isn't this a big deal in the art world or whatever? Sé wants to go 'cause a few of his friends are showcasing their short films there too. He says it's as big of a deal as Sundance."

Imani nodded, suddenly feeling an overwhelming sense of dread. She remembered mentioning the festival to Melody in passing, but she wasn't banking on really talking to anyone about it, especially just before going to see one of her favorite performers of all time.

"I just gotta focus. And, I will... after tonight," Imani said, holding up her glass of wine. "I'm not tryin' to think about that right now."

Melody's kohl-rimmed eyes squinted.

"I'll let it go...for now. But, don't forget to invest in yourself. You have it going on outside of being DeAndre's wife. Okay?"

"Go easy on her, Mel," Shanice said, projecting a little higher than necessary. "DeAndre showers her with so much, I'm sure. Probably can't keep up with even half of it. His pimp hand's too strong, but guess it's not trickin' if you got it, right?"

"Girl, stop—"

"Don't you ever talk about my husband like that," Imani said, interrupting Melody, and staring right at Shanice in the eye.

All chatter and cackles ceased as everyone stared. Kaylee, who was sitting next to Imani, dropped her eyes to her plate. Imani didn't know she even said it loud enough for the entire table to hear, but she could care less. She didn't want any allusion of a pimp to her husband in the same sentence. Imani had to nip that in the bud quickly.

"It's about time for us to head out anyway," Melody said, breaking the awkward silence.

Making their way to the venue entrance, the ladies were escorted to their VIP seats in the darkened theatre as the DJ hyped up the crowd of mostly women. As Melody promised at dinner, two bottles of champagne on ice sat in a bucket on a small table across from a plush couch. Not even a few minutes later, the man of the hour ascended from the stage floor, garnering a host of screams and shouts once he greeted the crowd.

Halfway through his set, Imani grabbed onto Melody's shoulder as she sipped her third glass of champagne while they sang to each other off-key. Melody stood up suddenly, swaying to the music, singing each lyric with inflection to Imani and Kaylee. The spotlight followed Usher as he danced off stage, interacting with the crowd while they intensely watched his every move. From her peripheral, Imani saw him standing a short distance away behind Melody, sizing her up. Melody continued dropping her hips and raising her hands in the air with her eyes closed, with no regard to anyone watching, even with the spotlight spilling on her as Usher drew closer.

Imani was hysterical, filming the entire thing on her phone, tapping Melody on the leg to get her to turn around. As if on cue, Melody turned, slowing herself down to a sensual grind as she beckoned Usher seductively with her fingers. Imani couldn't think of a time when Melody wasn't ready for the spotlight - she relished in it and didn't even pretend to be shy about it.

Usher was now in front of her, moving in close. He kept a respectful distance as he held her hand above them, watching Melody drop low to the ground, the audience eating it up.

"Alright now..." he said to Melody, giving her his signature dimpled smile before turning to Imani.

"Y'all having a good time tonight?"

Imani nodded, her champagne glass tilting in her shaking hand. She wasn't about to embarrass herself and scream in his ear, so she took another generous sip for courage. He sang a bit to both her and Kaylee before making his way back to the stage for the rest of the high-octane show that was a bevy of neon stage lights, video projections and energetic choreography. An hour later, Usher thanked the crowd, bowing in front of them as he danced off the stage.

Melody led them to an elevator away from the crowd and as they entered, Imani fell into a corner, feeling straight lucid from the copious amounts of champagne she had consumed. She laughed along with Melody and the group who were all feeling the effects of the night as they rambled about how good Usher looked and their favorite parts of the show. Once on Melody's floor, the women stumbled out, singing at the top of their lungs in call-and-response style.

## A Month of Sundays

Melody was on her phone a second later, in the midst of the loud commotion, singing into her phone in exaggeration. She held it in front of her, allowing Imani, who was beside her, to see Hosea's name on her screen.

"When I get home tomorrow, I'm about to ride you until the fuckin' wheels fall off..." she said to her husband. "I cannot wait to slob knob all up and down your dick..."

She was speaking low enough, but Imani was getting more than an earful, clutching her stomach in laughter at Melody's dirty talk, which wasn't even fueled by alcohol. Melody, still running her mouth in Hosea's ear, opened the door as her friends followed her inside. Imani waited beside the door to tap Kaylee - the most sober one of the group, before she walked in.

"I need to go walk this off now before we head back to our room," Imani said, taking a breath. "I'm beat."

As soon as they were in their suite, Imani kicked off her shoes and threw herself on the bed, shutting her eyes. Feeling the room sway, Imani opened them not even a second later. She took a breath, straightening up on the bed slowly, to unbutton her dress halfway and pull off her stockings.

"Hey, don't want to break the mood, but are you okay?" Kaylee asked. Imani focused on her, almost forgetting they were even in her designated room.

She smiled as her forehead dipped in the middle.

"Yeah, why?"

"Tonight at dinner - it got kind of awkward—"

Shaking her head vehemently, Imani swallowed and cleared her throat.

"I didn't mean to make it that way. I...didn't like that she said that. It was disrespectful."

Kaylee nodded.

"It was, but...you looked like you were gonna bash her head in if we weren't all there."

Imani sighed, her head dropping to the side before falling behind her shoulders.

"Have you brought up...anything to DeAndre?"

"Kay, I don't want to get into that right now. Okay?"

"Fair enough. I know. I just...want you to take care of yourself."

Imani looked at Kaylee, her heart drumming inside of her chest. What she wasn't about to do tonight was bring up her past. She had moved on from it unscathed, and her husband was helping her with that, unknowingly affirming her beyond what she even imagined.

"I am taking care of myself and that includes not dwelling on something that's not even a factor in my life anymore. I'm not that girl anymore."

Kaylee assessed her, with eyes slumped in empathy and nodded.

"I know, 'Mani, you aren't."

After taking a shower Imani was in bed, curling up under the covers as she looked out the window at the city that seemed as alive as it did earlier in the evening. She remembered being in bed in her New York apartment, staring out of a tiny window that faced the side of a brick building. Dark swirly shapes her mind concocted used to dance in front of her once she was up for at least 24 hours painting feverishly, chasing after validation so diligently, all because of one person.

Blinking away the memory, Imani grabbed her phone from the nightstand. There were no missed calls as she opened the text thread between her and DeAndre, besides she had no energy to even call him right now so she sent him a quick text.

*"Thank you for everything, baby. Miss you like crazy."*

Putting her phone back down on the nightstand, Imani turned over, pulling her legs closer to her chest as sleep finally took over.

∼

Hearing a phone ringing, Imani thought she was initially dreaming as she heard it blaring in and out of her subconscious. But it kept ringing, eventually stirring her awake.

Placing a hand on top of the black hotel phone, Imani sighed before picking it up from the receiver.

"Hello?"

"Hello, Mrs. Harrison. There's a delivery downstairs for you," a woman said, in a smooth, soothing feminine voice that thankfully didn't sound harried.

Tying her robe around her waist, Imani opened the door and crept out of her room, pitter-pattering in her slip-ons. Kaylee's room was on the other side of the suite, but she slept as light as a feather and would wake up from Imani's shortest footsteps when they lived together. When she got to the lobby, a woman at the front desk who gave her the most pleasant smile at 2 o'clock in the morning grabbed her attention.

"There goes my babbyyyyy, you don't know how much it means to call you my girl…"

Imani froze, butterflies fluttering in her stomach when she heard DeAndre's voice behind her. She folded her arms in front of her, grinning like the lovesick fool she was, before turning around.

"There goes my baby, with her pajamas and bonnet on lookin' like a snack."

Covering her mouth, Imani's cheeks were hurting at this point as she took in how effortlessly sexy DeAndre looked, even at this hour. Dressed in dark jeans and a varsity jacket over a simple black shirt, DeAndre had his head tilted and eyes closed with his hand behind his back, walking closer to Imani as he sang off-key for only her to hear.

"There goes my babbbyyyy, lovin' everything you do, hope she don't kick my asssssss."

Imani with her arms still folded, burst into more low giggles, shaking her head and willing herself not to ambush him like a madwoman fresh out of a psych ward.

"Don't you ever talk about my voice again," she joked moving closer to him.

Once he was close enough for her to touch, DeAndre looked down at Imani as a brilliant white smile spread across his face.

"My baby," he said, his voice piercing into Imani's heart. He pulled his hand from behind his back, revealing a bouquet of Birds of Paradise - her favorite flower. Imani gathered them in her hands, staring at the array of orange, blues and greens bursting in front of her.

"These are…so beautiful."

Imani grew emotional all of a sudden as a gnawing in her chest grew. It wasn't like they hadn't seen each other in a year, but it may as well have been that long. Distance from him didn't make Imani's heart grow any fonder, it just made her more uneasy, allowing her thoughts to run wild until she saw him again.

Pulling her closer by the small of her back, DeAndre enveloped her, his scent crashing stimulating all her senses at once.

"Seein' how sexy you looked tonight, all up on Instagram, I knew I had to give them to you in person. Didn't want room service to have the pleasure of seeing that look on your face when you got 'em."

Imani smiled at him, releasing a sigh of relief. Her prior concerns melted away gazing at him in real time like this. This was important...this was real, not whatever thoughts she had of a man who wasn't even wasn't even alive anymore. She looked down at her bouquet, brushing a finger against the petals.

"Tonight was out of this world. How did Stephanie do it and tell me you're giving her a bonus because of it?"

DeAndre pushed his head back with a chortle.

"For your information, she only took care of your clothes," he smiled, scratching his cheek.

"He was in LA around the time I was and someone in the crew was talkin' about how good the show was out here. Thought you'd be into it and Mel told me she was in town shooting for the week, so...I wanted to make it work for you."

"Well...it was perfect," she smiled as her eyes darted up at him again, penetrating. "I feel really good."

DeAndre observed her, putting his hands in his pockets.

"Good," he said, with a nod before mirroring Imani's own piercing gaze, his expression serious.

"Night's still young in Vegas. Whatchu tryin' to get into?"

Taking another quick glance at her gorgeous, one-of-a-kind bouquet, Imani took a whiff of them, staring at her husband with a mischievous smile.

∽

Rocking her pelvis back and forth to meet his strokes, Imani panted, feeling her orgasm brewing much quicker than the last two rounds. She pulled him closer by the shoulders, digging her fingers into DeAndre's back, gritting her teeth as her nipples hardened from the sensation.

"I - I keep cummin'..."

"Don't run from it, baby...Don't run from me."

His command danced in her ear just above a whisper, but Imani heard him loud and clear, slowing herself down to feel him filling her to the brim. DeAndre nodded, giving her a soft kiss on her neck before glancing down to where they were joined as one. Sliding his hands from her thighs to her waist, DeAndre raised her up just enough to see her moving back and forth over his shaft, his brows dipped in drunk-like consternation.

He rubbed his hands over her butt, cupping her cheeks as Imani kept herself up, throwing her ass back in swift twerking motions. Her gaze fell back on DeAndre with a fiery smirk tacked on. She could perform when she wanted to as well, especially when her husband was watching. He brought so much out of her within a matter of months.

"You're so fuckin' perfect, it's...dumb," he sputtered, letting out a half-laugh. "Makes me wanna give up on everything I'm doin' just to be in you all day."

Imani loved hearing him make proclamations like this, maybe because she had always wondered if it would ever be true. Feeling herself erupting, Imani crashed her lips into his as their tongues wrestled slowly and deliberately. Her orgasm surged below. Her legs - spread on either side of him - loosened and she let out the longest scream from the depths of her. When his deep growl followed a second later, Imani fell forward on top of him as he released in her with urgent force.

The warm feeling of him spilling into her was indescribable, like he was marking her on some territorial instinct that spoke to her deepest desires. All the heartache she had experienced up to that point in her life was healed when he was in her. He could split her in two and it wouldn't be deep enough.

His chest rose and fell as Imani lay on top, hearing the hypnotic rhythm of his heart slowing down.

"Damn." He rubbed the top of his fade, letting out a breath.

"Glad I booked another suite with all this shoutin' you doin.' Kaylee would've been knocking on the door, callin' the cops."

"You wish," she laughed, pinching him on his side, before rolling onto her back with her legs piled on top of his thighs.

Imani had never been with anyone before him sexually, but she just knew she landed on the Mount Rushmore of sex being with DeAndre. He pulled himself up, straightening the top half of his body on the bed before grabbing one of Imani's legs, his bottom lip folded under his teeth. He peppered small, slow kisses from the inside of her thigh down to her ankle as Imani pulsed with new desire all over again. Placing her hand on his head, Imani giggled, getting ticklish from the movement. Her hand fell to the side of his face as he gave her another kiss on the lips, this time, tenderly. Imani would give up everything she had, for them to be just like this forever.

"I'm sorry I didn't make it to the banquet and I shoulda been up front when I knew the change was happening."

Imani nodded.

"Apology accepted...and, I shouldn't have reacted the way I did about the donation. It was a nice gesture and funding is never not needed for the museum. So..."

Imani shrugged, as DeAndre assessed her carefully...

"So...I know you got a lot of work going on with the museum and with clients but, you think you could come with me to New York? I'm doing some press about the collaboration droppin' that week and want you wit' me."

Imani placed both of her hands on the sides of his face, tracing her thumbs underneath his chestnut brown eyes to his high cheekbones down to his beard, feeling the coarse texture at her fingertips. The one place she never wanted return to, if she could help it, was New York but, she'd go there for him. She always wanted to make herself available to him because who else would be if she wasn't? Imani knew there were seasons of give-and-take in any relationship. This just so happened to be the season for her to give.

"Of course I will," she smiled. "I'll be there."

# Saturday, 10:00am

"Good morning, Imani. How are you? This is your Aunt Ethel. It's Saturday morning, around 10am and I'm leaving this voicemail for you. This is now my... ummm...second attempt at calling you, baby girl. Glad your phone isn't cut off or anything. It's been about a month now since we last spoke and I just...need to know you're safe, Imani. I pray for you every day wherever you are. The last time we spoke, you said you were? fine. But, how come I'm not speaking to you more often if that's the case, Imani?

# Chapter 39
# Potential

Imani was in such a good mood a few days later at work, it felt like she was damn near skipping into the meeting she had with Lauri. She had just come from talking with a few of her coworkers, including Gloria, who flagged her down with questions about her weekend as Imani showed them a few of the videos that didn't make it to social media. With all of the commotion happening in front of her, Imani was thankful to see the notification of Lauri's email, requesting her to come to her office for their meeting a few minutes earlier than previously scheduled.

Sitting in one of Lauri's chairs now, across from her, Imani had her legs crossed, looking between Lauri and the two large canvases that had been dropped off earlier this morning.

"Imani, I just want to make sure you're...thinking all of this through. This exhibition can really put your work on the map and I want judges to see your potential."

Imani stole a glance at her boss before looking up at her work again. DeAndre had the massive canvases delivered so she wouldn't have to worry about getting them over to the museum later on. After Vegas, he didn't head back to Port Springs with Imani, remaining out of town but in the same time zone, thankfully, which allowed them to FaceTime each other this morning as she was getting ready. She was a heap of nerves, rambling about what she

## A Month of Sundays

hoped she wouldn't miss and excited about the work she'd been doing. Despite what she told Melody when she brought it up the night of the concert, she was working on her submission and it was...progressing, as she said.

"I don't think I know what you mean."

Lauri sighed, pushing up her glasses with her brows dipped in consternation.

"This direction...you're going with your work," she said. "It's just not something we discussed. It's a little...unexpected for someone who executes at your level."

*Unexpected?*

How did Lauri not see this...brilliance?

Imani was executing exactly at her level, something she had been striving to do for months now. Her work was so big now! So loud! So expressive!

She blinked, just thinking about how she rambled on and on to DeAndre about her work. And, he let her talk, too - he was always so patient like that, listening to her, only to encourage her once she was done speaking or rambling.

*I'm excited for you, baby. You're in your bag right now*, he had said.

Hell yeah, she was in her bag right now and no one could tell her otherwise.

There was so much she poured into her art on the daily now, just letting it take her beyond what she even thought. Her life was so different than she ever thought it would be. How could Lauri *not* see that she was an artist reflecting her experience?

She just didn't get it.

No, she'd *never* get it.

Lauri hadn't come close to the experiences that Imani had, all within a matter of months - experiences that people couldn't imagine having in years. Lauri wasn't the one just in Vegas to see Usher with *her* best friend on *her* man's dime before *her* man chartered a plane, *just* to have her in a separate suite all to himself. She'd never experienced that.

Imani only hoped to finally connect with someone who knew exactly what it was like to hold a *different* kind of power. Would Lauri ever feel the cool touch of diamonds draped over her while she was cumming that literally quadrupled her orgasm?

She'd never experience it or glean it in her art - because she didn't do anything *that* great.

Imani buckled her legs together, feeling her breathing shallow, already anticipating DeAndre coming home again. He was only home a handful of times in the month, but she was always ready for him. She stayed ready for him.

*When you think about me hard enough, do you cum?*

The question he asked her a few nights ago was planted in her mind and grew. Just like dandelion petals, Imani caught the thought, held on to it, and wanted to make a wish.

"I just want to know if you're taking this seriously?"

Lauri's question broke Imani out of her subconscious that was now in overdrive. She darted her eyes up to Lauri this time, fully aware of what she was going to say.

"I'm about as serious as you are...about second-guessing art done by your own kind."

Lauri was shuffling papers, but stopped once she heard her. She looked up at Imani through her thick black circle frames.

"Excuse me?" she asked.

*You gotta stand ten toes down on what you say and you gotta believe it. I'm the greatest because I say I am. No one's gonna stop that from being fact.*

DeAndre had said this on numerous occasions, in many variations, and Imani heard it from him a million times. A lot of people hated how braggadocious DeAndre always was, at least when he was playing. His self-confidence, though, turned Imani on to the highest degree and something about this moment made it all click for her sake.

She sucked her teeth before folding her arms in front of her.

"I always wondered why you'd never want to feature Black artists who weren't validated by White people. No disrespect to those Black artists...still geniuses. But, why can't you see their brilliance for yourself? Are you threatened by me or the potential you never reached?

"You know, they say those who can't, teach," Imani continued, doing a quick once over at Lauri, "or, in your case, manage a museum, gatekeeping real art."

Imani looked down at her hand resting at the crook of her elbow, watching the light hit the diamond of her ring. This week's manicure was a bright yellow polish that popped against the red undertones of her complexion. DeAndre had joked that her nails reminded him of yellow Skittles, she chuckled at the memory.

"I'm going to pretend that you didn't just say that to me," Lauri said. "Let alone in my office."

Imani unfolded her arms and placed her hands on her lap, giving Lauri the attention she craved. Lauri laughed, a hint of disbelief filtered through, and shook her head.

"You're good, Imani and, I know that," she said. "That's why I'm pushing you to get focused. You have Stella behind you and I'm on your side. Take a minute to assess what you're doing and come back to it. You think you'll be ready to submit next month?"

Iman cleared her throat, surprised at the direction this meeting was taking. But, she took a breath, choosing not to challenge Lauri any further. Her boss really was an amazing bridge she had no intention of burning. There was no time for her to fumble an opportunity like this.

"Yeah, absolutely."

∾

Imani sat on the living room couch, clicking on the remote, browsing through channels then through several movie titles on Netflix. She finally gave up looking for anything worth watching and placed the remote back on the couch.

Turning her head to the kitchen, she called out to the chef who was stirring two pots of food at the stove, a hand towel draped over his shoulder.

"Sebastian, do you mind if I turn on a Drake playlist?"

"As long as it's his stuff from the early-2000s."

Imani smiled.

"That's the only Drake I acknowledge."

With some of the rapper's hits from his debut album echoing through the entire wing of the house now, Imani set up the dinner table in the living room for one, thinking over her botched meeting with Lauri. She had been thinking about it all day since she stepped out of the meeting, her tail behind her legs at her ridiculous attempt at putting her boss in her place. What mental insanity had she stepped into thinking she could get away with that?

After work, she spoke with DeAndre over FaceTime and was going to tell him about the conversation when he had to cut their chat short.

"Baby, I gotta get into this interview real quick, but I'll hit you up when I get back in?"

"No, no," she said. "It can wait, anyway. Have a good night and I'll see you tomorrow."

Just when Imani had an inkling to miss him, she realized they'd be seeing each other again within a day or two for the *Late Night Show* taping in New York. They'd be able to talk... eventually.

Imani was pouring a glass of wine and placed it on top of her mat when the doorbell rang. She walked to the foyer, disengaged the alarm and was caught by surprise when she opened the door.

"Andele?"

Her mother-in-law, hands planted on her hips and staring out towards the driveway, turned around to face Imani. Sunglasses shrouded her eyes as usual as a light citrus scent of Chanel seeped from her pores.

"Imani, dear."

With a placid smile, she took off her glasses, her eyes bright with the energy of a woman who just recharged on an all-inclusive vacation.

"You look," Andele did a sweep of Imani's outfit, a stretchy loungewear set with fuzzy slippers. "Comfortable."

Imani's eyebrows hitched as she mustered a short smile.

"DeAndre isn't here tonight, so..."

The last time Andele and Imani were even in close enough proximity to one another was at the wedding. This was her first time making such an unexpected visit. Imani did her due diligence as her daughter-in-law to text her a simple greeting from time-to-time, which Andele had only responded to with a tapped-in thumbs up. It was sick how Imani had imagined developing a great relationship with Andele. But, she shouldn't have been too surprised. DeAndre barely had a relationship with either of his parents at all. She hadn't even met her father-in-law yet.

## A Month of Sundays

"Did...you and DeAndre have plans and got dates mixed up...or?" Imani asked, letting the question hang.

"No," Andele said, with a blink. "I'm here...out of my volition."

Imani's mouth formed into an 'O' as she stood there, taking in Andele's all-white outfit - a turtleneck with white bootcut jeans and knee-high boots. She cleared her throat, realizing she was being straight rude at this point. She didn't mean to...she was just shocked.

"Come in," she said.

About a half hour later, Imani and Andele were at the table, now set for two, as Sebastian walked over with a smile, their plates in hand with waves of heat streaming to the ceiling. He set each of them down before returning to the kitchen with Andele's back facing him from where he stood.

"Ugh, Sebastian," Andele projected, shaking her head. "You outdo yourself every time. Look at the food...this material."

Imani watched him blush and even found herself smiling at her mother-in-law's odd charm. She knew Andele didn't like her, but she was at least entertaining, just like someone with which she had fallen so madly in love.

Andele dug her knife and fork into her fish, picking up a piece to put into her mouth when Imani cleared her throat with a smile.

"What?" she paused, with a scowl.

"Me and DeAndre say grace."

Andele looked at Imani like she was witnessing a spaceship land on the moon as Imani gently took her mother-in-law by her delicate, supple hands. Hands, which probably hadn't endured any work in decades.

"Oh," her eyes narrowed, shifting from side to side, but not pulling her hands away. "Okay."

Imani and DeAndre weren't exactly hosting Bible Study, but whenever he was home, he made it known in subtle ways that he wanted to fall in line with her habits and rituals, one of them being to pray over their food. As someone who was once forced to cook without much of a choice, Imani couldn't express enough gratitude for the privilege of not having to do so at all now.

The two women raised their heads after Imani closed the prayer and drew attention to their decadent meals.

"So, what's new?" Imani smiled, raising her shoulders slightly for emphasis as she cut into her fish, tearing small slices.

"A friend of mine, Brenda, was here the other day and I just dropped her off at the airport this morning."

"Nice, how long was she in town for?"

"About a week. Cassandra was here the week before that, and we had just gone to Fashion Week at Springs Park, so that was absolutely fabulous. The collections are so loud nowadays, but every now and then, the designers stick to clean lines."

"Perfect."

"And, a month ago, I just got back from Belize with Betsey. The waters over there are just stunning. Pictures won't do them justice."

The more Imani listened to Andele speak, the more she realized that none of the activities she discussed were ones she did alone.

"Seems like you have a full schedule," she said, biting into her steamed broccoli. "I'd have to take a minute to myself to recharge, honestly."

"Oh, God, no," Andele blurted, taking a sip of her wine. As if detecting the tinge of vulnerability that seeped through, she looked at Imani, her eyes shifting.

"It's okay if you don't want to be by yourself," Imani started. "I'm here a lot more than your son, so…"

The two chuckled.

"You can just…call me anytime if you need company."

Imani saw the smallest smile play on Andele's lips as she cast her eyes to the ground, shifting them to the half-open door of her studio.

"DeAndre…ummm," she cleared her throat, "told me he was building a studio for you."

Imani's eyes widened.

"And…you haven't seen it yet."

"No," she said, her chin pointing slightly upward.

Imani chuckled. Andele's bark really was more than her bite.

"Do you want to?"

After finishing their plates and saying farewell to Sebastian, Imani led Andele into her studio, which immediately took her breath away.

## A Month of Sundays

"This is…"

Imani gave a faint smile.

"I know."

Andele's eyes toggled over to the handful of canvases, all in different modes of progress, near the back wall.

"Is…that some of your work?"

"Yeah, playing around here and there, depending on how the light comes in from the window."

Imani saw the question Andele asked without even vocalizing and nodded, giving her permission to peruse her work. Andele picked through each and every piece, her mouth slightly agape, taking in the various shapes, colors and figures that Imani let dance across the canvas.

"These are just…incredible."

If that was the closest thing to an 'I love you,' coming from Andele, she'd take it.

"Thank you."

"Are you…do you have representation or anything?"

Imani sighed, feeling the pull of anxiety at the pit of her stomach, twirling the tip of her foot against the ground.

"I'm working on it. My boss at work is helping me apply for the AireFete festival, so…"

Andele took in all of Imani's work, her eyes moving about as she walked gingerly around the perimeter of the entire space. For some reason, watching Andele's under-estimation of her crumble in real time was more satisfying than she thought it would be. That's what Imani loved about art - it spoke for itself.

"This is such good work, Imani." She turned to look at her, assessing her this time.

"Yeah, some of it was from my Aunt's house before I moved in and it feels like, I don't know, I could give them a new life here."

"How long have you been painting?"

"For as long as I can remember."

Andele's eyes then landed on a table that was the closest to her and she laughed, and full-on cackled within a matter of seconds. Andele placed a hand on her chest, one more guffaw breaking loose.

"Please forgive me. I just...didn't expect an artist with a capital 'A' to have a paint-by-numbers packet."

Imani laughed herself, raising her shoulders in mock innocence.

"I have to get out of my head every once in a while, what can I say?" she chuckled. "And, the newer ones are a lot better than they were even five years ago, so...there's levels to it, Andele."

Andele pursed her lips, another chuckle escaping.

"I wouldn't mind breaking one out now, if you want to," she said, conspicuously.

"Let's do it," Imani smiled.

After another glass of wine and about an hour into their paint-by-numbers masterpieces, Imani and Andele examined each others' work, impressed with the quality of the paint and consistency of colors as advertised.

"Looks like you're moving faster than me," Imani laughed as Andele nudged her leg.

"I've spent a lot more days trying my hand at these than I care to admit."

Imani stopped painting, looking at her.

"I didn't know when I'd be able to bring it up to you, but your photographs you took all those years ago were...brilliant."

After DeAndre told her about her photography, Imani did some research into Andele's photographs from the local Port Springs newspaper that has since shut down. The archives were stored at Artgo, allowing Imani to spend time going through the digital files.

Andele's lips crept into a side smile as she continued filling in the space with precision.

"Surprised they came from this old hag, right?"

Imani curled her lips, choosing not to answer.

"I know I...gave you a hard time in the beginning."

Andele dipped her paintbrush back in the tiny plastic pot and placed it back on the canvas again.

"So...how...are you faring?"

Imani shrugged. "It has its moments, but...I really do love your son."

Andele's eyes shifted to her, with an eyebrow raised. "Who doesn't?"

Imani chuckled.

"He…cares a lot about you, too. He loves exactly like his father."

Andele stopped painting, suddenly, her brows dipped in the middle as she stared beyond the table.

"It's amazing," Andele mused.

Imani sighed, taking another look at this project they committed to tonight.

"If my mentor found out I was doing one of these, she'd likely ring my neck," she chuckled.

"Who, your boss?"

"No, my mentor is another artist, Stella Rose."

Andele gasped as her eyes widened.

"No! That ol' girl!" she cackled.

"How is Estella Robinson doing?"

Imani's jaw dropped. "What? You know her?"

"I know her and all the men she stole from me back in college."

Imani laughed, stunned beyond belief.

"But Stella isn't even from the Springs."

"She was my roommate – this small-town girl who came to the second biggest city from New York to chase her dreams."

Andele chuckled.

"It worked out for her, though."

Imani chuckled, looking at her mother-in-law with the tiniest twinge of sympathy.

"Guess it did…for her."

Andele shrugged. "We all have our paths, right? Can't dwell on the 'what-ifs' and 'maybes.'"

Imani nodded, letting a small smile creep.

The women returned to their projects until it was complete - two images of a group of sunflowers in a field. They examined their work an hour later, walking out the studio and staring at the paintings on the ground in the living room, under one of the lights.

"This wasn't half bad," Andele said. "I'm damn good."

Imani laughed. "You are. Could be ready for auction."

Andele's eyes met Imani as they laughed together. Andele sighed before walking back to the living room table where they ate, picking up her bag.

"I won't hold you up any further tonight," she said. "I imagine you have to settle in to sing love songs to my son over the phone."

Imani chuckled with a shake of her head.

They walked down to the foyer as Andele shared her upcoming plans - plans that still didn't exactly include Imani. But tonight was a good first step in the right direction towards a different kind of bond.

She opened the door, allowing Andele to step out onto the front into the chilly evening air. Andele took in another glance outside before turning to Imani.

"You really have made this home...yours."

Imani smiled. She couldn't remember the last time she felt maternal love, but realized Andele had a unique way of showing hers and she finally felt a tinge of it. Imani watched her mother-in-law leaving as a thought came to her.

"Hey, Andele?"

Andele faced her again.

"You know that company you told me to get familiar with?" Imani's eyes filled with tears, thinking back to the advice Andele gave at brunch when her and DeAndre were engaged. "We're really acquainted now."

Andele stepped closer to Imani, and patted her cheek, with a knowing smile. She turned around and stepped further into the evening, leaving her floral scent behind.

## Chapter 40
# Late Night

Imani managed to finally unclench her jaw and take a breath once she was settled into the backstage area of the *Late Night Show* taping. Taking a generous bite of her croissant, she was proud of herself for not breaking down in a puddle of tears earlier once the plane landed in White Plains where a driver waited to take them to New York. Maybe she was going to do a lot better this time than she thought she would.

The backstage room she sat in with Stephanie now was well lit with an essential oil diffuser dispersing the calming scent of lavender and mint in the air. A monitor sat in the upper corner of the room, projecting DeAndre's interview with Chris Kerry happening live on television. Before today, Imani thought all of the *Late Night* episodes were aired live, but today illustrated that wasn't always the case. DeAndre's interview was happening now in front of a live audience, a little after 7pm, but would air on national television at 11pm.

"Our next guest needs no introduction. As one of the greatest athletes of all time, he's the 23-time Grand Slam champion and winner of more than 100 single titles and still ranked number 1 in the world of tennis. Please welcome the all-time great, my brother from another mother, DeAndre Harrison, ladies and gentlemen!"

The commotion from the crowd was muffled as Imani sat in the room, watching DeAndre walk out to the raucous applause before giving Chris dap as if he was greeting an old friend. Stephanie could've booked him for the later time slot on the show, but DeAndre wanted to make time for a celebratory dinner, commemorating his team for their hard work on the collaboration. Imani couldn't be any more elated for her husband, especially as he reminded her that any of his wins were hers. It was the sweetest sentiment, even though Imani was having a hard time taking it as truth.

"Before we even talk about the collaboration with Elite Athletics, which is incredible by the way, I gotta give you my congratulations and well wishes for marital bliss, man. Welcome to the club. Black love! Black love!"

The audience cheered as DeAndre showed a wide smile that looked close enough to a blush. Patting his hand against his side, he nodded to the crowd in appreciation.

"How is it? How're you feeling?"

"It's great. She's more than I could've imagined for myself. I don't have any complaints, man...you know, life is good."

"I had the pleasure of meeting your wife backstage earlier. She's beautiful, just model stunning."

DeAndre nodded with a smile.

"...and, all I kept thinking was...how in the hell did he get her?"

The audience chuckled along with the laugh track in record time, picking up on Chris's joke that even Imani giggled.

"I mean, I know you're decent...you get by, but c'mon. Let's be rational here."

DeAndre took the teasing in stride, laughing and shaking his head.

"I don't know. You gotta ask her that."

Chris smiled, nodding in acknowledgement.

"So, has she been to any of your games?"

DeAndre nodded, his brows dipped in the middle.

"Oh, yeah. For sure...But, I try not to...to watch her when I'm playin.' I love her man...I do - but the way her face tells me everything..."

The audience laughed as Imani shook her head, with a smile. In preparation for the interview, he let her know about the line of questioning Chris would have during the show. DeAndre promised he wouldn't reveal anything she didn't agree with, which would include anything that would embarrass her or make her the brunt of the joke. But, Imani wasn't worried about that. She never worried about how DeAndre represented her.

"You don't even have to say anything more. You know, I get it. I can just now decipher my wife's facial expressions and it's been 20 years. Don't worry about it, don't worry about it...she loves you, she's rooting for you, I'm sure of it."

"Can she play tennis?"

DeAndre scratched his jaw, chuckling, before looking out into the audience as if clueing them in on a secret.

"A'ight, don't tell her, but she's actually pretty good."

The crowd laughed for a moment before applauding, cheering with much more enthusiasm.

"Okay, so she could give you a run for your money?" Chris asked.

DeAndre's eyes widened playfully.

"I don't know about all of that...but, she's got somethin' in her, for sure. She's probably the only one who could give me a run for my money if I had to think about it."

Laughing at the two men's banter, Imani bit into her croissant again as her eyes fell from the monitor to Stephanie who was on her phone, grinning extra wide onto the screen.

"Glad someone is keeping a smile on your face," Imani said, from her position on the couch.

Stephanie, who was sitting next to her on the couch in the green room, paused for a moment before looking up with a blush that was much more apparent on her caramel face. She shook her head with a wave of her hand.

"It's..." she wrinkled her nose with a smile still present, "not a big deal."

Imani folded her lips, now even more curious than ever. Stephanie was always professional with DeAndre, which meant she deliberately chose to take the same course of action with her. But, Imani was more than willing to be Stephanie's confidant.

"It doesn't look like it," she said, her eyes plastered on her, moving closer like she was ready for any information Stephanie wanted to provide.

"It's a guy."

Stephanie sighed and looked at Imani before the two chuckled.

"It's always a guy."

Stephanie nodded and rolled her eyes.

"Always...anyway, I really, really like him. But, he comes with so much baggage. It's just...a lot."

Imani's brows dipped.

"How so? How did y'all meet?"

She cast her eyes to the ceiling as if caught red-handed.

"He's my client."

"Oh.."

"I know," she chortled. "I know...typical...but, I can't leave him alone."

Stephanie shook her head and sighed, rubbing her hands at the sides of her legs.

"He thinks he's so weak," Stephanie said, falling into a trance. "But, he's the strongest man I know."

Assessing her for a moment, Imani saw the tear that fell from her eye.

"Stephanie..."

Imani placed a consoling hand at her back as Stephanie swiped her face with her finger and sniffled.

"I'm sorry I'm not about to cry you a river on the clock."

"No, no. It's okay, really....We're so weak for these damn men."

The two women laughed before Imani pulled a tissue out of the box on the side table next to them, handing one to her.

"I just admire how you and DeAndre are with each other. You go by your own rules and it's so beautiful to see."

Imani smiled, taking in Stephanie's compliment that made her pause. She and DeAndre stepped into their relationship in their own way, making sure respect was of the utmost importance, but what rules did they really abide by?

The door swung open, pulling both of their attention to a producer with headphones and a mic in hand.

"Imani, would you be open to sitting in the audience? You won't have to say anything if you don't want to."

Looking back at Stephanie, Imani raised her eyebrows.

"Duty calls," she smiled.

A few minutes later, Imani was in the front row across from the sound stage, watching the last few minutes of DeAndre's interview on the couch. Other than pointing her out in the crowd as she blew a kiss in his direction, Imani sat in her seat, ready to head to dinner. Feeling the chill of the studio, Imani couldn't help the way her mind drifted back to memories of her former self drowning from the inside out, a passive onlooker of her own life. Imani wished someone would've told her all those years ago that the damage done to her, though it was only mental, would still come to her in the most random times - anywhere and anytime even during a bright moment for her husband.

Her phone buzzed in her lap, signaling two texts from Stella and Lauri, coming in at the same time.

*Be on the lookout for confirmation from the AireFete panel. Let me know how everything goes,* Lauri typed.

*So proud of you, my protege! No matter what, you should be proud of yourself,* Stella wrote.

After the wild meeting she had with Lauri and her surprising pep talk with Andele, Imani approached her application again with much more urgency, doing all she could to make it right, at least by her standards. She made the submission a few days before this trip to New York, and today would be when she would receive confirmation or rejection from the panel of AireFete judges. Imani was on the edge of her seat now, but knew she couldn't worry about it. For now, she needed to remain present and in the moment, with DeAndre. Tonight was commemorating his big moment, too - his historic brand deal with Elite Athletics.

After the crowd's applause for DeAndre once he was done taking pictures with Chris, Imani headed backstage to join Stephanie, Trey and a few of the associates on Elite's marketing and design teams. DeAndre returned backstage with Chris, who greeted Imani again with a kiss on the cheek and more well wishes. The entire group headed out a short time later and arrived at the Ritz Carlton, where they were staying, for a private dinner at the restaurant.

The gorgeous restaurant, with teal plush sofa seats and large pendant lights above circular tables with tea candles, overlooked the entire city of New York, known as the city of dreams. But, from Imani's experience, it was more like the city of nightmares.

"Hey, you a'ight?"

She turned to look at DeAndre, who didn't look like the long day they all just had. Bright eyed and clear with his hand resting on her lap, his handsome chocolate eyes stared with concern.

"Yeah," she smiled, before letting out a sigh. "I'm just a little tired from the flight. Glad we can finally relax, ya' know?"

Once the waiter arrived to take everyone's order a few minutes later, it didn't take long for the group to loosen up, discussing the excitement of the day and the process of perfecting the details of the collaboration. Midway through dinner, DeAndre stood from his seat at the middle of the table, tapping his fork against his glass to get everyone's attention.

"I know I've been sayin' it to y'all all day but, I really am grateful for everybody sitting here tonight, putting up wit' my picky ass for the last few months..."

The group chuckled as Imani thought back to the weeks after that meeting she attended with Elite. That time felt like so many moons ago that she couldn't believe how much the team had accomplished from that point to now. DeAndre was continuing his winning streak in sports and executing exciting projects like Elite while Imani was on her way to one of the top festivals in the world. She was proud of both of them.

"...so much that goes into what we do and I'm sayin' 'we' because I know that it's not all about me. I spent a long time thinkin' I had somethin' to prove or that there was somethin' I was missin' and I realize I don't anymore...."

Watching DeAndre continue his speech, she was reminded that she hadn't exactly given him much of an update about her work in progress and her submission to the festival. Imani hadn't even checked her email since they returned from the *Late Night* taping. Pulling her phone out of her clutch, she refreshed her inbox to find a new message from the Miami Art Association. Imani felt her heart race as she clicked the message, her phone shaking in her hands.

*Your AirFete Submission Update*
*Dear Imani,*
*Your work is truly that of the heart. Our judges were absolutely delighted by your skill, vision and message–*

"Oh my God...DeAndre."

## A Month of Sundays

Stephanie's shout of surprise pulled Imani's attention from the email as Stephanie, sitting directly across from them, held her chest, smiling from ear-to-ear at her phone.

"I'm sorry...I'm sorry to interrupt, but you were just picked for the Arthur Ashe Award..."

The entire group let out audible gasps, as DeAndre covered his mouth, shock registering on his face from the announcement.

"Don't play wit' me. Stephanie, Are you serious?"

She stood up from her own seat this time, with her phone in hand, her eyes darting across her screen.

"'On behalf of the Tennis League Association, we are pleased to inform you that you have been hand selected to be the recipient of the Arthur Ashe Lifetime Achievement Award, an honor bestowed upon recipients for their cumulative years of dedication and innovation to the sport and impact on the world at large...'"

Stephanie paused for a moment, holding back tears of her own, as she continued reading the message.

"...'Please accept the commemoration of this award in your honor at this year's Sports Awards Ceremony. You and your team should be proud of this incredible accomplishment.'"

The intimate area the group was sitting in struck in applause, whistles and shouts as DeAndre, overcome with emotion of his own, sat down and placed two fingers at the middle of his forehead, leaning on his arm.

Imani's heart leaped as she smiled, placing a hand at her husband's lower back.

"Congratulations," she whispered in his ear.

Apparently still in shock, DeAndre looked ahead of him, his fingers now on his chin as he stared in a trance without saying a word. Imani took the moment to continue reading her email, feeling a surge of adrenaline.

*We want to inform you that your work held our attention, but unfortunately, was not selected to be in this year's AireFete Festival. Our panel of judges took into consideration each individual application–*

Imani couldn't even continue reading as her eyes, blinking rapidly, filled with tears. She was so confident in her work, put her entire heart into it, and prayed over it before she sent it out. With everything she did up until this point, AireFete was meant to be the pinnacle of all of her hard work. She had both Lauri and Stella's blessings. How did she drop the ball?

"Baby...," DeAndre said, "this is insane."

DeAndre had apparently spent the last few minutes being showered with praise by his team before returning to his seat next to Imani. His brilliant teeth were beaming on full display until he and Imani caught each other's gaze.

"What's goin' on?" DeAndre asked, his smile fading and his forehead creasing.

Imani shook her head and sniffled, swiping her tears with a finger.

"I'm just...so proud of you."

With an emphatic gaze, DeAndre pulled her into his arms in a tight hug, his head at her shoulder, engulfing Imani with his entire scent. Imani held on to him, her heart lifted to the heavens. Just like always, his touch managed to lift her spirits on the cloudiest days.

"I don't want anyone else with me here but you," he said, low in her ear.

Pulling away from her with a smile, he gave her a kiss that Imani felt so deeply that she cradled the back of his head, thoroughly intoxicated. The gesture elicited even more applause from the group, who were still cheering and snapping photos of them on their phones.

The remainder of the night was such a blur for Imani as she finished the rest of her food, doing her best to stay engaged with everyone who was now on cloud 9. Imani worked to never compare herself to her husband. They were on two completely different paths, but to be in a sea of winners while she had lost was the oddest occurrence.

"A'ight, man, we headin' out," DeAndre said to one of Elite's brand managers sitting next to him. Everyone was finishing the 4$^{th}$ course of the meal - a chocolate crumble cake that Imani wouldn't have minded being alone with right now. All she wanted to do was cry, eating away all of her feelings in the process.

Imani was at their hotel room door a few minutes later, with DeAndre trailing behind her, fishing the key card out of her bag. As soon as her feet touched the carpet of the room, he was on her immediately, kissing her neck as

## A Month of Sundays

his hands caressed every inch of her frame. Imani turned to face him, meeting his intense gaze on her.

His touch was typically followed up by his words but, this time he was quiet. He openly assessed Imani as if seeing her for the first time. He pulled her face by the hands, kissing her much slower than they'd ever done. Imani's legs were suspended a second later as she wrapped them around him, waiting for him to take her completely out of this headspace she was in - a feeling so familiar she could taste it. Time had started, stopped and began all over again by the time Imani shuddered from her orgasm, melting underneath him like lava.

Lying across DeAndre, Imani made invisible infinity symbols with her finger, following the rise and fall of his chest. There were moments like this when she was so fixated on one part of his body that her mind snapped a picture of it to interpret on canvas. She had never painted a portrait of DeAndre, but maybe doing so would pull her out of the impending depression she felt caving in on her.

"When do you think you wanna try for a baby?"

Imani ceased all movement right then and there, her heart taking flight. She still felt the rumbles of his own chest as she looked up at DeAndre, his eyes glowing with a small smile on his face. She blinked, working to find her voice again.

"Today...uhhh...tonight," her eyes grew wild, filling with tears again. "Every....every night–"

DeAndre chuckled, placing a reassuring hand along her jaw. She hadn't mentioned anything else about having children since she brought it up for the first time when they were engaged. They had both been busy over these past few months, but Imani knew it was a subject she wanted to bring up before their first anniversary. Time was just moving so fast...so much had happened.

"I know I was hesitatin' about it," he rested his eyes in her gaze. "But I just started thinking...Why would I hold out being a father to my wife's children?"

Imani nodded emphatically, tears streaming down her cheeks, as she placed her hands around his neck.

"You're gonna be the most incredible father on the planet."

DeAndre's eyes shifted before they met hers again, this time filled, as the side of his mouth twitched.

"Thank you, baby," he rasped. "I know you're alone a lot...and that'll change soon."

Imani released a breath, overwhelmed by his words she had no inkling he even thought.

"I do...miss you, you know, when I'm not with you."

"I miss you," Imani started. "You're the first and last person I think about, always."

He looked at her, and Imani felt the rise and fall of his chest speed up. Lifting her slightly, he rolled her onto her back against the soft plush sheets and kissed her. When he entered her moments later, Imani softened all over again, her body more than ready to receive whatever he wanted to give. The point was they were now headed into a new direction - to start a family. Tonight was different. It had to be.

"You really miss me?"

"Yes," she said and blinked. "Of course I do."

She thought he was asking the question to be funny, but he was staring at her like she was speaking another language and, then it clicked.

*Has anyone even said that to you before?*

Imani moaned, suddenly hypnotized by every purposefully angled stroke, as his eyes pierced into hers.

"You've given so much...so – so-" she stammered, his strokes melting her. "So many things, but nothing compares and is as valuable as you."

DeAndre's eyes faltered as he focused on seducing her with every stroke progressively increasing his pace encouraged by the reward of her wetness. Imani fell deeper into ecstasy, gasping for air as she kept up with the pace he set, her face glowing with pleasure. He kissed her neck, settling in the spot that made her even wetter, moisture pooling out of her onto him. DeAndre interlaced his fingers with hers, squeezing her hand with just enough pressure as Imani felt her walls releasing gradually, allowing him to drive himself even deeper into her as they strove to climax together.

"Imani, baby," he said, his eyes boring into her. "Don't you ever think I can do this life without you...Baby...You hear me, right? Don't ever think that."

## A Month of Sundays

    Biting her bottom lip, Imani swallowed before wrapping her arms around his neck, their bodies rocking together with ease. Their passion-filled gasps flowing in a rhythmic frenzy before they released it all…for each other.

    "I love you," Imani whispered softly as they faced each other in bed, resting on their sides cuddling. She placed her hand on his cheek, already imagining his features imprinted on a little one made by the two of them.

    "I'll always only ever want you."

# Chapter 41
# Puzzle

Aside from his impeccable agility and top speed, DeAndre's strength as a player rested on his uncanny ability to calculate his opponent's next move. It was tougher to do on some players than others, but DeAndre always looked for a moment of hesitation before a serve or would assess an unexpected turn early in the game. And, once he found it, it was the missing piece of a puzzle that was part of the bigger picture.

Sitting in their bedroom now, DeAndre wedged a small square piece in the edge of its corresponding one, occupying himself with his favorite hobby, his only hobby, to keep his composure. He had moved up here, leaving Stephanie and her assistant downstairs to figure out the best public statement that could be released on his behalf. DeAndre didn't care what they came up with or even if they'd release anything at all. He had to make sure he was calm before Imani returned home.

Everything was so normal mere hours ago.

This morning, Imani raced upstairs from her studio, speed walking towards the en suite in nothing but small cotton shorts and one of his white T-shirts she cut, splattered with bits of dried paint.

"Shoot...I lost track of time. Me and Eve finally coordinated schedules, and we're having brunch in another hour. I gotta get out of here."

She kept the bathroom door open, allowing DeAndre to walk over from his seat across from his working puzzle and lean against the doorway with his hand, looking at her in the mirror. They had been back from New York for a week, and DeAndre was amazed at how much more he had fallen in love with his wife. New York had been such an emotional trip for them, marking the start of another level of their marriage. And, DeAndre was finally ready for it, much sooner than he even anticipated. She was washing her face at the sink, letting the water run as she went through her routine.

"You goin' out dressed like that?" he smirked.

Pulling one of the dry rolled up washcloths stacked neatly next to the sink, Imani, with her eyes still closed, scrunched her lips in his direction.

"Now, I can't wear what I want?"

"By all means, you can..."

Imani was bent halfway at the sink, when DeAndre pulled her ass into him.

"But, I'm gonna have to tap that before you go. Gotta leave my scent on you to let these knuckleheads know."

She let him grind against her slowly, taking the cloth away from her face to watch him through the mirror with a smile and shake of her head. He was a horndog at times, but he learned early on that Imani could handle it.

So, what did that make her?

"DeAndre," she giggled, straightening herself before turning around to face him. "I'm not starting anything else with you right now."

Imani, dressed beautifully in cherry red soft pants and a matching loose top tied in a knot moments later, gave him the most chaste kiss before heading out the door. It made him want to devour her right then and there.

"You're watching me leave for a change," she winked, positioning her sunglasses down to her nose. "I could get used to that."

She stepped out shortly after and Stephanie arrived an hour later, ushering in a much more frenetic energy.

"Is Imani here?"

He told her she wasn't but hearing her mention his wife was unsettling. Stephanie brought another young woman with her who she introduced as the intern for her agency. Scurrying to the nearest table in the living room with her intern trailing behind, Stephanie pulled her laptop out of her tote, typing in a flurry.

"I needed Ellie with me today because we gotta....we gotta go through this."
Stephanie turned to face him again.
"DeAndre, please tell me everything you can remember from these past few months."

∽

The night before his flight to Paris to play at the match qualifying him for the SW Tournament, DeAndre found himself in his hotel room in LA, restless.

He had just gotten off the phone with Imani, not out of his doing, but because his phone had cut off and died midway through their Facetime call. Yet, DeAndre wasn't exactly rushing to get back to her. They needed time.

His wife was pissed because he wasn't going to be with her tonight at her corporate banquet due to meetings he had here in LA and the match he had tomorrow. Well, it wasn't *her* banquet - he'd never forgive himself for that - but it was Artgo's and, just like plenty of functions he's attended like it, this one was just an excuse to get potential funders to open their wallets after being wined, dined and schmoozed by employees like Imani. DeAndre wasn't involved with the art world at all before his wife, but all of those events were the same as all money is green. She'd known in advance of his absence, but she didn't know he was going to make a direct donation to the institution.

"Did you even think about me when you gave that much?"

"Yeah, I thought it'd be a good gesture...since I wasn't gonna be there."

"Way to drive it home, DeAndre. By throwing money around."

"Isn't that how artists do their art? Ain't you a patron of your own industry?"

Imani pursed her lips, shaking her head. With a gold headpiece of chains hanging from both sides of her face, Imani looked like an art piece walking. A really angry art piece, but an exquisite one, nonetheless.

"You know how my colleagues see me anyway...I barely have a handle on being taken seriously since they now know I'm your wife."

In a few conversations they had since the wedding, Imani made it known that she'd heard coworkers of hers gossiping about DeAndre and his whereabouts when he was out of town, mentioning little rumors they'd heard about on social media. He tuned out the bits of conversation that fell into that territory, opting instead to redirect it to whether or not she wanted to continue working at Artgo in the first place. It's not like she needed to. But, Imani insisted she wanted to, which ended any further discussion.

"And...that's my problem?"

Imani rolled her gorgeous kohl-lined eyes.

"I'm not trying to get into an argument with you almost 2000 miles away."

"Well, I didn't think I was walking into one."

"You know what? I gotta get ready to leave. I'm driving–"

The call buffered as DeAndre angled his phone in various directions to get service. But, as soon as the screen blacked out, he released a breath, tossing it to the side.

He missed Imani every single moment he was away from her, and he knew his travel was doing a number on their communication. DeAndre was upfront with her about his schedule from the beginning. She knew exactly what she signed up for. But, what made him feel even worse about all of it was that she never guilt tripped him about any of it. For the first time in his life, he was with someone who truly didn't want anything from him but his presence, which funny enough, was the hardest for him to give.

Looking around at yet another massive, open-floor hotel room, DeAndre hooked up his phone to his charger and placed it on the nightstand before taking the remote and browsing through streaming service options. He was usually holed up in a hotel room around this time when he was away nowadays. Thinking back to his partying days, it felt like he was subconsciously searching for something and now, with Imani, even thousands of miles away, he felt like he found it in her.

But, after about an hour of watching a few mindless shows, he grew antsy, thinking about where he wasn't. His phone switched on, charging up, when he took a glance at the time. Even if he wanted to catch a flight to surprise her, she'd likely be on her way out of the banquet by now, heading home, and he still wasn't sure of her mood. As Imani had said, there was no need to puncture the wound of his absence, so he chose to keep his distance. DeAndre decided to check out a few take-out options nearby, instead, growing tired of the food designated at the hotel.

A text came through from Aiden – who had invited DeAndre to see his basketball game in Port Springs.
*If you're in town, I'll be at Neu Lounge in Hollywood.*
DeAndre tapped on the link Aiden sent along with his message, realizing that he really wasn't far at all and this spot, he's never heard of, had food. His plan was to grab a bite, say hi to Aiden then return to his room to chill and do last minute packing.

He and Trey pulled up to valet at Neu and were flooded with ongoing camera flashes that made DeAndre cover his face, once he stepped out of the car, as photographers recognized him. They walked past the long line of clubbers to the lounge door where a bouncer was inspecting every ID and face under the smallest flashlight. Hearing murmurs from some women ogling DeAndre in the line, the second bouncer at the door unlinked the barrier rope when DeAndre and Trey were close enough to step inside.

DeAndre was expecting it to be dark, moody and loud, with heavy bass reverberating, but this lounge had a completely different vibe. Stepping into Neu was like stepping into an aquarium as the lights were bright enough to radiate a soft ocean-like color that would rock anyone to sleep. With a lavender scent wafting in the air, the music playing was a mashup of hip hop hits and that alternative R&B which was more on trend nowadays. Women, wearing bras and sarongs made of tree vines twirled and twerked in cages, suspended midair, above the bar and tables around the room.

DeAndre spotted Aiden and his crew in the back towards the stage, in a slightly elevated, roped off section. Once there, he and Aiden dapped as DeAndre gave him a hug.

"What type of Cirque du Soleil shit you bring me to?"

Aiden laughed, shaking his head as they sat down. Trey held guard next to the gentleman standing in front of the roped off section.

"This is the spot!" Aiden said, opening his arms wide, before taking a sip of a smoking neon blue drink in a flute glass. "Found out about it through my boy who's messing with one of the founders. Plus, all the women folk done migrated here, so you know my ass had to be here."

Scratching the bottom of his neck, DeAndre took another survey of the room, watching it fill with the *women folk* Aiden was referring to, dressed in slinky dresses, sheer pants and small tops, looking barely over 21. It made sense Aiden would go with this flow - he wasn't even 30 himself.

Guess this is what it meant to get old.

"I'm gettin' myself somethin' to eat, then I'm out."

As a waitress, with bright orange eyelashes and an ivy sarong, stepped to their table, small welps and screams were heard near the front. She left shortly after they gave her their orders and Aiden stood to see what stirred the commotion. Usher walked past their section minutes later, with his own group trailing behind him.

"Aww, shit," Aiden mumbled with a smirk, sitting down. "There goes my chance of baggin' anything tonight. Dude must be on break from his show."

DeAndre, looking over his shoulder at the retreating group, suddenly had an epiphany. He needed to extinguish this fire with Imani before it grew much worse.

"Yo," he turned back to Aiden, "You know when he's back on the road?"

"You mean, Vegas? Yeah, he just extended the residency. One of my homies is his road manager. You tryna come through with wifey on Valentine's Day weekend?"

DeAndre did a quick assessment in his head, knowing good and well he couldn't, especially because he had a photoshoot with other players of the Tennis Association that day, which though annoying and tedious, was a mandatory requirement. It didn't mean she couldn't be there, though.

"Somethin' like that," he slid a hand across his chin. "I'll hit you up about it later."

The food arrived relatively quickly and the men talked about their hectic schedules, time spent away from family and friends and what they saw next for themselves in their respective careers. DeAndre, still determined to play for as long as he could, didn't see himself as this all-knowing mentor reminiscing on the days from yesteryear. But, he appreciated the loose friendships he had with other athletes. No matter if they played tennis or not, all of them reminded DeAndre of what it was like navigating his career as a much younger player. From his vantage point, Aiden seemed to be one of the promising ones and had a pretty solid head on his shoulders, all he needed to accumulate now was time and experience.

After taking the last bite of the steak he ordered that was seared to perfection, DeAndre looked around the lounge again, which was much more packed than it was when he initially arrived. The music was a little louder too and the mashup leaned more into the hip hop he was familiar with.

When he was on his way out the door, the night was finally getting started.

"I see someone on my team came through, I'll be back," Aiden said. "You stayin' for a little?"

DeAndre paused for a moment before looking at the time. It wasn't too late, plus the speed in which the food came made it feel like he was barely here for an hour.

"Yeah," he said, adjusting his chain, "for a few."

With Aiden gone, DeAndre watched the crowd packed at the level just before the stage, dancing hypnotically to the music under the soft lights that now included strobes. If Imani was here next to him now, she'd likely be swaying to the music in her seat for a few seconds before looking over at him with eyes that pleaded, *"please ask me to dance,"* which he'd willingly do without question, of course. His wife was so interesting to him.

At times she'd have the confidence of a lion, but then would turn as quiet as a church mouse in the next breath. Thinking of her now made him miss her all over again.

"So, you show up to my spot and don't come find me?"

DeAndre peeled his gaze away from the crowd back to his table, which Jazmine now occupied. She sat in Aiden's seat across from him as the men in Aiden's crew looked her over like she was one of the meals they ordered, and to be honest, DeAndre didn't blame them. With her hair still braided, Jazmine was gorgeous with her makeup done to perfection and dimples visible. He couldn't see her full outfit since she was sitting down, but she had on a lavender dress with a neckline that accentuated her ample bosom, a necklace cradled in her cleavage.

DeAndre's eyes widened in surprise as he looked around Neu again.

"Hol' up," he said. "This you?"

Jazmine chuckled with a nod.

"It's been an insane, few weeks," she said. "I had a chance to hire Raquel officially, so you might see her floating around too, but yeah...this is me. Not bad, right?"

DeAndre chortled. It wouldn't have been *his* spot, but he couldn't deny the crowd that looked like it wasn't letting up anytime soon.

"How long have you been open?"

"It's been under a year, so we're still young, but this was my dream for so long..."

Her eyes, shimmering with makeup, toggled back over to DeAndre.

"Thanks for helping me make it happen."

He looked at her, suddenly remembering the money he gave her, all the way back then. He assumed it was a drop in the bucket compared to all she needed to bring her business into fruition. But it must've helped.

"It was nothin,' Jaz. Surprised you didn't say anything after the match."

She shrugged.

"I'd rather you see it, than me just telling you. Lot of people talk a good game, ya' know?"

He nodded, suddenly feeling a shift in his countenance. She smiled at him, looking with such intensity that he had to look away.

"How long are you in town for this time? I see you around, but then you're always gone."

Right.

DeAndre was in his hotel room at *night* when he was out of town, but it wasn't like he never went to events during the day. The match against Liam wasn't the first time he and Jazmine had seen each other, either. He'd been seeing her off and on at some of the movie premieres, fashion shows and small listening parties he'd been to when he was around these past few months. They'd never have major conversations when seeing each other, but she'd wave from one corner of the room and he'd smile at her in acknowledgement from the other. Nothing to sing home about.

DeAndre shrugged.

"Was here on business for a few, but I'm heading out tomorrow for another match."

"Nice. Still on that winning streak. It's good to see you and actually...say something. I'm glad LA hasn't left a bad taste in your mouth."

DeAndre tilted his head.

"What?"

"Yeah, I mean, considering you were here when Rand died..."

He stilled.

"That was...a night." Jazmine took a breath, shaking her head. "DeAndre, you were so fucked up–"

"I'm not about to bring that up right now."

He looked to both sides of him, suddenly feeling everyone getting too close. He shifted in his seat.

"Why would you try to bring it up?"

"Because every time we see each other, you act as if nothing happened."

He squinted, not even trying to force his brain to think back on a night he had no recollection of.

"I've moved on, Jaz–"

"But I didn't."

They held each other's gaze as DeAndre grew more uncomfortable by the second, already regretting the minutes that ticked by between his initial decision to stay and now.

"Jazmine! What's up?"

Aiden's greeting jolted the both of them out of their stare down as Jazmine allowed a slow smile to creep up her face before turning around to talk to Aiden. DeAndre took the opportunity to seize the moment, as Aiden drew closer back to the table.

"Aiden, man," he stood from his seat, "I'm out."

The two pounded fists as Aiden looked at him, picking up on his urgency.

"Oh okay, cool. It was good catching up, though. Give the missus my regards."

"DeAndre," Jazmine's eyes dragged up to him as he stood. "Call me, okay?"

∽

When he left that night, DeAndre had no idea what any of what she said even meant. It jolted him for only a moment, but as soon as he woke up the next

## A Month of Sundays

morning, just like the night Rand died, he didn't think about it afterwards. He, for damn sure, didn't call her and he moved on.

But Jazmine was one hell of a random puzzle piece.

He told Stephanie the bits of details from that night as she and Ellie stood listening to him. Stephanie then pulled out her phone for him to watch the interview that went viral mere hours ago. DeAndre watched in straight disbelief.

*"I'm really not doing this to embarrass him; I've been trying to talk to him for months and he's been acting like everything is all good and it isn't. But, babies don't wait for anyone. He'll be here before we know it and I just need DeAndre to own up to his responsibility."*

*"So, are you and him aren't together, then? It was a one night stand kind of thing and you just know—"*

*"No, no. I mean...we...me and DeAndre have always gone by our own rules and it's never been defined as anything. But, the two of us know what's going on, so that's all that matters."*

The interviewer chuckled, narrowing his eyes.

*"Except he's married."*

*"Yeah, because he has to be,"* she took a sip of her drink through a straw. *"It's all a part of an image, right? I mean, he's got all these new deals now, he's got these awards now. Out of his entire career, he was never on primetime television. On a talk show?"*

Jazmine chortled, with an eye roll, as she rubbed her new extremely visible pregnant belly in her seat.

*"Yeah, he knew that his public reputation needed some cleaning up, so I think his team just pushed him in that direction."*

*"Okay, but..."*

*"I was with him all the way up to the point when he got married. Jonathan, you see the pictures! I'm right there next to him when he goes out, behind him, beside him. I was there...but, I didn't fit into his perfect image, so I was shoved away...went away quietly. But I'm sick of that. I'm sick of not being heard.*

*"You just want your child taken care of."*

*"Exactly, I want him taken care of,"* Jazmine said, choking up with emotion. *"I really do."*

DeAndre was two seconds from throwing the phone across the living room before Stephanie pulled it from his hands, as if predicting that exact reaction.

"This chick is fuckin' LYING!"

Stephanie watched him for a moment, her own eyes narrowing slightly.

"Wait, you don't believe me. Stephanie, when have I—"

"You know that it doesn't matter what I think. The only reason I'm bringing this to your attention is because it's catching so much buzz. If this was a year ago, I don't think people would care as much. But, now that you're everywhere... it's everywhere. I mean....DeAndre, she...really paints a convincing picture of you two."

Then, DeAndre saw all of the pictures. Right on Stephanie's laptop, he was presented with all of the optics. There were shots of them leaving and attending the same events, leaked videos of them waving to each other from across the room, screenshots of their direct messages, and even a photo of Jazmine and Imani that he never saw before.

Yet, the most culpable photos were candid shots of him entering and leaving Jazmine's latest venture, a business he looked like he actively supported. They were never officially together, but out of all the women that occupied his time before Imani was in the picture, Jazmine looked like the main one. They looked irrevocably linked publicly and, she ran with it.

Stephanie took a breath, placing a hand on her hip.

"Are you sure you didn't get this girl pregnant?"

∼

Connecting three pieces with the completed portion of the puzzle, DeAndre stood up from his seat and walked out on the porch off the side of their bedroom, gripping the railing. Imani pulled up to the driveway a few minutes later, stepping out of her Porsche looking like a flame of fire, slamming the door behind her. He thought to shout out to her, pleading his case before she even got to the foyer, but he stopped himself.

The last thing DeAndre needed to do was act guilty.

He hadn't cheated on his wife, the thought alone never crossed his mind, so there was absolutely nothing to defend. He knew Imani was upset at the news, probably more shocked than anything. But, there was no way she could actually believe this chick, this woman that she only really met in passing during his best friend's birthday party.

Taking one more cleansing breath, DeAndre stepped out of the bedroom and marched down the stairs, with confidence that he and his wife could talk about this amicably.

"Where the hell is he?!"

Imani's question echoed from the kitchen as she spoke with Stephanie who was working on keeping her own composure. Stephanie's eyes toggled his way as Imani turned around to meet his gaze.

DeAndre couldn't ever think of a time he saw Imani so visibly upset. There were no tears or sobs, just straight fury seeping out of her. She folded her arms across her chest as DeAndre stepped in front of her, folding his hands behind his back, quiet.

"Be honest with me."

"Don't I always?"

Imani's furious gaze on him faltered for only a moment as Stephanie glanced between the two of them then at Elle.

"We should go–"

Imani turned them.

"No, no, don't go, since now everything's come to light."

She glanced back at DeAndre.

"When you saw Jazmine at your match, was that the first time you'd seen her since we've been married?"

"No."

"Have you communicated with her *at all* since we've been married? On social, by phone, through a carrier pigeon, whatever?"

He swallowed, looking down at their mosaic flooring at his feet, before looking up again.

"Yeah."

"This girl is claiming that she's seven months pregnant," she said, tears pooling her eyes.

"Randall died seven months ago. Were you with her...did you sleep with her that night?"

DeAndre grazed his teeth against his bottom lip, taking a cautionary glance at Stephanie, her eyes disappointed. Out of everything Jazmine said in that video, the allegation that he fathered her child was her strongest argument. The math added up perfectly.

"Yeah."

Imani turned immediately, walking in the opposite direction back to the foyer and up the stairs. DeAndre rushed to catch up with her, but she was well ahead of him. By the time he got to her in their bedroom, Imani had pulled out a suitcase, speeding from their closet and back, shoving clothes in it.

"What're you doing?"

Imani looked at him, as if he was insane.

"I'm getting out of here, what does it look like?"

DeAndre pressed his hands together, pleading with her.

"Baby, Imani, I know this whole thing is lookin' crazy right now," he started, his heart beating a mile a minute. "But, you gotta believe that I didn't cheat on you."

She paused, pushing her hands against the temples of her forehead.

"I don't even know where to start. All I know is that I was literally eating with Eve, sitting down with her when she questioned me on how I was handling everything. I didn't know what the hell she was even saying until she showed me that video. And, just to save face, I had to act like I was okay. Did you know that interview was gonna happen? Stephanie is here. Was all of this planned?"

DeAndre's eyes grew opened wide in shock.

"What? No. Nobody knew. I don't even know how she laid out any of this."

Imani shook her head, continuing with her clothes pile.

"So, you just woke up the next day and thought....oh, ya' know, I think I wanna marry this girl who's been feelin' me for a while? Was that what it was?"

"Baby, I knew I wanted to marry you..."

"But, you also knew you could have your cake and eat it, too," she said. "I'd play your little obedient wife in this glass house while you split your time with her."

Imani zipped her suitcase, carrying it down the stairs. DeAndre followed behind, where Stephanie and Ellie were standing with their phones, wide eyed at Imani in front of them.

"Why didn't you just leave when you saw her around, like I asked you to? I don't ask anything else of you, DeAndre. All I asked you to do was that one thing!"

"Imani, if I spent my time thinking about all the women I dealt with in the past, being in the same room as me, I wouldn't be in any fucking room!"

Stephanie and Ellie covered their mouths with their hands, looking down at the floor.

He realized then that he should've said anything else besides that.

"I am *really* sorry we're here right now," Stephanie said, avoiding eye contact with both Imani and DeAndre. "Ellie, let's go."

This time when they went to leave, Imani let them. She stood looking at DeAndre, clear heartbreak in her eyes.

"A'ight, I shouldn't have said that, but baby, you gotta listen to me–"

"You have everything. You have the money, you have the accolades..." her voice broke.

"And the ONE thing I could've given you that no one else could've was a family...ONLY me! Not your mom, not your team, ME! I could've given that to you and now you gave this hoe that privilege? I thought you said I was your family. You said that to me – didn't you?"

"Imani," DeAndre closed his eyes for a second, rushing closer to touch her. He had to hold his wife but, she pulled away before he had the chance. "You are."

"I need to leave."

His heart sped up as she dragged her suitcase on its wheels at her side, rushing out the door to the front porch. Leaping into action, DeAndre ran to her, catching up just as she got back to her Porshe. She put her suitcase in the trunk then stormed her way to the driver's side. \

"Imani, baby, you're gonna leave me like this without talking it out first?"

She pulled her door closed, turning on the car. Fortunately, her window was down, which allowed DeAndre to grip the edge, pleading with his wife with all he had this time.

"I'm canceling my appointments, my meetings, all my shit for us to work this out."

She closed her eyes to take a breath before opening them again.

"You can't talk your way out of this one, DeAndre," she said, calmly, staring straight ahead. "Don't come after me. I'm so serious."

Without even looking his way, Imani sped off, leaving him in the driveway. DeAndre balled up his fists, exploding in the air.

"FUCKKKKKKKKKKKKKKK!"

For the first time in a long time, he was alone in his own home.

# Friday, 7:58pm

*Imani! Imani! You get back on this phone with me, girl [sobs]. You get on this phone right now and call me! He's lying to you, baby girl. You cannot go back to him. God, girl. How many times are you gonna keep following? You always jumpin' through that fire. I love you as if you were my very own child, I do. [sobs] Wherever you are, Imani, my door is always open to you. I love you, girl.*

# Chapter 42
# A Meeting of the Minds

DeAndre's phone vibrated incessantly once again, as Imani watched him pull out his cell from his back pants pocket.

"My bad," he said, looking at his phone then up at Imani again. "I gotta take this."

Opting out of rolling her eyes, Imani gave him a terse nod with her brows raised.

"I'll just tell her you'll join us in a minute. Watch your time, please," she said, before walking off without waiting for a response.

Even though Imani could barely tolerate much of anything DeAndre had to say right now, she returned home from an overnight stay at a hotel just in time for the two to drive to this private check-in meeting with Sister Coleman at the church. They were outside of the building in the parking lot together, standing in front of his light gray Panamera. He bought Imani a matching lavender one, one of the many random gifts he left her whenever he was away. Imani wondered in retrospect how many of those gifts were given out of guilt.

Imani walked across to the glass double doors of the church, her dark green midi dress swinging against her shins, not even surprised to have left DeAndre with another phone call that was a higher priority for him than this personal matter. Sister Coleman's request had taken Imani by surprise, the fact she was remotely interested in potentially giving marital advice to her son's ex-girl-

## A Month of Sundays

friend was unexpected. It hadn't even been a year since she and Michael ended their relationship. But, Imani assumed it was coming from a thought, toggling between genuine concern and slight curiosity. Maybe it was a sheer coincidence that this pre-scheduled meeting was happening not even a week after DeAndre's news hit the fan.

DeAndre hadn't been to church with her since they made their infamous debut as an engaged couple, and Imani assumed that everyone had seen the headlines by now about the mother of his soon-to-be-newborn. The initial pictures and videos Imani had seen of DeAndre and Jazmine hadn't stopped, either. There were now old photos of the two at different events together, alleged direct messages between the two of them and even Instagram Live replays of Jazmine's friends who applauded DeAndre for being "a nice guy every time he was around." Fortunately, members of New Leaf did their best to not embarrass or gossip about each other, at least to their faces. Yet, Imani saw the glances of pity from the corner of her eye or the forlorn smiles that landed when she met members' gazes. And, she knew Sister Coleman had more than enough prior knowledge of all of it. It was exhausting and made Imani pissed all over again.

On top of this news about her husband, Imani wasn't even sure what she was going to do in terms of her marriage. She couldn't imagine ending it so prematurely, but Imani couldn't deny her gut telling her there was a reason all these allegations triggered her in the first place. No matter how she thought through raising his child outside of their marriage even knowing a handful of relationships, like Melody and Hosea's, operated just fine this way, Imani still couldn't bring herself to let that happen.

Unlike Aaliyah who was a preteen when Melody and Hosea met, Jazmine was stepping into Imani and DeAndre's life with an entire infant in hand. Imani clearly was not the mother, but she'd passively have to watch this child grow up - developing, growing and morphing into a combination of both parents, one of which wasn't her. No matter how hard she tried not to think that deeply into it, the thought alone made her want to rip her hair out.

What Imani also didn't feel like negotiating was time, resources or emotional attachment to this baby. Who knows if Imani would connect with said child, but there was no way Jazmine would be easy-going if her son or daughter seemed to even remotely get along with Imani. She already made a point to air out DeAndre publicly. So, this whole co-parenting ordeal was bound to get ugly fast. Even with her client work on the back burner for right now, Imani didn't need the additional headache of drama even with her own image.

Pulling open the front door, Imani stepped into the vestibule, waving at the staff member sitting at the front desk.

"My husband's coming in a few minutes to head to the Pastor's office. You can look out for him."

Just six months ago, Imani took every chance she could to "my husband" everyone to death, saying it with so much pride that the tiny hairs across her arms stood up. But, referring to him as such now felt awkward and so convoluted, even with the insane, twisted and cloying love she had for him.

God, why was he so great until he wasn't?

Imani continued her ascent to the Pastor's office before hearing another office door on the right side open. Michael stepped out then, turning to lock the door before looking up, surprise laced in his features.

"Oh, hey," Imani said, awkwardly patting the back of her head. "Happy to...see you. How're you?"

As if jolted out of a trance, Michael cleared his throat, stuffing his keys back in his pocket.

"I'm hanging in there," he said, the smallest quirk of a smile lifting before dropping again. Scanning Imani, taking inventory of her Aminah Abdul Jillil leather platforms up to her Gucci A-line pleated dress, Michael nodded in acknowledgement.

"You look great...as always."

Michael pulled at his tie, but Imani didn't detect any of the scorn that was felt when they ran into each other months back. No, it was just awkward.

"What're you doing up here so late?" he asked.

"I have a meeting with your mom..." Imani nodded before swallowing. "With DeAndre."

Michael folded his lips, looking down on the floor with a nod.

"Right," he said. "Are things...well?"

Imani hiked an eyebrow.

## A Month of Sundays

"You really want to know?"

Michael took a breath, staring into her eyes.

"Things didn't work out with us, but I really did care for you, Imani."

Twirling her index fingers over each other, Imani's vision soon blurred before she blinked the impending tears away. What she definitely wasn't going to do was cry wolf to her ex about her husband. She still had some level of decency.

"It just isn't all I thought it would be, but I guess marriage is all about adjusting."

"Yeah."

"What's been happening with you, though?" she asked, a small smile appearing. "I mean, how's ministry? Still traveling a lot?"

Michael's face relaxed then, as he gave Imani the familiar dimpled smile she loved not too long ago.

"It's good...It's hard...I have one more meeting here tonight before I head home. But I feel fulfilled."

"I'm glad."

Imani looked at him over again, a feeling of relief settling over her. Even though years had passed since they first met, she still remembered the feeling of falling for him so gently, a complete contrast to how fast and immediate she fell for her husband.

"Mind steppin' about 10 feet away from my wife, bruh?"

Imani's smile dropped immediately upon hearing DeAndre behind them, placing his hand on her lower back once he reached them. Michael took a breath, nodding his head, his tight expression stapled on his face once more.

He looked DeAndre in the eye, void of expression, his chin raised.

"Not trying to disrespect...Brother Harrison."

As Michael walked off, Imani turned to face DeAndre with her arms folded and head tilted.

"I'm really not in the mood for your macho B.S."

Peeling an annoyed gaze off Michael's back, DeAndre turned back to Imani.

"Let me use the restroom first," she said. "I'll be there in a minute."

She pointed down the hall ahead of her.

"It's the last door on the left."

Before DeAndre could say anything, she turned around and walked to the bathroom on the opposite side of the hallway. Imani was washing her hands at the sink, watching the water spread across her gorgeous engagement ring and wedding band set. The time he proposed, she thought the curves, shapes and cuts of the ring were so appropriate for their relationship. It was a little unconventional, but it was theirs. She wasn't sure that was enough to keep her holding on to it though.

"Hi there, Sister Harrison."

Imani looked up at the mirror above the sink at Mrs. Coleman, who was smiling up at her as she prepared to wash her own hands. She was dressed in the most casual outfit Imani had ever seen her in - straight leg pants with a light pink blazer. Seeing her now before the meeting made Imani feel a little more at ease, like seeing Mrs. Coleman would give her the answers she so desperately needed to deal with this whole mess.

"I'm glad you both agreed to see me."

"Yeah, me too."

Imani dried her hands, looking at her in the eye for a moment in the mirror as Mrs. Coleman smiled. And, for some reason, Imani felt a thought get caught up in her head fighting to break free.

"Did you ever like me?"

Mrs. Coleman stood for a moment, surprise crossing her features as her smile faltered.

"Oh, Imani," she dried her hands, balling up the paper towel and placing it against her chest. "I never disliked you at all. I'm...so sorry you ever assumed that."

"It's just that...anytime you saw me, you always seemed to want to pull away from me or like you didn't want to be in the same room as me."

"It's because anytime I saw you, I knew you didn't want to marry Michael."

The echo from Sister Coleman's statement was the last thing Imani heard. She blinked as Mrs. Coleman gave her a forlorn smile.

"You had love for him, I know, but I never saw you look at him even remotely the same way you look at your husband."

Imani's eyes filled suddenly, as she stared down at her hands. The love she

## A Month of Sundays

had for DeAndre kept pulling her back to him, which is why she couldn't just throw her marriage away.

"And, look where that got me," she sobbed.

"Sweetie..."

Mrs. Coleman wrapped her in a hug that Imani willingly sank into.

"No matter what, you have to make sure it's all right with you. And, whatever you allow to happen will be, okay?"

Imani nodded.

"Now, I'm gonna go back to my office and greet Brother Harrison, you get yourself together here and we'll see what he has to say. How does that sound?"

∽

Imani watched Mrs. Coleman look between the two of them with the most pleasant smile despite the heavy tension in the room that could be cut with a knife. Her office was so quiet. The ticking of the Pastor's grandfather clock was the only sound in the room.

"Well...the first year of marriage is always...interesting," Mrs. Coleman said, taking off her light pink square rimmed glasses.

"And, from what you've both expressed to me...so passionately...you two have had quite a journey already, even under a year. But, there's always a chance for redemption."

Imani's eyes crept up to DeAndre, sitting in the matching leather seat next to her. Leaning back with his jean-clad legs sprawled and head tilted, DeAndre smoothed his hand over the top of his fade, exhaustion etched across his face.

This meeting wasn't going well by a long shot.

As soon as she closed the door behind her, sat in the seat next to DeAndre and Mrs. Coleman asked, *"so...how're things?"* Imani swore the initial argument they had was replicated. Between Imani's statements and DeAndre's counterpoints, the two hadn't let Sister Coleman speak for at least the first twenty minutes of the session.

Now, the smoke had cleared, at least on Imani's end - she already had a headache. They sat beside each other in stubborn silence.

"DeAndre, I know you claim that you didn't cheat...," Sister Coleman started.

"It's not a claim," he said, forcefully. "I didn't cheat on my wife. She's just refusing to listen to what I have to say."

"Okay, okay," she said, calmly as if speaking with an incessant child. "But, do you know why Imani may not *want* to hear what you have to say, even if all of this is untrue?"

DeAndre paused before toggling his gaze at her. Imani hated how even when she was angry with him, the slightest attention her way still made her heart beat double time.

"I don't."

Imani peeled her eyes away from him back to Sister Coleman who met her gaze.

"What's making you not want to see your husband's side of things? Don't you trust him?"

Imani closed her eyes, her memory going right back to bits of Jazmine's interview that she played on loop for an entire night, flashes of him and Jazmine in the corner at Randall's party mere months ago.

"He has so much history with this chick. There's so much more she knows about him than I do. I don't want to hear him clarify where he's been with her, what he has or hasn't done. I don't care."

"You really think that?"

Imani's eyes crashed directly into DeAndre, a tinge of pain flashed in his eyes.

"You have every single part of me...something that she never had."

"She was with you for one of the hardest days of your life. Wasn't she? You lost your best friend and you didn't even think about coming home! You didn't call me."

DeAndre pushed his head back, staring at the ceiling in exasperation.

"Did you forget that you told me to let you go? You told me to leave you."

"And, you came back, knowing you had all these women in the wings. You proposed to me, like...it was just a walk in the park or something. It was just another notch on your scorecard that, like an idiot, I fell for. You swept me off my feet and I fell for it."

## A Month of Sundays

Despite not wanting to lose control, Imani's eyes filled with tears, then. This pain was so visceral that she wanted to leave.

"Why did you have to get her pregnant? WHY?!" she screeched painfully, through a sea of tears.

Sister Coleman looked at Imani empathetically before reaching her hand across the desk.

"Honey, I know this must bring back so much for you," she said as Imani moved forward in her seat, extending her own hand to hold on to Sister Coleman's. Wiping underneath her eyes, Imani nodded, not all the way understanding what she meant by that.

"I really want to believe him, but I just...don't even know what to feel right now. I never thought I'd even have to think of a possibility like this. Think about someone else being in our life the way she's about to be."

"We don't even know if it's mine," DeAndre said, wiping a hand across his forehead. "I keep saying that we don't know."

Sister Coleman turned back to Imani.

"It's hard, but...you gotta learn that you can trust your husband. You can create a new family for yourself, even if this situation is familiar to you."

Imani choked back a sob, tilting her head as her chest rose and fell in spurts.

"What...what're you saying right now, Sister Coleman?"

The First Lady's empathetic smile dimmed, being replaced by guilt.

"Oh, I apologize," she said, taking a quick glance at DeAndre. "You didn't tell your husband?"

"What?"

"Well...about your father."

Imani paused, looking at DeAndre who was frozen himself, staring directly at her.

"What about my father?"

Sister Coleman leveled a look at her, straightening her gaze.

"Your father having you...outside of his marriage."

Imani's chest stopped immediately, her face growing warmer in an instant. She blinked, shaking her head.

"Wait...what?"

"Oh, Imani, I...um," Sister Coleman faltered. "I really thought Ethel told you."

Her words triggered a replay of images in Imani's mind of all those interactions with her parents as a child, specifically Helena. The distance she kept from her. The moments of hesitation she'd often have in small conversation. Imani just always thought Helena was timid; she had no idea that every day Helena stared into the eyes of a child who was the result of her husband's affair.

From her peripheral, Imani saw DeAndre turn to her, but refused to meet his gaze. Her marriage was literally repeating history.

Imani stood up, feeling herself dry heave, before opening the door to rush out.

"Baby..."

She heard DeAndre running after her, and Imani only made it halfway down the hall, before he caught up to her.

"A'ight...baby, look. I know this is...This is a lot and I can't imagine how you're feeling, but, baby, I'm here for you..."

Imani licked her lips, tapping her foot to prevent herself from slapping him dead across the face. If he touched her again, she wouldn't be able to hold herself back no matter where they were. As he kept talking, she pulled her gaze away from him to the end of the hallway where Michael had paused, his brows dipped in consternation.

"Wait a second," she called, speed walking ahead to her ex-boyfriend, ignoring everything her husband was saying.

Once in front of him, watching his eyes dance between her and DeAndre who still heading towards them, Imani pulled Michael's attention to her.

"Can you take me to my old apartment?"

Michael stood stock still for only a second before DeAndre's voice boomed through the hallway.

"I swear, nigga, if you touch her..."

Imani turned around then, ignited by his straight up audacity.

"...and, if you touch him, I will never talk to you ever again! Try me."

DeAndre looked at her, all fire in his eyes dimming. She stood between two of the most important men in her life aside from her father - each one exemplifying the highest level of restraint and confidence.

## A Month of Sundays

"Imani. I –"

Don't talk to me!" she shouted cutting him off as tears prickled the corners of her eyes.

Imani noticed Mrs. Coleman come up behind DeAndre and pat him on the back.

Turning back around to Michael, Imani looked at him, determined.

"I need to get out of here. Just drop me there and you could do whatever you gotta do after that."

With a nod, Michael opened the door for Imani, leading her to his car in the lot.

∽

"At least he didn't punch me in the face."

Imani turned to look at Michael who was checking the rearview mirror of his Toyota Camry where DeAndre was parked behind them, idle in his Porsche. Both cars were parked in front of Kaylee's apartment, without anyone stepping out of their respective vehicles yet. She didn't even bother turning herself around and wasn't surprised that DeAndre had followed them the entire way to her old apartment from the church. Imani was just thankful her husband didn't instigate an entire fight in the church.

"I could care less about anything right now, if I'm being honest," she said.

Folding her arms across herself, Imani wanted to literally disappear, away from DeAndre and everyone else. She was upset at her husband and now furious at her aunt for keeping this secret from her. There was no way Imani could even bring herself to be in the same room as Ethel right now.

"The parents I thought I knew turned out to not even be much of a family to me at all. How do I even reconcile with this?"

Imani told Michael everything on the way over to Kaylee's apartment just before Imani called her to ask if she could stay the night to sort things out in her head. She also didn't want to set foot back in her home anytime soon. Kaylee had promised she could stay as long as she felt the need to, but even Imani knew she didn't want to overstay her welcome.

"It's tough," Michael said. "But you gotta know that your aunt only wanted what was best for you. She sees you as more than her niece."

Imani turned to look at him in the driver's seat, a flash of déjà vu piercing her mind. He sat with a gentle gaze above a soft smile and Imani heard Ethel's words. *You had such a sure, reliable, steadfast husband-to-be in Michael.* Now that Imani was outside of their relationship, she realized how often Aunt Ethel's opinions influenced so many aspects of her life once she returned to Port Springs. She loved Michael, but it also helped that Ethel actively encouraged and approved of him, too. As reliable and sure as Michael was for her, Imani had to admit that her heart still didn't accelerate as quickly or yearn for him as deeply as it did for DeAndre.

That, unfortunately, was never going to change even now.

"Let me just get out of here," she said, tossing a half-smile Michael's way. "Thanks for the ride and I'm sorry I put you in the middle of all this."

Unlocking the door, Imani grabbed her bag.

"You'll always be the first woman I wanted to take care of."

Imani turned to him.

"I hate that I hurt you the way I did."

Michael nodded, looking over her features once more.

"I know. Take care of yourself, Imani."

Imani was not even halfway to the apartment building door when DeAndre stepped out of his car, hot on her heels in no time.

"Yo, you really thought that was a good idea to do?"

She turned around just as she received Kaylee's text that she was on her way downstairs. And, found DeAndre staring at her, his eyes narrowed.

"I clearly don't have any idea of what's happening in my own life, so might as well tack something else on for good measure."

DeAndre pressed his fingers to the corners of his eyes, shaking his head.

"Baby, you can't just run away from all of this like you want to," he said, looking up at her again. "You can't just run away from me."

He drew closer, his hands on her lower back, already making her melt all over as his Bergamot scent tickled her nose and his touch sent shivers up her spine. Just weeks ago, it was everything she ever craved and was the sweetest distraction. Even now, her body responded instinctually, but she couldn't stop the images of him and a pregnant Jazmine out of her mind, teasing her and poking at her.

Imani wiggled her way out of his grasp, pushing against his shoulders.

"I don't wanna talk to you," she said, looking up at him. "I don't even wanna be around you."

Behind them, the building door opened as Kaylee stood there, glancing between the two of them alert to ensure her friend was good before her eyes settled on Imani.

"I'm here, 'Mani," she said, before cutting her eyes quickly at DeAndre.

Taking one glance at Kaylee, DeAndre stepped closer to Imani again, being sure that this conversation would only be heard between the two of them.

"Baby, we can talk about this when we get home...let's go home."

Imani folded her arms, shocked that he was in denial since he couldn't just sweet talk his way out of this one. He was about to be a father to a woman's baby outside of their marriage and he was expecting her - apparently the child of an affair herself, as if him and Jazmine's baby wasn't enough to deal with, to help raise said baby for a kumbaya moment?

"I'm not coming home, you know that, right? You expect me to come home...with you?"

DeAndre glanced at Kaylee again before looking at Imani...realization of her intentions hitting him hard.

"So, you're gonna just stay here?"

"Maybe...I don't know...I just need to think...but I'm not staying with you."

"Imani, baby. Don't do this to me," he said blocking Imani's path to Kaylee's door.

She looked around DeAndre in Kaylee's direction, her expression filled with reluctance.

"I need some distance...some time...something. I need space to THINK...I can't do it when I'm around you cause I'm either mad or not thinking and that's not helping me."

When Imani went to step past him, he physically created a barrier with his body. Their eyes crashed into each other - battle of passion and frustration with DeAndre staring at her with defiance.

"C'mon, Imani, c'mon. All of this is gonna be handled the way it needs to be. Please, just...don't give up on us."

He hugged her, making it much more difficult for Imani to push him off. DeAndre embraced her tightly as if he were afraid to let her go, the pressure making it hard for her to breathe.

"You need to stop," she muttered through gritted teeth.

It drove her crazy how her love for him was as strong as her sudden repulsion of him. Imani couldn't even think straight – she was so damn mad at him – he had messed everything up!

"You already tried to leave me once," he said, pain drenched in his chords. "You left me already."

Imani finally pushed him away, literally feeling his weight leave her body. She looked at her husband, someone she revered more than any man she'd ever known, all of his confidence, prowess and elegance gone.

"Go away."

Finally stepping around him, Imani fell into Kaylee's extended arms and held onto her best friend with every ounce of strength she had, releasing every tear until she had none left to cry.

# Chapter 43
# Hitting a Brick Wall

"You low, down dirty dog."

Melody, now visibly several months pregnant, cast her eyes at DeAndre as she nursed a banana smoothie with a pineapple resting on the rim of the glass and bit into her massively round bowl of grilled chicken salad. Her squint his way could cut a knife.

While explaining all he could about his extremely loose "relationship" with Jazmine, Melody folded her arms in front of her and shook her head.

Even though DeAndre knew he was in for an earful, he also knew he needed to speak directly with someone who would relay information to Imani. The two hadn't been speaking on the phone over the past week -since Imani refused to answer his FaceTime calls - and the last time he saw her was when dumb-ass Michael dropped her off at Kaylee's apartment. So, DeAndre knew she was safe, but she never gave him an inclination on when she'd be returning home. He called Kaylee who was now the complete opposite of friendly, far from the smiles and encouragement she gave him when they surprised Imani all those months ago. Now she treated him like the enemy, not giving any answers, which meant Melody was his only option. She was also the only other person in Imani's life who didn't keep any secrets from her.

Melody continued shaking her head, chomping down her salad like she hadn't eaten in days.

"However all this pans out with ol' girl and the baby," Melody said, swallowing. "I hope you've learned your lesson to not put your business all out there on social media."

DeAndre nodded, taking a breath.

"We were posting a lot," he said, playing with his straw wrapper.

"We?!" Melody took off her yellow-tinted shades and placed them on top of her honey blonde waves, taking a sip of her smoothie. "*You* were posting about everything as soon as she said yes to you. And, yeah, you don't have her on full blast all over your page, but...amateur detectives are out there."

She pointed a long, stiletto nail in his direction.

"You know? The only difference between Jazmine and the other broads you've been with is that she ended up playing the long game. She got you comfortable to get your guard down."

DeAndre threw his straw wrapper on the table and couldn't even respond. Melody cut up the chicken in her salad and looked up at him again, her face laced with concern this time.

"Out of all the years I've known you...how could you make this one slip? It feels so amateur coming from you."

He put his forehead in his head, leaning forward on the table. "Mel, I was so gone that night."

"But, thought about proposing right after, huh?"

DeAndre let out a breath and pinched his nose bridge.

"I'm not trying to say I didn't hurt my wife, a'ight? But technically, I was still single when I slept with Jazmine."

As soon as he said exactly what he had been thinking all along, even when Imani was throwing his clothes everywhere like a woman scorned or wrestling out of his grasp at Kaylee's, he instantly regretted it. Melody looked at him in a way that could've killed him on sight, if that was at all possible.

"And, not even a month later, you were very engaged," Melody said. "And, three months later... what do ya' know? It coincides with the start of the second trimester of a pregnancy, you were married."

She narrowed her gaze, pointing a finger in his direction.

"You don't see the messiness in this timeline?"

## A Month of Sundays

DeAndre scratched his brow, unable to give an answer. He was still in disbelief that this one thing literally changed his reality in a heartbeat.

"Okay, so, homegirl clearly knows how to paint a picture," she moved on, not even waiting for his response to her previous question. "But, tell me those messages she had with you were all a lie?"

DeAndre's eyes shifted.

"No."

Melody's head dropped.

"What do you mean, no?"

DeAndre closed his eyes for a moment, preparing for Melody's vitriol. In the moment, it all seemed so innocent, but now, everything he had done incriminated him on all sides.

"A'ight...she..." he sighed. "She messaged me after the wedding to congratulate me and I thanked her, but Melody, all those messages she's putting up as evidence are a straight up lie. I never told her where I was or where she could meet me. She manipulated that shit."

Melody folded her arms, her jaw on the floor, giving him a look as if he couldn't be serious.

"It doesn't even matter because you be likin' that hoe's pictures," she cut her eyes at him, "don't you?"

"I'm not likin' or commentin' on thirst traps."

"But, it was enough for her to present evidence," Melody said, sucking her teeth. "We're in the age of AI, for crying out loud. People are out posting releases from me that I didn't even step foot in a studio to record, and that's not even from people who follow me."

Swirling her straw in her glass, Melody then tapped her nails against the table.

"I'm surprised Stephanie didn't tell you to do a sweep of all your followers or delete numbers, anyway."

DeAndre didn't answer, all those preliminary conversations Stephanie had with him coming back in spades. He dismissed pretty much everything she said, insisting that he had it handled.

When he didn't answer, Melody stopped and looked him over for a beat.

"She did," he said.

Melody laughed, sarcasm spilling over.

"Of course she did because she's a woman," she responded. "Well...just tell me you did all you just said while you were out of town?"

He sat back and shifted in his seat, not even able to keep eye contact with Melody.

"Wow, D," she said, shaking her head. "I had no idea you were such a...a messy bitch."

"You legitimately know every single person you follow or who follows you? You really trackin' it with the algorithms and shit?"

"Absolutely," she said, with pride. "And, do a purge of them at least once a month just because, thankyouverymuch."

He should've known. Melody's entire career was built on social media.

"Why does all this even matter?" He asked. "I'm not commenting on her shit or having any other direct interactions with her. For real, though, I'm not some 18-year-old tryna holla."

"No, but you're a married man, giving this chick an open side door," Melody said. "Might as well have delivered your dick to her in a box through FedEx. Ughhhhh...you men literally live in a world that's warped into your fuzzy-ass logic."

Melody shook her head, her left leg crossed over her right, shaking it in annoyance.

"I just don't get it," she said. "You harassed me to give you Imani's number all those years ago, which I'm so glad I didn't...but, you just couldn't let her go and she fell for your tall, lanky ass. Her nose was so wide open for you that you didn't even have to do the work of a formal engagement."

"Melody, a'ight. I messed up, but you know I've been about Imani since I met her...you know that, but-"

"Your dick was doing all the thinking," Melody deadpanned, shaking her head.

"And, all these damn pictures y'all have together," she said. "I think there's more pictures of you out there with her than with Imani."

DeAndre felt the blow in Melody's words, invisibly shrinking in his seat.

"Why didn't you even come back to the Springs that night? Eve said she was trying to get in touch and you lowkey ghosted her for like a week."

## A Month of Sundays

DeAndre sighed, exhausted. If he could turn back the hands of time, he would...that night felt like ten years ago.

"Come back and do what? Feel sorry for myself that my best friend died and I didn't know shit about anything? Imani wasn't even messin' with me then, anyway. She had cut me off for weeks by that point."

Melody looked him over, her mouth widening in shock.

"So, not only did you actively want to avoid reality, you also wanted to swoop in to get your girl in the process? All to not feel any of it? Wanted to just overdose on love to keep yourself from coming down to Earth? How romantic of you. No wonder she's had enough of you and your mess."

"I'm not sayin' it was the perfect next step. I just...couldn't be without her."

The night he found out about Randall's passing was a complete blur, but Imani was the first one on his mind as soon as he woke up from the straight stupor he was in. Now fully aware of being without his best friend, DeAndre knew the second most important person in his life needed to be with him, too.

"Well, now your ass is alone," she said, without an inkling of empathy in her tone. "How did you and Jazmine even hook up again?"

DeAndre leaned forward, looking over the view of the spring skyline on the rooftop.

"I was hangin' with her while I was out there, but...I'mma be real, Mel, I didn't even know how I ended up at her hotel that night."

Melody looked at him, giving a definite side eye. "What?"

DeAndre shook his head, still wondering exactly how he got to Jazmine's hotel.

"I swear I don't...I know we hung out that day and went out earlier at night, but I don't know when the hell I got to her room. I wasn't staying there with her."

Melody's eyes grew in sudden serious revelation and placed a flattened hand on her chest.

"DeAndre, wait, were you drugged?"

"What? Hell no."

"I mean, you say you don't have recollection of that night, but you woke up the next morning at a hotel you didn't book. Like..."

She let the last of her statements hang in silence as she looked at DeAndre, but he refused to get sucked down a rabbit hole of thinking that wasn't of his own doing. He heard about other men getting caught up with women who played them like a fiddle and was in denial that it could happen to him. Yeah, he had more than his fair share of escapades, but it never got to the point where he was beyond control. How *did* he let his guard down so easily?

"You're a mess," she said, simply.

DeAndre leveled a look at her. Melody was never known to mince words, especially when she felt like you were in the wrong. She had more than enough to stand on this time, too.

"Is my wife wit' y'all?"

The sound that women make when they feel like someone has the audacity to say or ask what they just did spilled from Melody's lips.

"Girlcode, fool," she said. "I'm not telling you anything, especially since you're in the doghouse."

The bite in her tone softened once she looked up at his face again.

"She's safe, fed and loved. That's all you need to know."

*I'm not even trippin.' I'll just call Hosea to tell me,* he thought.

She pointed her fork at him. "And, don't even let that lizard brain of yours convince you to call Sé..."

Melody pushed her head forward. "'Cause he's not gonna tell you anything neither."

"This is immature as shit, Melody! I know she's wit' y'all."

"Okay! Okay! But....just give her a minute, D, damn! Can you just...get off her for a second?!"

She stared at him straight in the face, all humor out the window.

"As I said, you gave this girl a rushed engagement that ended in a rushed wedding, which, although absolutely stunning, had *you* written all over it. You move her into your house, leaving her off-and-on for weeks on end, under the pretense that you were training for a season, which frankly, D, you're only participating in for your own ego 'cause how many more trophies do you actually need?"

Melody blinked.

"Don't you think she could use a fuckin' minute?"

As much as DeAndre tried to respond with a comeback, he couldn't. He couldn't deny Melody's points, especially since if the tables were turned, none of that would fly.

"It's literally been a whirlwind for her," she continued. "Are you going to the Sporties solo next week?"

Despite Imani's palpable annoyance with him, she agreed to attend the 65th Annual Sports Awards with him as his date. This year, to his genuine surprise, the Tennis League had chosen DeAndre to be honored with the Arthur Ashe award and he was its youngest recipient in history. DeAndre was so thrilled over the honor that he momentarily forgot how upset Imani was. When he told her over the phone, his request for her to be there was expressed as more of an expectation than a genuine request. But, Imani chose to appear on the red carpet with him, opting in to be beside him for on-air interviews as well. Of course, she then insisted on speaking with Stephanie to go over logistics, but her agreement to it in the first place had to prove there was still hope... right?

DeAndre shook his head.

"Still gettin' her right where you want her," she said, cutting him a side eye with her lips pursed. "Do you even know she entered that art exhibition and didn't get it?"

He looked at Melody, surprise settling in his features.

"She didn't say any...thing—"

"Of course she didn't... you know why?" she asked. "Your schedule is a distraction, your life is a distraction and, as long as she's physically present with you, then everything's just fine? Did you even ask her about it?"

The deeper Melody's words settled in, the more anxious DeAndre began to feel.

"...And, she's not above smoke from me, either, because I've been trying to keep her head on straight when you were gone. Girl is straight dickmatized over you, following behind you like a lovesick puppy when you were here...and, I get it, I was there, too."

Melody shook her head, releasing a sigh.

"But...y'all both need to decide what your marriage will be for the two of you, collectively. Compromises need to be made, DeAndre."

He squirmed in his seat, feeling uneasy about what Imani could even be thinking. Up until this point, he was well aware from her body language that she didn't like him being away, but she never explicitly asked him to compromise on any of his plans, especially because there were times when she couldn't be with him at games or see him out of town, neither. But, her being away from him didn't open a Pandora's box of news that had her hands tied. DeAndre couldn't shake the hurt he saw in Imani's eyes, after confronting him about the news and, on top of that, the shocking revelation about her father's wife not even being her own mother. Imani legitimately had every right to leave him, especially with how his own news would trigger her. Thinking about what Imani could be ruminating over, DeAndre realized he had no clue.

"What's wrong?" Melody asked. "Scared of losing her 'cause you didn't tighten your shit? You know, Imani's built different. Unlike you, she has two feet planted in reality. She might get some bruising in the process, but she could do well all by herself."

DeAndre's jaw tightened and his heart raced, on the verge of a panic attack. Melody watched him like he was writhing in pain tied up on a chair with his mouth taped.

"Good. Sit with this feeling and remember it."

## Chapter 44
# Reset

DeAndre pulled on the lapels of his charcoal suit jacket, buttoning the middle as Jeffrey back and turned to look at DeAndre's reflection in the mirror, smiling from ear to ear.

"Now..." Jeffrey said, looking over his bifocals with admiration. "That boy did good."

DeAndre laughed, glancing at himself in the mirror and admiring the side stitching of the designer suit he picked out for the annual Sports Award Ceremony tonight. Staring at himself in the mirror, he looked every bit like the winner he was.

Too bad he felt nowhere near it.

It had been a week since the emotional revelation about Imani's mom and Imani seemed to have shut herself out even more. Their phone calls were even shorter, with Imani barely saying a word as DeAndre did all he could to keep her on the line. Fortunately, she agreed to be his plus-one for the show, even opting to still walk the carpet with him as the dutiful wife in tow. Tonight would literally be the first time he put eyes on Imani in an entire week and he was bursting from the mere anxiety of it.

Once DeAndre finished tying his shoes, he walked out to the living room where Stephanie and Trey were waiting.

"Well, don't you look like a million bucks and not a dollar short," Stephanie said, smiling up at him with her phone in her hand.

She was dressed in a simple black off-the-shoulder cocktail dress that hugged her shape and her hair was gathered into a long, braided ponytail that narrowed the wide cheeks of her caramel face.

"Thanks," he said, already feeling his heart racing.

It was crazy how the anticipation of seeing Imani walk down the aisle and the anxiety of seeing her now were on two sides of the same coin. Without even realizing it, he was already looking ahead of Stephanie then behind him where Trey was sitting nearest to the front door.

"She should be here in a minute," Stephanie said tactfully, giving him a forlorn smile. She bit the bottom of her lip.

"Hey...I'm no one's therapist," she said. "But, just follow her lead."

He was going to take off his jacket to have a seat himself when he heard the front door behind him close. He turned around as Imani walked to them from the foyer looking every bit like a queen ready to sit on her throne.

Dressed in a long black crushed velvet gown with a Bardot neckline that accentuated her chest and long torso, Imani held the sides of a matching velvet cape with sleeves gathered up her arms, both decorated with stacks of diamond bangles of various colors that stopped just below her elbows. Her hair was now an icy gray silver that gave her a look similar to Storm from X-men without bordering into costume territory. One of the many things he loved about Imani was how effortlessly she presented herself. She was conscious of what she wore, but it never consumed her. Creativity poured out of her in different ways - she just had fun with the endless options available to her and Imani knocked it out the park every time.

DeAndre knew he dressed well, but his baby knew how to put that shit on.

She approached Stephanie and DeAndre, but still kept her distance from him, torturing him beyond measure. He was overwhelmed, just looking at her. Drop earrings with stars at the ends hung just above her shoulders, which were lightly dusted with the tiniest flecks of glitter, adding even more dimension to her deep brown skin. With her perfectly painted fuschia lips opened slightly and the bottom of her dress gathered in her hands, she looked like she was from another galaxy.

## A Month of Sundays

"Hi," she said, looking between Stephanie and DeAndre.

"Imani," Stephanie said, tone drenched in admiration. "You are–"

"My wife," DeAndre said, before she could even finish her compliment. He'd do anything to have her right now. How the hell had he let her get away from him?

Imani's eyes shifted between him and Stephanie, but she held her attention to Stephanie.

"Can we just go?" she asked without even cracking a smile.

"Of course..." Stephanie said.

DeAndre, Stephanie, Imani and Trey all walked outside to the Escalade that Clive had idling in the driveway. DeAndre opened the back seat door, preparing for Imani to step in first. But, when he turned, she wasn't moving.

With a stoic expression, Imani looked at Stephanie who was standing beside her.

"I'm not riding with him."

She might as well have slapped him across the face from the impact of what she said. DeAndre went to respond when Stephanie threw him a glance - shaking her head with wide eyes, signaling for him to stay quiet.

"Umm Imani," Stephanie soothed. "You agreed to walk the carpet with–"

"And, I will..." Imani responded. He couldn't remember ever hearing her voice so void of emotion, even over the phone.

"So," Stephanie continued. "We'd be running late...if you two were arriving–"

"I'm not riding with him in the damn car, Stephanie!" she yelled. "Either you or Trey is coming with me or I'll drive there myself. Figure it out or we'll be even more late."

Stephanie held her mouth open, aghast while Trey tugged on his ear. DeAndre just stared, flabbergasted.

"Yes, ma'am," Stephanie cleared her throat.

Imani and Stephanie waited while Clive called his co-driver to come and pick them up to head to the ceremony. DeAndre and Trey stood outside, both men with their hands in their pockets, with DeAndre playing the million and one thoughts in his mind.

"How long am I gonna be in this doghouse?" he asked himself out loud.

"Don't know what to tell you with that, my man," Trey said.

Once the car pulled up for Stephanie and Imani, DeAndre and Trey rode in their own separate vehicle with Clive. On the ride over, all DeAndre thought about were ways to get through to his wife. He thought tonight would be a reset for them, but from the straight fury in her eyes a moment ago, that likely wouldn't be the case.

They pulled up at the Kodak Pictures Auditorium an hour later, allowing Stephanie to escort DeAndre and Imani towards the press line for pictures and interviews. Just before DeAndre made it to the step-and-repeat where he and Imani would take photos, he turned around to face her, witnessing a heavy sadness in her eyes.

"We don't have to do this," he whispered, going in to touch her hand.

She pulled away, taking a breath before looking back at DeAndre, her expression serious.

"It's fine. You have to do press. Let's get it done, so we can get to our seats."

Imani balled her hand in a soft fist before taking DeAndre's hand this time. He looked down at their hands touching for a moment and swore he felt the exact same feeling he did when they first met. It was as if he had her for the moment, but there was no a guarantee he'd have her again.

As Stephanie escorted them down the line of journalists on the red carpet, Imani morphed into the quiet, proud wife within seconds who smiled graciously at compliments and blushed her way through the few questions reporters managed to ask her, mainly about what she was wearing and how she felt about DeAndre's award.

*"I'm so proud of this achievement for him. He deserves all...of the praise."*

She said a few statements similar to this when the reporters asked, and DeAndre saw the sadness still in her eyes, behind her smiles. Thankfully, Stephanie did pre-damage control and didn't escort them to any bloggers who would've brought up the allegations, but it still felt like a heavy cloud hanging over their heads.

Once inside the auditorium, DeAndre spent a few minutes greeting a few of his peers, some outside of tennis as well as a few of his previous opponents. Everyone was giving him so much love, praising him for a job well done but, none of it mattered. Watching his wife speak with the few people he introduced her to, smiling through light small talk, DeAndre wanted to literally grab her and run out of the auditorium. He wanted to spend all night professing all of the love he had for her, showering her with all the affection she could handle. He still didn't feel guilty, but none of it mattered when he was guilty by mere association.

The awards ceremony began a short time later, allowing DeAndre to finally sit down and be the closest he had been to his wife in weeks. They clapped and laughed at the appropriate points of the show, but he took every chance he could to observe Imani next to him. She watched the presenters and award recipients with unabashed focus, not even allowing her eyes to look at DeAndre. Nowadays, he had no idea what the hell Imani was thinking, but if her goal was to make him miserable, she was straight killing him. His stomach was tied in knots, just watching her quiet ease, as he finally placed his hand on her lap. And, instead of recoiling from his touch, Imani placed her hand on top of his, settling all of his nerves at once.

The crowd's sudden applause pulled DeAndre and Imani's attention as Serena Williams walked to the front of the stage to the singular standing mic. Her presence was a total surprise for everyone, considering her recent retirement and her decision to step away from the public eye for a while. And, from the applause that took some time to settle, she was still very much missed.

"Okay, okay," she said, "Let's focus."

The crowd laughed.

"I'm here tonight to celebrate an amazing peer of mine, an amazing friend of mine who has revolutionized the world of tennis as we know it. From his humble beginnings in Port Springs, DeAndre Harrison has proven himself to not only be a dynamic force on the court, but also be a world class champion reflecting the core values of the late great Arthur Ashe..."

Serena continued with her speech before a video montage with highlights of some of DeAndre's achievements as well as a few celebrities reflecting on his impact flashed before the crowd on the projected screen onstage. This entire presentation was put together so well, curated with so much intention and DeAndre was on pins-and-needles through all of it with his wife treating him like a complete stranger.

"Hey."

She turned to him for the first time tonight, her eyes glimmering from the lights just off the stage.

"Thank you for being here with me."

Imani sighed.

"You're welcome. You should be proud of yourself, DeAndre," she said, robotically.

"Stay with me tonight," he said, his breath strained. He felt his own intensity in his stare while Imani met his gaze with nothing but apathy.

"Please."

Imani's eyes narrowed.

"Since when do you beg?"

"...And, without further ado, I'm pleased to present this year's Arthur Ashe Award recipient, DeAndre Harrison..."

The two of them stood from their seats, as DeAndre saw Imani's face mustering just enough enthusiasm for the camera and lights that were now anchored their way. She joined the crowd's applause, clapping a little more gingerly, as DeAndre pulled her into him from her lower back, giving her a kiss on the cheek.

"I'll be on my hands and knees, if I gotta be," he said in her ear.

Her body stilled for a moment, before she pulled away, continuing on with her light clapping.

DeAndre walked up the stage steps and once onstage, took a moment to bow to Serena. They never had a chance to compete or play a doubles match together, but DeAndre never missed an opportunity to praise her publicly for her own legacy. He walked to the mic, seeing the faces of his peers and fans from the audience who watched him in admiration.

"I'm so honored to be here tonight," he started. "I'm humbled."

The crowd, knowing his reputation for being anything but, laughed.

"But, in all seriousness, I truly wouldn't be standing here tonight without my team, my entire crew and my wife. She's a girl from my 'hood who I chased like crazy..."

He chuckled. "And she's been such a blessing to me in the few months we've been together, just made my life so much more interesting. I love her beyond me, y'all."

## A Month of Sundays

DeAndre cleared his throat with his smile.

"I needed to get that off my chest from the jump, so y'all wouldn't catch me slippin'."

The crowd laughed again as DeAndre continued with his speech, and when his eyes landed on Imani, she watched him for a moment before granting him the smallest hint of a smile.

The rest of the evening sped up after DeAndre's recognition, but he decided to skip this year's after parties and festivities, per Stephanie's suggestion. He would've been in attendance with Imani at all of them, but DeAndre was now erring on the side of caution, not wanting to be associated with anything outside of this legacy he realized he'd built all along.

Stephanie, Trey, Imani and DeAndre all left the theater in separate vehicles at the end of the awards ceremony as Clive drove Imani and DeAndre back home. The Sports Awards were one of the few awards shows in close proximity to the Springs, which made it much more convenient for DeAndre to attend. After about an hour of the quiet car ride in which Imani had much to say, Clive pulled up to the front of their home.

"A'ight, stay safe tonight, man," DeAndre said, patting him on the shoulder as he watched Imani step out of the car, rushing inside.

DeAndre let his eyes roll as he shook his head, anticipating a long night. Clive turned to face him.

"It takes time," he said.

DeAndre gave him a closed smile as he climbed out the car, walking to the open front door and closing it behind him. He walked up the steps to the bedroom gingerly, feeling the hints of exhaustion he had earlier, hit him with full force now. Taking off his suit jacket, he stepped into the room and looked up to find Imani naked, draped with her diamonds in her ears, across her neck and on her wrists. Sitting at the edge of the bed with one leg crossed on top of the other, Imani looked at him with a hunger in her eyes now that he hadn't seen her in weeks.

"Beg for it."

Imani's signal set him off immediately as the two collided into each other, kissing so hard...with so much force that he couldn't breathe. Pulling his shirt so hard that she ripped off all the buttons, Imani pulled him aggressively by his waistband, backing herself up against the wall next to the balcony door. Her scent enveloped him immediately as he felt her hands travel from his bare chest down to his belt buckle. She paused for a second, making him chuckle. But, when Imani cut her eyes up at him, not even a hint of a smile was on her face.

"Are you gonna break my heart?" she asked, tears pooling in her eyes as she finally took off his belt, undid his pants, breaking his erection free.

"Baby, I'm not—"

"Are you?"

She cupped her hands around his dick, massaging it with just enough force to turn him on further.

"Why did you come back into my life just to tear it apart?"

Before he could answer, Imani kissed him again, pulling all of what he wanted to say out of him. It was clear to him within seconds that she wasn't in the mood to hear anything that came out of his mouth, no matter if it was the truth in her eyes or not.

Pulling her up to his waist, he entered her, moving into her gently as he kissed behind her ear, down her neck and shoulders. Her moans driving his desire, as he grew even harder from simply being in her presence. DeAndre wanted his love to be said through every stroke he gave.

With his eyes closed, he relished in how good it felt being inside of her again, feeling the familiar mold of her body and his intertwined.

"I love you, I love you, I love you," he whispered in her ear, peppering his affirmations with more kisses.

Suddenly, Imani pushed his head back, drawing his eyes directly to hers.

"Don't speak," she said, her face stoic, her chest rising and falling.

Imani continued thrusting her pelvis back then forward, distracting him from the sudden demand. Her movement accelerated faster until DeAndre couldn't see straight, couldn't even consider that his wife was using him for only one thing. And, the craziest part of it all was that he was willingly accepting it, accepting however she wanted to have him.

DeAndre fell asleep shortly after his own release, his arms wrapped around Imani's waist with her body pulled close.

When he opened his eyes the next morning, she was gone.

# Chapter 45
# Avoidance

Imani took a deep inhale, feeling oxygen fill her lungs, before finally letting it out through her mouth, keeping her eyes closed. She was sitting on a yoga mat in the middle of Melody's living room, waiting for cues from the yoga instructor projected on screen. The workday went by much faster than she anticipated, mainly because she spent half of the day avoiding Lauri. Imani didn't feel like hearing anything from anyone at this point, whether it was encouraging words or suggestions for next steps for what to do after her submission rejection. She needed to figure out what she was going to do with her marriage.

Imani heard the front door open and footsteps drawing closer to the living room. Feeling herself being watched, Imani took a beat before opening her eyes, allowing them to crawl up to Melody. Her Coca Cola bottle shape filled out her maternity leggings and sports bra set perfectly as she stood with a hand on her hip.

"Girl, you need to go back to your husband. You're lucky you're here during a week when Hosea is location scouting or your ass would've been out."

Imani took a breath and rolled her eyes. A few days had passed since the Awards Ceremony where she did exactly what she told Stephanie she would do - present herself as part of a united front for the public, showing that, without a shadow of a doubt, she was standing right beside her man. For what it was worth, Imani thought she could genuinely do it. But, as soon as she was face to face with DeAndre, all potential ideas of Kumbaya evaporated. She was pissed, straight fuming, in her seat for the whole evening - from the step-and-repeat to the extravagant presentation, fit for the reigning champion of his sport - that she didn't even know where else to place her anger.

And, when he whispered in her ear just before making his way to the stage, it was like a switch flipped making her feel like they were the only two people in the room all over again, she was beside herself, wanting to screw her brains out.

"I have gone back to him," Imani droned.

If she hadn't dropped her dress to give herself to him when they were back at the house, she would've probably slit his throat. DeAndre may have turned out to be a trifling, cheating husband, but he did more than satisfy her sexually.

*I could just keep having sex with him*, she thought.

"I'm not talking about using him as your walking vibrator," Melody said. "Now's not the time to get into your villain era. If he wasn't your husband, I'd salute you, but that's not the answer, sis..."

Her eyes narrowed as she placed both hands on her hips. "I see your little wheels turnin,' too."

Imani rolled her eyes, annoyed with herself for even telling Melody what she had done with him last night.

"Sweetie," Melody said, sitting on the couch and placing a hand on her leg.

"Jesus, I promised myself I wouldn't ask you this. But here I am."

She sighed.

"Is the thought of you co-parenting with this chick really the end of the world?"

Imani felt her jaw clench so tight, she thought her gums would bleed. She looked at her with such an intensity that even Melody straightened slowly.

"You and I both know this hoe will not go away, off into the sunset, Melody. She's made it very clear to publicly smear this for all its worth."

"But, you've now made it clear publicly that you're willing to still be with DeAndre. Maybe, the tactic is to just let her talk until she's blue in the face and doesn't get the reaction out of y'all that she wants."

Imani chuckled.

## A Month of Sundays

"And, she's gonna just keep talking. Did you see all the pictures they had together? With her family and friends? Like, how long has he even been with her?"

Feeling her emotions gathering in her throat, Imani swallowed. She was so tired of crying.

"Girl, I've known DeAndre for a long time and...he's just not that kinda dude. Yeah, he's had his fun, but he wouldn't have been with you in the first place if he planned on cheating."

Imani wanted to believe Melody in the worst way, but seeing Jazmine's messages with him on blogs and pictures of him showing up to her lounge out in LA made her think differently.

"Mel, this was the one opportunity I ever had to have a complete family that was all mine. I spent my life feeling like something was wrong with me, why I never felt connected to anything. This was my chance to create that with my husband."

Melody, with sympathy etched on her face, shook her head before reaching her arm across Imani's shoulders, hugging her to her chest.

"I'm not letting this go, Mel. I'm not."

Imani sat up in the bed in Melody's guest room later that evening, perusing Instagram, her gluttonous form of punishment. She had about five missed calls from DeAndre and counting, but she chose to simply ignore all of them, deciding to keep refreshing her feed to see if Jazmine was going to post any more images of her and DeAndre.

Scrolling through her timeline, another call from DeAndre came through and she sat and watched it ring a few times before finally picking up.

"Hello?"

"Imani, baby."

She was prepared to hang up shortly after picking up, wanting to make an excuse to end all conversation, but something in his voice made her pause. Her heart raced.

"Are you okay?"

"I'm not...uhh..."

He sounded dazed, like he had been crying or at least emotional.

"I...uhh...need to see my Dad."

# Chapter 46
# Lifeboat

Imani looked between DeAndre and his father, sitting across from each other at the steel gray table in Upper Port Penitentiary, and felt like she was seeing a physical snapshot of her present and future simultaneously.

DeAndre didn't have any siblings, but Mr. Harrison could have easily been one of them. Both men stood well over 6 feet tall with dark complexions, broad shoulders and angular faces. Even though David was 30 or so years DeAndre's senior, the only thing that truly teased his age was his eyes, wrinkled at the corners from time.

"So, you're the beautiful new addition to the family," he said, with the same subtle charm that his son encapsulated so effortlessly.

"Thank you...and yeah," Imani offered a forlorn smile.

She and DeAndre may have been on ice right now, but that didn't change what was fact and legally binded.

"Welcome, sweetheart, in case no one has said it to you, formally... I'm sure Andele 'bout had a fit."

Imani couldn't help but chuckle at David's spot-on assumption.

"It's gotten better," she smiled sheepishly, thinking back to Andele's surprise visit mere weeks ago.

She stole a quick glance at DeAndre sitting next to her, looking down at the cement. He had his legs spread and arms folded as Imani took a breath.

## A Month of Sundays

"It's really nice to meet you too, Mr. Harrison," she said.

David waved his hands in front of him.

"We gon' have to figure out somethin' else you could call me...too formal for someone worthy enough to inherit my last name."

Imani smiled, revealing all her teeth then.

"I'd like that."

Imani couldn't speak to the relationship DeAndre had with David, but within the two seconds she was with his father for the first time now, Imani already felt the most comfortable with the other half of her husband's parental unit. This was going much better than she assumed it would.

She looked over to DeAndre again, sitting exactly as he'd been since they got there.

"I'm sorry you couldn't come to the wedding," she said, turning back to face David. "You were definitely missed."

David looked at her, his eyes narrowed with a close-mouthed smile.

"That's sweet of you to say, Imani," he started. "But, DeAndre only fills me in on things, after the fact, like he's scared of what I'm gon' say."

Imani looked over to DeAndre, who propelled his gaze at his father, void of expression. She noticed his leg closest to her, bouncing frantically, and couldn't remember a time when she saw him so...anxious?

"DeAndre was telling me the doctors are saying you're not well?"

David sighed.

"Yeah, something about high blood pressure...blood levels," he said. He waved his hand dismissively.

"They always want to put us on some stupid ass medication, messing with your kidneys, just to kill you quicker."

Imani grazed her bottom lip with her teeth and grimaced.

"You had a heart attack, though," she said.

"I didn't pass out on the floor," he argued in defense. "I was still up and movin'."

Imani felt DeAndre shift in his chair, pulling himself up to the table.

"...because a doctor detected the start of it during a fucking checkup," he said.

## Jade Olivia

Imani watched David's face literally morph into stone. His eyes glazed over to his son, no other part of his body moving.

"You better watch who the fuck you talkin' to and how you talkin', son," David said, with the deepest baritone that sent a chill down Imani's spine.

She watched DeAndre push back from the table, his shoulders sagged, visibly shrinking in his seat to someone half his size. Seeing DeAndre being reprimanded from anyone *and* taking it was something Imani would never have predicted.

She looked between the two men before placing her hands on the table, folding them together. The silence between them echoed loudly in the room.

"I think we both want to make sure you're healthy, Mr. Harrison," Imani said. "We don't want anything to happen to you that would...umm...surprise us."

David looked back at Imani again, his eyes softening before a slow smile spread on his lips.

"Ookayyy," he said, raising his brows, pointing between her and DeAndre, "It's clear to me now. I get it."

Imani gave him an uneasy smile, not sure what that meant.

"I hear your concern, Imani," he said, pointedly, "but, I'm fine. I just need DeAndre to focus on his performance at the upcoming SW tournament. Can't get soft on me now."

DeAndre chuckled sardonically, shaking his head, but still refusing to say anything.

"Well, he is...focused," Imani started, "he always is."

David balled up his face, seemingly not impressed.

"He knows what I alwaysssss say to him. He's gotta stay aggressive. I can always tell when he's stuck in his head, gettin' all puffed up and showboatin'."

DeAndre released a sigh, pinching the side of his nose and looking everywhere else but at David.

Imani could agree that DeAndre was anything but a quiet player. When he played, it was easy to tell he was winning - he'd scream, shout to the rooftops, and pump his fists. It was always very apparent. He wasn't shy, but he had all his stats to back it up.

"I hear you, Mr. Harrison," she said, "but, with all due respect, your son has

## A Month of Sundays

a lot to show for how hard he works. I don't think the game would be as interesting without him...do you?"

When Imani's eyes bounced to DeAndre's, she had almost forgotten that the two of them were on shaky ground. His love for her was written all over his face and Imani centered herself so she didn't get caught in the moment with it.

"He'd have a lot more to show if he had won the SW Tournament last year," David said.

He turned his mouth to a contemplative frown with his eyes cast to the ceiling, scratching underneath his chin.

"Could also stop relying on a single serve location, too...and slow down on those forehands."

DeAndre continued looking off into space, dissociating in front of Imani in real time, and the only visible anger was his jaw tightening. She had never seen him so agitated, while actively refusing to say anything - a hostage biding his time, already accepting his fate.

David pointed to him, DeAndre's smile spread across his face.

"You remember that player, DeAndre?" he said.

David snapped his fingers before tapping them on his forehead with his eyes closed.

"Elli, Elliot....Ellison? Right!" He popped open his eyes in remembrance.

"Ellison. The one you played against in like '05?"

David shook his head, releasing a huff.

"That boy was good, DeAndre, wasn't he?" David laughed, dripped with forced amusement.

"Had you cryin' like a baby...he humbled you so bad. Got yo' ass weak in the knees. Aye, you still remember that?"

Imani looked over at her husband again, the light in his eyes dimming lower by the second. It was like he was morphing into a kid right in front of her.

*Is this for real?*

"Bet you hadn't 'til that knee of yours got hemmed up, huh? How'd that feel?"

Imani slammed her hands down on the table.

"Okay," she said, turning her attention back to DeAndre. "Baby, we need to get out of here so we can make our next appointment, right?"

His eyes were strained with stress when he looked at her. She was clearly throwing him a lifeboat and DeAndre nodded, blinking twice. Imani didn't even wait another second before she stood up, placing her bag strap over her shoulder. DeAndre followed, though much slower, wounded by David's straight disrespect. There was no way Imani would allow herself to stay there to witness any more of it.

David stayed in place as if already aware of their staged excuse for an exit.

"Guess I'll see y'all next year?" David asked, a mix of irritation and doubt present.

Imani stared at him, all earlier admiration for him gone. She couldn't even stand to look at him right now.

"You stay well, Mr. Harrison."

Imani and DeAndre were escorted out of the building by security who led them back to their SUV. The officer on hand thanked them for visiting as DeAndre spent a little time answering some of his questions and responding to the small banter that fans innocently engaged him in. Once the officer had shut the door after they were both settled in the back seat, Imani rested her head back and closed her eyes. She didn't even know how to even respond to DeAndre's ridicule, all at the hands of his father.

"When was the last time you came to visit?" she asked, still not looking at him.

"Last year," he said, his baritone the only sound filling the back seat.

Imani took a breath, finally turning to him.

"DeAndre...what the hell was that?"

She looked over at him now with his hand on his head, more exhausted now than he was when they were even in there. He shook his head, his eyes focused out his side of the window.

"I'm not even trying to bring anything else up," he said. "Already got enough mess between us as is."

Imani frowned now, narrowing her eyes at him. Now he was being avoidant all of a sudden? When he was the one always harping on her about omitting the truth and he was falling into the same habit.

"You seriously expect me *not* to talk about how your father just verbally

## A Month of Sundays

annihilated you?" she asked. "I don't care what *we* have going on, but I'm not gonna sit watching someone piss on you, then call it rain."

DeAndre continued looking out the window, his fingers over his mouth. Imani was getting increasingly frustrated, mainly because it felt like she was the only one capable of doing it. She found herself carrying the mental load once again. How could he deal with that abuse and dismiss it so easily?

Suddenly, so much was adding up in her mind. So much they either hadn't discussed or that Imani dismissed as minor things.

"Is this why you don't want to have...children with me?" she asked, already regretting the exact words when they came out, "..because of your relationship with your parents?"

DeAndre's eyes swept to Imani, this time with a touch of guilt.

"No," he said quietly. "I still...want to...with you."

It would've been safe to assume that DeAndre's words calmed her, but the knots in her stomach only intensified. She started internally shaking.

"So, that both mothers of your children could be pregnant at the same time?"

His entire face pried open in straight horror, looking at Imani like she grew another limb in the car.

"Yo, Imani," he said, disgusted. "What the hell?"

"I'm not letting you take me down a path that doesn't give me any answers," she said.

"Why aren't we talking about your Dad?"

"Why aren't you home?"

"Because I have to potentially deal with my husband having a family that isn't mine! It's not from me...not from my bloodline!"

Before she could even stop herself, Imani's hot tears poured down her cheeks. She pushed the bottom of her palms over her eye sockets, crying frantically.

"You hurt me...so bad DeAndre! I went along with you for every decision , even against my better judgment."

"Baby," DeAndre said, his tone gentle. "We don't even know if it's mine."

When he took Imani's hand into his own, the tinge of unease she suddenly felt being near him was startling and surreal. Pulling away from his grasp, she *never* thought she'd feel her passion for him waning.

"God, DeAndre! That's not the point!"

"I'm sorry...I'm so, so, so sorry. I'll say it to you every day if I fucking have to just please come home."

Earlier this morning as she waited for Clive to pick her up, Imani had foolishly thought that today would be the last day at Melody's house. Once she saw him, Imani thought she'd be able to face the potential of a new reality. She'd be both his wife and his child's stepmother. But, no matter how much she let it settle in her mind, it became more and more disturbing. She couldn't even face him now.

"I can't..." she said. "I can't go home."

"So, you're not stepping foot into our house until this baby is born?" he asked, this time in outright anger.

A fresh wave of tears fell as she continued sobbing, looking over at DeAndre, who was crumbling from the inside out himself. He fell further into his seat, placing two fingers at the corner of his eyes, covering his entire face.

This moment felt worse than the day she learned about the pregnancy allegations, beyond the night of the Sports Awards, beyond the FaceTime calls she finally yielded to. Imani really didn't know if being with him anymore would be in her best judgment. Being creative as an artist was becoming challenging when her happiness felt so distant and she felt her growth being stagnated.

She closed her eyes in anguish. She had forgiven him about the cheating, even thought the chances it likely happened were slim. But, that didn't absolve him of a new responsibility that could be staring them in the face in mere months.

"I just...can't...accept you being a father to someone else's child, DeAndre," she sobbed. "I can't be there...with you...to see that."

"Please...please...don't...tell me what I think you're tellin' me, baby," he croaked, not even looking at her. "Don't give up on me...don't give up on us."

Imani wasn't sure what she was even saying to him. She just couldn't imagine continuing her marriage at this point...not like this.

# Chapter 47
# Hideout

"I think this should be the last one."

Imani stood straight, assessing the cupcake she spent the past twenty minutes decorating to perfection, swirling the frosting around the top. Kaylee appeared, then in the kitchen then, holding a printed top and pants on a hanger.

"Great," she said. "We can finally eat one."

"I thought these were for your mom?"

Grabbing the cupcake, Kaylee took the largest bite, closing her eyes, satisfied in sugar euphoria.

After going back to the house with DeAndre from visiting his father, Imani walked out - once again, opting to stay with Kaylee to get more space, especially after what she witnessed. There was no way she was allowing the sympathy she had for him as far as his Dad was concerned to cloud her judgment. Imani would rather walk into a burning building before allowing herself to listen to anyone disrespecting DeAndre, but she couldn't let that be the deciding factor on their reconciliation.

"They are," Kaylee said. "But, there's no way she's gonna eat all of them."

Imani washed her hands before grabbing the outfit from Kaylee's hands.

"This is what you're wearing for church tomorrow?"

Kaylee nodded without saying anything as Imani did a quick assessment of the look. The pants were simple enough, but the top - a green paisley print - was an unusual choice for Kaylee. But, the more Imani stared at the top, a slow realization creeped in.

"We're actively taking each other's clothes now?" she asked, casting a side eye at Kaylee who froze, mid-bite.

"I had no idea it was gonna fit since the clothes I can shop for are US sizing," Kaylee shrugged. "But, lo and behold, I can also fit clothes that cost more than my rent...who would've thought?"

Imani shook her head, laughter spilling from her insides.

"You're lucky I love you," she said.

"You're lucky I don't charge you a pro-rated amount for rent at this point," Kaylee said, her mouth shaped into an 'O' from the jab she just unleashed.

"No, no," Imani said, laughing while taking the comment in stride, "You're absolutely right. I know I have to go."

"Well, let's get you through tomorrow," Kaylee said, with a smile. "Have you spoken to Aunt Ethel yet?"

Imani sighed, shaking her head. Her absence from church over the past few weeks had less to do with hiding and more to do with Imani's state of mind. She knew she had to get her mind right and actually open herself up to God's encouragement.

After the choir led the church through a few minutes of praise and worship, the congregation sat down, already preparing themselves for the sermon ahead. Imani turned to Kaylee to talk to her about her upcoming schedule of clients who had her busy well into the next few months. After turning down prospects over the past month or so, Imani finally felt ready to face the public again, no longer caught up in her personal emotions. She was just at the point of her slight depression where she was getting tired of her own self, exhausted from the self-loathing which made her spiral into emotions that kept her from moving forward, and even kept her from what she loved the most.

"...He was telling me that he wanted me to do a family portrait with all twelve of his relatives at their reunion," Imani was saying now of one of her prospective clients. "This'll be my first time in North Carolina, soooo...I was wondering if you'd like to come with me? Just so you could show me some of your old stomping grounds, maybe?"

## A Month of Sundays

Kaylee beamed.

"I was waiting for you to ask me," she laughed. "Of course! We gotta go to Max's when we're down there and the bookstore that's also a yoga studio that's also a bakery," Kaylee babbled excitedly.

Imani chuckled, pushing her arm through the crook of Kaylee's before resting her head on her best friend's shoulder.

"I can't tell you the name of it," Kaylee said, leaning her head on top of Imani's, "But it's been there since I was a baby."

With Kaylee's chatter receding into subtle background noise in her ear, Imani watched the choir sing a rendition of a Mary Mary song she hadn't heard in a while. It didn't take long for her mind to wander as tears gathered at the corners of her eyes. From the quiet life she had returning home four years ago to the whirlwind that's happened in the past eight months of her life, Imani was amazed at the way God not only carried her but was with her through it all. She had made so many risky decisions in her life and with each one, felt like she was going to be punished for it all - karma would have her in due time, she thought. Imani finally realized that she was the ultimate enforcer of her own punishment. She lied to herself about the love she truly wanted, she wasn't always honest with her friends and family and she was running away from her husband – the love of her life and the beginning of the family that she always genuinely desired.

After Pastor Coleman led the congregation through the benediction, Imani stood, her eyes landing on Aunt Ethel, who sat in her familiar place in the front row, fan in hand.

"Hey, mind waiting for me in the car?" she asked Kaylee.

Imani approached her aunt a few minutes later, taking a moment to stare at the woman who had lied to her for over fifteen years. What kept her from not saying anything?

"Hey Auntie."

Ethel stopped her chatter with another friend of hers in the church, looking up at Imani with a small smile. "I can imagine you're looking for some answers?"

# Chapter 48
# Faith

DeAndre stood in front of Ethel's apartment building, taking in the elaborate seasonal wreath with the light and airy colors of Spring. Taking a moment to clear his throat, he wasn't sure why he was so nervous, especially because he was the one who asked for this conversation. He was the one who convinced Ethel to give him her number all those months ago when they first met.

Back at the house after the insane visit with his father, DeAndre was fuming, pissed at Imani for a straight hour after she walked out the door, yet again. He hated his wife bearing witness to the awkward strain in his relationship with David, but DeAndre couldn't have gone through that visit on his own. He was learning more and more that he couldn't handle a lot of things on his own.

When Imani helped him, giving him a way out of his father's beratement, DeAndre caught it, holding it for dear life until they left the prison facility. He assumed that his wife was willing to stay with him and finally return home for them to figure it out. He had anticipated to take her down memory lane, recounting the many small ways the relationship he had with his parents changed. But, none of that happened. In fact, Imani seemed even more pissed, alluding to never being able to stomach DeAndre fathering a child that wasn't hers.

## A Month of Sundays

For what it was worth, he couldn't either. It seemed the more he thought of his wife's point of view though, the more he had to know exactly why she couldn't. It felt like it was much deeper for her than a hit to her pride – helping to raise a child that wasn't her own. He thought about their meeting with Mrs. Coleman and the shocking revelation of not being her mother's biological child. DeAndre knew Imani wouldn't want history to repeat itself, hell, who would? But there had to be more to the story than that.

He and Imani had never discussed each other's pasts, something that DeAndre felt wasn't even important…until now as Imani's reaction to this and a few other things made him wonder.

It felt like there were pieces of his wife still missing from the puzzle.

Since he had no in-laws to exactly turn to, he knew Ethel was his best bet at gaining any more insight into his wife. She told him to stop by on Sunday evening after church, reprimanding him a little for choosing not to attend in-person, but understanding how delicate his relationship with Imani was right now. There was no room to make any grand gestures that would just be distractions for everyone else and make things worse. Imani was having dinner with Kaylee now, so he had at least a good two hours to find out as much as he could from Ethel.

He stood at the door, preparing to knock, when it opened before he could. Ethel stood in front of him, a robe secured tightly around her waist.

"Sounded like you had a lot on your mind," she smiled, warmly. "Wanted to save you some of the fuss."

Placing down two mugs of tea in between a small plate of sugar cookies, Ethel sat down across from DeAndre at her dining table. DeAndre reached across and pulled her by the hands, bowing his head and leading them in a quick prayer. It had become so instinctual, thanks to his wife, and he knew how much he needed it now more than ever. He noticed the faint smile cross Ethel's lips.

"I don't know how much you know about all this mess that's come up about me—"

"Oh," Ethel chuckled. "I know. The girls in the church had a field day with it at choir practice."

"Right."

DeAndre took a deep breath, his head falling in shame.

"Ms. Ethel - before anything else, I just gotta tell you."

He had his eyes on the floor, gathering himself for the second time since being here, and shifted them to meet Ethel's gaze.

"I did not cheat on Imani."

For the first time, when he said it out loud, someone looked at him with assurance.

"I know."

DeAndre sighed with relief and let his back fall against the seat.

"I mean, don't get me wrong," Ethel said. "I was...surprised when your marriage lasted more than a month, but from the way you speak about her so publicly, I don't know...I believe you."

"But this girl...you were with...do you think it's yours?"

"I swear some days I'm sure it's not, then other days...I just wish I could be having this conversation with my wife."

Ethel let out a small laugh.

"Now, that...wouldn't happen. Imani could go along with so many things until she can't."

Ethel sighed, taking a sip of her tea. DeAndre watched her pause a little longer than she needed to before she covered her mouth with her hand, shutting her eyes with a sudden sob.

"Ms. Ethel?"

With her eyes filled, she wiped her tears before they fell, took another breath and looked back at him.

"But, you gotta know how important family is for her....My brother was so trifling. Got this woman pregnant who wasn't his wife, then convinced his actual wife to raise Imani as if she was hers. It was so painful for Helena, especially because she couldn't have any of her own. It was all crazy, then they both passed away in a car accident."

Ethel shook her head, pausing for a beat.

"It's not in my place to tell you everything, DeAndre, and I won't. But... Imani...she's been through so much."

# Seven Years Ago

\*\*\*

Pulling open the door of Tao's - the bar that Shawn invited her to, Imani stepped in, surveying the darkened establishment with small square tables littered throughout. It was a typical dive bar in New York, with sticky flooring and scribbled pen marks over random stickers covering the walls. Imani looked over at the bar and found Shawn waving, sitting further back to the right of the bartender with the two other interns they worked alongside.

"You made it," Shawn smiled, assessing Imani once she got close.

She thought Shawn was cool from the two months she had been working at Opendoor, a small gallery in the city that was her first official experience in the art world, but had a feeling he also thought of her as his competition. She learned very early that being in New York meant everyone was sizing her up as their competition. Artists weren't doing art for the love of it. They were doing it for survival.

"Yeah, I appreciate you inviting me out again," she said, tugging at her ear. "That client finally let me off the phone after she wanted every recommended art piece from the Baroque period."

Shawn, along with the two other interns, laughed as they fell into conversation about the plans they had tonight for the rest of the evening. Imani knew she wasn't planning on doing anything after this, but wanted to take a moment to get to know her colleagues and at least *start* making friends in the city. She was typically by herself for the majority of her time here and was semi-friendly with the barista at the coffee shop near her apartment who always gave her the right amount of Simple syrup. But, other than that, she didn't have many people to lean on.

"Rich, you got me for my shot, man?"

Imani froze as the deepest baritone she ever heard made the hairs on the back of her neck stand up. She was in mid-conversation with Shawn, whose attention ventured over Imani's shoulder, letting his eyes roll.

"Yeah, X," the bartender, Rich, said. "I got you, bruh."

"Hey, sweetheart?"

Imani felt a tap on her shoulder and turned around to put a face to a voice and, what a face it was. Even among the bevy of tattoos on his face, his hazelnut complexion and supple lips under a hive of locs atop his head seeped through, as he stared at Imani with deep set eyes like a bear who just found honey.

"You're actually in my chair."

Imani stared at first, speechless. His lips parted into a smile, and she saw that his eyelashes were the perfect curve and length, underneath rugged bushy eyebrows that she had a sudden urge to shadow in on a canvas.

"Hello?" he said, in an even lower register, dangling his head between his shoulders.

She blinked out of her trance.

"Sorry. I didn't know anyone was sitting here."

Imani just had never been so struck by someone like this before. He was literally a walking piece of art.

"Well, I wasn't really *sitting* there at the moment," he squinted, looking at her lips. "But, when I'm here, that's my spot."

He watched her so intently that Imani was convinced she had to move. There was something so intriguing yet intimidating about him at the same. It put her on edge.

Imani turned to Shawn, who looked at her in slight exasperation, then turned back to this man - X.

"I can move. I think we can move," she said.

He placed a hand on top of Imani's igniting a flame that took her forever to get out of her system for good. Her eyes descended and she noticed that just under his knuckles was a tattoo of a cluster of stars.

"You relax. We'll move."

He stood from his seat, heading further behind the bar that Imani hadn't even realized existed when she first walked in. Two women followed him, tailing him closely. Imani's attention wandered back to Shawn, who shook his head, letting out a breath.

"That guy creeps me out. He's been here a few times when we are, always with those women walking behind him like zombies."

Imani chuckled with a shrug. "Are we just having drinks?"

She chatted with Shawn and her colleagues for another hour or two before they got up, gathering their jackets, bags and personal items to head out the door. Taking another glance at the bar menu, Imani went back to the bartender Rich to make an order of sweet potato fries to-go.

"I could wait for you, if you want," Shawn said as the rest of the group stood at the door.

Imani shook her head.

"No, you go. I'm not too far from my apartment anyway. I just need something for the train ride back."

She and Shawn gave each other an awkward hug, bidding each other farewell and a safe weekend just before Rich called her back to the bar.

"Thank you so much," she smiled.

Pulling her denim jacket closer to her frame, Imani propped her bag strap on her shoulder, placing her hand at the doorknob.

"You know your name means 'faith'?"

Imani turned towards X's voice, surprised to see him and the two women he was with, sitting at a small table next to the front door. With his elbows on his knees, X gave her a small smile that drew her focus to a small star tattoo that rested on the top of his cheek like a birthmark.

"Yeah," Imani smiled. "My aunt told me that when I was little."

Twirling a ring on his finger, he continued looking her over, from head to toe.

"So, what things are you gonna have me believing that I can't see?"

As an artist himself - X, a moniker he went by, was well known in the underground art scene in New York from parties he attended and those he threw in his Harlem loft. Imani's focus was visual art on canvas whereas X was a self-proclaimed, "multi-hyphenate" - someone who didn't stick to just one medium but decided to dabble in many mediums when he saw fit.

"My moms named me Rudy," he said to her, "But, who'd really listen to what I had to say with that kinda name?"

"I like Rudy, though."

He smiled. "Then, you're the only one who can call me that. It's just for you."

They started going out together as friends after that night, at Rudy's insistence, meeting up with each other on the weekends or any early evening after Imani's internship. Rudy told Imani from the beginning that he wanted to get to know her as a friend first and he always kept a respectful distance from her because of it. But he was the most fascinating person she'd ever met. Everything he said to her in the beginning was always so simple yet seemed so profound.

"I never want to limit my expression. There's so much more you can accomplish when you open yourself up to it.

"We're all just conduits, right?" he asked her one night as they walked along the streets of the city. This night was one of the handful of instances where the two women she had first seen with him at Tao's those few months ago weren't with them.

Imani learned that Bella and Bria were Rudy's protégés - two sisters from a small city in the Midwest who, like Imani, came to New York to pursue careers in art. Whenever they were with Imani and Rudy, they didn't say much to her at all aside from a shy hello and curt head nods. Their hair was braided in long ropes of yarn with various colors and their faces were painted and decorated with the brightest shimmer eyeshadows and heavy black eyeliners. They dressed in all-black, similar to Rudy. If Rudy was in a band, Bella and Bria would clearly be his background singers.

"How long have you been helping them out?" Imani asked. The two weren't walking anywhere in particular, as usual, but Rudy loved taking her to random places in the city for her to discover and try.

"A few years," he said. "They're almost where they need to be...just need a little more direction."

## A Month of Sundays

"Is that something you think I need?"

Rudy looked at her, pointedly. Imani showed him her work shortly after their first few hangouts together, feeling as though his opinion would mean so much. Here was a professional working artist, living in the best city for art and willing to get to know her. She thought he'd have advice or feedback to give, but he remained quiet. He looked over at rows of canvases grouped against a wall in her bedroom, pulling them one-by-one without uttering a word.

"I think you're special," he said. "You have a gift and I want other people to see that."

∽

Imani, cradling her phone between her shoulder and her ear, walked to the front door of their apartment, listening to the latest voicemail from her aunt.

The third one within the week.

*Imani, sweetie. How're you? It's me, you're Aunt Ethel. It was good talking to you the other day but you didn't answer all my questions. Where are you staying, again? Where're you working? I saw the pictures you sent, too. And, baby girl, you're just....so pretty. You always have been, but I think I was surprised to see...all those tattoos. Call me old-fashioned, but, why would you wanna cover up all that beautiful skin of yours, huh? Cover up that temple you've been blessed with? And your hair....are they braids, like the box braids that the young girls wear? They look a little thicker than that, though. Anyway, you're smiling in the picture, baby girl, but are you at peace? Call me.*

Hearing the squeak of her Black Doc Martens on the stickiness of the building floor, Imani smelled the stench in the hallway that was suffocating tonight, especially when it was the night before trash day, or the day when trash was *supposed* to go out. She took one step on the dingy welcome mat, the only one on their floor, and heard the crushing of glass. Lifting up her foot, Imani saw the tiny shards of glass spread like confetti in the mat's course fibers. The pit of her stomach dropped as she took a breath and closed her eyes.

Imani thought she timed out her day perfectly. She had been at the coffee shop all day, taking a full 12-hour shift, starting at 7 in the morning, just to avoid potentially running into another one of Bella's Johns. But, she couldn't just stand out here or leave. Those options were never viable.

She had to have food ready for Rudy and her family.

Cradling her canvas under one armpit, Imani threw her yarn locs over her shoulder and rummaged through the bottom of her tote to find her keys. She opened the door and closed it behind her, throwing down her bag and keys on the tray table next to the long low couch. Imani was peeling off her black leather moto jacket when she heard muffled sounds from the closed bedroom door across the loft. Rudy's loft only had one bedroom and even with the large open space of the main area, everything could be heard.

"That's right...that's it. Right...you're always my best money spent...."

Imani felt the familiar bile rise in her mouth as she walked past the door and into the kitchen. She washed her hands at the sink before pulling a pot from the cabinet and filling it with water.

Today was Friday, and Fridays were Pasta Night, when Imani would boil the pasta at just the right amount of time and brown the ground beef long enough for the pink to disappear. Bria used to be on pasta duty until Rudy saw the pink in the meat just before she added pasta sauce. He beat her face in so hard that night, it was just as red as the meal. It was so brutal, the way he beat his daughters like that. But, just like always, Imani managed to calm him down.

She heard the bedroom door open, but kept stirring the pasta now submerged in the pot. A man dressed in a dark blue wrinkled suit waddled out of the room, tucking his shirt into his pants as Bella, dressed in a holey black t-shirt and tan underwear, followed behind him to the door. Imani looked up, still not saying a word, as the man turned around and said a few words to Bella before tapping her on the ass and walking out.

Bella turned, a few bills in hand that she counted, before looking up to meet Imani's gaze. Even from her distance in the kitchen, Imani saw how red they were. Bella sniffled, wiping her nose against her shirt sleeve.

"I got a little extra," her lips twitched.

"Think I could use it to leave?" she asked, looking into Imani's eyes with the same desperation as she always did when Rudy wasn't around.

Imani nodded. "Eventually."

The problem with being with Rudy was that everyone, including Imani, knew how much of a psychopath he truly was. Bria and Bella were sisters, and not related to Imani or Rudy at all. But, however he did it, Rudy managed to get into each of their minds, convincing all of them they were the found family that each of them truly desired. What they had in common was they were all orphans in some way, searching for a group of people who understood them. It was the hardest to escape because Rudy convinced each of the women he was the only one who understood all of them.

Tucking her bills into her bra, Bella walked over to Imani sheepishly, standing next to her at the stove before wrapping her arms around her waist.

"Day 582," Bella said.

Imani placed the spoon down against the pot, resting her arms around Bella.

"Day 420," she said, as they stood in each other's embrace.

While Bella and Bria had been living with Rudy just shy of two years, it had been about a year and two months since Rudy sunk his teeth into Imani, eventually convincing her to quit her internship, move in with him and work on her art under his "tutelage." Rudy started getting much more aggressive with his advances on Imani once she moved in. But, the two still weren't having sex nor did he trick her out the way he did Bella and Bria.

All of Rudy's clients and patrons knew Imani was off limits. He didn't keep Imani close, deem her as the "Mother" of their "daughters," to have sex with her, either.

His violation of her was much more specific.

"Wanna spark up for 420?"

Imani chuckled. "No, Bella."

The door opened again as the two of them heard the familiar heavy footsteps of the man they were all tied to.

"Bella!"

She went to loosen her grip around Imani's waist as Imani pulled her in tighter.

"Stay here," she said to Bella, her own heartbeat accelerating.

"Bella!"

He stomped further into the loft, into the kitchen, a drug-induced fury in his eyes. He blinked a few times when he saw Imani, though, calming down a little. He pointed a finger at Bella.

"Where is it?"

Bella blinked.

"I'm not sure what you mean?"

The advantage Bella had over Bria and Imani was that she was the smallest one out of the three, which allowed her to be the "baby," and typically be treated as such. But, Rudy didn't baby anyone when it came to his money. He had eyes on the back of his head to count that.

"Don't play stupid with me. I just spoke to Don and he told me you charged him less, cut him some deal. I know he made it up to you in tips."

Rudy looked at her, his eyes cold.

"Give it to me."

Bella shook her head, pulling away from Imani fully this time. They stood side by side at the stove.

"He didn't give me anything," she said.

Placing his finger down, Rudy continued his gaze on her for a beat before walking up to Imani, giving her the softest kiss on the lips.

"I missed you all day, my beauty," he whispered, their lips just barely touching. Imani could smell the bitter odor of cocaine against his jacket as she fluttered her lashes up at him, offering the faintest smile. She hated him so much for how much she loved him. They spoke each other's language.

"You, too."

He smiled at her warmly and when he gave her smiles like this, Imani swore she saw the Rudy she met at Tao's so long ago. The one she should've ignored but couldn't.

"I saw your painting next to the door."

Imani stilled, her smile fading.

"Don't look like that, beauty," he smiled. "It's good."

Imani perked.

"It is?"

He nodded. "Come here for a second, let me show you."

Rudy placed his hand behind Imani's neck, warming the area of her freshly-done ink. Rudy didn't believe in marriage, but he did tell her that matching tattoos proved their commitment to one another - a burst of stars to represent the most passionate connection he ever had with someone.

Imani swallowed, suddenly feeling like his hand weight thirty pounds against her slim frame, as she, Rudy and Bella walked into the living room space. She learned early on to *never* question Rudy's critiques of her art. He knew exactly what he was saying, since he was the one who sold it at his auction parties and he was the one who had much more experience in the art world than she ever did. Rudy was the divine while Imani was merely the conduit.

He took a breath, placing a hand at his chin and rubbing it, staring at Imani's piece. He, Imani and Bella were standing side by side with one another - one family, one sound.

"The balance and saturation of the colors are incredible..." he said.

Imani folded her hands together, placing them in front of her, not saying a word.

"The rhythm is so clear..."

She smiled then, her heart rate slowing.

"But, beauty..." he stopped rubbing his chin, looking at her in the eye. "It's all useless."

Tears gathered in Imani's eyes as her nostrils flared like he just punched her square in the face. But, that was how he dealt with her - forcing her to produce work when she didn't want to, pressing her to think outside of the box, only for her to miss the mark. She was almost there, but never quite achieved the goal. She was still a beginner, but she never advanced. But she didn't need to worry, Rudy was there to show her the way.

"Useless?"

"Yeah," he nodded, like he was stating the obvious. "I've seen this so many times from you. It looks...average.

"And, what do I always tell you about average?" he chuckled.

Imani looked at the piece she had spent three days perfecting, as a tear she managed to wipe away quickly, fell.

"I'll...umm...attempt it again, then."

Rudy nodded, his eyes cast on the floor with his arms folded. Taking a quick breath, he suddenly dropped his arms and slapped Bella across the face.

Imani gasped, placing a hand to her mouth as Rudy continued his hitting Bella.

"Did you make her do this?!" he yelled. "Did you?"

He grabbed her by the shirt collar, shaking her like a rag doll. Even though she tried not to, Bella screamed, sobbing profusely.

"Rudy, Rudy," Imani placed a hand at his shoulder, her voice trembling in a whisper. "Sweetie. She wasn't with me. She didn't....she didn't make me do anything. It was me. It was...what I thought you wanted."

He looked at Bella, his nostrils flared and eyes bloodshot before narrowing his gaze again, shifting it to Imani.

"You did that piece of shit?" he asked.

Imani felt her chest tighten. "Yes X, it was me. I did all of it."

He stared at her for what felt like an hour as his right eye twitched. Sniffing, Rudy pushed Bella away, walking past the two of them back into the kitchen.

"Is dinner ready, beauty?"

~

Imani collapsed on the bed, rubbing her hands against the sequins of her black cocktail dress, with her eyes closed. As usual, she was exhausted after hours of hosting the family's weekly art party - a chaotic and frenetic gathering of artists, critics, entrepreneurs of all industries who indulged in women, drugs and all the activities they could in one open space. The rules at the party were simple. It was required that each guest paid for something, either for entry, sex or the art. Those who paid for neither would never be invited again. Imani didn't use drugs the way Rudy, Bria and Bella did, but she did consume just enough alcohol to be buzzed enough to socialize. She drank to the point where the pounding of the music was muffled in her ears.

But, now she had a headache.

Placing a hand at her neck, Imani tilted her head from side to side as Rudy walked in, clapping aggressively.

"This is what I mean! This is what I mean," he said, pacing the floor in front of her. Imani took off her earrings, gingerly, her eyes following him across the floor of the bedroom they shared.

"Did you see how much we made tonight?" he asked, beaming. "Did you see it?"

They raised enough money from the party to finally cover this month's rent. But, there were still other bills- lights, heat, air, cocaine. It was all necessary to keep the house afloat.

"I did, Rudy."

Imani looked at him, quietly assessing him like she learned to do so well. Whatever he'd say, she'd agree, then listen, and wait until it was her time to answer. Rudy loved how well Imani listened and it was the one skill she knew had kept her alive.

"See, what happens when you listen to me?" he asked, smiling at her like a father reprimanding their child innocently.

"...see what happens when you work on your composition, the balance, the proportion? That's when our work shines."

Imani blinked before casting her eyes on the cold brown floor and massaging her temples. Rudy's favorite word was *our*, even when she had done all the work. The best trick Rudy ever pulled was getting Imani to believe him - believe him about her career, believe him with her art - all to sell *her* art as his own.

When she first noticed him doing it, he managed to convince her that her time would come to shine, he just had to negotiate the deal first. All she had to do was stay ready for her moment. But, for Imani, that moment never came.

*"Daddy will always take care of you,"* he said to her. *"But, you gotta earn your keep here just like everyone else."*

Imani had gone along with it, for every party up until this point, being the sweet, quiet girlfriend hanging on his arm. There were never any pictures or video allowed at Rudy's parties, so Imani never saw what she looked like.

But tonight was different.

A patron from the makeshift bar near the kitchen sauntered over to one of Imani's special portraits, one that she swore she'd never paint, but it snuck out of her anyway.

"*Who are these people?*" the guest squinted, swaying back and forth with his drink in hand.

Imani, standing next to him, took another sip of her wine. Rudy always told her not to say anything to guests who were looking at the art. She didn't have to do any convincing. Her looks were enough to get anyone to do almost anything. But Imani couldn't fight the need to respond to this guest who was staring at the portrait of her parents with a look of admiration in his eyes. She didn't have many pictures of them, except the small one she kept stuffed in the corner of her wooden drawer.

"*It's a family,*" she said, quickly.

"*You know who they are?*" the man asked, still staring at the brown faces looking straight at him.

"*Well—*"

"*Harry, my man,*" Rudy said, walking over to put his arm across his shoulders. "*Seein' something you like? What's up?*"

"*Yeah, I'm so...impressed by this one right here.*"

"*Ooohhh, now, this is a special one that took quite some time.*"

Imani watched Rudy straighten up, clear his throat and begin the familiar rant he did every time, saying the same thing, swapping out words depending on the art.

"*I had this dream several weeks back that I couldn't shake off about this family...*"

Imani stilled, her drink midway to her lips. This wasn't Rudy's usual rant at all.

"*This family of brown faces who spoke to me about their need to be together again, their need to see each other. What you're looking at, Harry, is them finally being reunited. You see their smiles of satisfaction?*"

Rudy shifted his gaze to her, a challenge in his eyes daring Imani to say anything opposing his words, the words Imani first said when he asked *her* about this creation.

"*They each had a tough road ahead,*" he continued, "*but, they made it back home to one another.*"

This portrait was the first Imani had ever done that made Rudy cry. It was the one piece that made her feel as if she finally reached the standard and yet he kept her making even more art. He said that tonight was the evening to release it to the world. It was also the night before the week that rent was due but, Imani knew by now that two things could be true at once.

Something about the way he explained the portrait...her portrait dedicated to *her* late parents, made her blood boil. He had no idea what went into its creation, the heart it took for her to get out. He knew none of it because he did none of it. She was so tired of this hell she was in, a hell she wasn't sure how she got sucked into in the first place. Imani thought she was smarter than this, but just like her aunt had said to her - she always jumped straight through the burning fire because of its allure.

"I feel so good, beauty," Rudy said now, looking at Imani sitting on the edge of the bed. He walked closer and sat, placing his hand on her knee and rubbing it in the softest circles. Imani's breath shallowed as he moved his hand further up her leg, stopping just before her middle.

"I think I just might give it to you tonight," he grinned, watching the desire on her face. "Would that turn your frown upside down?"

Imani's eyes closed halfway in pure ecstasy from his touch alone as she felt herself throbbing for him in desperation. Rudy loved teasing Imani with sex like a dangling carrot because he knew her kryptonite - physical connection. It was something Imani hadn't learned about herself until now. Rudy was never going to have sex with her, especially because it was something she wanted so badly.

He chuckled. "We'll see."

Rudy took his hand away quickly and stood as Imani squeezed her eyes shut, her head spinning. On any given day, she was either scared for her life, turned on or heartbroken.

*Lord, if you take me out of this hellhole, I will never chase again.*

A knock against the doorway frame made Imani open her eyes slowly. Bria, with nothing on but a pair of panties, sauntered in with a small glass mirror in hand, a smile plastered on her face. Rudy hated the expression she had on her face and slapped her up one night until she finally made the right one.

"For you, Daddy," she said, walking over to Rudy.

When Imani looked over at her, their gazes met and they smiled, genuinely. Imani took note of Bria's ample bosom and curved waistline. She was so beautiful, so soft that Imani wondered what light she'd carry if she was loved properly, by a man who really cherished her.

That's what Imani wondered for both Bria and her sister. What would it look like for them to be turned on? She'd pay money to see that.

"You're so kind to me, Bria," he said, bending over the mirror to snort the thin lines of white powder once, twice, and a third time.

As Rudy shook his head, his eyes brightening in pure adulation, Imani looked away. Whenever Rudy was high, it usually meant Imani would be up all night, painting and having to listen to everything that came from his mouth.

"Well, shit..."

Rudy stumbled on his feet for a second, something he had never done, which drew Imani's attention. He coughed and shook his head once more.

And then, he collapsed.

Imani jumped up from the bed, with a gasp.

"X! Oh my God - X!"

His body convulsed violently, contorting every which way on the ground as Imani's heart raced, assessing what to do. She ran over to him, preparing to push him on his side to keep him from choking when Bria pulled her by the arms.

"Bria, we have to—"

She stared at Imani, placing a finger against her lips, and shaking her head. Rudy continued convulsing, his eyes rolling to the back of his head, until his breathing stopped. Within seconds, he wasn't moving at all.

"Leave. Now," Bria whispered, not moving her hands away from Imani's arms.

Imani, with a trembling breath, stared at a now lifeless Rudy, sprawled on the floor with his eyes wide open.

"No. You...you and...and Bella. I need to be here with you."

Bella rushed in the room just then, scanning the floor until she saw Rudy.

"Just head out, Imani," Bella droned, glaring at the monster that had terrorized their lives.

Rudy had never mentioned his own family or friends before, claiming he was from another dimension unrestricted by time and space. He answered all of their questions with riddles, but someone had to have been looking for him.

## A Month of Sundays

For Imani, her Aunt Ethel sure enough was.

Bella reached into her jeans pocket and took out two wads of rolled up cash that she dropped in Imani's hand.

"Here, this should at least get you a bus ticket. You're from Port Springs, right?"

Imani nodded, feeling relief and guilt. Bella was funding her escape, but what would they get in return?

She grabbed her phone from the nightstand with a shaky hand.

"Here...here...my aunt's number," Imani said, nervously. "Y'all can call me if you need help or if you need to come where I am—"

Bella covered Imani's phone with her hand.

"You have a stable life waiting for you," she stared at Imani, unwavering. "I suggest you run to safety and hold onto it."

From Bella's statement and Bria's silence, Imani knew the three of them would never see each other ever again.

For Imani, it took her a solid three years to get her family from New York out of her system. 1095 days in counting. Even after she returned to Port Springs, moved in with Aunt Ethel and shaved her head of her nest of yarn locs...even after she entered her first healthy adult relationship, Imani still dreamt of Bria and Bella from time-to-time, praying for their safety in the shadows of the night.

# Chapter 49
# Recovery
## Present Day

Imani wasn't sure if it was Pastor's message or the conversation she had with Ethel shortly after service, but something in her told her to return home to DeAndre after she and Kaylee went out to eat.

Looking at the front door from Kaylee's passenger seat, Imani took a breath.

"This kinda feels like déjà vu," Kaylee said. "Please don't pop up with another husband."

Imani laughed and shook her head before reaching over her seat to hug Kaylee.

"Thank you for just...never judging me."

"'Mani...I would never do that. You're my sister. Plus, we're all trying to figure this life thing out."

"Yeah."

"Feeling better about what Aunt Ethel told you?"

"Still annoyed that I never knew, but...at least I can make peace with the knowledge I do have - it's a process, I guess."

After service, Ethel opened she and Imani's conversation with an apology of her own, explaining the doubts she had about DeAndre and their entire union. She regretted letting her pride get in the way of not seeing her niece walk down the aisle. But, Ethel also knew the two would have a test in their marriage.

## A Month of Sundays

"I'm not telling you this to justify all that pregnancy stuff, but I just...knew marrying him had the potential of bringing up so much of your past hurts that you tried shoving under the rug. But, I continued praying for you, just like I always did. I didn't know how to prevent it – how to protect you."

Kaylee smiled now, placing a hand on top of Imani's.

"Well, I'm here until the second," she said, shifting gears, "Then, I'm back home in North Carolina for a month. My grandmother wants to talk to us about her house. Had it in the family for years, and I'm the only lawyer *in* the family....so...who knows? But, I'm game for anything. God's got me."

Imani watched her best friend for a moment, the only consistent friend she's had since moving back to Port Springs. She was working on being more like Kaylee, if she was being honest with herself. Letting things be and running *towards* the unknown instead of away from it.

"Let me know when you're back in town."

Once Imani stepped into the house, she felt like it had never been so quiet. She should've been used to that by now but walking through the foyer and to the front door of her studio, she felt so different.

Imani walked into her studio, not having been there in weeks, observing all of her work-in-progress with much more intention. She finally caught up with Lauri who damn near bulldozed time on her calendar last week with a mandatory meeting that had to be conducted before the end of Friday. When Imani stepped into Lauri's office, she found her boss speaking with a man she didn't recognize.

*"Here she is,"* Lauri said, turning to her with a smile. *"Imani, I'd like you to meet Marquis Smalls, an agent who's a good friend of mine."*

Glancing at a portrait of a woman running, her hair spread behind her, Imani thought of the question Marquis asked her in that meeting.

*"What do you think you have to say now?"*

Imani hadn't answered it, asking him for time to think on it, instead. But, the question was in the back of her mind all weekend. Her life had been so different only a few months ago and the change hit her like a thunderbolt. The issue was that she didn't take the time to process it at all, didn't take the time to set boundaries for herself or within her marriage. But she could now.

Stepping out of the studio, Imani walked to the foyer and turned to the steps. She didn't think through exactly what she wanted to say to her husband, but she was opening herself up to the possibility of setting a new tone for their marriage. They really could create a family on their own terms. She knew for a fact that their love would certainly always be there, no matter what.

Imani pushed open the door of their bedroom and found DeAndre sitting at the edge of the bed, his hands on his knees with his head down and eyes closed. It was only when she closed the door that he looked up at her, his eyes strained. She rushed over, sitting down next to him on the bed, pulling the sides of his face by her hands.

"DeAndre–"

He looked at her, still, his eyes plastered onto hers before he broke down into his own tears.

"I'm so sorry I haven't been here for you."

Imani's eyebrows dipped in the middle as she swallowed.

"You're here for me," she said, her forehead opening. "It's just in different ways."

DeAndre turned his head away from her gently, standing up from the bed with his head down. She watched him turn to her and kneel down in front of her, taking her by the hand.

"You've had to adjust through so much and you bring so much light to my life and I brought you even more drama."

Imani watched him, her eyes narrowing. She knew this situation with Jazmine was a lot, but DeAndre was referencing it with much more gravity. Was he just talking about Jazmine? Were there even more alleged baby mamas hidden somewhere?

"I mean, it's a…surprise, for sure," she started. "But, I've done some thinking and…we can create the family we want and the one we need to be."

DeAndre brought her hand to his lips.

"I love you so much that I'd pull down every star from the sky for you. But I love you enough to let you go…for you to heal. I will love you through that, but if you gotta leave me, I'll let you. And not on some bitter bullshit, either. But to really let you go for you to thrive."

Imani's eyes widened.

"What're you even talking about?"

His eyes shifted.

"You know, baby," he started. "I've just been thinking about you...with your parents and how that...made you feel. And, then you gotta see me here with a kid that ain't yours?"

He stood up, pacing in front of her.

"I was so selfish with you and that's not fair to you."

"Well, I also didn't," Imani twirled her fingers. "...exactly tell you everything, either."

DeAndre paused and looked to her again. He sat down next to her, placing his hand on her thigh. "You know you could tell me any and...everything...right?"

Imani assessed him openly, taking in every handsome feature that captivated her from the very beginning, years ago when they first met. She grew to love him and was more than ready to move forward with him.

Imani placed her hands around his face again.

"I'm not leaving you, nor did I ever really want to, I don't think," she said. "Your love lifted me so much higher than I ever thought possible. But I know there are some things...we have to talk about."

DeAndre nodded, his eyes softening.

"I'm retiring."

She blinked, stammering. "Wait. What do you—"

"I'd been thinking about it even before we connected again, for real. Just wasn't something I had a reason to pull the trigger on."

Scratching the side of his neck, DeAndre looked at her before casting his eyes to the floor.

"I always knew I had to do somethin' different with you," he looked back up at her, "and, I want to."

Out of all the things Imani thought to suggest, having him step away from his calling, his gift was never one of those things.

"Are you sure? I mean, I don't want you to make any snap decisions based on any of this."

"Like I said, I didn't just start thinking about it and I might as well do it when I'm still on top..."

A small smirk grazed his face. "When the game still needs me and everything..."

"DeAndre..." Imani chuckled, knocking him against the shoulder, grateful to now be lighthearted with this crazy sexy man of hers again.

His smirk fell slowly as he rested his gaze on her.

"And, it's time for you to get poured into," he said. "You got stuff to do, you know, a career to grow...art to show around the world...you still tryna stay at the museum?"

Imani shook her head, her eyes blinking in succession. She stared at him, hearing Minnie Ripperton and hummingbirds singing in her head. Imani never felt like she didn't have his support but hearing him say it right now made her grow wings. In that moment, she could never imagine not being his wife.

"I'll have all ten of your chocolate babies," she said, her head tilted, hypnotized in love.

He shot his head back, eyes wide.

"Too soon?" she deadpanned.

They laughed.

"But, that definitely sounds," Imani sobered, "...different."

She looked at him, questioning. "What're you gonna do?"

"I don't know...maybe pay a shrink to cry on their couch...processing my issues, talkin' about my Pops or whatever."

His eyes crept to her.

"You think you'd wanna come with me?"

"Maybe."

A knowing look passed between the two of them that Imani couldn't quite describe, but she felt all the same.

He dragged his hand across the top of his fade. "I could...maybe actually go to church regularly...see what that's hittin' for?"

Imani nodded with a small smile.

"Let's take it one step, one day at a time."

# A Year Later

"**T**his has been such an enlightening discussion about identity and heartbreak and love in your work. On behalf of the Smithsonian, we couldn't be more thrilled to have your exhibition here until the end of this year...ladies and gentlemen, Imani Harrison."

The crowd in the auditorium cheered as the head curator for the Smithsonian Museum shook Imani's hand. The two stood for pictures in front of the couch where they discussed Imani's showcase that was now a part of the iconic museum's summer programming. It was the third one Marquis had a hand in placing her in, although having Stella as a reference certainly helped.

Taking a deep breath, Imani walked off the stage as the auditorium cleared. She was extra careful to use the side railing as she went down the narrow steps.

"My bad, baby, let me get you."

Imani saw DeAndre by her side as he grabbed her hand, and tucked his phone in his pocket, having probably taken approximately 1,764 photos of her tonight. She knew he'd want to go through almost all of them with a fine-tooth comb once they got back home now that he had a little more time on his hands. He still played local charity matches for the tennis league from time-to-time but most of his days were spent working with Elite, spearheading the creative direction of the lifestyle brand.

A museum volunteer approached the two of them with a smile.

"Hi Mrs. Harrison, the space is ready, would you like to step inside to see it first?"

Today was also the first day of Imani's art exhibit and the museum provided special access for close friends and relatives of the artist to take in the exhibit before the general public. Imani wasn't sure how she was going to feel stepping into the large room with several of her paintings displayed, but as soon as she did, all she could do was close her eyes and pray.

This life of hers was beyond anything she ever imagined for herself. But, with each heartbreak came a blessing around the corner. Even when thinking about the ultimate false accusation of DeAndre being Jazmine's son's father, Imani felt like they went through that season of their lives as a wakeup call and to bring forth newness.

"Imani, darling, I don't mean to interrupt, but you must meet a friend of mine."

She opened her eyes slowly to her mother-in-law who escorted one of her "friends" to Imani, all to brag about her exceptionally gifted daughter. Andele still hadn't quite said 'I love you' to Imani, but the fact that she talked her ear off every other week over the phone didn't go unnoticed by her. DeAndre was getting better with her nowadays, finding subtle ways to connect with her more often. The relationship with his father was still tough, but DeAndre was at least working on it, even if he had to keep a healthy distance away from him to do it.

Once Imani was finished making small talk with Andele's friend, she stood watching the small crowd of onlookers until her eyes landed on DeAndre again. She approached him, looking over his elongated frame.

"What do you see?" She asked, her eyes gliding to the portrait of her parents.

The canvas still had scuff marks on the side from the bumps and turns it withheld on the bus ride from New York all those years ago. Imani hadn't left with much back then, but she couldn't lose her best work.

"I see..."

DeAndre's gaze narrowed slightly, his eyes still on the portrait, as he took her hand next to him and moved himself behind her to pull her into an embrace, both of them facing forward at Imani's work.

## A Month of Sundays

"My family," he whispered.

The warmth from his mouth pierced behind Imani's neck as she leaned on his shoulder, tears welling up her eyes. They had been going to therapy to collectively work on their individual baggage, but Imani found that hers was heavier than she realized. DeAndre was patient with her, though, allowing her to open up to him about her past with however much time she needed.

"Your art makes me fall in love with you all over again."

He moved his hand further up Imani's belly to a hardness that felt strange, but thrilling. They chose not to tell anyone here about her pregnancy for the next few months at least until she couldn't hide it anymore. And, Imani wondered if she'd be able to keep their gift between the two of them longer than that, if covered under larger clothes or heavier jackets.

"You know what other name came to me a few days ago?" he whispered still in her ear, dropping his head on her shoulder, rocking her from one side to the next. Imani pulled her head back, swiping at a fallen tear and narrowing her eyes at his profile.

"If it's another name starting with 'D,'" she chortled. "I swear..to you..."

"But, Imani, baby, that's the thing," he said. "Those are the names speaking to me. Wait until I tell Kaylee again. You lucky she's overseas. See, my sister's got my back...C'mon, c'mon..check this out, baby, for real..."

Imani laughed, only halfway listening to his rant on baby names. When she had initially surprised DeAndre with the announcement, Imani was prepared to explain why she wanted to keep it a surprise at least for a little while. But, he understood. This would be just for the two of them, finally just for the two of them to share.

"Excuse me? Can I have your autograph, Mrs. Harrison?" Melody projected, wiggling her fingers in Imani's direction as she, Hosea and the kids approached. Imani hugged Hosea and kissed Melody on the cheek before locking eyes with the person she *really* wanted to see.

"My sweet Eli is here," she squealed, pushing her hands under his tiny arms to pull him up. "He's awake this time, too."

With Melody and Hosea's son, Elijah, in her hands, Imani smiled, before more tears fell down her face.

"Awww, girl," Melody said, placing a hand on her shoulder, "You ok?"

She asked the question in concern, but also like she was waiting for Imani to confirm a hunch. Like always, Melody had eyes in the back of her head. Imani continued smiling, though, before her eyes met her husband's across the room. He was standing with Hosea, the two of them surveying one of Imani's pieces, but her husband's eyes toggled between her and Elijah in her arms, with a smile.

She thought about what he said a few days ago after going back to the store to exchange another pair of maternity jeans that were still too large and unflattering.

"Crazy to know that our heart is just gonna be walking around outside of us. What're we gonna do with that?"

She didn't have an answer then, and she didn't have much of an answer now. Yet, Imani knew she was finally exactly where she was supposed to be.

# Acknowledgments

This book was a ride! I thank God that he entrusted me with this story and allowed me to see it through. This gift is a privilege I'm grateful for and will continue to fine tune.

**Here's the part where I thank my parents**

Thank you, Mom and MOD. (I told y'all you'd have a shout-out. Happy? LOL) Thank you to family and friends who've popped up in various ways, letting me know they see what I'm doing. Every DM, text and voice note were appreciated.

I gotta thank my OGs! My best Jessica; Annmarie, Phylicia and the Page Turning Homies crew.

To my peers, Nicole Falls; Necole Ryse; Briyanna Michelle; Lily Flowers; Rae Lyse; Brookelyn Mosley..so many others I can't even name. Some of y'all were there from the beginning of this story (whether you knew it or not) and some towards the end. Either way, y'all helped me get out of my *own* way.

To Jenine, thank you for putting up with my tears with kindness and humor. Even when I wasn't sure how all of this would turn out, it turned into something much more than I imagined. Thank you.

To Greg and Talulah, I love you more than I can truly put into words. Thank you for teaching me in your own way while accepting me just the same.

To every single last reader, thank you. Thank you for taking a chance on me. I pray this story meets you exactly where you are.

# About the Author

Jade Olivia is a Pennsylvania-based author with a passion for weaving stories that explore love, humanity and the experiences that shape us. When not crafting worlds on paper, Jade enjoys traveling, finding new restaurants, and spending time with her family.

Subscribe to my newsletter!
Instagram